COZY MYSTERY

All I Got Was the Headache

HISTORICAL ROMANCE

Summer Fancy
Fortune's Fancy
The Snow Queen (not yet re-published)

FANTASY AND GOTHIC ROMANCE

The Highwayman's Daughter
The Wild Swans
Fire and Ice (not yet re-published)

CONTEMPORARY ROMANCE

Merry and Her Gentleman (a Christmas novella)
'Twas the Night (writing as Kate Holmes with co-authors Sandra Hill and Trish Jensen)

FUTURISTIC ROMANCE

A Distant Star
All's Fair
Far Star
Hidden Heart
Dream Seeker (novella)

ROMANTIC SUSPENSE (WRITING AS ANNE WOODARD)

Dead Aim
Operation Rescue

ALL I GOT
was the
HEADACHE

An Amelia Fantastica Misadventure

Book 1

ANNE AVERY

To my sister Shawndra

For everything…

—A NOTE FROM THE AUTHOR —

I was having a rotten day at work. A really rotten day.

"You know what I need?" I said to myself. "I need a fairy godmother. The kind with a magic wand who grants wishes and finds me a handsome prince and all that good stuff. That's what I need."

"Hah!" said myself, who is a much more practical person. "The way your life is going, your fairy godmother would be a drunk or an incompetent idiot or both, and then where would you be?"

"Hah!" said I right back because I didn't want to admit that myself was probably right.

And then I said, "Hmmmmm," very thoughtfully, immediately followed by, "Hey! That's not a bad idea for a book!"

And that's how Amelia and Maxine and River City were born.

I hope you have as much fun reading about them as I did writing.

(Myself says I should just have settled for picking up carryout and a good bottle of wine on the way home and forgotten the whole thing, but, really, what does she know?)

CHAPTER 1

The folks who dink around with fairy tales? You know, Disney and the Grimm brothers and that French guy—what was his name? Perrault? Him especially!—they got it sooooo wrong.

I suppose you can't blame them. You can't blame the general public, either. They've all been brainwashed to believe that's what fairy tales are: tales. Stories. You know, *fiction*.

They've never had to face what some of us have to deal with every single day of our lives: Knowing it's all *real*.

Okay, maybe not *all* of it. The stories with giants and ogres and magic bean sprouts and stuff, those really are pure fiction. But the stories about fairy godmothers and the mess they can make of your life? Those stories are *real*.

I know because I've got one of 'em. A fairy godmother, I mean.

Yeah, yeah, I know what you're thinking. You read Cinderella and you watched the Disney movie, like, a million times, and now you've got your three little girls, who deserve better, watching the darned thing, too. And you're thinking that if you only had a fairy godmother, even a bumbling one, life would be a whole heck of a lot better than it is.

Well, I'm here to tell you, it wouldn't.

In fact, if *your* fairy godmother were only half as incompetent and annoying as *my* fairy godmother, you'd go off on the whole idea altogether.

1

To be fair—or at least scrupulously honest, which is a whole other thing—there probably are some decent fairy godmothers in the world. Bound to be. Sweet, hard working, dedicated fairy folk who'd never, *ever* think of dropping by when they aren't wanted and who always make sure their gifts will make their godchildren's lives better and happier and safer and all those other good things. And most would never, *ever* touch so much as a drop of spirituous liquors—I'm talking the alcoholic kind here, not the magical stuff.

And then there's Amelia.

Amelia Pomeroy Fitzgerald Fantastica, to be exact. (I suspect the Fantastica part is her own fabrication, though she swears not.)

Amelia dropped into my life (literally—she'd been dipping rather deep in a cask of twenty-year-old single malt they'd just broached in Glengarlie) the day I turned eighteen.

Up until then, my life had been pretty well perfect, despite the zits, the extra ten pounds that I was sure was keeping me from having a body to die for, an unreasonable mother (what mother isn't?), and a pair of boobs that had only just, barely, made it to a B cup. (I'd been close to suicidal before I finally managed to move out of trainer bras at sixteen.)

And then I turned eighteen, a day I'd been eagerly awaiting because it meant I could get a job, an apartment, and move out on my own, and Amelia showed up.

My life has been a hell of a long way from perfect ever since.

Take right now, for example.

Right now, my chief client (all right, my *only* client), Jameson John Montgomery the Third, was lying on the floor in my office with what looked suspiciously like my letter opener through his heart.

Fortunately, he hadn't bled much. Getting blood stains out of that old carpet would have been a bugger.

Unfortunately, he *was* very dead.

And then Amelia showed up.

As if that weren't bad enough, her style for the day was a too-tight pink sweater and short black leather skirt skimming thigh-high, high-heeled boots. If the folks at Disney could have seen her, they would have had a cow, right then and there. Flora, Fauna, or Merryweather she most definitely is not.

The red hair didn't do much for her, either. Never has. But she never listens to me.

"I could make him disappear if you like," she said, eyeing Jameson with beady-eyed interest.

"Like you made my neighbor across the hall disappear?" I said.

"That was a just a little glitch," she said airily, waving her wand dismissively. "Oops!" she added as my coffee pot exploded. Good thing there was only the dregs of yesterday's coffee in there. It could have been a real mess, otherwise.

"How many times do I have to tell you?" I demanded wearily. "Put the wand away."

"Not to worry. I'll just fix—"

I snatched it out of her hand before she could do any more damage. "No, you won't."

"But—"

"I'll buy a new pot. It's safer that way."

"Anyway, I got your neighbor back, didn't I?" Amelia could be easily distracted, but she always returned to the point of contention eventually.

"Three days later. After he almost lost his job because he didn't show up at work when he was supposed to."

"I fixed that problem, too!"

I snorted. I do a lot of that when Amelia is around.

"You sure did. He says they'll be releasing his boss from the psychiatric care home next week if everything goes well."

She huffed in irritation. She does a lot of *that* whenever *I'm* around.

"Spells of forgetting are really very tricky. You know that."

Boy, howdy, do I know that. I still haven't decided if I really

3

want to find out what happened that weekend I spent in Bermuda with Bryan Marsh. It's been two years, yet he still makes a point of crossing to the other side of the street whenever he sees me coming. Even if it means jaywalking in rush hour traffic three seconds after the light turns green.

"Let's concentrate on the problem in front of us, shall we?" I said.

Amelia frowned at me, then she frowned down at Jameson, and then she squinted. She should have gotten glasses years ago, but she's way too vain. (I haven't told her about the wrinkles when she squints.)

Taking care not to poke myself with the wand—Amelia insists on having a pointy gold star on the end of the thing, even though she admits it's not strictly necessary—I crossed my arms, and then I frowned even more than Amelia. (I'm not vain, so I don't worry about the wrinkles.)

Jameson was still there on the floor in front of us, and he was still very, very dead.

Clearly, this was not going to be one of my better days.

CHAPTER 2

I probably should explain that I'm an Investigations Agent. People hire me to investigate stuff. Or they used to, at any rate.

Business has been a little slow lately due to fallout from an unfortunate incident with a Mrs. Carruthers and the son she hired me to track down. I managed the tracking him down part just fine, but I accidently broke his arm and smashed his nose when I tried to keep him from getting away again, and Mrs. Carruthers has made a point of telling the whole world about it ever since, which hasn't done a thing for attracting new clients.

The bodily harm part wasn't really my fault. (It wasn't Amelia's fault, either. For a change.) If he'd just stayed put like I'd told him, I wouldn't have had to chase him. And if he'd been in better shape and a whole lot faster, I wouldn't have been able to catch him, let alone tackle him like I did. It was just his bad luck he hit the sidewalk instead of the grass on either side when I brought him down.

The problem was, little Bobby Carruthers was running a profitable side business of cooking meth in that dump of a trailer he rented, and he wasn't real eager to have anyone, especially not the police, who were right behind me, have a chance to talk to him about it.

Of course, Mrs. Carruthers blames me for little Bobby's arrest. She says he was framed—probably by me, though she's had a little harder time making a case for that part of it since the narcs already had him on their radar when she hired me—and keeps demanding that her lawyer file a wrongful arrest and imprisonment suit against me. Her lawyer keeps pointing out that it'd be hard to file something like that since I'm not the one who arrested him and dumped his butt in jail, but that doesn't deter Mrs. Carruthers.

She might have had a little more luck with a suit for grievous bodily harm, but Bobby, instead of just admitting he'd lost, made the mistake of kicking one of the cops where it really hurts and planting a fist in the face of another when they tried to drag him to his feet, so he came out of that little melee in worse shape than he went in. He also got resisting arrest and assaulting an officer added to all the drug manufacturing and trafficking charges. Which explains why Mrs. Carruthers' lawyer has declined to file a bodily harm suit against me in addition to not filing the wrongful arrest and imprisonment.

Anyway, he's so busy trying to keep little Bobby from a conviction with twenty years to life on the tail end of it that he probably doesn't have the energy to deal with me. No matter how much Mrs. Carruthers bitches.

Word is, he's losing interest in representing Mrs. Carruthers, anyway. I hear the betting pool down at the court house is running five to two against her right now, with the odds of her hanging on to him getting longer by the minute.

Not that it's any comfort to me. In the six months or so since little Bobby and his mom totally screwed up my business, it's been tough just making the rent. I stopped dining out on anything other than value meals ages ago, and if Jameson Montgomery hadn't come along, the value meals would shortly have become a thing of the past, too.

Of course, given that Jameson's dead on the floor of my office with my letter opener through his heart, I may not have to worry about value meals, either. I hear county jail serves a mean corned beef hash. They say you can even find real meat in it, every now and then.

"You *sure* you don't want me to disappear him?"

Amelia's question yanked me out of my bleak musings. There are worse things than jail hash, and dealing with the fallout from one of Amelia's magical disappearances was one of them.

"Absolutely sure," I said firmly. "You so much as hint you're going to disappear him and I'll snap your wand."

"Which you're still holding," Amelia pointed out. "Not that I'm worried. You've tried that before, remember?"

"Forty-third time to charm," I said, but reluctantly handed the thing back to her. It might look like some cutesy toy, but it would take the combined efforts of The Rock and Schwarzenegger in his prime to break it. If then. I know, because I've tried.

Amelia sniffed dismissively. To my relief, however, she stuffed it into that magic pocket thing of hers. I've never ceased to be amazed at what she pulls out of that pocket without even looking. And never so much as a bump to mar the line of her dress. Or her mini skirt, as the case may be. Hermione Grainger couldn't manage it better with that purse of hers, and she really *is* pure fiction.

"So what are you going to do?" Amelia insisted. "About him, I mean."

I sighed. "The only thing I can do," I said, and pulled out my phone.

It's never a good sign when you have the cops on speed dial, but there they are, right at the top of my favorites list. Even above my mother.

Okay, I'll admit I'm not sure why my mother ranks second. I try not to call her, ever, unless I can't possibly avoid it.

I punched the entry, then tried not to look at Jameson while I listened to the call going through. It wasn't easy. It's not every day a girl has a dead body on her floor. Not even me.

"River City police department."

The no-nonsense voice on the other end of the line was all too familiar.

"Hey, Rob. It's Maxie. Listen. I've got a little problem..."

THE COPS IN THE BLACK-AND-WHITE showed up first. Lights flashing, sirens blaring. Of course. Probably wanted the whole neighborhood to know there was trouble at the Maxie Peterson Investigations office. Again.

There were two of them, and they didn't get two feet through the door before they both stopped dead, enthralled by my new office decoration.

I perked up a little at the sight of them. It could have been a whole lot worse. Only one of them hates my guts.

"Hey, Maxie."

"Hey, Fred. How're you doing?"

"Not too bad. Better than you, by the looks of it."

"Yeah, well. Has Sharon popped yet?"

Fred beamed. He's a big bear of a guy, and he absolutely adores his wife, who has to wear heels in order to reach pint size. Except, these days, for the belly. They were expecting their first child, a girl, any day now.

"She wishes. Big as a house. Her words, not mine. Swears if the kid doesn't show up soon she's going to march into the emergency room and start raising a ruckus until they agree to induce. Doc says one more week, at least. She threatened to shoot him."

"Probably not a good idea. She's a lousy shot."

"Yeah. But I had to promise not to come to her next appointment in uniform, just in case."

"You two girls done gossiping?"

Gracie O'Mallon is two inches shorter than me and a good twenty pounds lighter, but she makes up for it in mean. She's also a whole lot better looking, though she's the only one who cares. She's hated me from the first moment we met, and I pretty much return the favor. No reason for the hostility, really. We just rub each other the wrong way, and neither one of us is at all inclined to do anything about it.

"Sure, Gracie," Fred said placatingly. "Maxie was just

asking."

"Yeah, well, try and focus, okay?"

Fred and I kept silent. We both know better than to argue with Gracie.

Neither one of them mentioned Amelia because they couldn't see her. Which was just as well, since she'd taken a seat perched on the edge of my desk and was glaring at both of them with unfeigned dislike.

Amelia hates cops, though she refuses to tell me why. Probably just as well, which is why I don't push it even though her attitude has complicated my life more than a few times.

Beyond the usual, I mean.

"So," Gracie said. "Who's the stiff?"

She'd hooked her thumbs in the front of her utility belt—she wore it a little lower on her hips than regulation so the world could appreciate her tiny waist—and was rocking back and forth on her heels. She did that so much—the foot rocking, I mean—that the heels of her shoes were worn down at the back.

I've never been able to decide if it's a sign of nerves or satisfaction. Could be both. Gracie enjoys seeing me in trouble, which happens often enough to keep her as mellow as she ever gets. But she isn't nearly as sure of herself as she'd like the world to believe, which explains at least some of her general hostility toward me and everyone else around her.

"Bitch," said Amelia.

I had to fight not to smile at that. Sometimes, in spite of everything, my fairy godmother is okay.

"The deceased," I said primly, to cover my amusement, "is Jameson John Montgomery the Third, and he's my client. Was my client," I amended. The urge to smile vanished.

Gracie's eyebrows rose appreciably and her eyes got wider. "*The* Jameson Montgomery the Third? The guy who inherited millions and millions on top of the family business?"

I nodded unhappily. "That's the one."

I'd been counting on a small percentage—a *very* small

percentage—of those millions to pay my bills this month. Now I'd probably be lucky if his bevy of lawyers didn't use those same millions to get me convicted of his murder.

Fred gave a small, appreciative whistle. He wasn't big on news and society gossip, but even he knew that having Jameson Montgomery hire me was a really big deal for me.

Having him murdered in my office with my letter opener through his heart is an even bigger deal, but not in a good way.

"Why'd he hire *you?*" Gracie's emphasis on the "you" made it clear she wasn't as interested in his reasons for hiring *any* investigator as she was in why he'd waste time and money hiring *me.*

I didn't take it personally. I'd been wondering the same thing.

"I don't know."

"You don't know?"

"No. I—"

Before I could finish, the outer door opened and a man I'd never seen before walked in. He hadn't bothered to knock.

At sight of him, I sucked in a breath and hoped my eyes weren't popping out of my head. I've never mastered all the rules of polite society that my mother tried to drill into my head, but I did learn that staring at perfect strangers just isn't *done.*

If Amelia ever had a mother to teach her good manners, she'd paid even less attention than I had.

"Hubba, *hubba!*" she said, grinning. She jumped down from her seat on my desk and tugged that ridiculous short skirt into place. "Well, helloooo, cutie!"

CHAPTER 3

Gracie didn't stare. Her spine stiffened and her eyes narrowed and her mouth thinned to the point that her lips all but disappeared.

"Trueblood," she said.

I'd never heard so much loathing in someone's voice before, not even hers.

If the new arrival noticed, he gave no sign of it. He gave her a brief, dismissive nod, said, "Officer O'Mallon. Fred," then turned his attention on me.

His eyes were that startling clear blue-gray that sucks you in. You know, the color that only really beautiful people ever seem to have.

I couldn't help it. I cleared my throat, straightened my shoulders, and gave a surreptitious tug to the waist of my pleated slacks to make sure they hung properly.

"How many times have I told you?" Amelia demanded. "Pleated slacks do absolutely *nothing* for a woman with hips like yours."

It was all I could do not to tell her to shut up. Though maybe they'd be nicer, when they arrested me, if they thought I was a nut case who conducted conversations with thin air and so deserved a little more care and sympathy than the average murderous investigations agent.

"And you must be the individual who called this in," the new arrival said. He had a great baritone voice. The kind that makes you think of things no self-respecting Investigations Agent should be thinking at a time like this.

"Maxie Peterson," I said, sounding all crisp and professional and totally unimpressed. Thank God for those acting classes my mother made me take in summer school. You never know when that sort of thing will come in handy. "Of Maxie Peterson Investigations." His eyebrows rose the tiniest fraction of an inch. "It's on the door."

"I noticed."

"And who are you?" I demanded. I was beginning to understand Gracie's reaction. No woman likes a man who can turn her brain to mush just by walking in the door. Me? I tend to get downright hostile. Amelia says it's a character defect. I say it's basic self-defense.

Pisses me off, that kind of reaction, but what's a girl to do? It's hormones and pheromones and probably a dozen other mones I've never heard of. It's not *me*. Honest. I wouldn't do that. Ever. Not if I could help it, anyway.

The edge in my voice didn't appear to bother him any more than Gracie's obvious dislike.

"Ben Trueblood." He didn't offer to shake hands, which was just as well, since we would have had to lean across Jameson to do it.

"New detective on the squad," Fred explained. He was the only one unfazed by Trueblood's entrance. But then, he's a guy. What would he know?

"I figured," I said.

Gracie settled for silence and a stony-faced expression that didn't do a thing for her usual come-hither air. Which, come to think of it, was a little odd. Gracie was usually the first to move in on a new guy, good looking or not.

Which meant he was probably married. Or he'd been totally uninterested in her advances

I really hoped it was the latter, but chances were good it was the former. That's the way things go when you're a single woman past twenty-five. All the good ones are taken. (And, yeah, I know. You've heard that one before. Doesn't mean it's not true.)

I couldn't help glancing at his left hand. No ring, which didn't prove a thing, one way or the other.

It was a nice hand. Tanned, masculine. Long, strong fingers.

"And this," Trueblood said, turning his attention to Jameson, who was still flat on his back on the floor and still very, very dead, "is our victim."

"Nothing like stating the obvious," Amelia said. Since everyone else was looking at Jameson, I risked shooting her a warning frown.

"Right. That's Jameson John Montgomery the Third," I said.

Trueblood didn't look impressed, which probably meant he wasn't from around here. Everyone knew about Jameson.

"He's my client. *Was* my client."

Trueblood nodded without taking his gaze off Jameson. His expression was impassive, but I had the sense he was the kind of guy who saw a lot more than you maybe wanted him to. Good trait in a detective, but not if you were his most likely suspect.

"And before you ask, that's my letter opener sticking out of his chest. *Probably* my letter opener," I amended. Accuracy is important in this kind of thing. "I haven't gotten close enough to be sure."

"So you haven't touched anything?"

I glared at him. "You're kidding, right? It's my office. I've touched *everything*."

Amelia snickered approval.

"But not him?"

"No. And not the letter opener. At least, not since someone stuck it in his chest."

Trueblood squatted on his haunches for a closer look. Despite his size, he made the move look easy, which meant he kept in really good physical condition.

Not that I needed any confirmation. I'd already checked out

the way his butt filled his slacks, despite the sport jacket that hid all the best parts. It had only taken a glance to know that the man didn't spend all his time in front of a desk.

It was a great butt. I should know, I'm a connoisseur.

Of course, Amelia would say that's because the only good look I get at a guy these days is while they're walking away, but we won't go there, okay?

"What's he doing in your office?"

"We had an appointment this morning, but that wasn't until nine. I don't know what he was doing here before then. And, no, he didn't have a key, and, no, I didn't let him in. He was like this when I got here. And, yes, the office door was locked. I didn't see anything that looked suspicious."

"Until you walked in." That was Gracie, always helpful with the obvious. Probably couldn't stand keeping her mouth shut any longer, even if she didn't have anything useful to contribute.

"Right. I did notice a little problem *then*," I said, even though sarcasm is totally wasted on her.

"Next chance you get, shoot her," said Amelia.

Amelia knows I don't own a gun, which, along with my utter lack of a sex life, is a continuing disappointment to her. Fortunately, she hasn't yet been tempted to remedy that particular defect herself. The operative word being 'yet'. Her attempts at recruiting males to help resolve the sex life part of it have been nothing short of disastrous.

Trueblood ignored both Gracie and me. He'd have ignored Amelia, too, if he'd had any idea she was there. He cocked his head to the side, still studying that damned letter opener.

Now I thought of it, the letter opener *was* rather interesting. Or, rather, the way it stuck out of Jameson's chest was interesting. Straight up, which meant it had gone straight in if he'd been standing when the killer struck. And that meant the murderer was probably a lot shorter than Jameson, but fairly strong.

I'm no expert, never having attempted the thing myself, but

I understand it takes either a fair amount of skill and force or an awful lot of luck to stab someone through the heart first try. Even if you're using something as finely honed as my letter opener.

That thought made me sweat. I hoped Trueblood never asked me what I was doing with a letter opener that sharp. The crime scene team was bound to find the whetstone I kept in the lower left hand drawer of my desk, but that didn't mean anyone would necessarily make a connection between it and the letter opener. That drawer is so full of miscellaneous junk that I always have a hard time finding anything, even if I know what I'm looking for.

Thank heavens I'd loaned my favorite Bowie knife to my brother last week. That really *would* raise a few eyebrows.

Still squatting, Trueblood scanned the room in front of him. Which meant he could probably see the dust bunnies that always accumulated under the desk, despite my dedicated efforts to vacuum them out at least once a year or so. He could see the stains in the carpet that had been there since long before I signed the lease on the place, as well as the scattered burn holes from a previous tenant who'd smoked too much and been way too careless with his butts.

Trueblood could also see the shattered coffee pot on the floor in front of the beat up old credenza that served as my combined filing space and office kitchen. The dregs of yesterday's brew had already seeped into the carpet, leaving dark, accusingly damp blotches behind.

Which reminded me: I hadn't had any coffee yet this morning. Maybe that explained the headache that was threatening.

"You try to make coffee this morning, Ms Peterson?"

"You're kidding, right? And before you ask, there would have been some coffee left from yesterday afternoon. I don't bother dumping it out until I make new in the morning."

"And you didn't break that pot."

"No." Which was absolutely true.

I believe in the truth and nothing but the truth, but that doesn't mean I feel compelled to share the *whole* truth if I don't have to. Besides, they wouldn't have believed me if I had.

"I really am sorry about the pot," Amelia said. "I'll get you a new one, I promise."

I waved her away. She's only ever sorry about the trivial things, never the big ones. She's never once apologized for Bryan Marsh, for example. I'm pretty sure she owes me big time for that.

Trueblood caught the gesture. He got to his feet in one smooth move, not even so much as a fingertip to the floor to help push off. Impressive.

"You have a problem, Ms Peterson?"

"Other than a murdered client, you mean? In my office with my letter opener in his chest? Not to mention the broken coffee pot? No, no problem."

Whatever else he was going to say was interrupted by the sound of heavy footsteps on the stairs and the thump of cases and equipment banging into the walls. At a guess, the elevator was out of order. Again. I prefer the stairs so I'm not always up on the most recent failings of building services.

"Crime scene folks," said Fred helpfully, as if the rest of us couldn't have guessed.

Trueblood nodded. "You mind letting them in?"

Since he'd left my office door half-open, I wasn't sure why they needed to be let in, but that was his business, not mine.

"Sure," said Fred amiably. He ambled out into the hall to verify the new arrivals' identities. "In here, guys," he called, then pushed the door all the way open.

He didn't offer to help the team with their gear. They wouldn't have expected him to. For all I know, they wouldn't have trusted anyone but themselves with their cameras and other assorted toys. In my experience, those guys can be awfully territorial.

First one in the door was Betsy Sharanski, which just goes to show that Fred knows his stuff. Betsy is my best friend and has been since grade school, but she won't let me touch so much as a cotton swab from her kit without strict supervision. The woman is a fanatic about her equipment.

She frowned when she saw me. "Hey, Max."

"Betsy. How's tricks?"

"Me? Fine." She glanced at Jameson, then looked back at me. "Doesn't look like you're doing so good."

"Ah, you know. Some days are better than others."

I didn't miss the way Trueblood's left eyebrow arched. I wonder if he'd practiced it, growing up. I'd always thought Spock had a good thing going there, but never managed to get the hang of it myself.

Betsy wasn't one for wasting time on friendly chit chat. She was already directing her team to set up.

"ME's on her way, so if you guys are done here for now...?" she said to no one in particular.

"No problem." Trueblood didn't seemed bothered by being booted out of his crime scene. Maybe because with him, me, two cops, a dead body, and one fairy godmother nobody but me knew about, the place had already been a little crowded. Betsy and her crew would make it impossible to move.

"How about we move out in the hall for right now," he added. "Unless you've got a better suggestion?"

He was looking right at me when he said it. Those eyes could send a shiver down a girl's spine at fifteen paces. This close...

"Nope. Hall's pretty much the only option," I said. "Unless you want to try the women's restroom? It's got a little more space. Four stalls, no waiting."

Gracie rolled her eyes. So did Amelia.

At least they agreed on something.

All right, so my sense of humor leaves something to be desired. This wasn't exactly what you'd call a normal situation, even for me. The lack of a morning coffee didn't help.

Trueblood stood aside to give me room to pass. I suppressed a wince as Amelia opted for the direct route, right over Jameson.

For the first time, it occurred to me to wonder if Betsy's crew would be able to detect some hint of her presence. That ought to be interesting, explaining Amelia to people who couldn't see her and wouldn't believe in the existence of a fairy godmother even if they could.

Pushing aside that problem for the moment, I led the way out into the hall.

CHAPTER 4

With me in the lead (Amelia was ahead of me, but if you can't see her, I figure she doesn't count), we migrated to the end of the hallway, away from my office and the stairs where there was now a steady flow of uniforms and Tyvek-suited crime techs going up and down.

I couldn't help wondering if Mr. Yaguchi, the building sup, had shut down the elevator precisely because there were so many people who wanted to use it. I wouldn't put it past him. The only skinflint I've ever met who's flintier than Mr. Yaguchi is the owner of the building, Mrs. Huffelwitz, who hired him in the first place.

I heard a chair creak behind one door, but none of my neighbors so much as poked their heads out, which didn't surprise me. Those who could had probably already relocated to the Last Caff, which has lousy coffee but really good wi fi. The rest would have barricaded themselves in and would probably pretend they weren't even there when the uniforms inevitably started canvassing the building's occupants.

If past experience was anything to go by, I'd be hearing a lot of complaints about the disruption and loss of business caused by my utter lack of consideration for others, but for right now, the less contact, the better, as far as I was concerned.

In my defense, that loss of business thing is a joke—most of my neighbors are struggling to make ends meet, the same as me.

The ones who aren't struggling definitely aren't going to be complaining to the cops about anything, for any reason. In fact, police attention is the absolute *last* thing they'd want.

I'd be hearing about *that*, too. Guaranteed.

I had enough experience with this sort of thing to know.

Well, not with murder—Jameson was my very first corpse—but there'd been a few incidents over the years. Not all of them my fault, I hasten to add. Amelia had a hand in two or three. Or a wand, as the case may be.

I sure hoped she hadn't had anything to do with this.

"Best I can do," I said, calling a halt to our little procession. "No chairs, but at least we're out of the way of everyone else."

Then I took a breath and instantly regretted it.

"Phew!" said Amelia, wrinkling her nose in distaste. "What's that stench?"

"Place smells like a urinal," said Gracie. "Didn't you say you had restrooms in this dump?"

"Locked to keep out the riffraff," I said. I was pretty sure they could all tell my smile wasn't nearly as friendly as it looked. "If you've gotta go, you might try the pool hall across the street," I added helpfully.

Wild Bill would kill me if he knew I'd suggested that a uniformed cop should so much as stroll past his front door, let alone use his restrooms.

"This is fine," said Trueblood. "A bit crowded, though. Maybe you could go help set up the team canvassing the building's occupants, Officer O'Mallon?"

Gracie was off like a shot, but not before giving me a look intended to shrivel me where I stood.

"And Fred, maybe you—"

"On it," said Fred, cheerfully avoiding the issue of what, exactly, he was going to be on.

That left me, Trueblood, and Amelia, who currently had her head out the window, breathing in exhaust fumes instead of ammonia. I'd long since gotten used to the fact that she didn't have to open the window first.

"Maybe if I open the window here...?" Trueblood reached for the bottom of the sash.

Amelia got her butt out of the way just in time. "Watch it, buster! Keep your hands to yourself, will you?"

Actually, she'd probably have been just fine with him feeling her up, she just wouldn't appreciate him being completely unaware of it when he did.

She tugged her skirt down, then adjusted her boobs. That pink sweater was waaaay too tight.

"Urrff!" said Trueblood, straining at the sash. "What the hell?"

He checked that the rotating lock on the sash was free, then tried again. With the same result. That window wasn't going to open before the second coming, if then.

"Don't bother," I said. "Far as I can tell, those things were painted shut when Ike was president and haven't been opened since. Same goes for pretty much every other window in the building."

Except for mine. I'd chiseled my way through the paint the second day I was in the place. I hadn't had much choice, not with an air conditioning system that doesn't work worth beans fifty-one weeks out of the fifty-two, and then only if the outside temperature drops below freezing.

Too bad my office wasn't an option right now.

"Maybe we could move a little ways back down the hall?" Trueblood suggested.

"Or maybe she should move to a whole new building uptown?" Amelia had been trying to get me to move out ever since I moved in.

The topic is definitely a sore point between us. *I* maintain that any decent, competent, self-respecting fairy godmother should have figured out a way to get me a nice office in a modern building with paying clientele by now. *She* maintains it's the sort of problem I should be able to solve on my own. At least, that's what she says *now*.

I do *not* want to talk about what I went through when she tried to help.

I shot her yet another warning look and debated the wisdom of remaining right where we were. Maybe the smell would drive her off.

I looked at the bustle of people at my end of the hall, then at the closed doors on either side. A flickering fluorescent in one of the ceiling fixtures was beginning to give me a headache.

And then I made the mistake of breathing.

"Look," I said, "I know this isn't strictly procedure, but there's a coffee shop on the corner. I would *kill* for a cup of coffee right now. I don't mean that literally!" I added a heartbeat later, mentally kicking myself.

The combination of Amelia, murder, and a serious lack of caffeine was *not* a good way to start the morning.

"You're right, it's not procedure," said Trueblood. And then *he* made the mistake of breathing. "But in this case, I'll make an exception. How about we avoid the crowd and use the fire escape?"

"That's not—" But I was too late. He'd already opened the door.

The man *definitely* works out. That door's so warped it's usually impossible to open unless you slam your shoulder into it a few times.

He took two steps through the door and came to a screeching halt.

"What the hell?"

"Er... Storage?" I knew *exactly* what had stopped him.

He turned to give me a gimlet-eyed glare. "This is a *fire* escape."

"Well..."

"There are *boxes* on these stairs. Boxes *filled* with papers. On every. Single. Stair."

I was getting the feeling he didn't approve of Mr. Yaguchi's

22

storage solutions.

"Maybe not *every* stair."

"You *know* about this?"

"Why do you think I keep one of those emergency ladders under my desk? You know, the metal chain kind you hook on the window sill? Ninety-nine fifty at Jankowski's hardware store three blocks over. I can probably get you a discount if you're interested."

His eyes narrowed even more. "Those are for a maximum of three stories."

"Right."

"You're on the fourth floor."

I shrugged. "My office overlooks the garbage bins. I figure they'll cushion my fall."

He looked at me like I was out of my mind.

It was a look that was all too familiar. Didn't mean I liked it. Especially from him.

"Shit." He looked back at the stairs. "Come on, then."

"You don't want to use the main stairs?"

"Call it part of the investigation. Though I'm pretty sure your murderer didn't come up this way."

I eyed the mess spilling down to the next landing. If you craned over the railing, you could see the same disaster, all the way down.

"How can you be so sure of that?" I demanded.

"If you look closely, you'll see there's mildew and dust on the surface of these papers. If someone had come up this way, they couldn't have helped dislodging some of the papers on the top and exposing the drier, cleaner papers underneath."

He was right, though I hated to admit it. I should have thought of it first. In my defense, finding my only client dead on my office floor not two hours before meant I was a little more distracted than usual.

Actually, make that a whole lot more distracted.

He started down, one hand on the railing.

He didn't strike me as the kind of a man who ever needed to hang onto a railing, but in this case, I couldn't blame him. A lot of the boxes had split and dumped their contents across the stairs, which made for some serious slip hazards.

Dangerous or not, the stairwell and the boxes that filled it had their uses. I wasn't about to tell him, though. I was pretty sure information like that would be tallied on the More Reasons to Suspect Her of Murder side of the page.

With a sigh, I took hold of the hand rail and followed him down.

Despite a couple of slips and a few sections of railing that were a little wobbly—one piece broke off in my hand when I grabbed it too hard to keep from falling. I didn't say anything, just tossed it on top of the nearest box and kept on going—we made it to the bottom without serious mishap.

Trueblood, however, was not impressed. He clearly didn't appreciate a miracle when he saw one.

"Five of those safety lights aren't working," he said.

"But three were," I pointed out

Mr. Yaguchi deserved *some* credit, after all. Usually, none of them worked. I never tried to go down these stairs without a flashlight, or at least the flashlight app on my phone.

"You sound surprised."

Sarcasm. I think he was starting to like me.

I ignored him and went to dig behind a pile of boxes beside the outer door. Mr. Yaguchi might not maintain the stairwell and lights and doors like he should, but he never leaves us completely without resources.

"Here," I said, brandishing an ancient two-and-a-half pound ball-peen hammer. "You're going to need this for the door."

"You're kidding." He didn't offer to take it.

"Nope."

"You can't get a bigger one?"

"They don't make 'em any bigger than this," I said, hefting it for my swing. Darned thing's so heavy it takes two hands. "It's

pretty easy, actually. You've got to whack the bar right...there."
The panic bar on the door didn't budge. "Okay, sometimes you
have to hit it here, too."

That did the trick. With my ears ringing from the metal-on-
metal clang, I forced the bar down and shoved the door open,
then stepped aside to let him go past.

"Ladies first."

More sarcasm, but at least it was *polite* sarcasm.

"Thanks, but I've got to put the hammer back."

He muttered something under his breath that was probably
rude, but did as I suggested.

Given enough time and the right circumstances, I could
probably learn to like the guy, even if he was a cop.

I returned the hammer and started to follow Trueblood, then
stopped as I realized there were now only two of us. Amelia was
nowhere in sight.

I couldn't help smiling. My day was looking up.

CHAPTER 5

The optimism didn't last long. Amelia was waiting for us at the Last Caff.

"I saved us a table," she said cheerily, rising from one of the premo tables for four in front of the window.

I didn't waste energy wondering how she'd managed that. I really didn't want to know.

Trueblood scanned the room, oblivious to all the appreciative female (and occasional male) attention he was drawing. I tried not to preen. The Caff's regulars aren't used to seeing me in the company of eligible males, especially eligible males who look anywhere near that hot.

I also didn't waste energy wondering what they were going to say when they found out who he is and why we're together. I already knew.

"Maybe that table at the back?" he said, indicating the least desirable—and therefore least occupied—corner of the room. The only time that corner got crowded was when there was a queue for the uni-sex john.

"Great!" I said, and meant it. One table, two chairs. Worked for me. Amelia would just have to settle for another table, which would annoy the devil out of her.

I couldn't stop her from eavesdropping on my private conversation with Trueblood, but I could at least take satisfaction from knowing she wouldn't dare start a panic by moving a chair closer when nobody but me could see her do it.

"What are you having?" Trueblood's question brought me back to attention.

"My suggestion, my treat."

"Thanks, but no. Can't accept favors from a suspect."

Suspect? "Not even a cheap brew of the day?"

He shook his head. "Not even. Which means I'm buying, so what'll you have?"

Suspect??? I'd known him all of—what?—half an hour, and already our relationship had been through more ups and downs than a roller coaster. Right now, it was decidedly down.

"I'll take the giant mocha caramel with extra whipped cream and caramel. Edna knows how I like it. And a grilled ham and Swiss croissant while you're at it."

Coffee's a must in the morning, but I've always considered breakfast optional...unless someone else is buying. Especially if they've just insulted me when they don't even know me. At all.

He grimaced at the mocha caramel, but I'm pretty sure he got the point. All he said was, "Right," and headed toward the counter.

I, on the other hand, claimed the back table we'd agreed on.

"You could at least move that chair closer."

Amelia might be annoying, but she isn't stupid. She knew exactly what I was doing.

"Nuh huh," I said. I kept my head down and my voice low so no one would think I was talking to empty air. "As far as everyone here's concerned, there's only two of us. They see me moving a third chair up and they'll think I'm crazy."

"You could put your purse on it."

"One, I didn't bring my purse." Good thing Trueblood was buying, after all. I hadn't even thought about the purse or the wallet in it. "Two, you hate having anything in your way when you sit down."

"Pretend it's to put your feet up."

"Then keep them on the floor? No way."

I took the seat that gave me the best view of the room, which meant Trueblood's back was going to be towards her. She'd hate that, too. She liked staring at good looking men. Especially since they couldn't stare back.

Unfortunately, that meant *I* had to look at her.

I frowned down at the table, studying the graffiti carved into the wood. The Last Caff had been around for years, which meant there was a fair amount to look at.

"Tsk," I said. "People are still using that old 'for a good time call' line? You'd think by now someone would have come up with something a little more original, wouldn't you?"

Amelia snorted. "With the clientele in this place? Not a chance."

"I'm clientele here," I objected.

"My point exactly."

Further debate was cut short by Trueblood setting a steaming cup of whip cream-lathered coffee in front of me. "Edna will bring your sandwich in a minute."

"Thanks." I may be greedy and unprincipled, but I am polite.

"You're welcome," he said, setting a small regular coffee on the table, then taking the seat across from me.

"That all you're having?" I asked, surprised. I thought all cops swilled coffee in the same quantities I do.

"That's all I could afford."

"Really?" I said, brightening.

The corner of his mouth twitched.

He had a very nice mouth.

"No."

My shoulders slumped. "Oh, well. At least I tried."

"You're not taking this personally, are you?"

I should have asked for *two* croissant sandwiches. Breakfast and lunch.

"Of *course* I'm taking this personally. What do you think?"

He took a sip of coffee and considered the question. "I think you could be dangerous—"

Dangerous? I perked up at that. I liked dangerous.

"...but only with that mouth of yours." And down I went again. "I can't see you stabbing a client right in your own office."

I thought of some of the clients I'd had. "Not before the first cup of coffee, anyway."

"So why was Montgomery in your office so early?"

"And how did he get there? I don't know if you noticed, but I have a decent deadbolt on that door."

"You should ask for your money back," Amelia said.

"I noticed," said Trueblood. "It's not an easy lock to pick."

"That's good to know," I said, ignoring Amelia and focusing on him. "I paid a fortune to have it installed."

"Who has keys to it?"

"Just me."

"Nobody else? Not even the building superintendent?"

"Mr. Yaguchi? You're kidding, right? You saw that stair well."

At least he had the grace to look properly abashed. "Fair enough. But I checked. I didn't see any scratches around the face, so whoever got in, they're either really good at picking locks, or they had another key."

He'd checked the lock? The man thought fast and, from what I'd seen so far, moved fast, too. That meant I was going to have to think and move even faster if I was going to keep one step ahead of him and out of jail.

"I have the only other key."

"You're sure?"

"Absolutely." Was I? I tried to remember the last time I'd seen it, and where, and drew a blank. Not a good sign. "I've never given a key to anyone else. Ever."

"All right, we'll leave it for now. So we're back to the question of why Mr. Montgomery was there in the first place."

"I have no idea."

That eyebrow shot up in disbelief.

"Okay, that's not quite true," I amended. "He was there so

we could talk about why he'd hired me and what he wanted me to investigate."

"And what was that?"

"He wouldn't say. That's why we were meeting this morning,

"And the appointment?"

"Was for nine. I got there around half past eight. Door was locked, just like it was supposed to be. But I already told you that."

"Were the lights on or off?"

I frowned, trying to remember. "On. I think."

"You think?"

"I was thinking about coffee, not evidence. I hadn't had any."

Edna chose that moment to sidle up with my croissant sandwich. I say 'sidle' because even though my back was to the wall, she was trying to approach at an angle that would give her a full frontal view of my breakfast companion. And him a full frontal view of her. I might have struggled to grow into a B cup, but Edna had passed B at about age thirteen and kept on going.

"I added mustard," she said, setting the plate down in front of me. She almost missed the table and dumped it in my lap because she was looking at Trueblood, not at me.

"I hate mustard," I said, scowling at the sandwich.

"She loves mustard," Edna assured Trueblood, beaming. She hadn't once looked at me.

"*I* love mustard," Trueblood assured her, reaching across the table to snag half my croissant.

"Hey!" I objected. He ignored me and smiled at Edna.

Edna's smile turned blinding. I swear, she hadn't blinked once. And then she ran her hands over her hips, smoothing the Last Caff apron she wore over her jeans and T, and I remembered how I'd wanted to do the same to my slacks when I first met him.

Hormones are a bitch. In any reasonable world, they'd be outlawed altogether.

"Well," said Edna, still smiling and staring and going absolutely nowhere.

"Thank you, Edna," I said, using a smidge more emphasis than strictly necessary.

"Twit," said Amelia. She'd been following the whole exchange with her usual disapproving frown. For someone who pays an awful lot of attention to guys who can't even see her, she wasn't very sympathetic to other females doing the same.

"Let me know if you need anything else," Edna told Trueblood.

"I will, thanks."

"Well," said Edna again, and then she looked around, a little dazed, as if she'd just realized where she was. "Better get back to work."

"About time," said Amelia.

Edna wandered off, still dazed. Trueblood took a bite of my sandwich. His eyebrows arched approvingly.

"Good sandwich," he said around a mouthful.

"Do you always do that?" I demanded.

"Do what?" he said, and took another bite.

"Turn women's brains to mush just by looking at them?" Amelia choked.

Trueblood stopped chewing and stared at me. "Excuse me?"

"You heard me."

He grinned and started chewing again. "Almost always. My sex appeal doesn't seem to have quite the same effect on women who haven't had their morning coffee, though."

"Huh," I said and took a big sip of coffee. I can't resist a challenge. It's a personality flaw, I'll admit, but a useful one.

"You going to eat the other half of that sandwich?" he asked, eyeing my plate.

"Yes."

"It's got mustard."

"I'm still eating it," I said, and took a big bite just to spite him. Even with the mustard, it was a really good sandwich.

"Have some more coffee," he said.

"Focus, Trueblood," I said. "You're grilling me about a murder, remember?"

He finished off the last bite of the half he'd snitched, then casually sucked the crumbs off the tips of his fingers.

I'm pretty sure it was deliberate, but I pretended not to notice.

"All right, if you won't do your job, Trueblood, I will," I said.

"Thank you."

"You're welcome. So, Ms Peterson, could you repeat your previous testimony?" I said in a deliberately high, prissy voice. "Why, of course, Detective Trueblood, I'd be glad to."

I drew a steadying breath. Enough with the games.

"Like I said, I've never given anyone a key to my office, I think the lights were on but I won't swear to it, Jameson and I had an appointment for nine, no, eight, and, no, I still don't know why he hired me."

"Any guesses?"

Plenty of guesses. Not one single, solitary fact I could hold on to, and definitely nothing I was willing to share with him. "No."

He looked hopefully at my plate. "Are you *sure* you're going to eat the rest of that sandwich?"

"If I give you the rest of the sandwich, will you go away and leave me alone?"

"No."

"Then get your own sandwich. This one's mine." I eyed the half remaining on my plate. The half with a big bite out of it. "Even if it has got mustard."

"All right." He settled back in his chair. The Last Caff's chairs are extraordinarily sturdy—they have to be—but his chair still creaked. He was a very big man. Not fat, just...big. "If you hadn't discussed why he was hiring you, why are you so sure he did? Hire you, I mean?"

"He sent me a check as a retainer in the same envelope with the note requesting my services and setting the appointment for this morning."

"Have you cashed the check?"

"Yes." It was either that or bounce my rent check. "It's just good practice, and I run a very tight, efficient business."

I give him credit for some self restraint. It was the perfect opening for a nasty crack about my office arrangements, but he let it pass. "How much was it for?"

I told him. His eyebrows rose. He gave a low whistle.

"That's a pretty substantial retainer."

"My services don't come cheap." I must have said that a little louder than I intended because Amelia, who'd been looking bored with the conversation suddenly sat up straighter. When she gets bored, she tends to doze off, no matter how impolite that is.

"You must have some suspicions."

I shook my head. "I told you. Not a one. And—I'll save you the trouble of asking, because I'm helpful that way—I can't figure out why a man like Jameson Montgomery would hire me, either."

He generously let that one lie. "You still have the letter that came with the check?"

I snorted. "What do you think?"

"Did you save the envelope, too?"

"Of course. They're both in the file I started, along with a photocopy of the check he gave me."

"You photocopy your client's checks?"

I shrugged. Given some of my clients, it's proven to be a wise precaution.

"What about the letter opener?"

"Tacky, ugly thing," said Amelia, wrinkling her nose with disdain.

If she'd hated the thing so much, she could have given me a gold one encrusted with jewels, right? Isn't that the sort of thing fairy godmothers are supposed to co for you? It might have been a little too fancy for the neighborhood pawnshops, but I could probably have off-loaded it for a nice chunk of change at one of the classier jewelers uptown.

"A weapon of opportunity?" I suggested, dragging my attention back to the man on the opposite side of the table. "I can't believe someone actually *planned* to murder him. Not like that."

"Where do you normally keep it?"

Another shrug. "Wherever I dropped it the last time I used it."

Or stuck it, but I wasn't going to tell him that. I used to use it for target practice whenever I got bored or was trying to think, but I got tired of staring at the holes it left in the wall. I'd patched the holes and repainted the whole office a few months back during another lull in business. The place had needed it.

"I assume I left it on top of the desk," I added, "but I can't swear to it."

He frowned at the wall over my right shoulder. His eyes took on the unfocused look of someone who's trying to think and not having much success.

"I know," I said. "It's not much to go on, but it's all I've got."

"Mmmm," he said, still staring at nothing over my shoulder.

I took a sip of coffee, then grimaced. It had gone cold, and a room temperature mocha caramel with extra whip cream is not all that appealing. I told myself I'd brew a new pot when I got back to the office, then remembered that Amelia had killed my pot and it was going to be days before I was allowed back in my own office. If then.

I needed to get my purse back, too. I couldn't forget that. It had my car and house keys as well as my cash and credit cards. Not to mention the knife that wasn't quite a switchblade so was perfectly legal. Sort of.

Trueblood came back to the present. "You have a business

card?"

"Yeah. In the office. Tell your crime scene guys to fish a couple out for you. They're in the top left-hand drawer at the back. Whole box of them."

The fact that I still had two-thirds of the five hundred I'd bought a year ago wasn't important to his investigation.

"I know I can't get into my office yet," I added, "but can I get my purse back? And my phone? And my car keys?"

"Probably. Unless the crime scene guys find something interesting."

"They won't." I hoped.

He glanced at his watch. "They should be done with it by now. I'll tell them you're going to drop by in a bit, shall I?"

"You don't have any more questions for me?"

"Not right now."

I waited for him to say something like, "But I want to follow up with you," or "I'll *definitely* keep in touch," or something like that.

He just pushed back his chair, almost creaming Amelia's knees in the process, then got to his feet. He fished a business card out of his jacket pocket and dropped it on the table.

"You think of anything useful, let me know."

Useful? What'd he think, we'd been talking about the *weather?* I ignored the card and the jibe. "Thanks for the coffee."

I did mention that I'm polite, right?

"You're welcome." He snatched the rest of the sandwich off my plate. "Great sandwich," he said, and started to walk away.

"Hey!" I said. I'd wanted that sandwich, even if it did have mustard.

"Huh," said Amelia, and stuck out her foot and tripped him.

He staggered, regained his balance, then looked around for what he'd tripped over.

There was, of course, nothing for him to see.

I stared, fascinated, as a faint wave of color washed across his face under that tan. The man was actually blushing. Who'd

35

have thought?

He recovered fast, though. He pushed in a chair that hadn't been anywhere near his feet, as if that were the culprit, then nodded coolly and swaggered away.

I wasn't the only one watching him go, which annoyed me.

I dragged my attention back to Amelia. She was watching him, too.

To me, Amelia is as solid and real as the chair I was sitting on, but for most people, she's not only invisible, she's also completely insubstantial. If she's not paying attention, they can walk right through her. I understand it's not pleasant—for her or them—though not nearly as unpleasant as if they'd walked through a ghost.

But sometimes, when she wants to, Amelia can make herself sufficiently solid that she can touch them and they can touch her. She says it takes way too much energy and usually isn't worth the effort. Note the 'usually'.

"Thanks," I said, and meant it. Sometimes—not very often—she's good to have around.

"You're welcome." She sniffed disapprovingly as she readjusted her boobs. "The least he could have done is say he'd be in touch."

CHAPTER 6

I got rid of Amelia eventually—she does have other godchildren, though she absolutely refuses to talk about them, thank heavens—and headed back to my office to retrieve my purse and phone. The crime scene team was still working, but Jameson's body was gone and, as far as I could tell, so were most of my neighbors. A building crawling with cops is never good for business, especially not in this neighborhood. I was definitely going to hear about it from the building's other residents, but with my office off-limits for a while, I had a good excuse for avoiding them until they cooled down a bit.

Fortunately, the media hadn't yet gotten hold of the news that Jameson Montgomery was dead. The minute they discovered that he'd not only been murdered, but that it had happened in the rather shabby offices of an unknown, down-market investigations agent, all hell was going to break lose. I didn't want to be anywhere around when it did.

An earnest looking rookie was posted at the base of the third floor stairs with instructions to prevent anyone from getting anywhere near the fourth floor, but when I explained who I was and what I needed, he obligingly abandoned his post to fetch my belongings.

I, of course, took advantage of the opportunity to sneak up the stairs after him.

Unfortunately, there wasn't much to see. The spaces

between the scarred old wood banisters allowed me a peep at what was happening halfway down the hall where my office door stood open, but the sight of a couple open equipment cases and a floor-level view across a carpet that should have been replaced twenty years ago wasn't very helpful.

Trueblood wasn't anywhere in sight, but that didn't mean he wasn't in there, going through my drawers. Sadly, they weren't the kind of drawers I might have enjoyed having him explore.

There were, however, two or three sexless, shapeless human beings stuffed in full-body zip suits wandering in and out of my office. Other than differences in height and girth, there wasn't much to distinguish one from another. I couldn't tell if Betsy was one of them or not, and this far away, I couldn't catch any more than an unintelligible murmur of conversation. Nothing that would tell me they'd discovered anything worth knowing, or what it was if they had.

I would, of course, ask Betsy later, but I knew exactly where that would get me: nowhere. Betsy and I have known each other since grade school, but she wouldn't tell me there was a mass murderer living right next door if she wasn't supposed to. Still, I like her in spite of her faults. There were other ways she might be useful.

I was considering the advantages of strolling in unannounced to demand an update when the rookie who was fetching my purse stepped back into the hall—hard to miss those shiny black shoes. The shoes meant they must have finished up some of the investigation, at least. They wouldn't have allowed him in there without protective booties, otherwise.

That didn't mean they'd be done any time soon, however. I'd be willing to bet that someone was going to be stuck with going through a lot more than the one file I'd opened for Jameson.

The thought of anyone, especially Betsy, finding out just how close Maxie Peterson Investigations was to moving operations out with Hector, the old drunk who lived in the packing crate behind the trash bins, made me grimace. I had friends on the police force. I really didn't want word getting out I wasn't nearly as successful as they assumed. Besides, I didn't know where I was going to find a packing crate as good as Hector's. He'd told me, more than once, that they just didn't make 'em like they used to.

Probably the best I could hope for was that it was Betsy who got to dig through my files. She might not tell me anything, but she wouldn't tell anyone else anything, either. Not unless she had to, anyway.

By the time the rookie made it back down the stairs, I was standing right where he'd left me, casually propped against the wall as if I'd been there since forever, blankly staring at the wall opposite. He bought the act, bless his innocent little heart. Trueblood wouldn't have, but then, he'd never have left me alone like that, either. Or believed I was who I said I was without checking first.

Trueblood was going to be a problem.

He didn't strike me as the kind of idiot who jumps to the easiest conclusions, but that charm and those good looks could be dangerously distracting. He knew it, too. If there was one thing I didn't need right now, it was a brain addled by all those raging mones.

The problem of Trueblood, however, would have to wait. I might not have an office, but I definitely had a job: Find out who'd killed Jameson Montgomery and why before I got arrested on suspicion of murdering the only paying client I'd had in ages.

THE CHALLENGE was figuring out where to start.

Even dead, Jameson Montgomery inhabited a world I couldn't easily enter without an invitation or, better yet, an escort who could open doors even an engraved invitation wouldn't budge. Which meant I couldn't just go strolling in asking questions of all and sundry, like family, friends, or similarly wealthy and powerful business colleagues.

I wouldn't do a whole lot better with the working stiffs who helped ensure his life went round in its usual well-ordered and very expensive routine and his business continued to mint the kind of money that kept him in big houses, fancy yachts, and fast cars.

With a few exceptions, those people were often pretty much invisible to Jameson and his ilk, but they were also frequently required to sign non-disclosure agreements when they were hired. Those agreements came with terms that made it harder to get information from them than from your quarry's reclusive, demented great aunt.

So how did I find out which ones were at least less inaccessible? And how did I get to them? And what was I looking for when I did?

Before I'd cashed that check Jameson had sent me—and it had been very tempting to cash it two seconds after I slit open that envelope, no questions asked—I'd done some research.

He hadn't said why he wanted to hire me, or what it was he expected me to do for that hefty sum, and he definitely hadn't provided any hint of why he would choose a struggling investigations agent whom no one in his world would ever have heard of when he could have hired the cream of the crop.

So, why me? Why so much money? And why deal directly with me? He'd sent me a personal check, and the note setting the appointment had been handwritten. Why go to the trouble when he could have summoned one of his minions to do everything for him, no questions asked?

My search hadn't turned up any answers, but I'd found enough intriguing hints to decide to go ahead with the whole thing.

Even the best of us makes a mistake now and then.

Jameson John Montgomery the Third was the only son of—wait for it!—Jameson John Montgomery, Jr., who was, in his turn, the only son of Jameson John Montgomery, Sr., who managed to make a mint during the Second World War by supplying the troops with sexy essentials like blankets and socks and really ugly underwear.

After the war, Senior parlayed that initial entrepreneurial success into manufacturing companies that happily churned out the consumer products that were in such demand. From there, he expanded into building housing for the growing middle class, then heavy construction for the expanding industrial base of a recovering Europe, and, later, a growing international market.

Senior eventually went the way of all flesh, but not before turning control of his growing empire over to his only son, Junior, who'd managed to snag a degree in electrical engineering, with honors, from M.I.T. No mean feat, that. Junior quickly proved he not only had the brains but also the drive and determination to take over his father's empire and make it even bigger. Not to mention make himself far, far richer.

JM Industries, the holding company that now controlled the various segments of the Montgomery world, had offices on five continents. (I think there are five continents, right? And Australia? Or does that make six continents? We're definitely not counting Antarctica here.) These days, its president and primary stockholder was—you guessed it—my client, Mr. JJM the Third himself. Jameson had taken over from his father some seven or eight years back when Junior's brilliant brain began to give out and he started having trouble with the Legos and Lincoln Logs his caretakers gave him to keep him occupied.

From what I could tell, the business world pretty much mourned the loss of Junior and wasn't all that happy that number Three was now the guy running the show. Or rather, the guy who ran it yesterday but who had now taken up temporary residence in the River City morgue

I had no idea what the majority were going to say about Jameson's change in residence, but there were definitely a few who weren't going to be overly upset about it. In fact, I'd be willing to bet there'd be more than a few bottles of expensive champagne uncorked very shortly, once word of Jameson's demise started making the rounds.

Unlike his father, Jameson the Third had not only *not* graduated with honors from one of the world's toughest schools, he'd never graduated at all. He had however, been booted out of some of the best. He'd started with Harvard (the reasons for his departure hadn't been available through a quick, legal, Internet search), then moved on to Yale (explanations also lacking). By the time he'd been shown the door at Stanford, however, even Junior couldn't keep the press from reporting that his son had a hankering for the company of pretty ladies—whether they wanted his company or not—and absolutely no compunction about cheating on his exams rather than wasting time studying for them.

Senior probably never had any qualms about handing control of his empire to his son, but Junior couldn't have been happy about his own son's less than promising performance. From the published information I could dig up in a few hours' searching, I couldn't tell if Junior had been so wedded to the idea of a dynasty of Montgomerys at the head of JM Industries that he'd chosen to ignore his son's shortcomings, or if he'd made the all-too-human mistake of thinking that, a) he was going to live forever and, b) his son would eventually shape up and be the kind of model human being a father could be proud of.

Whichever it was, by the time he was declared incompetent by the courts (following a petition filed on Three's behalf by a team of very competent and *very* expensive lawyers) it was too late. Control of the fifty-one percent of JM Industries stock held by Junior passed to his son, who already owned five percent in his own right. A team of very competent and *very* expensive caregivers took up permanent residence in Junior's house; and Three took up residence in the CEO's office at JM Industries. And that, as they say, was that.

Only, of course, it wasn't.

Turns out Jameson wasn't quite as useless a CEO as many had expected. He wasn't the business genius his father and grandfather had been, but he wasn't the incompetent no-good his college career had suggested he'd be, either.

His personal life was still a mess. Two divorces, a third pending—my guess? That was going to be one very happy, very *rich* widow. Timing is everything!—plus agreements for support of two out-of-wedlock daughters by different mothers that he hadn't wasted time and money contesting. But somehow JM Industries was still expanding and still putting more money into the Montgomery personal coffers than was going out to the Montgomery exes, both legal and not.

Which didn't mean that all was well on the business front.

It hadn't taken a lot of digging to catch the rumblings through the business press about lawsuits being brought against JM subsidiaries on three of those five (six?) continents. Charges of polluting (air, water, soil, or all of the above), plus bribery, tax evasion, labor disputes—you name it, someone somewhere was suing JM Industries over it. In the normal scheme of things, JM's lawyers (and there had to be a boatload of them, at every level) would have been very, very busy.

Nothing new in any of that, right? These days, you can't open a newsfeed without reading about one major multinational or another behaving badly and being sued for something, somewhere.

But here's where things got interesting.

Jameson had started out by following in his father's and grandfather's defiant footsteps, preferring protracted and expensive court cases rather than cede so much as an inch to anyone for any reason whatsoever. And then, with no explanation, a year and a half ago he abruptly reversed course, saying JM should accept responsibility, pay up, and invest in the improvements and operational changes the various plaintiffs were demanding. For all of it.

I'd been grateful I'd been sitting down when I read that. I'm no news geek, and I'm certainly no business expert, but I've never heard of any company, anywhere, being so willing to concede before the cases had worked their way through every appeals court possible, and even then it often requires the threat of government action to get them to pay up. Yet here was Jameson saying his company and its subsidiaries would accept responsibility for everything, pay up, fix the problem, follow the law, and all the rest of it? All without spending millions of dollars and countless years dragging through the courts first?

All those plaintiffs in all those countries must have been pretty happy, but the other forty-plus percent of JM Industries stockholders? Not so much.

With Jameson controlling a majority share of the business, there wasn't much those stockholders could do, but that didn't stop them trying. And Jameson, from all I could tell, was fighting them every step of the way.

Which is where things stood when I opened my mail and found his note and that great, big, fat check.

Nothing I'd read explained why Jameson John Montgomery the Third would even know about my existence, let alone want to hire me, but I really wanted to find out. Two hours after I'd started digging, I called the number he'd given in his note. Nobody answered and the recorded messages was one of those automated ones that says you've reached the number you just dialed, which is always so helpful. I left a message agreeing to this morning's meeting, and then I went out and deposited the check and prayed there'd be a bunch more to come.

Too bad things weren't working out as well as I'd hoped.

In fact, it couldn't have worked out much worse if Amelia had arranged the whole thing for my benefit herself. Most times, I wouldn't hesitate to blame her, but murder is going a little far, even for Amelia.

CHAPTER 7

I decided to start my investigation with a visit to Garr Analytics, a computer firm specializing in helping companies make sense of all the customer and sales data they collect so they can get even more customers and make even more money.

Garr Analytics is owned by a geek genius friend of mine, Gareth Garr. He houses his business in the next to the top floor of a renovated old apartment building two blocks from my much shabbier digs. He reserved the top floor for his personal residence—he doesn't like long commutes—and leases out the rest to companies and individuals that never, ever seem to have any trouble making the rent.

As if to underline the differences between us, Gareth's building elevator worked, his office door was brass-trimmed glass without so much as a smudged thumbprint marring its perfection, and the reception area was sleek, modern, and expensive, just like his services. The receptionist looked up, prepared to be snooty and exclusive, but at the sight of me, he smiled, instead.

"Hey, Maxie. Haven't seen you in a while."

"Hey, Douglas. Nice tie."

"Nicer suit." He stood, posed, then turned so I could admire the superb cut across the back. He looked over his shoulder to check my reaction. "What do you think?"

I cocked my head and frowned consideringly. It was for

effect only. I don't have much style sense, and Douglas knows it.

"Very nice," I said after I'd given it the requisite appreciative review. "Armani?"

His chin came up. *"Puhleeze!* Bespoke, from Jordan Brothers. Three months on the waiting list, just to get measured!"

My whistle of surprise really was appreciative. A bespoke from Jordan Brothers would have set me back a whole year's office rent and then some.

Douglas is always trying to get me interested in a little self-improvement, but I keep telling him my black turtlenecks and blouses paired with black or tan slacks have a certain professional neatness. Goes with my hair (black) and eyes (brown). It also makes getting dressed in the morning a whole lot easier—just look for whatever's still clean. Relatively clean, anyway. Some days I can't afford to be picky.

Gareth, to Douglas' never-ending despair, is worse. He likes Ts and worn blue jeans and sneakers, with the sneakers optional, more often than not. So far as I can tell, that's the required uniform for just about every geek genius on his way to being a billionaire, but Douglas hasn't given up hope. I swear that's why he keeps refusing Gareth's offers of marriage—it's his only remaining leverage in his efforts to convince Gareth he should *look* like a smashingly successful entrepreneur, not just *be* one.

"Gareth's in a meeting," Douglas said, now that the important matters were out of the way. "It may be a while, I'm afraid."

"That's okay. I was really looking for Lucille. Is she in?"

Douglas' eyebrows rose. He has as great an appreciation for Gareth's great aunt's specialized skills as I do. "Something interesting?"

"I'll tell you all about it, I swear, but I need to talk to Lucille first."

"Promise?"

"Cross my heart and hope to die," I said, accompanying the childish oath with the necessary cross over the heart and raised right hand. "But I gotta talk to Lucille first."

"Go right on back," Douglas said, buzzing me through. "You know where to find her."

As promised, Lucille was burrowed into her corner office, the one with a really good view of the cross streets and the neighboring apartment and office buildings.

Potted geraniums lined the window sills, though she'd taken care to leave clear viewing angles for the top-of-the-line, tripod-mounted Nightforce Xtreme spotting scope at the front window, and the similarly high-powered Leupold at the side. She's still trying to decide which of her three night-vision scopes is going to be her go-to device when she doesn't feel like going home and wants some entertainment.

I'd used her infrared scope one night when I was hanging around, waiting for her to work her magic, but didn't care to repeat the experience. Especially not if the scope was focused on the four-story brick building three quarters of the way down the block. There are some things you just don't want to know about your neighbors.

The rest of the office is furnished in crowded, grandmotherly kitsch that matches the geraniums more than the scopes. Lucille has a fondness for framed family photos and lots of them, as well as for lace doilies, china shepherdesses, and cat sculptures of every shape, color, and style, with quantity always taking precedence over quality. The cats are her compensation for allergies that make the real item an impossibility. None of us can understand the shepherdesses because Lucille hates sheep and is allergic to wool as well as to cats.

The wall across from the main spread of windows is dominated by an Early American-style sofa half buried under the crocheted afghans she's forever working on. In the corner, two Lazy Boy recliners angled companionably in front of a surprisingly small flat-screen TV.

Lucille's husband, David, has been dead for over twelve years, but she says having the recliners and small TV like that make it seem as if he's just gotten up to go to the bathroom and will be back at any moment.

The two had been sweethearts from grade school. They'd married at eighteen and immediately settled down to raise a family in an apartment four floors below this one. David had been an electrician for the city, Lucille a full-time homemaker, and they'd been very much in love. The only real sadness in their lives was the discovery that they couldn't have children, but they'd compensated by helping out with the neighborhood kids, instead.

They'd been in their late forties and comfortably settled into unchanging routine when Gareth's parents died in a car crash and they suddenly became guardians of a precocious four-year-old boy. Gareth admits he pretty much made their lives hell, especially at first, but Lucille only chuckles and says it wasn't quite *that* bad.

David lived long enough to see Gareth gain early enrollment in the advanced math program at Stanford—the flight to California to settle him in was the first time either Lucille or David had been on a plane or more than a hundred miles from home. Lucille still likes to talk about what a thrill that had all been, and how proud David was of Gareth's achievements.

What neither of them told their great nephew was that they'd invested every penny they had in his education, including their small retirement savings, and then they'd borrowed more. It might have worked out if David hadn't suddenly dropped dead of a heart attack on the job. Unfortunately, Social Security and the widow's pension Lucille received from the city weren't enough to cover her expenses along with the loan they'd taken out for Gareth. She was on the point of being evicted for nonpayment of rent when Gareth discovered the truth.

He immediately dropped out of Stanford, flew back to River City, and bullied the landlord and social services into helping her out. And then he'd started his data analytics business in the tiny bedroom he'd occupied since he was four years old. Three years later, he bought the entire building so Lucille would never again have to pay rent or worry about eviction, and moved his business out of his old bedroom and into the renovated space it now occupied. For her part, Lucille had refused to budge from the apartment she and David had shared their entire married lives, but she had let Gareth buy her a new stove.

It took a couple more years for Gareth to realize that his great aunt had her own brand of genius—she was, bar none, the best Internet sleuth for gossip of anyone in the nine boroughs, possibly the state. She says there's a fifteen-year-old girl in the little upstate town of Burke who can beat her, but that's about it.

Right now, she was hunched over one of the 1000-piece jigsaw puzzles she's addicted to, squinting over the top of her trifocals at a piece she was trying to force into place.

Lucille may be a whiz on the Internet, but she sucks at puzzles. She also cheats.

I craned over her shoulder, studying the board. "That's not going to fit, Lucille," I said mildly.

"Of course it will, punkin'," she said, not bothering to look up. "You just have to be firm with these things."

Firm meant mashing the piece into place with her thumb. "You see?"

"Mmm," I said, studying the results. At least she had the pattern going in the right direction. "Better than usual, but it still doesn't fit."

"Foo," she said, pushing back from the table. She may like her Lazy-Boys, but she loves her fifteen-hundred-dollar, adjust-to-any-angle office chair. Since Gareth now pays her a substantial retainer on top of covering all her expenses, she can afford it. "How are you dear? Haven't seen you in weeks."

"I've been busy." Watching the phone, waiting for it to ring with paying clients, but we didn't need to go there.

She beamed. Lucille has the sweetest smile. Makes you feel good, just seeing it. "That's good. Young people should be busy. Keeps them out of trouble. So what brings you here now?"

"I'm in trouble and I need your help."

Her smile widened. "Take that chair and tell me all about it."

TWO HOURS LATER I had photos and the full names, addresses, emails, private Facebook accounts, and phone numbers—business and private—of Jameson's wife, ex-wives, and the two (acknowledged) mothers of his children. (No telling who might pop out of the woodwork now Jameson wasn't around to defend himself.)

I also had a mountain of dirt on what the wives, at least, felt about him, each other, and their unwed rivals with the kiddies. The moms had been a great deal more discreet, but I'd be willing to bet that was due more to the small print in their child support agreements than to any reluctance to trash the others.

It never ceases to amaze me what people will post on some of these social media sites, especially when they think only their very very best friends are looking. If they had any idea just how often those same best friends passed along those scandalous little tit bits, and to whom, they'd probably feel compelled to change their names and move to Bora Bora.

In addition to the ladies' contact information and their views on their nearest and dearest, I knew the names of their hairdressers, favorite dress shops, preferred coffee shops, lunch spots, and all time favorite shoe stores.

Did I mention that Lucille is a genius?

Judging by everything she'd dug up, the women in Jameson's life not only hated him and each other, they also cost him a fortune just keeping them in lattes and lacy undies.

Lucille had asked if I wanted their Social Security numbers, too, but I'd politely declined. Even I don't cross that line if I don't have to.

"I should have a substantial number of his staff and business contacts by tomorrow," Lucille said, interrupting my train of thought. "Do you want me to print them or email them to you?"

"Print." Without a laptop, I didn't really have an option. I'd never gotten used to reading emails on my phone, which was the smallest and cheapest available under the cheapest plan I could find.

"You *sure* you don't want to borrow one of my laptops, punkin?" This was the third time she'd offered.

"Not right now. Thanks, anyway."

She never believed me when I said I didn't want a second slice of her famous double chocolate devil's food cream nut cake, either. (In that case, she was always right—it was my waistline that didn't want that second piece, not me.) But I really didn't want the laptop. Since I no longer had an office and would have to lug it around with me, I didn't want to be responsible for even one of her costly little toys.

Besides, she's way better at this kind of thing than I am. Once she gets started on JM Industries and Jameson's out-of-character swing to social responsibility, I'm betting she'll dig up all the bits I missed. The ones that would have made me opt for moving into a packing crate next to Hector's instead of cashing Jameson's check without knowing why he'd sent it.

As if reading my mind, Lucille said, "What I don't understand, dear, is why you wanted the information on all those women first. Why not follow the money, instead? That's what they do in all those detective shows, isn't it?"

"Probably," I said. "Most of the time, though, the money's harder to track, and the people that control it generally are very, very good about not talking to people like me. But Jameson had a taste for flashy women who liked the limelight. What do you think is the first thing they're going to do when they hear Jameson's been murdered?"

"Check with their lawyers to make sure they get a good chunk of his estate and that the child support continues even now he's dead?"

She had me on that one.

"Okay. The *second* thing they're going to do?"

"Get on the phone and tell everyone they know?"

I gave an exasperated huff. "The *third* thing, then."

She just looked puzzled.

"They're going to talk to the press."

"They will?"

"They will if the call is from a very sympathetic reporter from that nice magazine or gossip column that just covered them in such a flattering way."

Lucille glanced at the folder with all the printouts of those same magazines and gossip columns.

"So you're going to pretend to be a writer with one of these magazines?"

"That would be lying. But sometimes, when you say things in a certain way, people jump to conclusions and think you said something you didn't."

Lucille frowned. "And saying things with the deliberate intention of misleading isn't lying?"

"Not really."

"Not really isn't no, dear."

She had me on that, too, but I wasn't going to admit it. "Come on, Lucille. Focus, here. I'm trying to keep out of jail."

"Hmm," she said, considering. But Lucille is way too sweet to argue for long. "What if they won't talk to you?"

"Then I move on to plan b."

"And what's that, dear?"

"I haven't the faintest idea," I admitted.

CHAPTER 8

Before I left Garr Analytics, I updated Douglas on everything. He ran a quick check to see if news of Jameson's murder had hit the media—it had, and it wasn't pretty—and promised to keep an eye on how my part in the whole mess was being covered. So far, there weren't any details. I wasn't even mentioned. Yet. But I would be, and I was pretty sure the media was going to enjoy the part about Jameson hiring me, then ending up dead in my office.

They say there's no such thing as bad publicity. If you haven't already noticed, sometimes "they" get it dead wrong. Once word got out, Maxie Peterson Investigations was toast. The burned black kind that gets dumped in the trash.

Still, sufficient unto the day and all that. I'd worry about looking for a new job later. My first priority had to be making sure I wasn't arrested for murder.

Step number one, work my way through all those telephone numbers Lucille dug up for me. I didn't expect much, but you never know.

I didn't intend to use my personal phone, though. It's one thing to leave a call-back number if you really want someone to call back, quite another to leave a number the cops can tie to you if they start wondering who's harassing their suspects. Which meant I needed a public pay phone that wasn't too public. There aren't very many of those left, but they aren't completely extinct.

Murphy's Pub is a grubby little place that caters to the

serious drinkers in the neighborhood, guys who value cheap booze and wouldn't recognize an ambiance if it jumped up and bit them on the butt. It's owned by Mikael Konstantin, a Russian immigrant who arrived in the U.S. with a few kopeks, a talent for running illegal stills, and a number of old family connections that the FBI, among others, keeps a close eye on.

As always, I hesitated a foot inside the door, waiting for my eyes to adjust to the dim lighting and my nose to start packing up from the choking smell of beer and stale cigarette smoke. The city banned smoking in public places years ago, but if anyone ever told Mikael and his clientele, they'd long since conveniently forgotten. The place reeked.

This time of the day, it was half full with lunch customers who preferred to take their meal in liquid form. Not one of them paid any attention to me, or anyone else for that matter, which suited me just fine. From his spot behind the bar, Mikael noted my arrival, but without much interest. If the cops ever asked if I'd been there, he'd give them a shrug and the same blank, uninterested stare he was giving me now. The man has an amazingly short memory, at least when it involves the comings and goings of his customers. I'm not the only one who finds that useful every now and then.

I claimed an empty seat at the bar and, when Mikael eventually ambled my way, ordered a glass of the house red and ten bucks' worth of quarters. The red, as I knew from experience, was over priced and pretty much undrinkable, but Mikael wouldn't have handed out the quarters any other way.

The phone was on the wall at the back. Despite what you see in the movies, it wasn't anywhere near the rest rooms. As a courtesy to customers who found it a convenient place to conduct business, Mikael had placed a table and two chairs beside it, and moved everything else a discreet distance away. I set down the wine and Lucille's folder of notes, chunked two quarters in the slot, and started dialing.

The first call went straight to voice mail. "This is Christine.

Please leave a message." I hung up. I hadn't really expected anything else. Christine is Jameson's current wife, and chances were good she'd already learned she's now a very, very rich widow. She has other things to do than answer her phone.

Another two quarters. "Montgomery residence." Plummy voice, very cultured, with just a hint of superior, nose-in-the-air disdain. The butler or someone close to it. I would have expected a secretary or house maid, which must mean the senior staff were already on alert.

"Mrs. Montgomery, please." I tried for equally superior and ever so slightly bored, but didn't quite pull it off.

"Mrs. Montgomery is unavailable. May I take a message?"

"Please. Mr. Montgomery was supposed to meet me—"

"Who is calling?" There was a sharper urgency to that question.

"My name's Maxine." I couldn't help wincing when I said it. I hate the name my mother inflicted on me when I was too young to defend myself. "I—"

The plummy tone vanished, replaced by a nasty, hard edge. "Don't bother calling again. I'm setting incoming calls from this number to be automatically identified and recorded."

The bang of the phone slamming down made me jump.

Touchy, touchy. He hadn't even let me finish, which must mean they knew *where* Jameson had died, as well.

I hung up. I hadn't really expected anything else, but you'd think high-priced servants would be a little more polite about slamming the phone down, wouldn't you?

The next calls, to Mrs. Montgomery number two, then number one, then the newest mama, didn't fare much better. Number two had a maid who was downright insistent I leave a name, number, and explain my business, but I couldn't tell if that was because she knew about the murder or because she was supposed to be unhelpful and borderline rude to any unknown callers. Mrs. number one and mama number two were more voice mail. I didn't leave any messages.

I was getting low on quarters when I finally struck pay dirt with mama number one.

"Hello?"

I sat up straighter. The throaty, rather tentative voice didn't sound like anyone's idea of a high-priced maid or personal assistant. The slight thickness said the speaker had been crying. I quashed a surge of guilt and plowed forward.

"Ms Carmody?"

"Yes?"

"My name's Maxine. Do you remember the piece that *High Style* magazine did on you last April?" I said, resolutely pushing down a twinge of guilt. I've never quite worked out the ethical nuances of relying on suggestion and innuendo in an investigation, and I hope I never do. Sometimes they're the only way to get the response you're after.

"I remember."

Of course she did. If you're in fashion and you want to get noticed by people who are crazy about clothes and have way more money than they know what to do with, *High Style* is the place to be. According to Lucille, anyway, who knows all about these sorts of things.

Katie Carmody had been a high fashion model when she met Jameson Montgomery. She wasn't quite at the level of models who were automatically offered the cover of *Vogue*, but she probably would have made it if she hadn't gotten pregnant first. Not that *Vogue* has anything against pregnant women on their covers, mind, but Katie hadn't quite made it to that level of fame where she could be allowed to be fat and beautiful and on the cover, all at the same time.

Jameson didn't stay with her for long, however. He was in the process of divorcing wife number one when they met, so Katie probably figured an offer of marriage was right around the corner. It wasn't. By the time the baby was born, Jameson had wandered off, but Katie's lawyers managed to drag him back and didn't let him go again until they had his signature on a paternity support agreement and Katie had the first of a string of nice, big, fat checks in her bank account. From everything Lucille had found, it had all been fairly amicable, as such things went.

Evidently, Katie liked her new role of kept woman. The job of mama, not so much. She'd packed her daughter, Julia, off to day care the minute she was old enough, then to an exclusive girl's boarding school that took them really young. So far as Lucille could find, Katie had made no effort to return to her modeling career. She had, however, recently started her own clothing line, launching it with a major showing during the last fashion season.

Her style—bright, wild, and with a lot of bare skin showing in unexpected places—wasn't everyone's cup of tea, but then, neither was the price. *High Style* magazine's profile of her as the new, wild designer to watch, wouldn't have hurt. Assuming the new business was a success, Katie would be sitting pretty since she was still receiving a couple million a year for Julia and would until her daughter turned twenty-one or graduated from college, whichever came last.

I was guessing Julia would eventually be encouraged to go for a doctorate in something or other, maybe even a post-doc. If they worked it right, Julia would be in her thirties before those payments came to a halt. By that time, Katie would be sufficiently well established in her fashion career that she wouldn't miss those regular millions. Much.

So I'm a cynic. Sue me. This job will do that to you.

"Given the tragic news this morning," I continued—the sound of a stifled sob came clearly over the line—"*High Style* might find it interesting to explore how you left your extraordinary modeling career for Mr. Montgomery—" (They might! I wasn't claiming they *did*. I hadn't actually *said* I was from *High Style*, after all. If Katie Carmody wanted to connect a couple of unconnected dots, that was her problem, not mine.) "...then raised your daughter on your own, then, you know, how you built your business success without his assistance—"

I stopped, worried I'd gone too far.

Sometimes, I worry too much.

"It's true! I did!" There wasn't a hint of tears any more. "*All of it! All on my own!*"

It had probably helped that she'd had the bulk of that two million dollar child support payment to play with, too. Lucille had looked up the cost for that boarding school. It cost more than I made in a year, but that still left a lot of room for fun.

"Of course you did! That's why I thought, if you could spare me a little time..." I let the suggestion dangle.

"When do you want to do it?'

"Ahh, as soon as possible?"

"Right now? Would now be good?" I could almost hear her wiggling in excitement, right over the phone. "I mean, for the interview. I'd need a little more time to prep for a photographic shoot, you know?"

"Now would be great. No photographer." Probably not ever, but you never know.

"Let me give you directions...'

KATIE CARMODY'S HOUSE was in one of the tonier River City neighborhoods. Not quite top-tier mansion stuff, but still way beyond my league. I parked my eight-year-old Corolla in front, but instead of getting out immediately, I craned forward, studying the place.

"Not bad. Not great, but not bad."

If I hadn't had my seatbelt on, I'd have bumped my head on the roof liner. I whirled around to glare at Amelia, primly seated in the middle of the back seat and frowning at the house.

"What are you doing here?" I demanded. "I don't want you here. I didn't invite you. Go away.'

She dragged her attention off the house so she could frown at me instead. "Of course you want me here. You need all the help you can get."

"Don't."

"Do."

"Do not."

"Poo!" said Amelia with an airy wave of her hand. "Of course you do."

I slumped back in my seat and stared bleakly out the windshield. I did not want Amelia anywhere near me at any time, regardless. I especially didn't need the distraction now, but there was absolutely nothing I could do about it if she insisted on staying. In fact, she'd be more inclined to move in with me for the duration if I put up too much resistance.

And don't think using reverse psychology does any good, either. Been there, done that, and have the psychic scars to prove it. I'd probably be in counseling if I weren't afraid I'd be committed for observation and forced medication about two minutes after I tried to explain the problem.

"Don't you have other godchildren that need looking after?"

"Taken care of," said Amelia. "You're my top priority now."

As if for emphasis, she leaned forward and poked me with her wand. Hard. A second ago it'd been tucked in that magic pocket of hers, now here she was, physically abusing me.

"You should be grateful," she said. "You're ten times more trouble than all the rest put together."

"I do my best," I muttered under my breath.

Another poke. "What was that? Are you complaining?"

"Who? Me?" But I know when I've lost. I pulled the keys out of the ignition, unfastened my seat belt, and picked up my purse. "Shall we?"

Amelia was already on the front porch, impatiently tapping her foot, by the time I made the sidewalk.

Just as well. It was the first chance I'd had to notice what she was wearing, and I needed time to get my expression under control before I knocked on Katie Carmody's front door.

Amelia had abandoned this morning's boots and black leather for what looked like a personalized homage to Katie

Carmody's designs. She'd made a few critical concessions—a little more fabric in a couple of strategic spots and a lot stronger straps and belts and strings to hold it all in place—but it wasn't a style that suited her. And that's a serious understatement.

I'd never have thought I'd say it, but I preferred the boots and leather.

"What do you think?" Amelia asked when I reached the porch. She held out her arms and did a three-sixty so I could appreciate the overall effect.

Give me credit. I didn't snort or gasp or anything. All I said, when she came to a halt facing me, was, "Too bad Ms Carmody can't see you."

I meant it, too. Sort of. The shock alone would have her babbling things she'd never tell me, otherwise.

Amelia beamed. "You know, I could arrange it," she said, then hauled out her wand and poked the button on the security panel by the broad front door. "But I won't."

I was breathing again by the time Katie Carmody opened the door and let us in.

CHAPTER 9

It's a good thing I hadn't brought a photographer for that article I never actually said I was writing—even Katie's considerable skills at makeup hadn't quite managed to hide the evidence that she'd been crying. Maybe she really had cared for Jameson, in spite of everything.

Amelia gave her a sharp-eyed once over, then pouted in disappointment. The cream colored slacks and loose, satiny cream blouse Katie wore were elegant, but subdued. Not so much as a hint of the Carmody flair.

Since Amelia never had to pay for anything—that pointy-starred wand may look silly but it has some serious advantages—it would never occur to her that the simple slacks and blouse had probably set Katie back by the average monthly income for a family of four.

Katie led us through a broad, marble-floored foyer into what she no doubt called the living room. There was about an acre of white carpet, broad, low white couches that no one in his right mind would want to lounge on, and a wall of windows that looked out on a pool that could have held a hundred in a pinch.

As if to complete the picture, there was even a tanned, broad-shouldered, golden-haired pool boy in tight racing swim trunks, carefully skimming leaves out of the pool.

Unfortunately, reality doesn't always get the details straight. This pool boy might have had broad shoulders, but he couldn't have been more than fifteen or sixteen, max, and was so skinny you could see his ribs and the knobs of his spine. He had a phone stuck in the waistband of his trunks that was connected to earbuds, and his head was bobbing along to whatever beat was rocking his boat.

As if realizing the kid was spoiling the whole House Beautiful thing, Katie glided over to open one of the glass doors.

The boy looked up, then tugged the right earbud out.

"Ricky? Do you mind? I have some guests so…?"

He shrugged, but pulled his pole net out of the water, stuck his earbud back in his ear, and ambled away.

Amelia looked askance. "Isn't that illegal? Child labor or something?" she demanded.

I ignored her, but Katie must have picked up on my godmother's disapproving vibes because she said, "That's Ricky. He works for his dad."

I nodded. I didn't care. Ricky might be scrawny, but he didn't look abused. Kid has to earn his pocket money some way, right? Even my mom doesn't know all the things I did to earn a little extra cash when I was his age, and she knows *everything*.

"Lovely house," I said instead. All the way here I'd been trying to decide how I should handle this. Coming right out and asking her if she'd walked into my office this morning and killed the father of her only child didn't strike quite the note I was looking for.

I almost added, "Don't bounce on the sofa, Amelia," but caught myself in time.

Amelia can be amazingly rude. (The rest of the time she's just plain rude.) Katie hadn't even asked me to sit down.

"Nice sofa," Amelia said, leaning back and propping her feet on the glass coffee table in front of her.

"Please," said Katie. "Sit. Can I offer you something. Tea? Coffee?"

I wondered if something stronger was often on the menu around here. Somehow, I doubted it. Booze contains an amazing amount of calories and does absolutely nothing for the complexion. It only took a glance to know that Katie Carmody wasn't struggling with either.

"Coffee would be nice, if it's no trouble."

Amelia made a face. She thinks it's silly to worry about causing other people trouble, perhaps because she does it all the time and never, ever apologizes. For anything.

"You know what?" Katie said before I could stake out a spot on a sofa. "Let's move to the kitchen. Kitchens are such comfortable places to talk, don't you agree?"

"Absolutely," I said.

I wouldn't know. My kitchen's the size of a hatbox so I tend to avoid it as much as possible—even canned tomato soup requires more effort than it's worth. But I liked the idea of a comfortable place to chat. I wondered if maybe Katie was a little more down-to-earth than all the gossip magazines had led me to believe. Those rags have been wrong before.

I followed Katie out of the living room, through an equally impressive dining room with table and chairs for ten, and into a gleaming modern kitchen almost as big as my entire one-bedroom apartment, six-by-six basement storage space included.

While Katie ground some (no doubt expensive) coffee beans and started water heating for the fancy French press, I perched on one of the tall stools set at the end of the broad, granite-topped center island and took a look around.

Maybe it's just the class of people I consort with, but the kitchen didn't look anything like a normal person's kitchen. No coupons or kids' drawings stuck on the fridge with funky magnets; no dishes, washed or otherwise, in the sink; no hodgepodge of stuff cluttering the counters because it couldn't be stuffed in the already over-crowded cabinets and drawers. I'd give her a break on the kids' drawings since her daughter was thirteen and spent most of her time at boarding school, but no coupons? Not even two-for-the-price-of-one pizza coupons?

Definitely not my world.

"Do you take cream in your coffee?" Katie asked, dragging me back to attention.

"Thanks. Can't manage without it."

"I'm with you. I try and be good on most things, but I can't stand coffee without the cream. And sugar," she added, setting out a glass container of the latter, along with a spoon and square tea napkins for both of us. Cloth, and beautifully pressed. No cheap paper stuff for Katie Carmody.

I got a glimpse of the interior of her fridge while she dug out the cream. Gleaming clear plastic bins filled with fruits and veggies, neat glass containers with who knows what, all neatly arrayed on the gleaming clean glass shelves. No cheap wine, no beer, no carry out, and not so much as a hint of something forgotten at the back that might be growing fur.

Forget the same world. We don't inhabit the same *universe*.

It was only as Katie was digging in a cabinet, trying to decide between mugs or cups and saucers, that I realized Amelia was nowhere in sight.

That is never a good sign.

I wasn't wasting energy hoping she'd simply gotten bored and gone somewhere else. She was up to something, and I was pretty sure I wasn't going to like it once I found out what.

Best not think about it. There wasn't anything I could do to stop her, anyway. Believe me, I've tried.

"Do you do much cooking?" I asked Katie instead.

"Not really." She almost sounded sorry. "My life's so busy I don't have time, you know?"

"I can imagine," I said. Me, I'm just lazy. I'm also a lousy cook. "Thanks," I added as she set a mug of steaming coffee in front of me.

Mugs were good. Casual. The sort of thing you chose when you were ready for a little girl-to-girl chat.

The coffee smelled wonderful. I dosed mine with cream and sugar, then took a cautious sip. Hot, rich, and very smooth. Even better than it smelled. I didn't care about the house or fancy clothes or her stunning good looks, but I envied Katie's ability to buy really expensive coffee beans anytime she wanted.

Katie claimed a stool across from me. I savored my coffee and kept silent while she stirred in the sugar and cream. Sometimes silence is the best goad to conversation.

It worked this time, too.

"You're probably wondering why the big kitchen since I don't cook."

I'd figured it was because it came with the house, but now that she mentioned it...

She looked around, nervously rubbing her left wrist as if missing a wrist watch that wasn't there. "Jameson really liked this kitchen, you know?"

I sat up straighter on my stool. "Did he?"

She nodded. I could see the faint glint of the tears that were starting to well, but she blinked them back. Maybe she was just being stoic, but tears wouldn't do a thing for the mascara, and she'd already had to redo her face at least once before I'd shown up. I could tell because she'd missed a tiny smudge in one corner.

"You wouldn't have thought someone like him, who was used to people taking care of that sort of stuff, would care, but he did. It was perfect for parties. Caterers love a space like this, you know?"

"Do they?" What else was I supposed to say?

"Yeah." She was still fiddling with her wrist, but hadn't touched her coffee. She must have seen me noticing because she abruptly pulled her cuff down, picked up her teaspoon, and started fiddling with that, instead. "There's an extra big fridge in the pantry, a freezer, serving pieces, dishes for dozens and dozens. Before we even moved in, he had an assistant help me pick out all the things he wanted."

I wondered what his assistant had thought of the assignment. How do you even advertise for a job like that? Must type, take messages from my wife, and set up house for my mistress?

"I'd never really had a house before," Katie continued, "just apartments. New York's all apartments, you know. I had a fabulous flat in Paris one winter when I had a string of assignments in Europe," she added, brightening at the thought. "You could see Notre Dame from the balcony off the living room and master bedroom. It was amazing."

I managed to stifle an appreciative whistle. I wasn't familiar with Paris real estate, but I'd bet that apartment had set somebody back a hefty chunk of change.

I was pretty sure Katie wouldn't have paid for it. She definitely hadn't paid for this place. (Lucille was very particular about getting that kind of detail right.)

"But it was different for Jameson," Katie continued. "He was used to big spaces, lots of staff. He wanted the same thing for our house."

Our house?

"Lot of work, making a home for two," I said carefully.

"We wouldn't have had to worry about any of that, but his wife was being difficult." Katie's features hardened. "She didn't want to move out, even though it was *his* family's house, not hers."

"Mmmm," I murmured disapprovingly.

"It's not even really a house," she added fiercely. "It's a *mansion*. It's got servants quarters, not just a maid's room like this place, and *two* kitchens, and a ball room, and I don't know how many bedrooms and bathrooms. It's even got real stables!"

"Wow!" I said. I was on pretty firm ground with that one.

"Yeah. I could have given *fantastic* parties with a ballroom to work with. We *needed* that space, because there were all his business friends and my fashion friends and everything! I mean, even *Town and Country* covered a party he gave there, you know?"

I let my eyes widen in appreciative amazement. Lucille had missed that bit, and from the way Katie said it, having *T & C* cover your party was only a touch less prestigious than having the Queen for tea.

"But he got her out eventually, right?" I said. "His wife, I mean?"

We were talking about Jameson's first wife here. Since then, he'd gone through another wife and was getting rid of the third when somebody changed his plans. Not to mention another pregnant lover. Yet here was Katie, still clinging to her fantasies thirteen years after he'd walked out on her and her unborn child. It didn't argue for a firm grasp on reality, on her part.

"Yeah, he got her out. Eventually. As it happens," she added, a little too casually. "I might just be moving into that place, anyway."

"Really?" I didn't have to fake the surprise.

She nodded violently, that perfect mouth flattening into a hard, ugly line. Her grip on the spoon tightened until the thing started to bend, ever so slightly.

"Absolutely. Don and I have talked about it."

"Don?"

"My lawyer. Don Larson. I was talking to him just before you called. He totally supports me on that. After all, I'm the mother of Jameson's only child. Julia *definitely* should inherit that house. *And* the money. *All* of it. Though I'll have to take care of it for her for quite a while, of course."

Of course.

I didn't say it. I did say, "I thought Jameson had another child?"

"Hah! That lying bitch?" She slammed the spoon down on the counter top hard enough to send ripples across the surface of her still untouched coffee. "Angelina's like a cat in heat and always has been."

All the brave, misty-eyed grief of a moment ago was gone. If it had ever been there in the first place. I had a feeling I was getting my first glimpse of the real Katie Carmody.

"Angelina said Jameson was the father," Katie continued spitefully, "but there was never any DNA test. The way she slept around, that kid of hers could have had a half dozen fathers."

"Really?" I said, with what I hoped was the right note of sympathetic appreciation.

I wasn't going to waste time in a discussion of basic biology, but I couldn't imagine Jameson would have accepted paternity if he hadn't known he had no other option. I *definitely* wasn't going to mention the inheritance prospects of wife number three, whom Jameson hadn't quite managed to divorce before someone changed his plans. Permanently.

Not for the first time, I wondered if Jameson had left a will. At this point, his lawyer was the only one who knew for sure, though Trueblood might have ferreted out the answer by now. It had to have been right up there near the top of his list of Things To Find Out.

Even if a current will existed, it could still be contested in court—there's never any shortage of lawyers willing to take on a case that's guaranteed to make them a lot of money, no matter who wins. None of the women Jameson had loved and left had been shy about making their demands while he was alive. Now he was dead, there wasn't anything to stop them getting even louder, shriller, and whole lot more litigious.

Time to change the topic.

"How did your daughter react to the news of her father's death?" I asked.

Katie's eyes widened and her mouth dropped open. Not her best look, really.

"Oh. My. God," she said. "I forgot about Julia."

Yup, this was the real Katie Carmody. Took time to talk to her lawyer about the financial spoils but couldn't remember to tell her daughter.

"I didn't mean that, exactly," she added, suddenly remembering that she was talking to a woman she thought was a reporter. "I mean, I'd been focusing so much on how awful this was going to be for her—she loved him so much, you know. And he loved her, too. It's all been so hard…"

She set down her coffee mug and brought a trembling hand

to her lips. The tears were coming back. She snatched up her napkin and delicately dabbed at her eyes.

It was beautifully done. Tender. Vulnerable. Brave despite the emotional devastation of loss.

I wondered if she'd gone to acting class, too. She'd have been an A plus student for sure.

"That woman is *definitely* oversexed."

I almost spewed my coffee. Amelia was standing in the doorway, hands on hips and looking *very* disapproving.

"You should see what she has in her nightstand," she continued. "Packets and packets of those rubber thingees for guys and not one but *two* of those giant electric cigar thingumabobs."

Condoms and battery-powered dildos. That was not an image I wanted in my head right now. I turned my attention back to Katie.

"How did you get the news?" I asked. I'd been digging for motive. Maybe I should have been focusing on alibis.

"I need to call Julia," Katie said, not looking at me. I wasn't sure she'd even heard my question.

She slid off her stool, then tugged her clothes into place. It was an automatic gesture, but it was also like she was girding herself for a fight.

"She can't come home," she muttered. "They can't let her come home."

That last wasn't for me. Katie was so focused on whatever was going around in her head that she seemed to have forgotten I was there.

She was halfway to the door when she remembered. She stopped and turned back to demand, "You can see yourself out, right?"

She didn't wait for an answer. Amelia had to jump to get out of her way.

"How rude!"

"And prying in people's nightstands isn't?" I shot back.

Amelia sniffed dismissively. "I was looking for evidence." She swept the kitchen with what she no doubt considered a steely gaze. "Find anything in here?"

"She has a very clean refrigerator. And somebody irons her napkins."

Amelia frowned. "That's not evidence."

"Neither is any personal stuff she keeps in her nightstand."

"Yes, it is."

"No, it's—" I sighed. I should know better than to argue with her. "Come on. Let's get out of here."

"You're not going to search the place?"

"I assume that was what you were doing. You were gone long enough."

"*Somebody* had to. And I have an advantage, you know."

"Yeah. No scruples."

"That's not what I meant."

She meant that nobody could see her poking her nose— literally—in places she had no business looking, but it would annoy her a lot more if I played dumb or, better yet, ignored her altogether.

Trouble is, ignoring her just makes her behave more and more outrageously, until you *have* to pay attention.

"I gotta get my purse," was all I said.

Amelia reluctantly followed me back to the living room, but when I headed toward the sliding glass doors and the pool rather than the front door, she exclaimed, "Hey! I thought she said you should show yourself out!"

"She did," I admitted, stepping out onto the slate-paved patio. "But she didn't say which door."

"Hah!" Amelia scrambled after me before I could slide the door shut in her face.

Not that she can't walk through a closed door as easily as an open one, but she still hates it. Especially if she suspects you of deliberately shutting it in her face.

Some people are just so suspicious.

CHAPTER 10

"What do you expect to find out here?" Amelia demanded when she caught up with me.

"Nothing. But that doesn't mean I don't want a look around, anyway."

I kept my voice low in case there was anyone lurking in the bushes or around corners who might wonder why I was talking to myself, and what, exactly, I was saying.

Actually, I was hoping to find our pool boy, Ricky. Or his father. Or maybe a maid, hanging out the laundry or beating the rugs or something. *Somebody*. Anybody who might tell me if Jameson Montgomery ever dropped by the house to see his former lover and their daughter.

Not that I had any idea what difference it would make if Jameson actually spent any time with his eldest child or not. He paid the bills, which was all the law required. It didn't demand that he actually be a loving father, too.

I found Ricky around the side of the house. He still had the pool net, but instead of scooping leaves, he was furiously thrusting the blunt end into a hedge like a spear-wielding gladiator making sure the enemy was well and truly dead.

"Ricky?"

He jerked around, startled, eyes narrowed, hard and glittering. Whatever enemy he'd been slaughtering in that hedge hadn't stood a chance.

The expression was gone in an instant, replaced by the distant, frozen mask of a servant who knew his place.

"Ma'am?" he said. The response was courteous and respectful. The way he squared his shoulders, on the other hand, said he was game for a fight if I was.

"Do you have a minute to chat?" I said mildly.

"He's just a kid," Amelia objected, leaning close and keeping her voice low as if she didn't want him to hear. "What would he know?"

Maybe a lot.

He shrugged. He had a lot of attitude for a scrawny pool boy. "Sure."

He crossed to me, the pool net still in his hands. The long pole was a great excuse for keeping his distance—no one could accuse him of being rude, yet he was well out of reach.

Or maybe I was way too suspicious and he just didn't want to have to retrieve it.

"You that magazine lady here about Mr. Montgomery?" he asked.

I hadn't expected that. "Uh... Did Ms Carmody say I was?"

Another shrug. "She said there was a lady from some fancy magazine coming, and I was supposed to make sure everything looked all tidy and neat."

"And she mentioned Mr. Montgomery?"

I was having a hard time ignoring Amelia, who was standing there with her arms crossed over her chest, impatiently tapping her foot.

Ricky frowned. "No, but I figured she'd have told me yesterday if it was anything else. She likes everything all polished up when reporters come, you know."

Amelia snorted. "Of course she would. It's all about the image with these fashion types, never the substance."

For the first time I noticed that she'd changed out of the Katie Carmody outfit into something resembling the tight sweater, black leather mini, and boots combo from this morning.

Never thought I would have considered it an improvement. Katie was officially out of favor with Ms Amelia.

I turned my attention back to Ricky.

"Why did you think this was about Mr. Montgomery?"

"He's dead, isn't he? That's what they said on the radio."

I glanced at the phone still stuck in his swimming trunks. "Yes, he's dead."

"Murdered."

Another snort from Amelia. "Like a letter opener through the heart is a popular choice for suicides."

"I don't know if they've made an official determination yet," I said.

"So that's why you're here, right? Because he's dead?"

I nodded, wondering where this was going. I'd thought I'd be the one asking questions.

He hesitated, evidently weighing his next words. "Do they know about Julia? The cops, I mean. Do they know about her?"

"Mr. Montgomery's daughter? Probably." Almost certainly. Family would have been the first thing Trueblood checked on. If spouses were at the top of the list for suspects, former spouses and lovers had to be a solid number two. At least to start. Which meant the kids ended up in the tally, too.

Ricky's face darkened in a scowl. "She didn't even call her," he said.

"Who didn't call her?" As if I didn't know.

"Her mom," he said bitterly. "She didn't even call to tell Julia her daddy was dead."

"How do you know? Did you call Julia?"

He nodded. "Soon as I heard. Somebody had to."

"Smart kid," said Amelia. "Got ol' Katie's number, doesn't he?"

I was more interested in the fact that Ricky not only had Julia's number, but that he'd cared enough to call her with the news when Julia's own mother hadn't thought to. The only interest Katie seemed to take in her daughter's existence was the leverage it gave her with Jameson's bank account. And his estate.

"How is she? Julia, I mean?" I said.

That was a mistake. The shutters slammed down at the reminder that he was talking to what he thought was a member of the press.

"Fine," Ricky said. "Anyway, you had a question, ma'am?"

So we were back to *ma'am*. If I'd had any chance of getting answers from him, I'd killed them with that question on Julia. Still, nothing ventured…

"I was just wondering if Mr. Montgomery visited here much. You know, to see Ms Carmody and Julia."

"I wouldn't know, ma'am. I just work here sometimes when my daddy needs me. Anyway, Julia's at school."

"So you didn't see Mr. Montgomery often?"

"I'd best get back to work. Ms Carmody doesn't like me bothering her guests."

"I'm not a guest—"

"Gate's right over there, ma'am" he said pointing politely. "Just follow the path."

And with that, he shifted his grip on that net and marched away without a backward glance.

Amelia snickered. "Told *you*, didn't he? You shouldn't have asked about the girl like that."

"Thanks," I snapped back, irritated. "I already figured that out."

"Too bad you didn't figure it out *before* you asked."

"Whatever would I do without you?" I asked. My sarcasm quotient goes way up whenever Amelia's around. I can't help it.

"I honestly can't imagine," Amelia said, and vanished.

UNFORTUNATELY, she was already installed in the passenger's seat by the time I got back to the car.

"Don't you have someplace else you need to be?" I demanded, reluctantly sliding behind the wheel.

"I canceled my appointments."

"You make appointments? Since when?" Amelia's never given *me* any warning that she's planning to ruin my day.

"All right, I canceled my *plans*. Satisfied? You're my top priority now," she added, as if that were any reassurance.

My phone rang before I could say anything I'd regret. "Maxie Peterson Investigations," I said automatically.

"Jancie Jarrow of the *River City Courante*, Ms Peterson. I—"

I hung up before she could finish. "Shit."

Amelia beamed. "This is great! You're going to be on all the news. The girls will be sooooo jealous! Nobody else has a goddaughter who's famous!"

I groaned and started the engine. Someday I'd figure out what I'd done to deserve a fairy godmother like Amelia, but I wasn't going to waste time stressing about it now.

"Where to next?"

I consulted the folder Lucille had created. "Wife number one."

"Why not number three? If she inherits everything—"

"She'll have to wait. I couldn't get past the butler when I called. Guaranteed I won't get through security at the Montgomery mansion."

"Mansion?"

"That's what Katie called it. She's already planning her first big bash in the ballroom. She's convinced her daughter's going to inherit everything," I added by way of explanation.

"The daughter she dumped in boarding school when she was five?"

"That's the one."

"Poor kid. Maybe I should put her on the godmother waiting list. Agatha's up next, I think. A bit scatty but she's good on wishes. Kid deserves a break."

A break, maybe, but *not* a fairy godmother. Nobody deserves one of those.

I didn't say it.

Besides, maybe Agatha was one of the good ones. There had to be one or two that could successfully manage the modern equivalent of glass slippers and Prince Charming, right? I'd met a couple of Amelia's buddies. They scared the hell out of me, but that didn't mean all fairy godmothers were like them.

What I *did* say was, "Let's concentrate on finding Jameson's killer, shall we?"

Not to mention keeping me out of jail, rescuing Maxie Peterson Investigations from certain doom, and justifying that big advance from Jameson currently sitting in my checking account. What was left of it, anyway.

Wife number one was Mrs. Annalise Dougherty Montgomery. Neither one nor two had remarried, and they'd both chosen to keep Jameson's last name. Probably came in handy when they were making dinner reservations, among other things.

Annalise lived in a lovely little townhome (or as little as it gets for two point eight million) not far from Katie's bigger but slightly more down market home (two point two five million and change—as a friend of mine in real estate keeps saying, it's all about location). Her proximity to Katie was the reason she was my next stop. That and the chance I might be able to talk my way past security.

In the meantime…

I fished my bluetooth earpiece out of the clutter in my console and popped it in. Because River City cops view fines for cell phone use while driving as a convenient source of revenue, I waited until the next traffic light had me pinned before calling a number I knew by heart.

I was in luck. Sort of. My good buddy Betsy Sharanski, the crime scene investigator, picked up on the third ring. That, however, was where the luck ran out.

"You shouldn't be calling me.'

"Is that any way to greet a friend you've known since grade school?"

"It is if she's a murder suspect."

"That's harsh."

"It's the truth. Don't tell me you're surprised."

"Why do you think I'm calling? What's going on? Did you find any suspicious fingerprints on the letter opener?"

"Give us a break, will you? We've haven't had time to enter everything in the database, yet, let alone check for prints and DNA."

"Bummer. Did you?"

Betsy sighed. "Yeah. There are prints. Yours."

"But they were smudged, right? Like somebody with gloves or something?"

"Maybe."

"Maybe? What do you mean by 'maybe'?"

"Hold on, Mom. You're fading out. Let me go find a better signal, okay?"

It was my turn to sigh. Betsy wasn't alone, she couldn't tell me what was going on, and so far I was still their best—probably their only—suspect. This was not what I'd hoped to hear.

"You still there?" Betsy sounded like she was in some sort of echo chamber. My guess? She'd taken cover in the fire exit stairwell.

For the record, that's a lousy place to have a confidential conversation. It's not just the echo, which means you can be heard a lot farther away than you think, it's that you don't know who could be lurking on a different level, out of sight yet listening to every word you say.

I made a mental note to explain the risks to her another time. Right now, the last thing I wanted to do was antagonize my best and most reliable source of information inside the investigation.

"I'm here," I said. "You have *any* good news?"

"Not really. Someone did a half-assed job of trying to wipe off the prints—door, desk, chairs. That sort of thing. Whoever it was missed a couple, though. Both yours."

"But I didn't stab him! I wasn': even there!"

"I know you didn't stab him. I'm just telling you what they'll say about the prints. It doesn't clear you, and it doesn't give us a hint about who *did* kill him."

"What about the other stuff? Hair and dirt from shoe treads and that sort of stuff?" I watch detective shows, too.

"Plenty of dirt. You really need to get a new vacuum, Maxie. Or use the one you've got a lot more often."

She's worried about my housekeeping skills at a time like this?

"Maybe next week. What else? Hair?"

"Several hair samples, but that's not going to do much good, either."

"Why not?"

"Come on, Maxie. I've been in your office when half your neighbors have come wandering through, cadging a cup of coffee or saying hi."

I heaved another sigh even though it wasn't my turn.

"I suppose I'm lucky you didn't find any of your hair there." Betsy has long, gingery red hair. Not the sort of thing you see a lot of. "If they'd had any idea you'd been there they'd have taken you off the case, and…."

I didn't finish the sentence. I can be real slow sometimes, but I get there eventually.

"They *didn't* find any of your hair, did they?" I said. It wasn't really a question.

"There's not a single sample of my hair in the collected evidence."

"Which isn't the same thing as saying you didn't find any to begin with."

My best friend Betsy Sharanski, who sleeps, eats, and drinks rules and regulations, had deliberately withheld evidence she'd collected at the scene. Granted, it was evidence that she'd been there, too, but it was still evidence.

"Thanks, Bets. I owe you one.'

"No, you owe me about a hundred." Her voice had dropped until it was barely a whisper. "They know we're friends. The only reason they let me work the scene is because they were really short-handed this morning, and because they know I *never* cheat. Ever."

This kind of infraction would be killing her, yet she'd done it anyway. She's right. When we're wheeled into the old folks' home together, I'll *still* owe her for this.

"If it weren't for you," I said, "I'd have no one to tell me what was going on."

"You'd have Gracie."

"Now you're being mean. Gracie would plant evidence *against* me if she thought she could get away with it."

"Exactly, so be grateful you've got me. Listen, I gotta get back. I'll keep you posted if I can, Maxie. But for right now, don't call me, okay? Not even at home."

"Okay."

"Promise?"

"Promise," I said, but I was already talking to a dead connection.

"Not good, huh?" Amelia didn't even try to pretend she hadn't been listening to every single word.

Before I could say something I'd regret, the phone rang. That was a mistake.

"Don't hang up, Ms Peterson! The *Courante* would love—"

I hung up, and then I turned the phone back off. Jancie whatever-her-name-was from the *River City Courante* might be the first reporter to find my number, but she wouldn't be the last. That Yellow Pages ad hadn't even paid for itself and now it was going to ensure that any and every nut case in River City—and I was including the media in that—would be calling to ask questions I couldn't answer.

I didn't have time to dwell on it in any case because we had arrived at the elegant wrought iron gates of Eddington Estates.

I have no idea who Eddington was or why he'd have a

bunch of very expensive houses and townhomes named after him, but it didn't matter. The guard wasn't letting me in, regardless.

"I'm sorry, ma'am," he said even though he didn't look it. "Without a name, I can't announce you to Mrs. Montgomery, and since it appears she hasn't given you the gate code..." He shrugged, palms up, in a gesture of friendly helplessness.

"He's not sorry," Amelia huffed. "He's rude. And you even said please."

"I understand," I said, smiling apologetically at the guard while trying to ignore her. "It's a surprise visit, but it won't be a surprise if—"

The guard's eyes suddenly went wide and vacant, and he jerked upright like he'd been pulled on strings.

"Go right on through, ma'am," he said in a flat voice that didn't sound at all like it had thirty seconds earlier. As he spoke, the gates majestically swung open even though he hadn't moved an inch.

"Bear left," he added, still in that same flat voice, "then right on Stonybrooke. You can't miss it." He wasn't even looking at me.

"Close your mouth, Maxine, and do as the man says," said my fairy godmother primly.

"What'd you do, Amelia?" As if I didn't know. We'd been through this sort of thing before. It never turned out well.

"A little befuddlement spell, that's all. It will wear off soon enough."

"When? The last time you put that spell on someone—"

"Would you rather I shut the gates and left you to figure things out on your own? Just how far do you think you'd get with that approach?" She was getting huffy now.

Huffy and Amelia is not a good mix.

I drove through the gates, then grudgingly followed the poor man's directions. If he wasn't back to normal by the time we returned, I didn't know what I'd do. Demanding Amelia reverse a spell can easily make things much, much worse.

As I drove, Amelia provided a *sotto voce* accompaniment to my thoughts. "Ungrateful little...*mumble mumble*...anyone else would be...*mumble mumble*...and to think I could have...*mumble mumble mumble*...and I mean it!"

Fortunately, Stoneybrooke Road and number 219 weren't all that far away. There wasn't quite enough time for Amelia to get seriously wound up before I parked the car.

After a few seconds' inner debate, I turned off the engine and unfastened my seatbelt. I hate not leaving myself an out in case I need one.

"You're going to leave this to me, right, Amelia?" I said. Firm but not threatening. It's hard to strike just the right balance when you're dealing with my fairy godmother, perhaps because she's basically unbalanced to begin with.

"*Right?*" I said when she didn't answer.

She heaved a deep sigh to make it clear that she was the injured party here, then said, reluctantly, "If you insist."

"Great."

"Even if you will make a hash of it just like you did with the last one."

"I didn't make a hash of it," I said, stung.

"You didn't get a confession, either."

"I wasn't trying to get a confession!"

"My point exactly."

"I'm getting out now."

"I'll wait here," she said, looking put upon and abused.

"Perfect," I said.

Amelia? Wait? It was never gonna happen.

I grabbed my purse and climbed out of the car, then pointedly locked the door. You can never be too careful, even in a place like this.

Plus, it would annoy Amelia, even though the lock didn't really stop her. (By now you've probably figured out that I enjoy annoying my fairy godmother. It's absolutely the only satisfaction

I get out of the relationship.)

Mrs. Montgomery number one had bought into one of those developments that doesn't approve of front-stoop neighborliness, and reinforced that opinion by building tall garden walls around every single townhome so that all you could see were the roof lines and an occasional tree that had been chosen because it never got too tall, too shady, or dropped too many untidy leaves.

Despite the broad, beautifully landscaped public walks that fronted the row of townhomes on either side, there wasn't a soul in sight.

If Annalise socialized with her neighbors, it was probably at the racquet or golf club, not here It wouldn't be reasonable to expect otherwise, not when she was reduced to living in one of these modest little two-bedroom, three bath, six thousand square foot bungalows (not counting the maid's rooms). Which might be one of the reasons Jameson had had such a hard time moving her out of his mansion, way back when Katie first started eyeing that ballroom.

I hadn't been able to reach Annalise by phone earlier, and there was no guarantee she was here now, but I didn't have any better idea. It was too early to start staking out the dress shops and hair salons. The coffee shops might be an option if this approach didn't pan out, but I'd cross that bridge when I came to it.

Amelia, despite her avowed intention to stay put, had already vanished. I wasn't wasting energy hoping she'd taken the hint and left. I'm never that lucky.

To my surprise, I only had to wait a couple of minutes before a voice on the intercom at the gate responded to my buzz.

"Yes?"

"Mrs. Montgomery?"

"Yes?"

I drew a deep breath, crossed my fingers, and said, "My name's Maxine Peterson. I'm investigating Mr. Montgomery's death. I wondered if you had a few minutes to talk?"

To my even greater surprise, there was only a moment's hesitation before she buzzed the gate opened. "Come in."

Wow! Honesty really does work every now and then. Not that I'd ever had any doubts.

The patio courtyard was about what I'd expect for the bucks, elegant slate-paved walkway, manicured decorator plants in imported decorator pots, a couple of upholstered patio chairs set by a burbling fountain (easy enough to manage when you have someone else to haul the cushions in out of the rain and fish the leaves out of the fountain).

By the time I reached the carved double doors at the entrance, they were open and Annalise Montgomery, Jameson's missus number one, was waiting for me.

Like Katie, Annalise was tall, fine-boned, and gorgeous, but her hair was black, not blonde. She was dressed in a chic black sheath that would have easily run to four figures off the rack, and she stood in the middle of that open doorway as stiff and straight as if she were facing down a charging herd of ninja assassins.

"You're Maxie Peterson?" she said. "Of Maxie Peterson Investigations?"

"Yes, ma'am," I said, my heart sinking. The Maxine thing can't be expected to work all the time, but I'd hoped it would get me in the front door, at least.

Annalise drew herself up even straighter. Her dark eyes narrowed menacingly.

"Did you kill Jameson?"

"What! Me? No!"

"No?"

"No! Honest!"

"Oh," she said, visibly deflating. "Shame."

She eyed me up and down. I didn't get the feeling she was much impressed.

"Well," she said with a resigned sigh. "As long as you're here, you might as well come in, anyway."

CHAPTER 11

It was an hour before I finally managed to escape. I'd consumed gallons of a vilely healthy green tea, listened to Annalise's detailed review of her husband's manifold failings, apologized— twice—for not having had the gumption to murder him myself, and barely avoided dropping my teacup when Amelia abruptly reappeared to announce that, unlike that other hussy, Mrs. Montgomery had absolutely nothing disgusting in her nightstand.

I'd only needed a quarter of that hour listening to Annalise badmouth her ex-husband to know that Jameson had had the right idea when he dumped her for Katie. If the green tea hadn't been sufficient reason for making the switch, Katie's excellent coffee and apparently extensive collection of condoms should have clinched the deal.

Regrettably, I was pretty sure Annalise hadn't killed him. If she'd been going to do it, she'd have nagged him to death years ago.

Which meant it was two down, at least three more of Jameson's girls to go, and I wasn't any closer to figuring out who had killed him than when I'd started. And I hadn't even begun on his disgruntled Board of Directors, hostile stockholders, and, for all I knew, former best friend who'd swiped his mistress or something. Not to mention, I hadn't even started on the possibility of more recent mistresses who hadn't attracted the same gossip column coverage as the wives and mamas.

All that might have depressed me, but life was not without its good news: Amelia had disappeared not long after ransacking Annalise's cupboards and drawers. And when I discovered the guard at the security gate, though still dazed and confused, was showing signs of recovering, I felt good enough to turn on the radio and start singing along to Lady Gaga, who was complaining about paparazzi. (All right, I do the papa-paparazzi part, then hum the rest. But it seemed appropriate, under the circumstances.)

By this time it was late afternoon and I'd had nothing to eat since Trueblood had bought me that sandwich. Given that he'd eaten half of it before I got my first bite, then snatched the rest, I didn't think that even counted.

There wasn't anything edible in my own kitchen, and, with the current uncertain state of my finances, it didn't seem like a good idea to splurge on Pietro's All You Can Eat Italian Buffet, my pig-out place of choice. Which meant that value meals were not only back on the menu, they were the *only* menu.

I did go a little upscale by parking and dining in rather than driving through. That way I could get free refills on the Coke and have a chance to mull things over. Even if everyone in the place had been following the coverage of Jameson's murder, they'd never notice me huddled in the back corner booth.

Forget those dark, smoky bars of the old detective novels. For true anonymity, nothing beats a brightly lit, shiny clean place like Mickey D's.

A packet of medium fries, one burger, and a medium Coke plus refill later, I still hadn't thought of any solution to Jameson's murder that made any sense. Alive, he kept making money and paying alimony or child support. Dead? Why would you bump off the guy funding the gravy train unless you were absolutely, positively, no-doubt-about-it sure that you were in his will for an even bigger pay day?

That thought inevitably led to wondering again if anyone, other than his lawyer, knew what was in Jameson's will.

Not counting Trueblood, of course. And he might not know yet either.

I should probably give him a call.

On the plus side, I could ask him about the status of the investigation and share some of my hard-won insights and bits of insider information, and he could tell me that of *course* I wasn't a suspect and never had been.

On the minus side.... There were an awful lot of minuses.

For starters, my pluses were pure self-delusion. Trueblood wasn't going to tell me squat about the investigation, let alone reassure me that I wasn't a suspect And if he did talk to me, he'd be a whole lot more likely to grill me about why Jameson had hired me, and what was he doing n my office, and why didn't I have any better answers than I'd had this morning?

By now, he probably knew I'd been to see Katie and maybe Annalise, as well. Didn't take a genius to figure he'd want to know what we'd talked about, and how I'd managed to track them down so fast, and why I'd been sticking my nose where it didn't belong.

So...no calling Trueblood. No Betsy. No... I frowned at the crumpled burger wrapper I hadn't realized I was shredding.

Who *could* I call who would know what was going on *and* be willing to tell me? I could think of a few people who fell into the first category, and a few more that fell into the second, but other than Betsy, no one I knew covered both bases. Even Fred, who was one of the friendliest, chattiest guys in River City, knew how to keep his lips zipped when he had to.

I couldn't think of anyone else to call. Lucille said she'd have the stuff on Jameson's business and business contacts tomorrow morning. I could nag her about it, but right now she'd be deep into her afternoon TV game shows and wouldn't appreciate the interruption. Besides, since she never charged me a dime for her research, I didn't want to abuse the relationship. I certainly didn't want to know what Douglas was seeing on the news, but he'd make a point of telling me everything, regardless. For my own good, he'd say.

Clearly, if I got out of this mess and still had a business, I was going to have to make a few new friends.

The thought of friends brought me up with a snap. I'd been focusing on who had a motive to kill Jameson, only belatedly wondering about alibis. I hadn't once thought about *how* they'd killed him. Or, rather, how they'd gotten into my office without so much as scratching that lock.

I hadn't thought about the people I knew in the building who might have seen or heard something. Though they'd all done a bunk this morning, before the cops moved in in force, at least some of them ought to be back and working by now. Murder might happen down the hall, but it would be business as usual in the rest of the place.

And if it wasn't, they'd blame me, regardless.

Fortified by fat, carbs, and sugar, and with at least an idea of what to do next, I got moving.

THE COP CARS WERE GONE and parking on my street was back to normal, as in, there wasn't any. I debated the rival merits of double parking or cramming into the space in front of the fire hydrant, but the sight of our neighborhood's favorite person, the meter maid, headed my way decided the point. (Derick Johansen is five foot ten, two hundred fifty pounds, but everyone still refers to him as the meter maid because they know it annoys him.) I sucked it up and paid for a space in the basement garage two buildings over from mine.

It's not so much that the hourly rates there are exorbitant. (They are.) The whole place creeps me out: dark, dank, with low, massive-beamed ceilings that make me feel like tons of concrete are about to come down on top of me. If I were making a movie, I'd have a serial killer staked out there on a permanent basis.

Like the on-street parking, my building was back to normal. The tarnished metal letters above the main entrance still spelled out "Huf elwitz ffice Buil ing" ust as they had when I first signed the lease on my office three years earlier. The front door buzzer was jammed, the elevator was out, and the four flights of stairs to my office showed their normal collection of footprints and trash. The crime scene team hadn't carried everything out with Jameson's body.

The sight of the crime scene tape across my door almost made me miss a step. Even though I'd expected it to be there, that bright yellow really stood out against the ninety-seven shades of dirt brown and gray that made up the building's normal color scheme.

To my relief, the doors to a couple of offices were standing open, and I could hear phones ringing and the murmur of conversations and clank of metal file drawers opening and shutting from behind the others. People still needed to make a living, no matter who got murdered right down the hall.

I started with Jimmy Jones, two doors down on the left, on the premise that surviving an encounter with Jimmy meant all the other interviews would seem like a piece of cake in comparison. Besides, his door was the first one open.

Jimmy runs Jimmy's Friendly Bail Bonds. On a good day, he's about as friendly as a grizzly with a sore paw and a real bad attitude. I wasn't expecting this to be a good day. His clients, in general, aren't too fond of River City's finest. Having a herd of police traipsing up and down the hall this morning wouldn't have done his business a bit of good.

Jimmy had his feet propped up on his desk and a cheap fan blowing stale air straight at him. Judging from the spreading sweat stains under his arms and across his chest, the fan wasn't doing much good. It was, however, slowly stirring the strip of aged wall paper peeling away from a ragged hole in the wall behind him.

A few months back, one of his more excitable customers, who'd recently enjoyed a visit from a couple of Jimmy's more persuasive debt collectors, had stormed into Jimmy's office to object. To reinforce his objections, the man had pulled a small caliber handgun on Jimmy. When Jimmy just laughed, the guy had shut his eyes, wrapped both hands around the gun, and shot a hole in the wall. A couple days later they moved him out of the hospital and back into jail, no possibility of bail. Jimmy had never bothered to patch the wall.

"'Bout time you showed up, Peterson," he snarled when he saw me. "I'm billin' you for lost time and business. What the hell you mean, invitin' the cops in like that?"

There wasn't a beer in sight, so add hot and thirsty to the bad attitude.

"Nice to see you, too, Jimmy," I said. "Way I heard it, one of your clients came looking for you and ended up killing my client, instead."

"Sheeit. Since when you got clients? Especially millionaires, huh?"

"Doesn't matter, since I'm not going to have any clients, millionaires or otherwise, if the cops can't figure out who killed him."

"Way I hear it, they think you did it."

"That make sense to you?" I shot back.

"I been in this business since before God made dirt. Most things don't make sense, and that's a fact." He swung his feet off the desk and heaved himself out of the chair. "You want a beer?"

"No, thanks, but I appreciate the offer."

I really did. That was an olive branch I hadn't expected. I waited for him to fish a can out of the little box fridge he kept behind his desk, then pop the lid and settle back in his chair before I asked the next question.

"You hear of anything that might help me figure out who did this?"

Jimmy wouldn't have been here when Jameson arrived—he usually starts his day down at the jail—but he's as good at gathering scuttlebutt in his world as Lucille is in hers.

He frowned, then took a swig of beer while he considered

the question. "Not sure. Trudeau says he heard arguing, but he figured you and Yaguchi were going at it."

"Trudeau? Why would he think that?"

Trudeau is a legend around here. He runs some sort of investment business—at least, that's what the sign painted on his door says, "Investments"—but you hardly ever see him, and you certainly don't see any clients. Vi Chambers, with Dickson & Dickson Accounting, three doors past my office on the right, swears he's a Commie Spy. But that's just Vi.

"Why would he think I was arguing with Yaguchi?"

"Said he didn't figure it was a client since you haven't had any."

I couldn't argue with that, though it was depressing to think that even Trudeau, who didn't talk to anybody except Jimmy, knew that Maxie Peterson Investigations had been foundering.

"He mention the time?"

"Nah. I doubt he'd have told me that much if we hadn't both ducked into Wild Bill's when we saw all the black and whites parked out front."

"You saw Trudeau on the *street*?"

"Nobody sees Trudeau on the street. Probably wouldn't have noticed him in Wild Bill's either, but sometimes, ya know, ya just get lucky."

And sometimes you don't. I was in the "don't" category, and Jimmy knew it.

"You hear anything else?" I said. I still had a number of offices to go and it was getting late.

"No, but I'll let you know if I do."

"I'd appreciate that." I didn't believe it, but I did appreciate the thought.

If Jimmy learned something he figured might earn him a few points with his contacts in the police department, I wouldn't be the first to get the news, and I wouldn't get it from him. Business, as Jimmy is the first to say, is business. At least he never pretends it's otherwise.

CHAPTER 12

The next open door, one past mine on the left, was William Watson, Esq., Attorney at Law.

Bill and Jimmy sometimes pass each other clients, which keeps the business in the family, so to speak. Since Bill occasionally hired me on a case, I thoroughly approve of the sharing. We all send clients to Dickson if they need an accountant, and so it goes. Around here, we're all one happy, incestuous little family on the theory that what goes around, comes around.

Which is why we all take our personal business needs elsewhere. No one in his right mind ever lets his family know the details of what he's up to.

Bill is one of the more successful tenants in the building. That means he makes enough to hire full time help. In his case, though, they're definitely not hired for their brains, professional skills, or maturity. The current incumbent, Wendy Rosenstein, being a case in point.

At my entrance, she looked up from filing her long, purple enameled nails, shifted her gum from one cheek to the other, and said disapprovingly, "Bill thought you'd be in jail by now."

"Nice to see you, too, Wendy." I said, claiming a chair in front of her desk. "Sorry to disappoint. I take it this means you're already out of the running on the betting pool."

It was a shot drawn at a venture, but I'd been in this building long enough to know how things worked. I'd participated in a couple of the pools myself. Never won anything, but, you know, part of the family and all that.

"Yeah, well." She sighed. "It was a five dollar pool, too."

"I'm flattered. Who's holding the pot?"

"Janice down on two. You know?"

I nodded. Janice was our go-to betting expert. She's especially good if you're interested in the horses, but she'll take a flyer on anything. The funny thing is, for a hard-core gambler, she's rigidly straight-laced about money matters. There were a few folks around who'd been suspected of skimming a little off the top of a pool now and then, but if down-to-the-penny Janice was running this one, the pot was likely to be substantial.

"Thanks for the tip," I said. "I'll drop by on my way out and buy in."

Wendy shrugged. "Nobody's taking the 'never get arrested' option, you know."

Personally, because I am basically an optimistic person, I was going for Friday noon, but I wasn't telling her that. If I wanted to be realistic, I'd go for early Thursday afternoon, latest, which gave me tonight and all of Wednesday to figure out who killed Jameson.

Time to get down to business. "You see or hear anything this morning, Wendy? Before the cops came, I mean?"

Her eyes widened in mock innocence. "Me? What are you talking about? I wasn't here."

"Sure you were. You must have been. Nobody came past my office after I found Jameson, yet when I walked down this hall with Detective Trueblood afterwards, I heard a chair creak even though the door was shut and everybody was pretending they weren't really there."

Absolutely true. I just couldn't remember *which* office I'd heard the creak from.

Wendy wouldn't appreciate the distinction even if I explained it to her, however, which suited me just fine.

"I heard voices," she admitted at last. "A man and a woman's. I figured it was you arguing with Mr. Yaguchi about the rent or something. "

I suppressed a wince. Was there anyone in this building who didn't know I'd been going through a financial drought lately?

Stupid question.

"Shouting?" I said instead. "Did you catch anything they said?"

She shook her head. "Nah. They weren't shouting, just talking loud. But not so loud I could hear, okay? Only as I was walking by, though. Couldn't hear once I got through our door."

"Anything else?"

"Nuh huh."

"Did you hear anyone come in afterwards?"

Another shake of the head, a little sullen this time. I was pushing harder than she was willing to go.

"No one?" I insisted. *Not even me?*

"No."

"You tell that to the police?"

She eyed me resentfully. "Mr. Watson doesn't like me talking to the police."

Which meant she'd avoided them so far. She wouldn't have had a choice if they'd actually been able to find her.

Not that they would learn anything helpful when they did. Helpful to me, that is. A man and woman arguing, but nobody can make out the words or positively identify the voices?

The police couldn't arrest me on that kind of shaky evidence, but they wouldn't scratch me off their list, either.

IT DIDN'T GO ANY BETTER with anyone else I was able to talk to. Most hadn't been here at the time of the murder (or said they hadn't). Those who admitted to being present either hadn't heard anything or just heard a man and woman arguing.

Eventually I gave up and trailed down to Sturmond Shipping

on the second floor.

Janice Zemelkis was in her usual hideaway, half hidden in the warren of ancient metal shelves and filing cabinets that had formed Sturmond's office cubicles since long before the idea of cubicles was invented.

The woman is seventy if she's a day, tiny, bird-thin, with yellowing grey hair in a shade that's beginning to resemble some of the old shipping notices that have been pinned on the walls since Truman trounced Dewey. She always looks as if she'd dressed for church, drinks Earl Grey with lemon from a rose-covered Royal Doulton tea cup with saucer, and can calculate the changing odds and payouts on a trifecta faster than the bookies can manage with a computer.

She looked up at my entrance, then primly set aside the pile of documents she'd been working on and pulled a large manila clasp envelope from a drawer.

"I'd just about given up on you."

"Sorry. I've been delayed."

I already had a five dollar bill out. I'd considered a tenner, but Janice disapproves of hedging a bet unless you're talking specialized investments, which rumor has she's also pretty good at.

"I don't suppose the option, 'not arrested,' is still available, is it?"

That made her clasp her hands over the envelope and look up at me with the same kind of disapproving frown that Mrs. O'Shaughnessy used to give me in the third grade.

"I know this is just an office pool, Maxine, but I still do not advise putting your money on frivolous entries that have very little chance of winning."

"Thanks for the vote of confidence," I said dryly.

"My advice has nothing to do with my belief in your guilt or innocence, Maxine—and for the record, I do *not* believe you murdered that Mr. Montgomery. But if you are going to participate in a betting pool, then you should participate with the intention of maximizing your chances of winning."

I couldn't help but laugh. "Sounds like good advice."

"It is. So..." She handed me a pen, then opened the envelope and pulled out a sheet of legal-sized paper with a grid printed on it. She set it on the corner of the desk so I could see it clearly.

Vertically, down the long side of the paper, the grid was divided into twenty-four hours broken into hour increments. Along the top, the days of the week starting with today, Tuesday, and ending with Tuesday of next week. A lot of the spaces were already filled in—most, I noted wryly, for today, tomorrow, and Wednesday. Nobody had me making it past Saturday afternoon.

Wendy hadn't expected me to make it to her afternoon coffee break. Jimmy, bless his curmudgeonly heart, had given me the longest odds. He had the last entry—noon on Saturday.

I debated, pen hovering over the available spots. Thursday was more likely, but I couldn't quite bring myself to be that pessimistic. Friday at noon, my personal preference, was already taken. I frowned, considering, then wrote my name in the block for Friday at two.

I handed pen, form, and my five dollars to Janice. She stuck the money in the already bulging envelope, then pulled a five out of her middle drawer, picked up the pen, and neatly wrote her name in for Thursday at noon. That done, she stuffed her money and the form in the envelope, closed the clasp, then slid the envelope into the right hand desk drawer.

Janice always did advise gathering as much information as possible before placing any bet. Good to know she takes her own advice.

"I'll lock it in the company safe before I go home tonight," she said.

"Wish me luck," I said.

"Of course. Now, if you'll excuse me...?"

I took the hint and got out of there. I didn't want to think about that grid and what it implied, anyway.

When I asked Janice to wish me luck, I meant with solving

the murder, but winning the betting pool would be good, too. I might need it as a first payment for a good criminal attorney. I sure as hell wasn't hiring Bill Watson, and I probably wasn't going to need Jimmy's services. Given my uncertain financial state and the status of the man I was suspected of murdering, bail, if it was granted at all, was likely to be set at a level only slightly below the national debt.

Once out on the street, I hesitated, uncertain what to do next. I still had two wives and one mama to track down, but I was pretty sure any attempt to call the three women was doomed to failure—by now, they were being hit by the media as hard as I was. If I couldn't get through this morning, I certainly wouldn't get through now. Not to mention that tomorrow, when Lucille gave me the info on Jameson's business contacts, I'd have an even longer list of people who wouldn't talk to me.

I considered heading home. I hated the thought of paying for another hour in the parking garage, but I hated the thought of sitting in traffic even more. Besides, I wasn't going to learn anything looking at the dingy walls of my second-floor walkup.

Which left calling my mother and explaining why her only daughter was in the news as numero uno on a list of murder suspects.

Reluctantly, I pulled out my phone and turned it on, wincing at the number of missed calls and voice mails I'd have to sort through later. Or never.

Before I could bring up my favorites list, the darned thing rang. I didn't recognize the number, but I'd seen it before: It was repeated multiple times on the lists of missed calls and voice mails.

Ignore? Or answer?

I gritted my teeth and answered.

"So you're finally picking up." The voice was male, deep, and somehow familiar.

"Who is this?"

"Ben Trueblood. I've been trying to reach you for the past

couple of hours."

My heart sank. "What do you want, detective?"

"We need to talk."

"Now? I'm really busy—"

"No you're not. You've been standing in front of your office building for the past five minutes, staring at your phone, doing nothing and going nowhere."

"What!" I almost shrieked. "Where are you? Are you—? *Shit.*"

He was leaning against the side of the building opposite, long legs casually crossed like a man who was perfectly comfortable watching the rest of the world go by—or stand stupidly on the sidewalk opposite going nowhere at all.

He broke off the call, then shoved upright, stuffed his phone in his pocket, and crossed the street toward me.

CHAPTER 13

"You were spying on me," I said, glaring.

"I was coming to look for you There's a difference. Put your phone away," he added helpfully.

I cut the call, shut off the ringer, then dropped the phone in my purse. "You should have called "

"I did. You never answered."

"I turned it off."

"I noticed."

He was looking amused rather than annoyed, but that wasn't much comfort. And he was standing way too close.

I forced myself not to take a step back. "The media were starting to call."

"Please don't tell me you're surprised."

"I'm not surprised," I admitted grudgingly, "but they wouldn't have gotten on to me so fast if you hadn't given them my name."

"We put out a press release saying victim's name not released pending notification of kin, everything under investigation. I didn't give them your name *or* Montgomery's *or* the location, and neither did anyone else in the department."

"Then how did—?" I stopped, blinked.

He cocked his head, studying me, dark brows mockingly arched.

I shrugged, irritated. "Any one of the people in this building could have heard your people mention Jameson's name. They'd all know it happened in my office, and half of them would be happy to talk to the press."

The other half would sooner have had their tongues cut out, but I wasn't going to mention that.

"I knew you'd get it eventually."

He was beginning to annoy me. "Don't make fun of me, Trueblood. I'm not having a very good day."

Did I mention he was standing too damn close? The man was too handsome for his own good, and he knew it.

"I'm not making fun of you. If it's any comfort, I'm not having a great day, either."

"Are you suspected of murdering someone in your office, too?"

"No, but—"

"Well, then," I said. I shifted the strap of my purse higher on my shoulder, then pointedly walked around him and stepped off the curb.

He fell into step. "We can walk and talk, no problem. I need the exercise."

"We talked this morning."

"That was a friendly chat. This time, I've got more questions."

"Which means this conversation won't be so friendly?" When he didn't answer, I added, "What if I don't have answers?"

He shrugged. "I suppose it will depend on which answers you don't have. We could always do this down at the station, you know. I could even call a black-and-white if transportation's a concern."

"You're a prince."

"I know, but we all have our crosses to bear."

I couldn't help it. I laughed.

"Much better," he said approvingly. "Where are we going?"

"Wild Bill's," I said, pointing.

"I'm still on duty."

"Yet another cross. It must suck to be you," I said, and pulled open the door.

He laughed and followed me inside.

He had a great laugh. It went with that sexy deep voice, I suppose.

"Coffee okay?" I asked.

"Beer would be better." He sounded resigned.

Wild Bill was behind the bar. His bushy eyebrows shot up at the sight of me, then crashed together at the sight of Trueblood right behind me. The man can spot a cop a mile away.

He couldn't do anything to stop one from walking into his bar and buying a drink, however, even if it was only a coffee.

"Coffee, please, Bill. Black," I called, leading the way to a table at the side. "And a red wine.'

I didn't get a response, but that was Bill.

The place was beginning to fill up with the sort of after-work crowd that had never heard of a mojito and would have been appalled at the idea of diluting good booze with anything other than ice, and even that would be pushing it. From the back room came the murmur of male conversation and the click and rattle of the pool tables. It would take another hour and a few more beers before the conversations back there moved up a notch to rowdy.

The waitress who brought our drinks was new to Wild Bill's but had the hard edges of a woman who'd spent most of her adult life in places just like it.

"Wine's you, doll, right? An' a coffee for the copper."

"Thanks. Separate tabs, please." I said.

Her eyes got hard and slitty. "You shittin' me?"

"He's on duty, and I'm a murder suspect, so I can't look like I'm bribing him with drinks. He'll tip triple for the both of us," I added helpfully.

She eyed Trueblood. "Yeah?"

To his credit, he looked only mildly annoyed. "Sure." Once she was out of earshot he added, "She didn't blink at the murder suspect bit, but I thought she'd spit at the separate tabs."

"Woman knows her priorities," I said, taking a sip of the wine. Drinkable. Just. Unlike Murphy's, Wild Bill's offers quality plonk.

Trueblood took a sip of his coffee and choked. "Jeeze. That stuff'll put hair on your chest."

"You need any help in that department?" I said, and immediately wished I hadn't.

He eyed me for a minute as if debating his response, then took a deliberate swallow. This time he didn't even blink.

"No," he said, expressionless.

I knew I shouldn't have asked. He was going to be asking me about Jameson's murder, and I was going to be thinking about what was under his shirt.

"Good to know," I said, just as expressionless.

He looked just the tiniest bit disappointed at my aplomb, which made me want to smirk. I managed not to, but only just.

Anyway, he's got dark hair and dark-haired guys always have hairy chests, right? Personally, I don't have enough up-close-and-personal experience to know, but maybe I should pay a little more attention in the future. Assuming I have a future. There's probably not a lot of chest hair in a women's prison. If there is, I hope I never find out for sure.

I took another sip of wine and plunged in. "So, what did you want to ask me?"

"You visited Annalise Montgomery and Katie Carmody this morning."

"That's not a question."

"What did you talk about?"

"Annalise wanted to know if I'd killed him."

"Did she? And what did you say?"

"No, of course. And then I had to apologize for being so remiss. I think she was wanting to congratulate someone for a job well done. Katie, on the other hand, wanted to know how soon I thought she could move into his house."

That got his attention. "*Did she*? What gave her the idea that she could?"

"She seems to think her daughter's going to inherit everything."

"What about the current Mrs. Montgomery? Or his other kid?"

"She didn't really say anything about the wives, current or otherwise, but, according to her, Angelina Mestes, mama number two, is a slut and slept around so the kid's not Jameson's."

"Then she'll be sorry to hear that not only did Jameson acknowledge paternity of her daughter, but Ms Mestes has a perfect alibi. She's been in England for the past week. The guest of a very wealthy Russian who's slumming in some duke's former estate that he just bought."

"Nice. She take the kid with her?"

"No. That's what nannies are for."

"Sounds like Katie and Angelina have a lot more in common than they'll admit." I explained about Katie remembering to talk to her lawyer but forgetting to inform her daughter of Jameson's death, and how the pool boy actually thought of it first.

"Lovely," Trueblood said. "You get any sense of how Jameson felt about being a father?"

"He adored his daughter. That's according to Katie. As far as I could tell, neither one of them ever paid much attention to the poor kid." I couldn't keep the disgust out of my voice.

"You're awfully young to be such a cynic."

"I'm over twenty-one. And some of us would call that being a realist.

"So they weren't great parents. It's not what you'd call a motive for murder," said Trueblood.

I couldn't help it. I sighed. "Nope. It would have been a lot easier if Katie or Annalise had just confessed."

"Now you know how us cops feel."

"Tough."

"And that's it? Did you talk to anyone else?"

"I couldn't get through to the current Mrs. Montgomery or Mrs. Number Two. At least now I know why Angelina didn't answer."

"Shannon Montgomery—Mrs. Number Two, as you put it—was in Florida with friends."

"So you've scratched her off your list, too?"

He shrugged. "Possibly. Your number twos, both Mrs. and mama, could have hired someone else to kill him for them."

"But you don't think that's likely."

"Let's just say, I think it's more likely you killed him than that they arranged a hit."

"Since I didn't kill him, that makes three of us that are off the hook, then."

He ignored that. "You talk to anyone else?"

I hesitated for a moment, but decided full disclosure was the best policy. He'd find out, anyway.

"Everyone I could in my office building," I admitted.

"And...?"

"And nobody heard or saw anything. All right, some of them thought they heard a man and a woman arguing—"

"And thought it was you and Mr. Yaguchi."

"If you already know, why'd you ask?" I demanded resentfully.

"They might have told you something they wouldn't tell us."

"Well, three people thought Gracie was pushy and rude, everyone liked Fred, and that young officer—"

"Jamie."

"Him. Dolores on third thought he was really sweet and wants to introduce him to her granddaughter. Do you think you could arrange it?"

"I'm not a dating service. What else? That pertains to the case, I mean."

"Oooh, pertains. Nice word."

"Ms Peterson?"

All the women you talked to thought you were hot.

I wasn't about to tell him that. Especially since I agreed.

"The betting pool is strongly tilted toward you arresting me by tomorrow at the latest."

He tried, but couldn't repress a lopsided smile that made a little dimple at the corner of his mouth. I really wished he hadn't done that.

"Nice to know your friends have such confidence in you," he said. "What'd you choose?"

"Friday at two," I said with dignity. "I would have gone for noon, but that was already taken."

"I take that to mean you don't have any confidence in *me*." He was teasing.

I was pretty sure he was teasing.

"How'd you guess?"

"No guessing. I'm a good detective, even if you don't believe me."

"Listen, for the record, I did *not* kill Jameson. But if you are going to arrest me, I'd really appreciate it if you'd do it at two on Friday. I hear it's the biggest pool they've run in ages, and I'm going to need the money."

"The criminal justice system is not run for your convenience, Ms Peterson."

"Obviously. If it were, you'd be out looking for the killer and leaving me in peace."

"I *am* looking for the killer, which is why I have no intention of leaving you in peace until we find him. Or her."

He was getting just a little peeved. Which didn't come close to how *I* was feeling about it.

"All right, so what have *you* learned so far? There are a lot of you out asking questions and only one of me."

"You know I can't tell you."

"No quid pro quo? I answer your questions, you answer mine?"

"You wish."

I couldn't help sighing. Again. "Yeah. At least tell me if you have any suspects other than me."

"We have a lot of possible suspects—" That perked me up, for all of two seconds, then he added, "but none with the means and opportunity that you had."

"But I don't have a motive."

"That we know of."

"We've been over all this."

"And we'll be going over it again until we have some answers. Which leads to another question. I took a look at the murder weapon. It doesn't look like a letter opener. It looks like a dagger."

"It does, doesn't it?" I said cheerfully. "But it's a letter opener."

"An awfully *sharp* letter opener."

"Ever tried using a dull one on some of these modern envelopes?"

"You don't need them that sharp. And there was a whetstone in your desk."

I was hoping they wouldn't notice that, but with Betsy on the team, I should have known better. "Score one for your team. But with the whetstone, you would also have found a folding knife that I use for slicing up apples and stuff. Those fancy colored things just don't hold an edge, you know?"

"Mmm," he said, which might have meant a lot of things, most of them not nearly as helpful as I'd like. "We also found a knife in your purse. Both it and the one in your desk are strikingly similar to a switchblade."

"Which is illegal."

"Yes."

"They're not switchblades."

"No. Not quite."

I studied him. "Your point is...?"

"You seem to have a bit of a thing for...sharp implements."

"Of course I do. It's hard to cut an apple with a spoon. Never mind the envelopes. Besides," I added, "my mother doesn't approve of knives and daggers and stuff."

Which is the honest-to-God truth. Mom always says, if you have to have a knife, get one designed for fighting, not fancy. She hates that letter opener. She also says things like, never take a knife to a gunfight, and, if you're close enough for knives, you did something wrong. Such as not shooting first. But I was pretty sure comments like that wouldn't help my case.

"You always listen to what your mother tells you?" Trueblood said.

"Always. That way I can be sure I ignore all of it."

He came close to straining something, trying not to smile. "Another honest answer."

"You see? You should have more faith in me."

"I'm a cop. You want faith, you need a different profession."

I couldn't take it any longer. I shoved my chair back and stood. "When you get some, let me know."

"I'm not finished."

I picked up my purse. "I am."

"We can continue at my place, if you prefer. And I can always call for transport."

There wasn't so much as a hint of a smile left. It was amazing just how square and hard that very masculine jaw of his could get.

I put my purse down. Then I put my rear back in the chair. "What?"

"I had two reasons for wanting to talk to you."

I crossed my arms over my chest. I figure there's nothing like a little petulant body language to get your point across.

"The first was to find out what you learned from Ms Carmody and Mrs. Montgomery."

I tilted my chin upwards and tried to look bored. I don't think it worked.

"The second was to warn you not to try that with anyone else. Let us do our job."

"I am. You should do it faster."

"I find you're harassing any other—"

"Did they complain that I was harassing them?"

"No, but someone will. Don't do it."

There's nothing more guaranteed to get me doing something than telling me not to. My chin went higher.

I know, childish, but there you go.

"Promise?" Trueblood insisted

"No."

"At least you're honest."

"I try to be. Everyone should have at least one virtue. That's mine."

"I'll remember that."

I bet he would, too.

"We done *now*?" I said.

He eyed me for a minute. It's rather amazing just how dark those blue-grey eyes can get when they're narrowed into annoyed slits. "For now."

This time, when I stood and picked up my purse, he didn't try to stop me.

I was a good ten feet away when he called, loud enough for half of Wild Bill's patrons to hear. "So, Peterson. What're your vices?"

I shot him an annoyed look of my own, then turned around and marched out without so much as a word or a backward glance.

I was in my car and easing into traffic when I remembered that I'd neglected to leave the money for my glass of wine.

That cheered me up so much I was singing by the time I hit the first traffic jam between me and home.

CHAPTER 14

I was considering the wisdom of splurging on a six pack of my favorite artisan beer, Twisted Torment, when my phone rang. Before I'd driven out of the parking garage, I'd turned it off mute again and checked the messages. Even more unfamiliar numbers, and one repeated number I recognized and chose to ignore.

That earlier urge to call, just before Trueblood called me, had been an aberration. My mother would wait. She doesn't like it, but she should be used to it by now.

But this call I didn't want to ignore. My baby brother never bothers me unless he has something worth saying. Well, almost never. I put in my earpiece.

"Nic!"

"Hey, Max. How many times have I told you that you should let me manage your advertising. In case you don't know, this is a lousy approach to getting eyes on your business."

Nic is a junior account executive with River City's most influential ad agency. He's brilliant, charming, and drop-dead gorgeous, knows what tie to wear with which suit, the best wine to serve his clients, and, when he's not working, is busy breaking hearts among River City's young and beautiful females. Although people swear we look a lot alike, I'm convinced he must have been switched at birth. I adore him, but we couldn't be more different if we tried.

"Thanks for the vote of confidence, little brother," I said

dryly.

"You talked to mom?"

I winced. I couldn't help it. "What do you think?"

"Don't do this to me. You know she calls me whenever you don't answer."

"I know. And I really appreciate your support."

"It's not support. I just can't turn my phone off all the time like you do."

"That's the price you pay for a nice, fat paycheck."

"Are you going to be needing some of that paycheck to pay a lawyer? I've already called Bernie Carswell, just in case."

There's a lot of reasons I always take my brother's calls. His willingness to help me out of a bind is just one of them.

"Even you don't earn enough to pay Bernie Carswell," I said.

I had to blink back some tears, though. Nic plans to be a multi-millionaire by thirty and, despite what looks like a wild lifestyle, is a dedicated, savvy investor—almost as savvy as Janice, who's given him a few pointers now and then. For him to offer to dip into his stash to help me out is...well...pretty fantastic.

"Besides," I added, before I got maudlin, "it's not that bad yet."

"Yet?"

"It won't get that bad," I amended. "I know it *looks* bad, but there's a detective on the case—"

"Single? Good looking?" For a man who loves playing the field as much as Nic does, he's worse than any normal mother about trying to play matchmaker for me.

"Good looking. Don't know about the single." I almost added, 'don't care', but that would have been a lie. "But I get the feeling he's pretty good at his job. He's not the one who released my name to the press."

"I know. Jerry in media recorded it, along with the reporter who followed up by saying that they'd 'been able to learn' the names of the deceased and the chief suspect. Guess which one you were."

I scowled at the world through my windshield, which needed washing. The whole car needed washing, if it came to that. I'd run the thing through a car wash six months ago. It was way too early for a repeat.

Maybe I ought to ask Amelia—

I cut that thought short. Knowing Amelia and my luck, she'd turn the Corolla into a muddy duck boat. The kind that's actually made up to look like a giant yellow rubber ducky. Parking around my office was impossible with a normal car. I didn't even want to think about what it would be like, trying to find space for a duck boat.

Although, if the thing were big enough—

I cut that thought short and got back to Nic. "Was there a point to this call other than to tell me I'm in deep doo-doo?"

'Doo-doo' had been one of the first things he'd learned to say, right after 'want!' and 'mine!' As an elder sister, it was my job to remind him of stuff like that whenever he tried to start bossing me around or blaming me for something that was *definitely* not my fault.

"Yeah. A couple of us here were thinking this was a great opportunity for you to get some name recognition for the business."

"You mean, other than being arrested for murder?"

"Well, okay. Yeah. But you can't buy this kind of media coverage, sis. The trick is to turn it to good account, you know what I mean?"

"You're kidding."

"No. I—"

I killed the call. I'd kill him if he tried anything of the sort.

The trouble with Nic is, he inherited our mother's love of jumping into a fight with all four feet. The only difference is, he uses words. Mom prefers her Glock and a few crippling karate kicks. I've never developed the knack for either approach. I'm what you'd call the pacifist of the family.

Unfortunately, my approach wasn't getting me very far.

Doubly unfortunately, I didn't know what to do next. Downing an entire six pack of Twisted Torment sounded like a start, but then I'd be up and down all night peeing. Assuming I could sleep for worrying, which I doubted.

"I was thinking we should cruise by his mansion. I could cover you if you wanted to break in, you know. A couple befuddlement spells—"

I jumped a foot, which is hard to do when you're strapped in with a seat belt, and then I swore.

"Amelia, damnit! Would you quit popping in like that?"

My fairy godmother had settled into the back seat like a woman who'd moved in for the duration. It took another moment for her outfit to sink in: black everything. Shoes, stretch pants (not the best choice for either of us), turtleneck top. Gloves. This was not the Amelia I knew. I didn't like the change. It worried me. A lot.

And then she held up a black balaclava.

"I've got two of 'em," she said. "One for you and one for me."

"One for me?"

"If we're going to break into whatsisname's place, you're going to need it."

"We are not—" The traffic started to move again, which meant I couldn't launch myself into the back seat as the first step to strangling my fairy godmother.

By the time I and the other four thousand drivers trying to get home ground to a halt at the next light, I had my murderous urges under control. Sort of.

Strange how no one else provokes that kind of urge to violence in me. Not even my mother.

I checked the rear view mirror. Amelia was still there.

"What makes you think we're going to storm Jameson's mansion?" I said.

"You have any other ideas?"

I glared at the car in front of me.

"I didn't think so. If you had, you wouldn't have wasted three hours talking to all those losers in your building."

"They're not losers. And my time wasn't wasted."

"That's right. You did get a slot with the office pool."

I ignored that. "Are you *trying* to get me arrested?"

"You won't be. I wouldn't let that happen."

I glanced in the mirror again.

"Trust me," Amelia said, and waggled the balaclava so I could get a better look.

Another light change, another few hundred yards while I fumed helplessly. And then we all ground to another halt. I hate rush hour.

Amelia was still in the back seat. She'd pulled one balaclava over each fist and was pretending they were puppets talking to each other.

"Some people are just *really* ungrateful," said the right hand, frowning fiercely.

"*Especially* considering they don't have a single useful idea of their own," sneered the left hand.

The hands really did seem to be talking, but that was probably just the hallucinatory effects of breathing in all the exhaust. Which annoyed me even more. Amelia can use magic to make a couple of ski masks talk but she can't use it for any practical purpose, like vacuuming my carpet or cleaning my windows? Or, say, starting the day over by bringing Jameson back to life so I could forget this nightmare?

I drew a deep breath, then another one, so I wouldn't be tempted to tell her so. When it comes to Amelia, honesty is definitely *not* the best policy.

"It's not that I'm ungrateful," I said, resorting to a little grammatical obfuscation. "It's just that I really don't like the idea of having breaking and entering added to the murder charges when Trueblood arrests me."

"You worry too much." At least Amelia was the one talking and not her fists.

"I've heard that before."

"Then maybe you ought to start listening."

"I don't listen to my mother. Why should I listen to you?"

She didn't have an answer for that one.

Traffic moved a whole two blocks before we hit the next light. Congestion was easing. By the time I came to a complete stop, Amelia was in the passenger's seat beside me.

I couldn't help it. I blinked. "What happened to all that black?"

She shrugged. "Not really me, you know?"

"The polka dots are quite...eye-catching."

She preened. "Think it will catch on?"

Not if there is a drop of good taste left in the world.

"Don't ask me. No sense of style, remember?"

She eyed my own basic black. "You wouldn't even need to change. The mask and a pair of gloves—"

"Not going there."

"Fine." She hunched down in the seat and propped her feet on the cowl. "Where are we going, then?"

"*I'm* going home. I have a frozen dinner waiting. Salisbury steak with corn and mashed potatoes. There might be a mac and cheese, too. Want to join me?"

Amelia can eat human food if she wants, but she usually chooses not to. Too bland, she says. No pizzazz. I haven't dared inquire into what qualifies as culinary "pizzazz" if you're a fairy godmother. I'm pretty sure I don't want to know.

"Party pooper," she said.

"It doesn't occur to you that I might be just plain pooped?"

I wasn't—if anything, I was still overdosing on adrenaline—but it was exactly the right thing to say.

"Well, if you're gonna be that way..."

The last word trailed off into nothing as Amelia vanished.

MAYBE I SHOULDN'T have been so quick to get rid of

Amelia. I stopped for a six-pack of Twisted Torment and was half a block from the nondescript brick apartment building that I call home when I realized there were two TV camera vans and a dozen people I didn't recognize milling around in my parking lot.

As if annoying the tenants in my office building wasn't enough, now I was going to be hearing from a lot of irate neighbors, too.

No help for it. I ducked into the parking lot for another apartment building, worked my way around to the alley behind it, then out through the parking lot of the apartments on the other side.

The side street was quieter. As soon as I found a space to park, I pulled over, then sat drumming my fingers on the steering wheel and staring out the windshield at absolutely nothing, desperately trying to think.

I might work as an investigator, but tracking down the lost heir to a few grand is a very different thing to figuring out who killed a multi-millionaire in my office.

I'd left the police force after three long years on patrol, then earned my PI license by working for a private investigations firm that did a lot of work for one of the big law firms in River City. Until now, the trickiest thing I'd ever handled was an irate wife whose ex was trying to prove she'd remarried and therefore was no longer entitled to alimony. Tricky, not because confirming the marriage had been that hard, but because she'd had a mean upper cut and I hadn't been expecting violence from a leading light in the Junior League.

Over the past couple of years I'd been working at building the business. All I was aiming for was more of the same, just with a better class of clients who could afford to pay me a whole lot more than the clients I had. Now, all that was circling round the drain. Even if someone else was charged and convicted of Jameson's murder, the big-spending clients I'd been aiming for weren't going to want to deal with an investigator who'd attracted so much of the wrong kind of attention.

But if *I* could be the one to solve the case, there was a chance I'd not only save my business, but could turn it to my advantage, as well.

You'll note I said a chance. Janice Zemelkis wouldn't think much of the odds, but it was the best I could hope for.

Doing nothing at all would definitely sink my floundering little ship, because after all, who wants to hire an investigator who stands on the sidelines on something like this?

I'd hoped that a TV dinner and a couple bottles of my favorite beer might help the old grey cells start working a little more efficiently, but our distinguished media representatives had just sunk that approach. Which left me...what?

I'd lost the research I'd originally done on Jameson when the police confiscated my laptop. Lucille would have a lot more for me first thing tomorrow, but until then I was pretty much on my own, and, with the second wife and second mama both off the hook, the only lead I hadn't yet tried was wife number three.

And of them all, guess who had the most motive for wanting Jameson dead?

I sighed, then put the Corolla into gear and pulled away from the curb. I hate it when Amelia's right.

CHAPTER 15

I was parked down the street from the entrance gates for Jameson's mansion, studying the situation and wishing for a little useful magical intervention, when Amelia popped into existence beside me. I should have remembered that little adage about being careful what you wish for.

"Told you so," she said smugly.

"Yeah, you did. Happy now?"

She thought about that for a minute. "You should say you're sorry."

I thought about refusing, then opted for the safer, if more demeaning, approach. "I'm sorry."

"You should have listened to me."

"I did. I'm here now, aren't I?" There's just so much groveling I'm willing to do.

She eyed me narrowly for another minute, then evidently decided she'd gotten about as much from me as she was going to.

"Apology accepted."

"Thank you."

"So, what're we going to do?" She craned forward, studying the guard at the tall iron gates. "Want me to—?"

"No! That is, I've got another idea," I said, improvising fast. "If you befuddle the guard, we still have to get through more guards, servants, maybe guests. I mean, who knows how many people might be in our way, right?"

"Right…" She dragged that out slowly, as if considering the implications.

"And Christine—Mrs. Montgomery—would be bound to notice if half the staff are standing around looking like brainless zombies, right?"

"I thought rich people didn't pay any attention to the servants," Amelia said doubtfully.

"Maybe not, but if everyone around her is befuddled…"

"Okay. Maybe." Amelia didn't like agreeing with me any more than I'd liked apologizing. "So what?"

"So…what if she *wanted* to talk to me?"

"Why would she want to do that? You probably rate right up there with the servants she doesn't pay any attention to. If you make it that high. At least the servants'll open the doors and fetch, right?"

"Maybe. But what if someone gave her a magical nudge, convince her she wants to talk to me? A really *tiny* little nudge?" I added hastily. "Could you do that? You know, like when you kept encouraging all those poor guys in college to ask me out for dates? Only not quite so much."

"You told me not to do that anymore. Got downright snippy about it, in fact," Amelia huffed.

Oops. I hadn't realized she was still nursing a grudge over that, but, really, having a dozen guys lined up outside your dorm room door wanting to ask you out is more than just a little embarrassing. Especially when some of them are known to be dating busty cheerleaders or the campus beauty queen, who didn't take it well at all.

"This is different," I said. "And you wouldn't have to work nearly as hard at this one. Just a teensy, tiny drop of magic. A hint, you know. Just enough to make her really glad to get my call so she tells everyone to let me in when I show up at the front gates.

"You're the only one I know who can do that, Amelia," I

added, resorting to outright wheedling. "Please?"

"Okay." Amelia loves it when I grovel. "Give me a couple minutes…"

"Just a *little* nudge," I said nervously. "A *very* little nudge."

She shot me a disdainful look. "What'd I say about you worrying too much?"

I tried to look contrite, but couldn't stop myself from showing her my right thumb and forefinger pinched together. "A teensy *weensy* little nudge."

She gave a dismissive wave with her hand, then turned her attention to the gate. "Don't interrupt when I'm trying to focus."

I was already regretting my impulsiveness, but it was too late to back out now. Besides, in twenty minutes of staring at that gate, I hadn't come up with any way to get into the house to talk to Christine Montgomery that didn't involve the risk of bodily harm or the instant summoning of police.

"There!" said Amelia after what seemed an eternity. "That should do it."

"Great," I said. "So what do I do now?"

"Give her a few minutes to tell the butler or whoever that she's expecting your call and to put you through immediately, then…you call her. Simple as that."

"Great," I said again. "So…what'd you *do?*"

"I just made that teensy little suggestion you were talking about."

"Just a suggestion?" A suggestion didn't sound too bad.

"All right, maybe it's a little more accurate to call it a compulsion."

Uh oh.

"I kept it light, just like you asked. But, trust me. Mrs. Montgomery is going to want to talk to you. She won't be able to help herself."

AMELIA WAS RIGHT. Mrs. Montgomery definitely wanted to talk to me.

When I eventually presented myself at the front gate, the guard practically leaped to buzz me through. The butler—a very stern and proper butler right out of an old movie—was standing at the open door, waiting, when I drove up. If he disapproved of the interruption, he was too well disciplined to show it. So maybe it hadn't been him on the phone this afternoon, after all.

I didn't have more than a couple of seconds to tug at my slacks and make sure my blouse was properly tucked in before I was being escorted through the vast front hall, up a truly impressive grand staircase that looked like it took a small army of maids to keep dusted, and into a library that seemed to have been snatched out of some English mansion whose owners had a decided preference for massive mahogany desks and a lot of red leather.

As the butler opened the double doors to let me pass, I heard a, "But, Christine, this afternoon you said—" cut short as Christine Montgomery abandoned the gentleman who was speaking and rushed across the room, hands outstretched to welcome me.

She was as tall, slender, busty and beautiful as all the other wives and lovers in Jameson's life, but there was an elegant sophistication to her I hadn't noticed in the photos. I had the feeling she'd normally treat plebeians like me with a cool condescension that would instantly put us in our place. When Amelia struck, however, normal went out the window, and Amelia, in this case, had definitely struck.

"Ms Peterson!" Mrs. Montgomery said, as brightly chipper as if I'd just told her she'd won the Super Lotto and added a few more hundred millions to the pot. "Thank you *so* much for coming! I can't tell you how *much* I appreciate it!"

"Told you," Amelia whispered with satisfaction.

"Mrs. Montgomery. Thank you for agreeing to talk to me."

"For you, anything. *Anything!*" She was beaming and shaking my hand with more enthusiasm than a used car salesman with his first sale.

Hoo boy. When this was all over, Amelia and I were going to have a heart-to-heart on just what an itsy bitsy nudge really means.

"Please, come in. Come in. Oh!" she added as her disapproving companion stepped forward. "But first, I must introduce you to Geoffrey. Geoffrey, say hello to Maxine."

Geoffrey was one of those tall, lean, distinguished older guys with grey hair and impeccable taste in clothes who were used to ruling their not so little corners of the world. I didn't need to have overheard that snippet of conversation to know he was Not Happy. In fact, Not Happiness radiated off him like heat off a furnace.

Amelia was focusing on other types of heat.

"He is *hot*," she said, unabashedly eyeing him up and down. "I like hot older guys."

I ignored her and held out my hand to Geoffrey. He didn't take it.

"Maxine?" he said. "Or is it Maxie? Of Maxie Peterson Investigations?"

I forced a cool, superior little smile. "That's correct," I said. "And you are...?"

He didn't seem inclined to tell me, but Christine jumped right in.

"Geoffrey Dawson," she said happily, as if that explained everything.

Actually, it did. Unfortunately.

"Of Dawson, Dawson, and Dawson?" I said.

"That's correct."

He didn't have to say more. Triple D was only the biggest, most powerful law firm in River City. Three brothers, each one colder, meaner, and more brilliant and cut-throat than the other, with hordes of junior partners and wannabes in the wings, eager to emulate their masters. The Dawsons knew the law inside out, upside down, and backwards, and when the law didn't cooperate, they were fully capable of pulling a few strings at the state house and having the law conveniently changed.

"Geoffrey is—was—Jameson's lawyer," said Christine cheerily. "He was very interested in meeting you, too."

"Yes?" I said. My mouth had gone dry. I wasn't sure it was safe to say more.

It didn't help that Amelia was circling him to get a better look. I didn't like the glint in her eye, but there wasn't much I could do about it now.

"I was not aware that Jameson had hired a private investigator," said Geoffrey, eying *me* up and down. His eyes narrowed, his jaw hardened, and his thin, patrician mouth turned down at the corners. "Had I known, I would not have approved."

The glint went out of Amelia's eyes as *her* mouth turned down at the corners.

Christine giggled. "Jameson could be such a *naughty* boy sometimes! Now stop frowning like that Geoffy—" That made him blink. Clearly he wasn't used to being referred to as Geoffy, certainly not from the elegant Christine— "and go away so Maxie and I can have a nice little chat."

"Christine, I don't think—"

"Go. Go!" said Christine, making shooing motions with her hands.

"Go!" said Amelia sternly, pointing toward the door.

Geoffrey did a stiff quarter turn on his heels and marched out the doors that automatically, and without human assistance, opened in front of him. A West Point cadet on parade couldn't have done it better.

Amelia shut the doors behind him a little more firmly than strictly necessary. Christine giggled.

"Geoffy wanted to marry me, you know," she confided.

"But you didn't want to marry him?" I said.

"Oh, I did. He's so handsome, and absolutely *marvelous* in bed, you know. And he's— Well, let's just say he's *very* generously endowed! Jameson, poor dear, wasn't nearly so…gifted."

I couldn't help it. "So why did you marry him and not Geoffrey?"

"Don't be silly," said Christine, giving me a playful poke. "Jameson had *ever* so much more money!"

"Ah," I said.

Amelia just snorted.

"Yes," said Christine. "And Geoffy says it's all mine now. Isn't that nice?" And then she giggled again.

"You bet," I said weakly.

Amelia's little nudge had acted like a truth serum, which might help me but wouldn't be fair to Christine if anyone else saw her like this. Dawson probably figured she'd overdone the meds a bit. Somehow, I was going to have to convince Amelia to undo the spell without causing more problems. I didn't expect that would go down well.

"How about we sit down here so we can have that little chat, Mrs.— Christine," I said.

She didn't resist when I led her over to an overstuffed, red leather sofa. I took the chair facing hers, but not before shooting a look of warning at Amelia, who was standing, arms crossed over her chest and toe tapping impatiently, glaring at our hostess.

"Those two deserve each other," she said. "Too bad the husband had to get killed first."

"So, Christine," I said, deliberately shifting in the chair so my back was to Amelia. Big mistake. I know better than that.

Christine's eyes widened and her mouth fell open. I jerked back around to find Amelia opening the drawers on that big desk. I could see her do it, but to Christine it would look as if the drawers were opening of their own accord.

"Amelia!"

"What?" Then she looked up to find Christine staring at her. Only Christine couldn't see her. "Oh. Sorry. It's just easier this way."

She quickly riffled through the contents of the already open drawer, then shut it and started on the next drawer down. Only this time she didn't bother opening the drawer first.

"Christine? Christine!" I said, more loudly this time. She jumped and turned her attention back to me.

"Silly me. I could have sworn..." The words died away. Even bewitched she wasn't going to admit she saw desk drawers opening and closing, all by themselves. I could tell she was trying to stare at the desk without appearing to stare. It made the whites of her eyes show a little too much. "Never mind. What were you saying?"

As long as she was going to be impulsively truthful, I might as well take advantage of the moment.

"Your divorce from Jameson. When would it have been effective?"

"Two weeks from now." Her smile faded. "I didn't want a divorce."

"But Jameson did."

She nodded. "He insisted. He said he was going to marry some little trollop he'd knocked up." Her chest—beautifully enlarged and resculpted by a master plastic surgeon (Lucille had dug out her rave review on her private Facebook page, where she'd boasted to her friends about the results)—swelled. "He was going to divorce *me!* The *nerve* of the man!"

"Who was he going to marry?" Lucille hadn't found so much as a hint about any planned marriage. Or another offspring.

"Who cares?" Christine gave the best sitting-down indignant flounce I've ever seen. "Some little tart from the wrong side of the tracks, I suppose, just like the others. My family have been leaders of River City society for *generations*, yet he was going to *divorce* me! But I showed him!"

I sat up straighter. Was she going to confess to murdering Jameson? And if she did, how was I ever going to prove it? Confessions while under the influence don't go down so well, especially when the only one who can testify to them is the chief suspect. "You did?"

"You bet! I socked him for a bundle. Five times what those other two bitches got out of him!"

"Did you?" I said weakly. As confessions went, it probably made Christine happy but didn't do me much good. Not for murder.

"*Pffft!*" said Amelia in disgust. From the sounds, she yanked open one of the drawers, then deliberately slammed it shut.

Christine didn't even notice.

"Annalise will have a cow when she finds out," she said with a satisfied giggle. Then she paused, clearly struggling to get a grip on her wandering thoughts. "But I don't care about that any more, do I?"

"Because now you get it all?"

She stared at me as a smile slowly spread across her face. "That's right. Geoffy told me. I get it all. Every. Single. Penny."

This time, she didn't just giggle. She outright guffawed.

"Silly twit," said Amelia. "I ought to teach—"

"Amelia! Let me handle it, okay?" I didn't take my eyes off Christine. She was laughing so hard I was afraid she might fall of the chair and choke to death.

"I could—"

I held up my hand in warning. Amelia shut up. Sort of. I couldn't catch what she was muttering. Not that it mattered. She'd give me a detailed recitation later.

"What happens to all the alimony for the other wives and the child support for the kids?" I asked. "Did Geoffrey say?"

Christine reluctantly dragged herself upright and tugged her clothes into place. She was trying to frown but Amelia's little 'nudge' seemed to be getting more potent, not less. She was struggling with recurrent bouts of giggling, sort of like hiccups that wouldn't stop. It wasn't doing anything for her powers of concentration.

"What did Geoffrey say?" she got out eventually, looking puzzled and silly at the same time. She giggled. Again.

"The alimony and child support," I said. "What happens to

those payments. Did he say?"

"Payments?"

"Alimony? Child support?"

She waved her hand like someone batting away a mosquito. "Jameson's dead."

"Right, and...?"

She yawned. A huge yawn that went on forever and almost dislocated her jaw. "Geoffrey says..."

"Yes?"

"He says—" another yawn. "He says I'm going to be very, very..."

"Christine?"

Like a child finally giving up the fight to stay awake, she curled into a ball and laid her head on the arm of the chair. Her eyes closed. "*Very* rich." It was barely a whisper. Her face relaxed into a contented smile as she passed out.

"Want me to wake her up?" Amelia asked.

"You think she has anything else to tell us?"

"I don't think she has another thought in her head right now, awake or sleeping."

We both stared at Christine, who was starting to snore.

"Not much help, was it?" said Amelia.

"Not really. I'm not even sure I believe the part about another kid."

"Why not? The man definitely had a problem keeping it zipped."

"Yeah, but a kid? After all this time?"

"It happens."

"Maybe," I said. "But she wouldn't have killed him over it."

"Of course not," Amelia snorted. "She'd already hit him where it hurts."

I shook my head. "I'm not sure money was the way to get at Jameson."

"What do you mean?"

"I don't know," I admitted. "It's just something that's been sort of... I don't know. Sort of teasing at me. Katie. Annalise. Christine. To them, it was all about the money. Sounds like Angelina was pretty much the same, and I'm guessing wife number two is just like them. But he never fought them on it. They demanded millions, and he paid without argument, right?"

"Right."

"And he was in trouble with his board of directors and his stockholders over wanting to pay off all the claims against their various companies, right?"

"So?"

I shrugged. "I don't know. It just doesn't seem as if money was what was driving him."

Amelia shrugged and turned her attention back to Christine. "It sure was what drove this one."

"Is she going to be all right?"

Another shrug. "Sure. Probably. Why not? Once she wakes up, anyway."

I could have given her several examples of why not, but now was not the time or place. "Guess we'd better go tell someone she's gone beddy bye."

That would take a couple minutes. Back on the road in ten. And then what?

I hadn't the slightest idea, and I sure hoped Amelia didn't either.

I should know better.

CHAPTER 16

"Now we track down wifey number two," Amelia said as soon as she'd settled into her seat.

"At this time of night?"

"Sure. Why not? My magic doesn't go away after dark, you know."

"Doesn't improve, either."

"What?"

"Nothing." Did I mention that I do a lot of muttering whenever Amelia's around? "Anyway, Trueblood says she was in Florida with friends."

"And you believe him?"

"You think he'd lie about something like that?"

Amelia didn't have an answer for that.

"What's she going to tell us, anyway? That she really loved Jameson and the money was just, you know, solace for her broken heart when he left her for that trollop."

"Nobody uses the word 'trollop' anymore. Even I know that!"

"Christine did." Okay, so she was loopy on Amelia's helpful little nudge. I shouldn't hold it against her. "I'm going home."

I thought longingly of the cold beer I'd planned on. The beer that had been sitting on the back seat of my car for the past two hours, getting warm. Well, it wouldn't be the first time I'd stuck a bottle in the freezer. Take a slow shower, get in your jammies, it's almost cold enough.

The energy that had made me flee those reporters and tackle Christine Montgomery was gone. I was exhausted.

I could always ask Amelia to disappear the reporters or make me invisible or something. Anything to get me past them and up to my apartment.

Were befuddlement spells wrong if they were used on members of the press who were hounding me? I could offer her a beer and— No, scratch that. The last time I shared a six-pack with Amelia, she accounted for five of the six. I've tried to forget the details of what came after.

I wasn't that desperate. Yet. If the reporters were still camped out in my parking lot, I'd run them over, then dash for my apartment while they were trying to regroup. No one could object to that, right?

"I'm still going home," I said.

Huh?" said Amelia. "You just said that."

I wasn't about to explain.

It was after ten by the time I got to my street. I was relieved to find the media had abandoned my parking lot.

Unfortunately, Amelia hadn't abandoned me. She'd spent the entire drive speculating on who'd killed Jameson, and why, with every scenario crazier than the last.

We were up to Geoffrey Dawson having stabbed Jameson in a jealous rage because he wanted his client's money and his wife. She couldn't, however, explain how Geoffrey, who was taller than Jameson, could have driven that letter opener into Jameson's heart like that. (At least, I was pretty sure he was taller. The only time I'd actually met Jameson he'd been stretched out dead on my floor, which rather skews your perception.) If the two men had been standing, the opener would have gone in at a downward angle. Pointing that out was, however, a waste of breath. Amelia never, ever lets logic spoil her theorizing.

I parked my car, turned off the engine, released my seat belt, then just sat there, head back against the head rest, eyes shut, trying to get up the energy to convince Amelia it was time for her to go home, wherever home is when you're a fairy godmother.

"You know, you should be glad you have me," said Amelia.

I opened one eye to glare at her. I was too tired to try both.

"That beer was getting awful warm, but I fixed it for you. Should be nice and frosty by now."

I opened the other eye. The beer was cold?

"It's after ten o'clock, Amelia," I said.

"Yeah, but it's six o'clock somewhere else. Perfect time for a beer. You've got to learn to seize the moment, Maxine."

Have that cold beer or argue with Amelia. One was late but doable, the other a losing proposition, right from the start. Besides, she'd turned it cold again. Or so she claimed.

"Right," I said, and opened my door. The dome light came on, I heard something hit my windshield hard and the sharp crack of a rifle.

It's amazing how fast you can think when you don't have time to think at all. I threw myself out of the car, rolling away and kicking the door closed behind me.

The dome light went out. The pavement was hard, something was poking in my back, my heart was pounding a mile a minute, and now I couldn't think at all.

Someone had shot at me? Seriously? At *me?*

"SOMEONE'S SHOOTING AT US!" shrieked Amelia "Help! Help! Police! Murderers! 911! Help!"

I rolled to my knees, then flung myself behind the nearest car. My heart was hammering so hard it almost drowned out Amelia. Too bad no one else could hear her and call 911 for real. Worse, my phone was propped on my console with my earpiece right beside it. Which means I waited right here until my would-be murderer hunted me down, or I did something about it.

"Help! Murder! Police!" I shrieked.

It came out as a choked croak that I could scarcely hear. I

couldn't breathe and my throat felt like it had squeezed shut.

Where was a good car alarm when you needed it?

Alarms.

Legs quivering and with a stomach that threatened to bring up the supper I hadn't had, I rose into a crouch and tried to push against the car. It rocked a bit, but no alarm. Not surprising, really, since most of my fellow-residents were like me and considered any vehicle under eight years old to be practically brand new. My car didn't have an alarm, either.

I hesitated, then tried to peer around the side. The low-wattage bulbs in the entrances to the two buildings and the dim lights showing behind a few window curtains, here and there, didn't provide much illumination. The open walkway that ran between the two buildings was a tunnel of black. A dozen assassins could have been lurking behind the scraggly bushes that passed for landscaping without anyone being the wiser.

I had no idea where the shooter was.

"*Psst!* Amelia!" She couldn't hear me for her shrieking. "*Amelia!*" I bellowed.

That got her attention.

It also got the shooter's attention. There was another sharp crack. The car I was hiding behind lurched and tilted as the left front tire died.

I squealed, then scuttled back behind my own car to find Amelia had already had the same idea. Give her credit—at least she hadn't abandoned me.

"Set off the horns," I hissed.

"The what?"

"The car horns. Make them start honking. Lots of them."

"Wha—? Oh!"

My car horn started blaring. The shooter put another hole through my windshield. A few seconds, another.

Oh well, once you've got one bullet hole, what's the harm in another dozen? At least I now knew that all the shooter had was a single shot rifle and not a semi-automatic with an annoyingly large-capacity magazine.

Mother would *not* have approved of their poor planning and lack of proper equipment. Thank heavens not many of us come up to her exacting standards.

"More horns."

Amelia, for once, didn't argue. Another car started honking, then another. More shots. I counted two more windshields and three or four, maybe five hoods and fenders that had new holes.

In the apartments, lights were coming on. Lots of lights.

Nobody stuck their head out to ask what was happening, but somewhere in the depths of River City's emergency ops center, I knew, the 911 operators' call boards were lighting up like Christmas trees.

Amelia had focused on the cars to our right, so I went the other way, scuttling behind the car with the new flat tire, then its neighbor. I paused, took a deep breath, told myself I was about to do something stupid, then crept up the far side of the car so I could get a better look.

Someone threw open a window.

"I've called the cops, you bastard! You mess with my car and I'll shoot you myself!"

The threat, issued in the quavery falsetto of a very old woman, made my heart warm. I recognized the dulcet tones of Mrs. Minsky in 222C. Everybody knew Mrs. Minsky. She was super protective of her fire-engine-red '78 Mustang and was probably the only person in River City who had 911 on speed dial.

That did it. A hooded figure carrying a rifle burst from behind one of the bushes, headed for the ink-black walkway between the two buildings.

Without thinking, I upgraded from stupid to really stupid and went after him. With the kind of day I'd had, the chance to take some of my frustration out on a deserving bad guy was just too much to resist. Even James Bond couldn't have reloaded a single shot on the run.

Fortunately, the shooter hadn't reloaded *before* he started running, and I had a lot less distance to cover. I still might have missed him, but he hadn't been prepared for the deplorable state of what was optimistically called a sidewalk that ran between the two buildings.

The shooter tripped on one of the broken squares of concrete that had heaved out of the ground and went sprawling. I heard an anguished "oof!" and the clatter and scrape as he lost the rifle. He gave another "oof!" as I flung myself on top of him, then a squeal as I grabbed an arm and twisted it up behind him. Sometimes those extra pounds that Amelia's so snotty about can come in awfully handy.

"Don't even *think* of moving, you jerk," I snarled in his ear, planting my knee in the small of his back. He tried to squirm out of my grip. I appreciated the effort. It gave me a good excuse for digging my knee in that much harder.

Besides, I owed him for scaring me so much I squealed.

"Ow! *Owww!* You're hurting me!"

"Not half as much as I'd like to. You *shot* at me!"

"Bitch!"

"You betcha," I shot back, and wondered if anyone would object if I smashed his face against the concrete. No one around here would object, but the way my luck was going, the jerk would sue me for bodily injury and win, and then where would I be?

I settled for planting my free hand on the back of his head so he couldn't gain any leverage by arching back against me, firm enough to prevent him from moving but not so hard he couldn't breathe.

I'm fairly tall and I'm not even close to fragile, but I might not have been able to keep him down even then except by now it was clear I'd nabbed a kid, not some full-grown Mafia assassin. He wasn't even that big—certainly not as big as me—and his voice was in that range where you couldn't tell if he was going to be a tenor or it just hadn't finished changing. For an instant, I wondered if it could be Ricky, the pool boy, but this kid wasn't near skinny enough. If I'd kneed Ricky in the back, I'd have permanent dents in my patella.

By now my heart had stopped pounding in my ears enough that I could hear the sound of sirens headed my way.

The kid heard them, too, because he started fighting against my grip again. "Let me go. I didn't hit you. Let me go, damnit!"

"You shot *at* me, you little twerp, and you killed my windshield. If you hit Mrs. Minsky's car, too, she'll shoot you herself."

I might have given his arm one last tug except spotlights suddenly hit us, almost blinding me even though I wasn't facing the parking lot.

"Put down your weapon, put your hands up, and step out of the shadows! Now!"

I had to let the little jerk's arm go to put up my hands, so it wasn't my fault if I kneed him a bit harder as I got to my feet. Honest.

Hands in the air, I backed a couple steps away, then turned to face the cops, squinting against the spots. I ducked my head, blinking and trying to adjust to the loss of my night vision, when my former prisoner shoved to a crouch, then tried to lunge forward, into the shadows.

I didn't have a choice. This time it wasn't a canted concrete block but all one hundred and thirty-two pounds of pissed-off woman that did the trick.

I sat on him.

CHAPTER 17

When the cops pulled me off the twerp and back to my feet, I made sure to keep my hands up.

"Next time he makes a break for it, shoot him," I said helpfully. "Her," I added in surprise as I got my first good look at my shooter. "Who the hell are you?"

"We'll ask the questions, ma'am," said the cop who'd dragged the kid to her feet. "What's your name, kid?"

"Julia Montgomery," the kid said with the kind of arrogance that only a privileged rich kid or a really cocky drug dealer ever manages. "Jameson Montgomery was my daddy."

"Yeah?" said the cop, a little more warily. "And you?" she added, turning on me.

"Maxine Peterson."

"Shit," said the cop at my back under his breath.

"Shit," said the cop holding Julia, loud enough for all of us to hear.

The two cops who'd stayed by the cars, providing cover, had abandoned their posts and strolled over in time to catch the exchange.

"Trueblood's got this one, right?" said one of them, clearly amused.

"Yeah," said the other. "He's gonna love it."

"I'll call in the update," said the first, heading back to the cars which still stood, doors open and lights flashing, in the middle of the parking lot.

By now, a crowd was forming as my neighbors cautiously emerged to make sure their vehicles had survived the carnage and enjoy the entertainment if they had. The furious howls from those who hadn't been so lucky just added to the spectacle.

"So, which one of you was the shooter?" the cop holding Julia demanded.

"She was," I said. "And her last name's Carmody, not Montgomery."

"I'm a Montgomery," Julia sniffed, indignant. "Carmody is my mother's name, not mine."

"The rifle's over there in the shadows, by the way," I added helpfully.

I wasn't about to argue with a thirteen-year-old who'd thought shooting at me was a good idea. Even if she did think I'd killed her daddy. At least, I assumed that was why she was shooting at me. I haven't had a lot of experience with barely-teenaged would-be assassins slaughtering my windshield.

"Where's the bastard that shot out my headlight?"

Before anyone could stop her, Mrs. Minsky burst through the crowd and charged us. The cops didn't stand a chance of stopping her—they weren't expecting five-foot-nothing of enraged old lady to be quite that fast, or that deadly with a rolling pin.

I knew better. Mrs. Minsky might be old, but she's sharp, remarkably fit for her age, and right now she was running on pure mad.

She barreled past Julia's cop, already well into her swing with the rolling pin. Julia just stood there, gape-mouthed and confused. I didn't stop to think, just stepped forward and shoved her back, out of the way.

I'd intended to duck under Mrs. Minsky's swing, then go for the rolling pin. Amelia almost beat me to it. She materialized behind the old lady, hand outstretched. She missed and grabbed the cop who was holding onto Julia, instead. The cop, already off balance because I'd pushed Julia, swung around to clobber whoever had grabbed her. Her fist went right through Amelia. With nothing to stop her momentum, the cop lost her balance and her grip on Julia, who made a break for it. Amelia, annoyed, danced out of the way. I abandoned Mrs. Minsky and went for Julia.

Never get distracted when dealing with vengeful, violent old ladies. Never.

Instead of dodging Mrs. Minsky's swing, I stepped right into it.

The rolling pin and the side of my head met. The rolling pin won. I went down like a rock as the whole world went black.

TRUEBLOOD FOUND ME sitting on the back steps of the ambulance that had been summoned on my behalf. The EMT was tidying away his gear, and I was waiting for the crowd to disperse so I could stagger up to my apartment, take a hot shower, and go to bed. Amelia, in one of her rare moments of insight, was keeping well out of sight. She knew as well as I did that I wouldn't have walked into Mrs. Minsky's swing if I hadn't been distracted, though she would never admit it.

Trueblood set a foot on the middle step, propped his elbow on his knee, and leaned in to study the damage.

"You're starting to have a couple nice bruises there," he said in the helpfully casual tone of someone commenting on the weather. "One on either side, actually."

"Thanks. Makes me feel a whole lot better, knowing that," I grumbled.

I was grateful there wasn't all that much blood since I'd hit the ground pretty hard after Mrs. Minsky konked me. I knew about that because the left side of my face was scraped and beginning to swell and because I had more sore spots than could be accounted for by one rolling pin.

Trueblood ignored my surliness and looked up at the EMT.

"What's the verdict?"

"She'll live," the EMT said curtly. He sounded sort of disappointed. He'd recommended a trip to the emergency room for observation for concussion, I'd refused, so we'd called it a draw. Medical types hate it when you ignore their advice.

The fact was, I had a headache, and it hadn't needed the man's warning to know that it wouldn't be a good idea to take aspirin or indulge in any alcoholic drinks for the next few hours.

I could cope with the no-aspirin edict, but the thought of that six pack of Twisted Torment still on the back seat of my car getting warm again wasn't doing anything for my disposition. The only consolation was that Julia wouldn't have hit it when she shot out my windshield—the angle was all wrong. Maybe I'd have one for breakfast, instead.

Trueblood turned his attention back to me. "Next time an old lady swings at you, I suggest you duck."

"I did. I got distracted."

"What distracted you?"

My fairy godmother. I wasn't about to say it. "I hope you're not planning on arresting me for this," I growled instead.

"Not for this. Julia's admitted she was the one doing the shooting."

I eyed him dubiously. I hated to admit that the vision in my left eye was just the tiniest bit blurry. But that might be the swelling from scrapes. "Are you're arresting me for her father's murder?"

"Not right now."

"Huh," I said. "What's going to happen to Julia? I assume her mother is going to pay for my windshield?"

"And the other damages. Eventually, anyway. Well, probably. Julia's been taken downtown and her mother's been called. I'm not handling that."

"Huh," I said again. "I hope you're not pressing charges against Mrs. Minsky."

"You want them to?"

"No. I'm pissed Julia shot out my windshield, but it's not Mrs. Minsky's fault I got in the way. If I'd had a car like her Mustang and somebody shot it up, I'd clobber them, too." Only I wouldn't settle for a rolling pin. For one thing, I don't own one.

"I saw the Mustang," said Trueblood. "I admit, I admire her restraint."

"Right," I said, getting shakily to my feet. I hated accepting Trueblood's help to navigate the ambulance steps, but I did, anyway. "If you're not arresting me for anything, I'm going to bed."

"You have someone who can keep an eye on you? Just for tonight?"

No. Nobody I cared to ask, anyway. "Sure. What are you doing?" I added when he took my elbow and started steering me toward the building entrance.

"Seeing you get there safely first."

I decided not to object. That entrance seemed a whole lot farther away than normal. Besides, he could carry the beer. I needed to retrieve my purse and cell phone, anyway.

I managed to get us up the stairs and through my front door before letting out a groan.

Trueblood set the beer down in a hurry. "You okay?"

"Yeah, fine." I wasn't the problem.

Amelia was sitting in yoga position on my couch, waiting for us.

"YOU'D BETTER SIT DOWN,' said Trueblood, trying to lead me to the sofa.

"I don't think so," I said. Amelia was patting the cushion beside her. "I'll take the arm chair. More support," I added before he could suggest I lie down instead.

He helped me settle, then stood back, studying me dubiously. "You want some water or something?"

I closed my eyes. The chair had been a bad idea. It was right across from Amelia. "Sure. Thanks."

"I'll put the beer in the fridge while I'm at it."

"You're a good man, Trueblood. Even if you haven't managed to catch Jameson's killer yet."

I caught a rude noise from the kitchen, then the clink of bottles being set in the fridge, followed by water running in the sink. He hadn't had to search for a glass—I learned a long time ago it's less effort to leave your dishes in the drainer so they'll be handy the next time you want them. At least they'd been clean. Some mornings I didn't manage that much.

Footsteps headed my way, then, "Here."

I opened my eyes to find Trueblood looming over me, holding out a glass of water. There was an awful lot of him to loom, all of it lean and well-muscled. His shoulders looked broader from this angle, too.

I took the glass and closed my eyes. Looking at him was disconcerting enough. Seeing Amelia behind him, eyeing his butt... That was just too much to expect of a woman who'd so recently been hammered with a rolling pin wielded by an irate ninety-year-old.

The water helped, but when I went to set down the glass, I found Trueblood still looming, this time with my cell phone in his hand. I'd forgotten he'd slipped it in his jacket pocket when we'd rescued my purse and the beer.

"I'm not leaving until you have someone here to watch you," he said, setting the phone on the arm of the chair.

And then he backed up and sat down on the couch two inches from Amelia.

She yelped and started to scoot over, then seemed to think better of it. I didn't like the satisfied smirk that was beginning to spread across her face, and I was pretty sure Trueblood wouldn't either if he could have seen it. Of course, if he'd known she was there, he wouldn't have sat down in the first place. In fact, if he knew her like I did, he'd probably have turned tail and run the instant he spotted her.

"You need a new couch," she said. "This one sags when he sits on it."

Several responses shot to the tip of my tongue. Since they were all vulgar, and Trueblood would probably call the EMT back on the theory that my brain was more muddled than usual, I kept my mouth shut.

I just hoped my eyeballs weren't popping out of my head from the strain of it.

"You going to call?" Trueblood said.

"I'm thinking." Or rather, trying not to.

"Of course," Amelia added, sizing him up, "if all that weight were distributed horizontally rather than vertically, like in the bedroom..."

That did it. I punched in my passcode, then the speed dial for Nic. Our conversation was short. I didn't need to explain—it was enough that I said I needed his help.

I just hoped I hadn't interrupted something more entertaining with his latest female companion. Under those circumstances, he'd still answer my call for help, but he'd make me pay for it afterwards.

"Satisfied?" I said, trying to focus on Trueblood and ignore Amelia.

"No," said Amelia. "Why don't you ask him to help you to bed?"

"I will be," said Trueblood, "once this Nic shows up."

"Fat chance," I said, intending it for Amelia. Blame it on the headache. Normally, I'm not that stupid.

"Are you saying he's not coming?" Trueblood demanded, frowning.

"Nic'll come," I said, closing my eyes and leaning my head back. I was in no condition to cope with this right now.

True to form, Amelia kept up a string of suggestive comments that only I could hear I only hoped my annoyance with her wasn't reflected on my face. Trueblood had gone above and beyond, and even though I wished he hadn't, I didn't want to make him regret helping me. No telling when I might need his help with something a lot more urgent.

Fortunately, Amelia eventually gave up and vanished (I peeked under my lashes to make sure), so all I had left to deal with was the headache and this damned, intense *awareness* of Trueblood's presence. He didn't talk, didn't fidget, just sat there watching me, and it was driving me nuts. Even under the pounding in my head, I'd swear I could hear him breathe.

It seemed like forever before I heard Nic's key in the lock. I opened my eyes and forced myself to sit up. For his part, Trueblood muttered a heartfelt, "Thank God," that he probably thought I didn't catch, then got to his feet.

Nic was two feet in the door when he realized I was not alone.

"Who the hell are you?"

"Detective Ben Trueblood," said Trueblood calmly. "I take it you're Nic."

"That's right. I— What the hell happened to you?" he demanded, crossing the room in three long strides to drop down on one knee in front of me. "Who hit you?"

He gently touched my temple, then my cheek and chin, which had begun throbbing in synch with my head. I winced.

"Mrs. Minsky," I explained.

"Who the hell is Mrs. Minsky?"

"Don't shout. She's a neighbor who got mad because someone shot her car."

That made him rear back indignantly. "So she took it out on you?"

"No. Yes. Sort of. It's ..complicated."

"Maybe I should explain?" said Trueblood.

That brought Nic to his feet in a surge of temper. "You'd damn well better."

"Nic—"

"It's okay," said Trueblood, making a "calm down" gesture

141

with his hand.

Nic isn't normally a physical kind of person, but he's tall and very fit and when he gets mad, he's downright intimidating. Trueblood didn't even blink.

I did, though. Looking up at two tall, broad-shouldered, incredibly handsome men squaring off at each other would be a bit unsettling at the best of times, and right now didn't even come close to being a semi-good time.

I grabbed Nic's hand and tugged. "Come on, Nic. Settle down. Detective Trueblood's trying to help."

Nic looked down at me, then back at Trueblood. "Yeah?"

"If you'll let me explain?" said Trueblood mildly.

At least, it sounded mild, but I had the distinct impression that he was just as much on edge as Nic, and if Nic lost his temper and started swinging, Trueblood wouldn't hesitate to swing back.

"Come on, Nic," I said again. I hadn't let loose of his hand and didn't intend to until he settled down. He might be my baby brother, but he's always been overprotective. There's never been any need for it, but since when does logic have anything to do with family?

Reluctantly, he settled on the arm of my chair, then put my hand on his knee and placed both of his hands protectively over it. "I'm listening."

Trueblood eyed his hold on me, then settled back on the couch and started explaining.

"She refuses to go to the hospital as the EMT recommended," he said at last, "and I didn't want to leave her until I was sure there was someone here to keep an eye on her, just in case. So she called you."

Judging from the look on Nic's face, he was torn between thanking Trueblood and yelling at me. He settled for, "Maxie, don't you think—?"

"Absolutely not. I'll be fine, Nic. Honest."

That last convinced him. He knew me. I didn't say "honest"

if I didn't mean it.

"All right then. Of course I'll stay. But that doesn't mean I don't think you should—"

"I know." I slipped my hand free—he hadn't let go of me the entire time Trueblood was talking—and wobbled up onto my feet. Both men got to theirs. Who says chivalry is dead? "Detective. Thank you. Now that Nic's here…"

"Of course," said Trueblood. "Keep an eye on her," he added with a warning frown at Nic.

My brother nodded grimly. I suppose I ought to have been annoyed, but I was too tired and my head hurt too much.

Trueblood let himself out, but just before he closed the door behind him, he leaned back in and said, "I'll give you a call tomorrow."

I couldn't tell if that was a promise, or a threat. I settled for waving weakly. It was all I could manage.

After Trueblood left, Nic gave me a few minute's privacy to pull on the only pair of pajamas I own—I normally sleep in the nude, but when your brother is checking on you, that option is definitely out—then came in to make sure I was tucked in properly.

I managed to stay awake just long enough to say, "You're the best, you know?" and to catch his, "I know," in response before I was out for the count.

CHAPTER 18

I came awake to the smell of coffee and an urgent need to pee. My mistake was looking in the mirror when I washed my hands afterward.

I couldn't help it. I screamed.

There was a loud, "What—?" and a crash from the kitchen. Three seconds later Nic, wild-eyed, flung open the bathroom door.

He took one look at me and swore. "You look like hell."

I dragged a shaky hand through the rat's nest of my hair and took another look in the mirror.

It was as bad as I'd thought. Not nearly as bad as I've seen on women—and a couple of men—beaten by their spouses, but bad enough. I had a nasty bruise on my right forehead where Mrs. Minsky's rolling pin had connected and another bruise and scabbed-over scrapes down the left side of my face where I had connected with the cement. Both sides hurt.

Nic's glowering gaze met mine in the mirror. "All this for a thirteen-year-old juvenile delinquent?"

"She shot out my windshield. And Mrs. Minsky's Mustang's headlight." I leaned closer to the mirror, squinting a little and gingerly pressing my cheek.

That was a mistake. I winced and backed off.

"It was dark," I said. "I thought it was whoever killed Jameson."

"So it would have been all right if it had been a grown-up killer instead?"

"The rifle was only a single-shot." Even to me, that didn't sound too rational.

Nic threw up his hands. "You get more like mom every day."

"I do not!"

"Do too. But I'm not arguing with you this morning."

"Better not," I muttered. I'd just started feeling a teensy bit guilty for last night, but that low blow wiped out all debts.

Nic sighed. He knows when he's not going to win the argument, no matter what. "You up for a cup of coffee?"

Okay, maybe not all debts. Which didn't mean I was going to let him off the hook completely.

"There's some left?" I said. "I heard something break."

"An empty cup. You screamed. I'm not used to women screaming. At least," he added, "not when they're my sister, and not usually first thing in the morning."

"I did not need to know that. Go away. I'm going to take a shower and get dressed. But there'd better be some coffee left by the time I get out!" I added, poking my head out of the bathroom to make sure he heard as he retreated to the kitchen.

I'M NOT USUALLY ONE to spend a lot of time getting ready in the morning, and I certainly don't waste any energy plastering on makeup—mascara and lip gloss are about as far as I'm willing to go, even when I'm trying. This morning, however, I made an exception.

Fortified by two aspirin and the steaming cup of coffee Nic had left beside the bathroom sink while I was showering, I tackled the challenge of disguising the damage as best I could.

My best wasn't very good, but at least I wouldn't frighten small children and dogs. Much.

Resigned, I dragged on the first clean clothes I came to in the closet, then ventured out, prepared to find Nic sitting at my kitchen table, swilling coffee and mentally girding himself for a protracted argument about wha⁻ I should and shouldn't do today.

Instead, I found him at the stove fishing bacon out of a frying pan and laying it out on a plate to drain. I almost swooned at the tempting smell.

"Bacon?" I said, wondering f brain trauma could lead to sensory hallucinations.

"And fried eggs and homemace coffee cake. Not to mention a fresh pot of coffee," Nic said, gesturing to the full pot on the counter. "Fill up your cup, then sit down. Everything will be ready in a couple of minutes."

"Where did you get eggs and bacon?"

If either of those items had been in my fridge, they'd passed beyond edible a long, long time ago. Forget the coffee cake. I never risk bringing any home because I can't stop eating it once I've started. Me passed out on the sofa from severe carb overload is not a pretty sight, even if there's no one there to see.

"It's all from Mrs. Minsky," Nic said, and grinned. "I asked the super where she lived, then made her cough up whatever she had that I could use for your breakfast."

"You what?"

"Little old ladies always have something in the kitchen. I figured she owed you. By the way, you need to get to know her better. She made the coffee cake herself and it's fantastic."

"She what?" I had no trouble picturing Mrs. Minsky swinging rolling pins, but Mrs. Minsky making coffee cake? My bruised brain, never at its best in the morning, boggled at the thought.

"Coffee. Now," he said, pointing. "You're repeating yourself."

The coffee cake was fantastic. So were the eggs and bacon. By the time I'd poured my third cup of coffee, I was feeling a whole lot fonder of Mrs. Minsky and had forgiven Nic for everything. If he kept this up, I might even forgive him for the time he ripped the cover off my pristine copy of *Mighty Man and the Temple of Doom* when he was five.

"Thanks, baby brother," I said at last, shoving my empty plate away.

"You can thank me by staying home today and letting Trueblood and his team handle this," he said.

"I owe you a lot, but I don't owe you *that* much."

He sighed. He hadn't really expected me to, anyway. He knows me too well.

"At least duck the next time someone shoots at you, okay?"

"I did. Duck, I mean."

"And *then* you went after them." It wasn't a question. Like I said, he knows me too well.

"What's on the news this morning?" I said instead. Nic is far more attached to his cell phone and its connection to the Internet than he is to any of the women in his life. I knew he would have checked.

"Nothing. Nothing new, I mean. More of the same from yesterday. Lots more. It's lead on every channel, front page on every paper."

My shoulders slumped. "So no one's been arrested for Jameson's murder."

"You knew him well enough to call him Jameson?"

"I never even met the man."

"Yet he ended up dead on your office floor." He hesitated, then added, "You should talk to mom."

"You really think that's going to happen?" It wasn't a question. He knows better. In my situation, he wouldn't talk to her, either.

"Trueblood called."

My spine stiffened. "He did? When?"

"While you were in the shower. Wanted to know how you were."

"And...?" I pushed when he didn't offer any more.

"He said they'd charged that Julia kid with a slew of things, then released her into her mother's custody."

"Big whoop. Doesn't find the killer."

"You can take it up with him when you see him."

"Oh, yeah?" I wasn't sure I liked the sound of that.

"He asked you to come by the station later today."

"Yeah?" I *really* didn't like the sound of *that*.

"But he said to call first, make sure he was in."

I sighed. "I guess that's better than saying he'll be right over to arrest me for murder."

"I believe it's called 'helping the police with their investigation.' You might try it."

"I have. It didn't help because I don't know anything. What's even more embarrassing," I added, frowning, "is I think Trueblood believes me."

"Most people would think that's a good thing."

"I'm an investigator. That's what I do for a living and—"

"You call this a living?" my going-to-be-a-millionaire baby brother said, gesturing at the cramped kitchen around us.

I shot him a warning scowl but forged ahead. "And I *should* know something. But I don't. Not anything useful, anyway."

Nic stared at me for a moment, clearly debating with himself whether to keep arguing or give up. Being a very smart guy, he gave up. "So what are you going to do next?"

"I need to talk to Lucille. She was going to have more information on Jameson's business partners and stuff this morning. I need to call my insurance agent and have them send someone out to replace my windshield. And then..." I considered the options, but my fuzzy brain wasn't being very helpful. I didn't have any idea about what came after, 'and then'. So I shrugged, instead. "Then it depends on what Lucille tells me."

Nic's met Lucille. I suspect he's actually hired her as a consultant a time or two, though he's never admitted it. Never share your business secrets, he says, not even with your family. He means it, too.

"Okay. Fair enough," he said. "How are you planning to get there?"

I hadn't considered the problem, but the solution was easy. "You're driving me. After I call my insurance agent about getting my windshield replaced."

"Bet he's gonna love that. And then what?"

"You ever hear of playing it by ear?"

He shot a pointed glance at my left ear, which was as scraped up as my left cheek, but wisely didn't say anything. Nic knows when he's not going to win, no matter what.

THE INSURANCE AGENT promised to send someone out to replace the windshield and start the paperwork to get Katie Carmody to pay for it.

"If they don't pay," he added gloomily, "you're still on the hook for the two hundred dollar deductible."

"They'll pay," I said.

I hoped. At least I didn't have to wait to hand over the keys—since the car was so old, with the windshield gone they could just reach in and unlock the doors. Of course, some of my neighbors might have done that already. Just to be helpful, you understand, not because they were interested in checking out the stereo or anything.

Lucille, unfortunately, had no magical solutions for me. A fat folder filled with contacts, financial information, juicy rumors, and lots of possible motives, but nothing that pointed to a murderer. After due consideration, I decided to start with the most active rouser of the rabble demanding Jameson's removal as head of JM Industries, one Leslie Postin, Esquire.

Postin personally held over six percent of the company's public shares, most inherited from his grandparents, who had been friends with Jameson's grandfather, the founder of the company. Six percent didn't come close to trumping Jameson's fifty-plus percent, but it was enough to make him a royal pain at stockholders' meetings and win the support of similarly disgruntled shareholders and directors.

The lawyer had been agitating for Jameson's removal from the beginning, first on the grounds that his college history proved him unfit for the job and later, when Jameson started talking reparations instead of lawsuits, on the grounds that he was bent on destroying the company altogether.

I figured if anybody had the dirt on Jameson and his enemies, it would be Leslie Postin. What I didn't expect is that Postin would actually be willing to see me. I got the feeling he shared Annalise's eagerness to shake the hand of anyone who'd played a part in removing Jameson Montgomery the Third from the scene, even if I hadn't committed the actual murder. It wasn't a happy thought.

My outlook didn't improve when I emerged from Garr Analytics and found Amelia outside, waiting.

CHAPTER 19

"You look like hell," said Amelia the instant I appeared.

I almost said, "So do you," but a strong sense of self-preservation kicked in first

Amelia was leaning against the building, arms crossed over her stomach, one leg bent, foot flat against the brick in an excellent imitation of a hooker waiting for her next john to cruise by. As for her outfit... Well, let's just say most of the hookers I know wouldn't have been caught dead in anything that skimpy or with that much glitter. And certainly not in that much orange.

It's a good thing the passersby couldn't see her because she'd have stopped traffic for two blocks in either direction.

As if the getup weren't bad enough, she was wearing fake eyelashes that probably created a mild hurricane when she blinked, and she'd added fat, eye-popping streaks of magenta, pink, and electric blue to her hair. The colors wouldn't have worked with all that orange if you were a blind man on the dark side of the moon. Out here in broad daylight, it was nothing short of painful.

For an instant I wondered if maybe Amelia was color-blind as well as near-sighted, but only for an instant. In this case, it wasn't her vision that was the problem, it was her taste. She didn't have any.

"Not this morning, Amelia," I said, setting off up the street. "I have a headache."

"I'll just bet you do." She shoved away from the wall and fell into step beside me. Well, into wobble. Even Lady Gaga wouldn't have tried walking in those shoes. "I can fix the headache, you know. And the bruises."

I could think of a half dozen cutting things to say about how it would have been more helpful if she'd prevented them in the first place, but I'd save that for another time. Or maybe never. With Amelia, sometimes never is best.

"The makeup sucks, too. It's all caked around those scrapes. Disgusting. Really. You *sure* you don't want me to fix you up?"

"Absolutely," I said, grimly plowing ahead.

The last time Amelia tried to improve my makeup job was two seconds before I walked into a restaurant for a first date for which I'd had real hopes. By the time I stuck out my hand to introduce myself, I had perky pink circles on my cheeks that looked like a six-year-old had gone wild with her mother's lipstick, and eyes rimmed in two pounds of night-black eyeliner.

The only person that style might have worked for was a Tim Burton ghoul. It definitely didn't work for me. My prospective date took one look at me and started babbling about an emergency call he'd just received, so sorry but he had to run, good-bye! If he'd moved any faster getting away, the carpet would have charred under his feet.

I never heard from him again. I wouldn't be surprised if he's still running.

This was not a good time to remind Amelia of that, however. Especially since she was already pulling out her wand.

"People who saw me like this would notice if the scrapes suddenly vanished," I said instead. "We don't need anyone asking awkward questions."

"Good point," she said, and reluctantly slipped her wand back in her pocket. "So, where are we going?"

"The subway," I said. "I don't have a car, remember?"

"No need to get snippy!"

"I wasn't getting sni—" I started to say hotly. I swallowed

the rest as I caught the eye of a man who'd flattened himself against a shop front in order to give me as wide a berth as possible. The instant I was past him, he scuttled off up the street as fast as he could go.

I couldn't tell if it was my face alone, or the sight of a battered woman babbling to herself that had set him off, and didn't care.

I couldn't do anything about the face, but I decided right then and there I was going to start wearing my bluetooth earpiece regularly instead of leaving it in the car. With one of those in your ear, nobody gives a second thought if you're carrying on a conversation with empty air.

"So what did that Lucille have to say for herself?" Amelia demanded, changing the subject. It wasn't that she'd noticed that man's reaction or given up on the original conversation, it's just that she has the attention span of a gnat.

"She had lots of names and contact information for me," I said. "She had Douglas run a few fast financials, too."

"And?"

I shrugged and dodged a stray dog who'd decided to claim the middle of the sidewalk to scratch at fleas. Amelia probably would have kicked him, but he must have sensed she was there because he quit scratching, growled in her direction, then slunk out of the way to pointedly pee on a parking meter. I could sympathize.

"Mostly, nothing new. Lots of people were mad as hell at him, but I can't see there was anyone mad enough to want to kill him."

"Then where are we headed now?"

"The offices of Leslie Postin, Esquire."

"Who has a name like Esquire?"

"It's not a name, it's a title. Postin's a lawyer."

"Oh. A *lawyer*."

I don't know why she was sneering so hard. She's never had to deal with them. I have. Some of them, I'm happy to report, are almost human.

"Postin represents a group of stockholders and directors who were trying to oust Jameson.'

"Can they do that?"

"That's what I'm hoping Postin will tell us." I had no idea what good it would do me if he did, but a girl has to start somewhere.

We had to wait a couple of minutes for the train I wanted. I fidgeted. Amelia amused herself by making the ticket machines spit out free tickets on a random basis until I hissed at her to stop. The last thing we needed was a riot as commuters tried to snag the loot.

The car was pretty well packed when we boarded, but I managed to grab the only empty seat, beating out a cute young thing in yoga pants and a very skimpy tube top. She snarled at me and used language that would have embarrassed my mom, who has a pretty ripe vocabulary herself. I smiled and settled more firmly on my seat. I had some thinking to do, and I do my best thinking sitting down.

I figured Amelia would either magically transport herself to Postin's office or, better yet, just disappear. Instead, she sailed through the doors just before they shut, wand out, pointy star ends glinting.

Wands, it turns out, have other uses than making magic. A pimply kid in jeans fourteen sizes too big blocked her way. Without hesitation, Amelia swung the wand and whacked him on the part of his butt hanging over the top of the jeans. Since that was most of it, she had a good-sized target.

"Move!"

The kid yelped and moved, spinning around to take a swing at his attacker. Yoga Pants was right behind him. He pulled his punch, but not soon enough. The spikey wrist band he wore snagged on the knit of her tube top, pulling it down to reveal what, for a kid his age, was as close to heaven as he was likely to get. He gaped. Yoga Pants screeched and socked his ear. He staggered back, tripped on the three yards of pants leg puddled around his ankles, and went sliding on his ass, which liberated his jeans from their precarious perch on his butt and pulled them down around his knees.

I sighed and pulled my feet off the floor, out of the path of trampling feet as the others in the aisle either tried to get out of the way, or surged forward for a better look.

Amelia, unfazed, sailed through the pandemonium she'd created and pointed her wand at the harried looking businessman occupying the seat next to me.

"You too," she said.

He blinked dazedly, then got to his feet and obediently shuffled closer to the door, brief case clutched tight against his chest, oblivious to the pandemonium around him.

"There, that's better!" said Amelia with satisfaction, settling into the newly vacated seat.

"That was rude!"

"So were those pants."

"I'm not talking about the kid, I'm talking about— Oops! Watch it!" This to a burly workman who was trying to inch past. Size thirteen triple-E steel-toed work boots are dangerous in a packed subway car. "I'm talking about the gentleman who had that seat first."

"Oh, poo!" said Amelia airily. "If he's a gentleman, he won't mind giving up his seat to a lady."

But you're no lady. I didn't say it.

By now, the passengers in the aisle were beginning to sort themselves out. Yoga Pants had pulled up her top and huffed off to the other end of the car, followed by multiple appreciative male gazes. The pimply-faced kid was on his feet and had pulled his jeans back up. Pulling them up hadn't presented a problem, but he'd lost confidence they'd stay up—this time around he was clutching a fistful of waistband and hanging on grimly.

Amelia looked around, clearly pleased. "I've never been on the subway before. I had no idea it was this much fun."

"Aren't you worried someone s going to sit on you?" I asked. "All they see is an empty seat."

"No, they don't. I put up a glamour. They don't see anything at all. Not even the seat."

What could I say to that? Fortunately, comments weren't required. Amelia was too engrossed in her new surroundings to pay any attention to me, a blessing for which I was duly grateful. When it comes to Amelia, peace doesn't last for long so you have to savor it while you can.

We got off in Woodbridge, one of the toniest sections of downtown River City. A hundred years ago, it had been a neighborhood of comfortably middle class families living shoulder-to-shoulder with the comfortably middle class families next door. These days, the families that lived in Woodbridge were way, way, *way* past middle class. The old townhomes sold for tens of millions of dollars—before renovation—and rents for apartments the size of a large coat closet ran to four figures a month.

The offices of Leslie Postin, Esquire, occupied the second floor of an elegant brick five-story with gleaming windows and bright red geraniums in sleek black pots on each step leading up to the building's front door. Secretaries, discreetly hidden behind closed doors, had the first floor while the numerous junior partners and lesser minions who conducted the day-to-day business of the firm filled every floor above that, all the way to the attic.

Clearly, Leslie Postin, Esquire, was doing all right for himself.

Amelia must have noted the upgrade in her surroundings— the orange hooker outfit and weird makeup were gone, replaced by a sleek black suit that was only a tad too tight and hair swept up in a blond knot on top of her head that would have taken a human hairdresser an hour to tease into place. The hairdo had gone out of style in the sixties. For Amelia, the combo was amazingly conservative.

I blinked. "Nice suit."

"Givenchy. I picked it up the last time I was in Paris."

Amelia had been to Paris? And she hadn't even brought me back a T-shirt or a teaspoon with the Eiffel Tower enameled on the handle? Not even a fresh croissant? Maybe I'd get a T-shirt of my own. I already knew what it would say: "My fairy godmother went to Paris and all I got was this lousy headache."

"Now *behave* yourself, Amelia," I said, changing tack. "No opening drawers or riffling through files. No playing with the blinds or rearranging the knick knacks. Nothing to upset Mr. Postin. Understood?"

"So, why do you need me?" she demanded, offended.

I bit back the *I don't* and said instead, "It's always good to have two people so we can compare notes afterward. Just don't do anything to make him suspicious, okay?"

"Okay, but I'm telling you—"

"Just *don't.*" Fortunately, we didn't have a chance for further argument. The snooty voice on the speaker that had responded to our initial buzz had evidently confirmed that I was expected because the door clicked open and the voice said, "Please, come up."

So we did.

CHAPTER 20

Some day, when I grow up, I want to inherit lots of money, then make even more in my job so I can afford an office like Leslie Postin's. Furniture that might have belonged to George Washington (assuming George could have afforded it in the first place), thick white wool carpets covered by an antique Isfahan that probably should be hanging in a museum, cut-glass lamps that glittered under their hand-made silk shades. Even Amelia was impressed.

I tried to pretend I didn't notice, but I'm not sure I pulled it off.

"Mr. Postin," I said, taking the soft pink hand the antiques' owner extended across his desk. I was surprised he could reach that far—the desk was huge and Postin was only a few inches over five feet tall. He was also completely bald, with a round, pink face and a shiny pink dome that gleamed beneath the crystal chandelier. You had to squint to see eyebrows and lashes so skimpy and pale they might as well not have existed. "Thank you for seeing me."

"Ms Peterson," said Mr. Postin in a rich baritone that would have made him a fortune if he'd gone into commercial voice-overs. So much for preconceptions. I'd taken one look at his short stature and fussy bow tie and been sure he'd be a squeaky tenor. "Thank you for coming." He gestured to one of the pair of silk-upholstered wing chairs in front of the desk. "Please, take a seat."

I settled into my chair and, after a stern glance from me, Amelia claimed the chair beside me. I declined the offer of coffee or tea, apologized for my somewhat battered appearance (a fall, I said, which was partially true—I didn't mention Mrs. Minsky's rolling pin), and we got down to business.

"It's most fortunate you called," Postin said. "I'd already asked my secretary to arrange a meeting."

"Yes?" I hadn't been expecting that. Even Amelia perked up.

He paused, studying me, his plump, pink hands pressed together as if in prayer. "You are a businesswoman, Ms Peterson, are you not?"

"Er...yes?"

"Of course you are. And I am a businessman. And this conversation? It is business, too. You understand?"

"No, I'm not sure I do."

"Quid pro quo, Ms Peterson. I give you something, you give me something in exchange."

"Okay," I said cautiously.

This wasn't going the way I'd imagined, but if it got me something I could use, I was all for it.

"What's he think?" Amelia grumbled from the depths of the wing chair beside me. "This is some sort of horse swap?"

To show her disdain, she swung her feet up to prop them on the edge of the desk. She's not a great judge of distance. If she hadn't been wearing those ridiculous platform shoes, she would have missed entirely, but the edge of the heels caught. After a second's struggle, she scooched lower in the chair and stretched.

I ignored her. "And what is it you want from me, Mr. Postin?"

"Why did Mr. Montgomery hire you, Ms Peterson?"

"Honestly? I haven't the faintest idea."

I explained about the letter and the check and the appointment we'd made to meet in my office yesterday morning. The appointment Jameson kept a little too early for his own good.

"So you accepted the payment without knowing what service was expected?" His frown barely moved those almost invisible brows. "That doesn't seem very...wise."

"I did some research on him. There wasn't anything that set off alarms, so, yeah, I deposited the check. Contingent on the conversation we were supposed to have yesterday," I added virtuously.

"Alarms. Hmm. Yes," he said softly, patting his fingertips together and staring vacantly at nothing over my right shoulder.

I kept quiet, wondering what was going on in that lawyerly mind of his and trying to ignore Amelia, who was rolling her eyes and circling an index finger at her head to indicate she thought he was crazy. As if she had room to talk. To maintain that insolent feet-on-the-desk thing, she'd had to scootch so low in the chair that her butt was half off the seat and her chin was on her chest from the awkward angle.

Too bad I couldn't take a picture—she doesn't appear in photos. Not even so much as a blur. There'd been a time early on when I'd been sure if I could just convince my mom that I was being harassed by a fairy godmother that she would take care of the problem. Amelia thought it was funny, so for a while she insisted on inserting herself into every single family photo going.

Postin's pale eyes came back into focus. "I'm sure you will not be surprised to learn that I've had my staff look into you and your business, Ms Peterson."

I was, actually. It was one thing for me to ask Lucille to do a little research into the leader of the opposition to Montgomery's control of JM Industries. It was quite another to find out he'd been researching me. Even if Jameson *had* been murdered in my office.

"Considering Mr. Montgomery's resources, you were a... How shall I put this without being...disparaging? You were a surprising choice."

"Yes, I was," I said agreeably. "And isn't that fact

interesting?"

The faintest of smiles lit his face, and I'd swear his eyes twinkled. "Indeed it is."

"I don't know what Jameson wanted, Mr. Postin," I said. "Do you?"

He just sat there smiling at me and patting his fingers together, *pat pat pat pat pat.* Evidently, my candor had earned me a few brownie points. I just hoped I could take advantage of them.

"Want me to give him a poke?" Amelia demanded, getting restless. She put her feet back on the floor and sat up straight, ready for action. I twitched my fingers dismissively, which was as close as I dared come to waving her off.

I leaned forward to stare Postin in the eye. He didn't blink, but his smile widened the tiniest fraction of an inch. I had the feeling he was waiting for me to answer my own question. Instead, I asked another.

"Why did Jameson suddenly insist on settling with all those people suing the JM Industries subsidiaries, Mr. Postin? Do you know?"

That faint smile vanished. "No, Ms Peterson, I do not. Not really. But it's the right question to ask. The only question worth asking."

I nodded. Jameson hiring me was easy enough to explain. He'd needed someone outside his normal world, someone with no connection to anyone he knew, and thus no hidden loyalties that might lead them to betray him. But that didn't answer the question of what he'd wanted me to *do.*

"As you can imagine," I said, "I've been spending a lot of time thinking about Jameson Montgomery recently."

Well, when I wasn't being interrogated by arrogant detectives, warned off, shot at, battered, bashed, or just flat annoyed, that is. The annoyed part was in danger of repeating since Amelia, who lacked even a three-year-old's ability to sit still and be quiet, was reaching for a carved quartz paperweight that sat on Postin's desk. It was the shiniest thing within reach, so of course she wanted to play with it.

Desperate, I reached across the desk and snatched it first. Amelia huffed and slumped back in the chair, arms crossed over her chest. Wearing Givenchy hadn't done a thing for her attitude. It's a sow's ear, silk purse thing.

"It's like this crystal," I explained to Postin, for all the world as if I were in the habit of snatching paperweights off the desks of perfect strangers. "There are lots of sides to it, and the closer you look at one side, the less you see of the others."

I set the thing back on the desk, well out of Amelia's reach, and continued, "When I was deciding whether or not to accept the job, the thing I kept seeing was Jameson's sudden insistence that JM *not* fight all those lawsuits being brought against it. Nothing else was out of the ordinary for a spoiled rich boy—not his multiple wives, his mistresses, his wild behavior when he was younger. But agreeing to payments that would total in the hundreds of millions, maybe more, when he wasn't forced to? Especially when he would take the biggest financial hit since he was the majority stockholder? That didn't make any sense."

"Very good," Postin murmured, watching me with interest.

"If I had more time I might work it out, but it would be a lot easier if someone with an insider's perspective would just explain it, instead," I said. "Someone like you, Mr. Postin."

"That's a substantial quid for your rather paltry quo, don't you think?"

Amelia snorted. I continued to ignore her.

"A bunch of words for another bunch of words. Doesn't seem like a bad exchange to me. You're not risking insider trading charges, if that's worrying you. If your staff did even a basic job of researching me, you know I haven't got a dime and couldn't take advantage of anything you might tell me, no matter how juicy."

"They did rather more than a basic job, Ms Peterson, and one of the interesting facts they discovered is that you'd be very *un*likely to take advantage, even if you could."

I blinked. I couldn't help it.

Amelia sat up straighter. "Whaddya know. The old toot's not as silly as he looks."

"Regrettably, I can't make a profit off it, either," he added.

The expression on his round, pink face was bland and eminently lawyerly, but the tiny quiver of his lips gave him away. Leslie Postin, Esquire, had just made a joke.

"The reason Jameson gave for his decision," he continued, "is a foolishly sentimental determination to, as he put it, 'secure his legacy for the next generation'."

"That's it?"

Postin nodded.

I couldn't help the surge of disappointment. "You're right, that's not very useful. For anyone."

"No. Understandable, perhaps, but not very useful. Montgomery was the third generation of his family to run the business. It would scarcely be surprising if, as he matured, he began thinking about what would happen after he was gone."

"No disrespect, Mr. Postin, but I'm not sure I buy it. Jameson has two illegitimate daughters. Beyond admitting paternity and paying the bills, he's never shown much interest in either one of them, so far as I can see. They don't even bear his name. That's not much of a legacy."

"You tell 'im," said Amelia, who'd been following the discussion with rather more attention than normal. Probably it was thinking about daughters and next generations and her wild suggestion that maybe Julia needed a fairy godmother of her own.

As long as it kept her from playing with things she shouldn't, I was all for it.

"True, but he needn't have been talking about his own offspring, you know," said Postin. "He could have been talking about a legacy in general. A successful business, respected reputation, that sort of thing."

"Maybe." In my opinion, that was a pretty big maybe. "He doesn't seem like the kind of guy who cared what others thought of him, let alone worried about dying."

He didn't seem like someone who gave much thought to others, period. What he'd been planning on doing sounded pretty noble and pure, but nothing I'd learned about the man so far made me think either one of those adjectives was likely to apply to Jameson John Montgomery the Third.

"I guess the question that matters now is, what will happen to the business now that Jameson's dead?" I said. "Do you know?"

Postin shook his head. "That's a question everyone's asking, including me. I assume his present wife inherits the bulk of the estate, but I don't know that for a fact. Until the will is read and the lawyers sort things out, business should continue as before. As the leader of a rather large faction among the minority stock holders, you may be sure I will be watching events rather more closely than most.

"In any case," he added smoothly, getting to his feet and coming around the desk, "the immediate question is who killed him, and why. Until we have those answers, everything else will have to wait. Ms Peterson," he added, extending his hand, "thank you for coming. It was a pleasure meeting you."

"Mr. Postin," I said, standing and taking his hand. The lowly hired help doesn't protest a dismissal by the mighty. Especially if the help is fresh out of useful questions. "It was a pleasure meeting you."

As if on cue, the office door opened and his snooty secretary came in carrying a silver tray with a dainty china teapot and matching sugar bowl, cream pitcher, and cup and saucer.

"Your tea, Mr. Postin," she said. "And a treat for liddle kittykins," she added in a childish voice, beaming down at the enormous Persian cat that was twining around her ankles.

At the sight of the cat, Mr. Leslie Postin, Esquire, possessor of inherited wealth, priceless antiques, and a law practice whose earnings would have supported a small duchy, at the very least, beamed and squatted on his heels and said, "Here kitty, kitty, kitty."

Liddle kittykins, perfectly aware of who was actually going to be doling out the treats he could smell on that tray, abandoned the secretarial ankles for more profitable brown-nosing.

He should have paid more attention. Amelia hates cats almost as much as they hate her.

With her inimitable dedication to being annoying, she'd paused to relocate the paperweight and riffle through the files and notepads neatly stacked at the side of his desk. Satisfied that she'd made her point, she turned to follow me and caught sight of liddle kittykins at the same instant he caught sight of her.

She shrieked. He spat and sprang backwards, right into the path of the secretary. The secretary squawked, staggered, and tried desperately to regain her footing without spilling the tea or the treats.

She might have managed it, too, if Amelia hadn't leaned forward to hiss at the cat, who yowled and dodged under the secretary's feet.

Tray, tea pot, and all the rest of it went flying.

It might have remained just a problem of cleaning up the mess on the Isfahan, but Postin made the mistake of reaching to help his assistant and ended up with a plate of cat treats on top of his head and a pot of tea down the back of his handmade suit. I didn't wait to check what had happened to the sugar and cream.

"Really!" said Amelia resentfully as I hastily shut the door on the devastation we'd left in our wake. "What kind of a person would keep a *cat* in a place like *this?*"

I didn't waste my breath trying to explain.

CHAPTER 21

I should have stayed to help clean up the mess.

Postin's front door clicked shut behind Amelia and me just as a woman and a man with a camera around his neck hit the first step. I didn't recognize the woman, but these days, cameras with fancy lenses generally mean only one of two things—a wildlife photography enthusiast or the media.

Powerhouse investment lawyers may be as deadly as a pride of hungry lions, but they're generally far less photogenic. That left one option.

I ducked my head and tried to scoot past without attracting their attention. I might have made it, too, if the woman hadn't made a point of checking me out as I went past.

She did a double take when she spotted the bruises and scrapes, but that didn't stop her. "Ms Peterson? Maxie Peterson?"

I scooted faster. She did a one-eighty and grabbed my sleeve.

"Ms Peterson! I'm Jancie! Jancie Jarrow of the *River City Courante.*"

Wonderful. She'd left about five times more voice mails than any of the rest of the media yesterday. Just my luck I'd run into the *Courante's* bulldog like this.

I pulled my sleeve out of her grip and kept going.

She skipped a step and fell in beside me.

"Why was Jameson Montgomery in your office yesterday,

Ms Peterson? Is it true you were investigating his wife?"

Wonder who dreamed up that one? Why investigate a woman you were already divorcing unless you thought you could wiggle out of the agreement your lawyers had hashed out?

"No comment." I hit the sidewalk and set off toward the subway as fast as I could go without appearing to be running away.

Amelia was still on the steps checking out the photographer. If it's male and over fifteen, it takes priority. Your fairy goddaughter being harassed by a pushy reporter doesn't even register.

"Were you investigating *him?*" Jancie demanded. "Did *you* kill Jameson Montgomery, Ms Peterson? From what I hear, it was *your* letter opener that was stuck in his chest. Would you care to comment on *that?*"

"No." How the heck had she found out about the letter opener? I was definitely going to have to call Betsy if she didn't call me soon.

"Be that way, then! It's gonna make a great front page photo, you running away." Without breaking stride, she called back over her shoulder, loud enough to wake up half the neighborhood, "Hey, Stewie! Get over here and get a photo. Get *lots* of photos!"

I ignored her and tried not to look like I was panicking. Stewie was going to have to do some running if he wanted anything other than a shot of my back side.

From behind me came the sound of running footsteps, headed my way. Give the man a point for energy, and a razzberry to Amelia for not tripping him as he was going down the steps.

I considered my options.

Option one. Start running.

Option two. Shove Jancie into oncoming traffic, *then* start running.

Option three. Answer Jancie's questions, which would give her a bunch of off-the-cuff quotes that would probably be dumb enough to indict me and give Stewie a great shot of me caught between wide-eyed panic and murderous rage.

Option two held a certain appeal, three was sheer lunacy, but there was still a fourth—yell for Amelia and damn the consequences.

I stopped, spun on my heel, and bellowed, "Amelia!"

"You don't have to *shout*," she huffed behind me. "I'm on it."

I spun back

Amelia was standing there, wand out and sparkling like crazy. Jancie Jarrow, eyes wide and mouth gaping unappealingly, was frozen in the act of turning to see who I was yelling at.

Too bad Stewie couldn't get a shot of it—he was frozen, too, camera clutched in one hand to keep it from bouncing, back foot shoving off the concrete, front foot still in the air. Judging from his form, he must have been a runner in high school, though he'd obviously let himself go a bit in the years since.

I sure hoped he still had a high school athlete's sense of balance because there was a better than even chance he was going to land flat on his face when Amelia's freezing spell wore off. Those things are more than a little disorienting, as I'd learned to my cost when Amelia finally unfroze me after I'd tried to clobber her with a tennis racket. In my defense, it was only a tennis racket. If a baseball bat had been within reach, I'd have gone for that, instead.

"Satisfied?" Amelia demanded, looking more than just a bit smug.

"Uh, sure," I said. "You bet. Thanks!"

I've learned not to be too difficult until that wand stops sparkling. Her magic is erratic enough without adding a sparkly wand to the mix.

I scanned the street to see if anybody had noticed our Disney cartoon moment here. The only person close enough was a little old man on the opposite side of the street who was waiting while an obese pug did his business on the sidewalk. Fortunately, the old gentleman didn't seem interested in anything except the state of the pug's bowels, so we had a minute or two to figure this out.

"How long till that spell wears off?" I asked.

Amelia studied her victims. "Hour?"

"An hour!"

She shrugged. "Maybe more. I hit 'em pretty hard."

Wonderful. "Why did you do that?"

"You were yelling. You never yell."

Well, not *for* her, anyway. I've been known to yell *at* her a time or two, but now was not the time to quibble about the fine points.

"Right. So, can you unfreeze them?"

"Sure. Then what?"

She had a point. They'd just come back to life—assuming Stewie didn't plant a facer on the sidewalk first—and have a dozen more questions to add to the mix. And this time Jancie might be a tad more hostile.

So that left…what? A forgetting spell? Befuddlement?

I thought of the guard at Annalise's gate yesterday, then frowned at Jancie.

No forgetting or befuddlement. Not that I had a problem with afflicting a reporter with either, just that someone might notice the after-effects and start asking uncomfortable questions. They wouldn't have a snowball's chance of getting close to the right answers, but just asking would lead them to me. Lots of people would know what Jancie was working on, and someone at the paper had to be aware that she and Stewie had set out for what I presumed was an appointment with—

That proverbial mental light bulb flashed on.

"Can you do a levitating spell on these two?" I asked Amelia. "And stop painting lipstick stains on the poor man's collar. That's not nice."

Amelia snickered. "He deserves it. He walked right through me when he came after you."

"He can't see you."

"It's still rude."

"Come on, Amelia. Can you levitate them?"

Levitation is one of the few spells Amelia can actually do well. "Well" meaning, the things she levitates actually levitate rather than blowing up or turning green or something equally unexpected. The consternation and occasional outright pandemonium that usually result when she does it are another matter, and not my concern right now. After all, Amelia can create a panic just by lifting a coffee cup when people can see the cup but not her.

Amelia eyed her two victims like a butcher calculating dressed weight on a side of beef.

"How high do you want them?"

"Not how high," I said. "How far. Can you levitate them up those steps and in through Mr. Postin's front door? You might have to open the door, too."

Amelia waved her wand dismissively. I couldn't help ducking even though the thing had stopped sparkling.

"Sure," she said. "Easy."

She waved her wand at Stewie, who promptly rose six inches off the sidewalk. He would have immediately pitched forward onto his nose if I hadn't caught him in time. Those running poses look great in a stop-action photo, but, to work, they require you maintain your forward momentum through the whole stride. Stewie lost all his momentum the instant Amelia froze him.

"Oopsie!" said Amelia cheerfully. She gave another wave so that Stewie, who hadn't moved a muscle, shifted to be properly balanced for a two hundred pound man floating in plain air. "The door's no problem at all."

Another wand wave and there was a flash and an electrical sizzling sound from the vicinity of Leslie Postin, Esquire's, exquisite front door.

"How's that?" she said.

As if in response, sparks shot out from around the fancy

brass door handle, immediately followed by a gout of thick black smoke as the door popped open.

"Great," I said. Which was a perfectly safe comment, despite the heavy sarcasm. Amelia's oblivious to the nuances of 'it's not what you say, but how you say it that counts'. With any luck, Postin would blame some random hooligan for the damage to his front door, not Jancie and Stewie, but I didn't have time to worry about such niceties right now. "Now levitate Jancie, too. I can drag them over there if you'll keep them up in the air."

"No problemo."

And it wasn't. I got a grip on Stewie's belt with my left hand and Jancie's elbow with my right and started towing them toward Postin's front steps and the still-smoldering front door. Amelia followed up in the rear, wand steady as she kept the two aloft.

The front steps presented a bit of a challenge because Stewie's outstretched foot kept bumping into the step above, but I solved that problem by spinning him around and dragging him up backwards.

Getting them through the door was a bit more difficult since Amelia had to strain to split her magic enough to allow me to maneuver first Jancie, then Stewie into the elegant vestibule, but we eventually got it. I just prayed none of the secretaries came out to see what all the banging around was about.

Fortunately, there wasn't a peep out of anyone. Probably couldn't hear anything through those thick walls and solid doors. They built things right a hundred years ago, for sure.

I parked Jancie in the middle of the hall, facing the stairs, and set Stewie close to the wall so when he eventually completed that running step, he fell into the wall and not onto the floor. They only wobbled a little when Amelia set them back down.

"How's that?" she demanded. She was puffing a bit, and I'd swear there were beads of sweat on her brow, but I wasn't about to mention it.

"Perfect," I said. Which wasn't a lie, exactly, since it was the best I could do. *We* could do, I amended. Fair's fair. I couldn't have managed without Amelia. And aside from that charred front door and shattered lock, we hadn't done any major damage. Always a plus.

Amelia eyed our living statues. "So, now what?"

"Now we leave. You can unfreeze them as soon as I hit the subway. Deal?"

"You're not worried someone will find them like this first?"

"I'll walk fast, I promise."

I didn't want to be anywhere in the vicinity when the two unfroze. They wouldn't remember anything from the moment they were frozen, but they were going to remember meeting me on the front step and Jancie chasing after me, demanding an interview. Which would leave them wondering how they ended up in Postin's foyer with a damaged front door gaping open behind them. Wondering, but unlikely to mention it. To anyone. Ever. Chances were good they wouldn't even admit their confusion to each other.

I'm just mean enough to wish I could be a fly on the wall to see it. Even if they were just doing their job. Serves them right for hounding me when I'm almost as much a victim in this as Jameson.

Notice I said *almost*. I'm sure Jameson is even more annoyed than I am. He's just not around to complain about it.

AMELIA ABANDONED ME as soon as we hit the subway and she'd unfrozen Jancie and Stewie I didn't object. Besides, she looked like she needed a nap. I, on the other hand, still had work to do.

While I had a signal, I turned my phone on and downloaded my calls. While we rattled through all those tunnels, I'd catch up on whatever I'd missed since I'd left Garr Analytics.

I hadn't missed much. At least, not much I was interested in.

Even though Douglas had brought me up to speed on media coverage since yesterday (in case you're curious, it wasn't doing my reputation any good whatsoever), he'd added to my joy by capturing some of the video and Twitter feeds and scanning the print stuff. It made for grim viewing. Thank you, Douglas.

(As an aside, I don't know where Jancie and the *Courante* got that picture of me that they put on the front page above the fold, but if a stranger recognizes me after seeing it, I'm asking Douglas to set me up with the best hair stylist and makeup artist he knows and damn the cost because matters are a lot more serious than I realized.)

Betsy had called but warned me not to call back, which was frustrating.

I kept on scrolling. Trueblood. Mom. Jancie. Station 4. Trueblood. Mom. Mom. My insurance agent. Mom. Jancie. CBS. Trueblood. NBC. Mom. Three more TV reporters. Trueblood. Mom. Mom. Trueblood. Mom.

My insurance agent was the only good news. He'd get someone out there today.

Trueblood left one message. It was short and to the point. "My office. Today. I'm serious."

When the cops stop saying please, you know you're in trouble.

Mom hadn't left a message. She knew I knew what she'd say.

You'd think she'd also know I wasn't having any of it, but that's mothers for you. They never listen and they never give up.

I deleted the whole list and turned off the phone. They'd all call back, sooner or later. Unless Trueblood sent a black-and-white after me, first. At least that would save me the cost of another subway ride.

I got off at the Curtis and Bond stop, which is right in the heart of River City's equivalent of Wall Street. JM Industries' main headquarters is in one of those sprawling industrial-slash-business parks in the suburbs, but Jameson had maintained secondary offices for senior managers here. It was probably just chance that Dawson, Dawson, and Dawson was in the same building, six floors down. My plan was to hit JM first, then Triple

D.

I hadn't figured out any way to determine if Jameson had been aware of Geoffrey Dawson's relationship with Christine. Trueblood could flat out ask, but I didn't have that advantage.

I couldn't see Dawson stabbing Jameson like that, though. Destroy him financially or in the courts? Absolutely. Kill him? Not so much. It's not much fun gloating if your opponent's too dead to appreciate it, and lawyers love to gloat.

I hoped I could get some answers here. I really didn't want to go all the way out to corporate headquarters. For one thing, the subway doesn't go that far, plus cops frown on you driving around with your windshield shot out.

I just hoped my insurance agent hadn't lied about getting it fixed today. I wasn't worried about anyone ripping off my stereo—no self-respecting thief would be caught dead with it— but there was a chance it was going to rain and the upholstery wouldn't like being drenched. If anyone wanted the floor mats, they could have them.

I got through the doors of JM and all the way up to the gorgeous young thing sitting behind the vast front desk without anyone stopping me.

"May I help you?" The woman's voice and diction were as coolly sophisticated as the dress she wore, which struck exactly the right balance between professional and slutty seductive. I wondered if she and Jameson had had a relationship. She was definitely his type.

"I was hoping to talk to Mr. Gurgain or perhaps Ms Demetrios," I said, identifying the board chairman and the chief financial officer. "Are they in?"

"Do you have an appointment?"

"No, but I think they might want to talk to me anyway." Hoped, actually, but I was trying to be positive.

"Your name?"

I told her.

Big mistake. Her eyes widened as she blinked back tears, and her mouth opened and closed like a fish out of water.

"Murderer! Bitch! *Murderer!*" The last came out as a screech that brought two uniformed guards running.

"Call more security! Call the police!" She pointed a finger tipped by a viciously long, blood-red nail at me. "She murdered Mr. Montgomery. She killed Jameson! Oh, my God! Bitch! Murderer!"

By now people were popping out of offices on all sides. One of the guards edged toward me, clearly debating the wisdom of taking on a murderer. The other guard seemed torn between tackling me and restraining the receptionist, who looked ready to launch herself across the desk at me and rip my throat out.

At least I had the answer to the question about her and Jameson.

Not that it helped.

"So you're saying Mr. Gurgain and Ms Demetrios aren't available?" I said, keeping my hands where the edgy guard could see them.

"No! I won't let you kill them, too! I won't. *I won't!*"

"Perhaps it's time for a break, Miss Sanders?"

The calm, clear voice easily cut through the receptionist's screeching. I turned to face a tall woman with graying hair and a third uniformed guard at her heels.

"Mr. Bakkins? Would you and Mr. Solon escort Miss Sanders to the break room, please? I'm sure she would like a nice hot cup of tea right now."

The first two guards closed in on Miss Sanders, who promptly collapsed into her chair, sobbing. "Jameson. Oh, Jameson!"

"Now, now, miss," said the third guard. "Ms Demetrios is right. A little break will be just the thing."

They didn't quite drag her away, but they came close. The woman was playing the prostrate-with-grief card to the max. Not to mention she had a great pair of lungs. Anyone who hadn't been rousted out of their cubicle by her screeching needed new batteries for their hearing aids.

"Mr. Leiberman, if you'll please take Miss Sanders' place? I believe the excitement is now over," Ms Demetrios said. She didn't raise her voice, but it was enough to send everyone scurrying back to their offices. Satisfied, she turned back to me.

"I take it you are Maxie Peterson?"

I nodded. I'd almost said, 'Yes, ma'am,' which would have annoyed me no end. I admire women with that kind of commanding presence; I just don't like it when it works on me.

"Come with me." She didn't bother looking back to see if I followed.

I did. Of course.

CHAPTER 22

Sharon Demetrios was chief financial officer for JM Industries, but you couldn't have told it by the cramped, windowless office she led me to. Even the stacks of financial reports and bulging folders that half buried her desk seemed more suited to one of the worker bees under her. Clearly, this was a woman more interested in the work than the trappings of power.

"I apologize for Miss Sanders," she said as we settled into the visitors chairs in front of her desk. "She took Jameson's dalliance rather more to heart than she should have."

"Dalliance?"

She shrugged. "An old-fashioned word, but apt for the majority of Jameson's affairs. Women never lasted long in his life. Not even his wives. I'm sure you already know that."

"You don't think one of them was like Miss Sanders and took it more to heart than he intended?"

"I assume most of them did. *Including* his wives," she added dryly. "The man could be enormously charming when he wanted. He was, however, quite adept at getting rid of them if they ended up clinging too much, even if he had to pay to do it."

"You didn't like your boss?"

The corner of her mouth quirked. "Actually, I did. To a degree." She studied me for a moment, then, "Why did Jameson hire you, Ms Peterson? What was it he wanted you to do?"

Finally, the reason she'd been willing to talk to me. She had the same question everyone else did. And I had the same answer.

"I don't know," I said.

As for everyone else, that wasn't the answer she'd wanted. "So, the media actually got that part right?"

I nodded.

"But you have a theory?"

"Lots. One is, it had something to do with the lawsuits against your subsidiaries that he wanted to settle."

That appeared to amuse her. "Why would he hire an unknown investigator with limited resources and no international experience to help with something like that?"

"You have a better theory?"

"I deal in facts, Ms Peterson, not theories. I always have."

"He wouldn't have hired me to help with getting rid of an inconvenient lover, Ms Demetrios. I don't take those kinds of jobs."

"I know. And that's a fact I find...interesting."

She knew? That meant she'd had someone research me and my business, just as Postin had. I didn't have anything to hide—well, not much, anyway—but I still didn't like it. Not that it surprised me. In their place, I'd have done the same.

"Why *did* Mr. Montgomery want to settle those lawsuits, Ms Demetrios? Do you know?"

"No."

"Mr. Postin says he wanted to, as he put it, 'secure his legacy'."

"Leslie said that?" She snorted. "Ridiculous. Oh, that's what Jameson *said*, but how Leslie can believe he actually *meant* it is beyond me."

"Mr. Montgomery didn't care about legacies?"

"Not beyond the substantial legacy he'd actually inherited. He had two illegitimate daughters and didn't seem to take much interest in either one, so far as I could see. He wasn't a philanthropist. To be honest, he always behaved like someone who didn't think the usual rules applied to him because he was rich and going to live forever. The notion that he was concerned about his legacy is absurd. I don't believe it. It would never occur to Jameson that he could die like any normal human being. He certainly wouldn't have expected anyone to murder him."

"I don't imagine anyone does," I said. "So what happens to the business now? Do you know?"

That made her go still. I waited, letting the silence stretch, and wondered. She'd brought me into her office because she wanted answers she thought I had. Once I'd admitted I didn't know why Jameson had hired me, she should have booted me out. So why hadn't she? Did she think I knew something I wasn't admitting to knowing? Or that I knew something important, even though I didn't know I knew it? Something she could pick out of the conversation even if I couldn't?

"Ms Demetrios?"

She cleared her throat. "What happens now? That's probably pretty straightforward. Since their divorce wasn't final, Jameson's controlling interest in the company goes to his wife, Christine. At least, we assume it will. Jameson was more a creature of habit than he liked to admit. He might not be able to keep his own schedule straight without the help of his secretary, but he always kept a handle on the money."

"Always?"

"Always. Whenever he was married, he left everything to the current wife. He also made sure in the pre-nuptials that they couldn't touch one single share of it while he was alive. When he divorced, he'd change his will so virtually the entire estate went to a charitable foundation his grandfather established before he was born. The Jameson John Montgomery Foundation. You can look it up."

"Rather a precarious approach to running a major business, isn't it? Having a majority of the stock floating like that?"

"Definitely. There aren't many family owned businesses the size of JM Industries, but in most cases, by the time the third generation takes charge, ownership is dispersed among multiple heirs so the death of one of them doesn't severely impact that business. The ownership of JM, however, is *not* dispersed."

"And more vulnerable because of it, I assume."

Her lips compressed into a thin line. Whatever her reasons for talking to me, she wasn't about to discuss the company's vulnerabilities with an outsider.

"JM Industries will continue to thrive, Ms Peterson. Jameson's murder is a personal tragedy, but there are many good people here who will ensure that the business goes on, regardless of who owns it. Now, if you'll excuse me, I'll just ask Mr. Bakkins to show you the way out.'

We both knew she meant Mr. Bakkins was going to make sure I was escorted off the premises with no opportunity to ask questions of anyone else, but she was much too polite to say so.

Which meant I'd have to find another way to talk to someone who could tell me what was really going to happen to the business now that Jameson was dead. Good people can do bad things if enough money is involved, and with Jameson John Montgomery the Third, there was way more than enough to be a great motive for murder.

WHILE I WAITED for the elevator that would take me down to Triple D, I fished out my phone. You'd think I'd have known better than to waste my time, but I kept hoping there'd be a message telling me the murderer had been arrested, my name was cleared, and life could go back to normal.

No such luck. Trueblood. Mom. Jancie, with what looked like an unusually long voice message. Two unidentified numbers that were probably the media. Trueblood. And mom. All in the space of half an hour.

These people have got to get a life. Including mom. No, *especially* mom.

When this is over, the two of us are going to have a little heart-to-heart. But only when it's over. Until then, she'll just have to tough it out without me.

Dawson, Dawson, and Dawson occupies three entire floors of the building. Just the thought of all those wolfish lawyers busily plotting corporate takeovers and income tax avoidance schemes and other perfectly legal but morally questionable shenanigans set my nerves on edge. Knowing Geoffrey Dawson hunts at the head of that pack pretty much shredded any nerves that were left. I wasn't looking forward to this interview. Assuming I could get in to see him, of course.

I should have had Amelia freeze him last night instead of marching him out the door. Then, once Christine passed out, Amelia could have unfrozen him for a friendly little chat.

But she hadn't, and we hadn't, so here I was. I stuffed my phone back in my purse, plastered a polite and professionally aloof smile on my face, and headed for the front receptionist.

The woman who guarded the portals of Dawson, Dawson, and Dawson was as young and good looking as Miss Sanders. Unlike Miss Sanders, however, she was dressed in a conservative grey business suit with pale yellow shirt buttoned right up to the top, and her ever-so-distant smile gave just a glimpse of sharp, white teeth. I gave her points for not wincing when she got a good look at my bruises and scrapes.

She also refrained from screaming, screeching, or hurling accusations of murder when I gave her my name. Instead she hummed, ever so slightly, at the back of her throat, thought about it for a moment, then said coolly, "Let me see if he's available."

Which meant that between the news coverage of Jameson's murder and the office water-cooler gossip, I rated as a Person Of Interest worthy to be considered for an interview with the great man himself.

While I was trying to decide how I felt about that, she was on the phone explaining the situation to a higher authority. Whatever she said, it worked. She set down the phone and stood.

"Mr. Dawson can give you a few moments of his time. If

you'll follow me?"

That's when my phone rang. I gave a silent curse and fished it out of my purse. "Sorry."

Cool professionalism instantly shifted to frosty disapproval. "You'll have to turn that off. Mr. Dawson doesn't appreciate interruptions when he's talking."

I glanced at the caller ID. Mom. Again.

"Not a problem," I said, and shut the thing off, then followed the woman down the hall.

Unlike Postin, Dawson didn't bother getting up when I walked in. His personal secretary, to whom I'd been handed off, left me standing in front of his desk like a school kid hauled before the principal. I was trying not to feel like a wayward kid, but that wasn't easy. The term 'steely gaze' was coined to fit him.

Except he may not have been quite as coolly unemotional as he seemed. I stiffened my spine and let the silence between us stretch. He broke first. He shouldn't have—lawyers with his reputation just don't do that kind of thing—but he did.

"What do you want?"

First points to my side. Yay me.

I claimed a chair, settled my purse, crossed my legs, and said, "Answers to lots of questions, starting with, now that he's dead, who gets Jameson Montgomery's controlling interest in JM Industries?"

"I won't answer that."

"But you wrote his will, so you know its terms."

"I won't answer that, either."

"The CIA uses the 'we can neither confirm nor deny' line a lot. You might try it. For variety, if nothing else."

Those thin, patrician nostrils flared as if at the scent of rotting fish. "Dawson, Dawson, and Dawson are not the CIA. We hold ourselves to a higher standard."

"And probably keep your secrets better than they do, too, I imagine. But I want to find out who killed Jameson as much as you do, probably more, so the questions stand." I leaned forward for emphasis. "Who benefits from his death, Mr. Dawson?"

That thin mouth thinned even further. "Everyone. The man was a disgrace to his name. The world is better off without him in it."

Whoa! So much for lawyerly discretion!

"Mrs. Montgomery is certainly better off. If they'd divorced, she would have only gotten the settlement. With him dead—"

"Christine would *never* stoop to violence! And if you think you can harass her—"

He was cut short by his office door being flung open so hard it slammed into the wall as Katie Carmody stormed into the room, little Julia firmly in tow.

"You bastard! You snot-nosed, head up your ass, slimy, cheating, lawyer bastard! What do you mean Julia doesn't inherit?"

Rage had transformed Katie Carmody, turning her into a wide-eyed, red-faced wild woman. That got Dawson on his feet.

Before he could get a word out, his secretary appeared in the open door. "I'm so sorry, Mr. Dawson. She got past security and I—"

"Thank you, Mrs. Lutz," said Dawson, coming around the desk. "I'll deal with this."

Mrs. Lutz left, closing the door behind her. I'm pretty sure I'm the only one who noticed. Dawson and Katie were doing their best to stare each other down, hoping the other would crack first.

Katie should have known better. Geoffrey Dawson ate pretty little ladies like her for lunch.

"Sit down, Katie," said Dawson.

"You said—" she wailed. That was all she got out.

"Sit *down*, I said. You too, Julia."

Julia just pulled her hand free of her mother's grasp and crossed her arms over her chest, the perfect picture of a sullen teen prepared to defy the world and every unreasonable, demanding adult in it. Bereft of her last support, Katie collapsed in the nearest armchair and broke into tears. Dawson simply stood there, staring at them both with distaste.

They'd all forgotten there was anyone else in the room, which suited me just fine. I shifted so I had a better view and waited to see what would happen next.

Julia didn't make me wait long. She threw a disgusted scowl at her mother, then turned her wrath on the lawyer. She was tall for her age and he was a grown man and a whole lot taller, but that didn't faze her in the least.

"Daddy promised the house would be mine," she snarled. "*Mine!* He *said* so, and you can't take it away from me!"

"*Your* house, yes," said Dawson. "The house you and your mother live in now."

That got Katie's attention. "What? No! That's *my* house!"

Dawson shook his head. "No, it's not, and you know it. You signed the agreement. It's all laid out clearly in there. Jameson maintained the house for the two of you until Julia turned twenty-one or graduated from college, whichever came last. At that point, all support for Julia stopped, including maintenance of the house. Unless, of course, Jameson died first, in which case the house and everything in it became Julia's property. Not yours, Katie. Julia's."

"What?"

"I don't care about *that* house," Julia objected. "I want my daddy's house!"

"Well, you're not getting it," said Dawson. I had the feeling he enjoyed saying it, too. "Beyond the maintenance you'll receive until you graduate, you get your house, free and clear, and a half million dollars. Before taxes, I might add, which means maybe four hundred thousand after. That's it. Your mother gets nothing."

"What?!"

I'd thought that first 'what?' had been loud. I'd been wrong. This latest was *loud*. I mean, hurting-your-ears loud. I was impressed. Katie didn't look like she had lungs that strong.

"*No!*" said Julia, stamping her foot. "Daddy's house! I want *daddy's* house! *And* his money! I'm his daughter, his only child—"

"Not his only—" Dawson started to say, but Julia wasn't listening.

"His *only* child. Mommy said so. And he loved me. Me! He *said* so!"

"She *belongs* in that house!" Katie cried. "*Her*, not that scrawny, stuffed up bitch he married! Julia is Jameson's flesh and blood. And I'm Julia's mother!"

Dawson's hands had curled into fists. Judging by the expression on his face, he was struggling against the urge to strangle them both. I could sympathize. If Jameson had meant to secure his legacy with his eldest daughter, he'd have been sorely disappointed.

Not that I blamed Julia. With parents like hers, the kid hadn't stood a chance.

"And anyway," Julia added viciously, swinging around to point an accusing finger at me. "What's *she* doing here? You're plotting against me, aren't you? *Both* of you. I know you are."

"Ms Peterson is—"

"Not shooting at you, for starters," I said. Now I'd been dragged into the conversation, I had a few questions of my own. "Where'd you get that rifle, Julia? And why were you shooting at me?"

That got Dawson's attention. He glared at me, then Julia, then back at me. "She *shot* at you? Julia? When?"

"Last night. In the parking lot outside my apartment."

"She didn't mean anything. She's just a kid!" Katie objected. "Nobody got hurt!"

"What do you call these scrapes and bruises?" I demanded, pointing. So much for being a spectator to all this.

"*Julia* didn't to it. The detective said so! And I said I'd cover everything."

"I didn't hit you, did I?" Julia sneered.

"Not for want of trying. How'd you even get there? Who

drove you? Your mother?"

"I had nothing to do with it!" Katie objected. "I didn't know anything about it. I didn't even know Julia had taken one of the cars until the police told me."

"That's 'cause you never know anything. You never pay attention to me, mom, do you? You don't care about me. You've never cared about *me!*"

"That's not true, baby. You know that's not true. You're my daughter. I love you!"

"No you don't. You just love the money daddy gives you. *I* know. I've *always* known."

"Julia shot at you? With a rifle?" Despite all his years in the courtroom, Dawson was having a hard time keeping up.

Julia eyed him disdainfully. "The rifle's mine. Daddy bought it for me because I was on the shooting team at school. And I drove myself. I know how to drive. Ricky taught me."

"*I* certainly didn't give her the keys!" Katie huffed.

Her daughter whirled on her, furious. "Of course not. You never give me anything! Ever!"

"Why would I give you my car keys? You're not old enough to drive!"

"So? Daddy would have let me. He loved me. He said so!"

"Jameson wouldn't—"

"I hope the hell you're not expecting *me* to represent you!" Dawson interjected.

That set both of them off.

"I don't need a lawyer! Nobody got hurt!"

"She's just a child! It was all a mistake! I—"

For the second time that morning, the office door burst open. This time, the first two through the door were dressed in the crisp blue uniforms of River City's finest. Mrs. Lutz trailed anxiously in their wake.

"What the hell?" Dawson exclaimed.

"Don't let them take me!" cried Julia. "I didn't do anything!"

"You leave my daughter alone!" screeched Katie.

"I'm sorry!" said Mrs. Lutz, wringing her hands. "They'd been called— I heard the shouting—"

By now, I'd gotten a clear look at the two cops. My stomach slid into my shoes. Fred, at the rear, looked worried and embarrassed, but his partner was grinning from ear to ear.

"Maxine Peterson," said Gracie, pulling her handcuffs off her utility belt. "You're under arrest."

CHAPTER 23

Despite my protests, I got that free ride to River City police headquarters that Trueblood had offered me yesterday. It was just my bad luck that Gracie and Fred happened to be the closest when the call came in. Something about following up on another case entirely.

Gracie didn't actually arrest me, though I could tell she really, really wanted to. She also didn't let me out of the handcuffs until she dumped me in one of the interview rooms, despite Fred's attempts to talk her out of it.

I wasted half an hour staring at the drab tan walls and fighting against the urge to cuss and stomp up and down before Trueblood finally put in an appearance.

"Took you long enough," I grumbled, settling back in my chair in a way I hoped was deliberately provoking.

"I could say the same," he responded pleasantly, deliberately refusing to be provoked. "I lost track of how many times I called you today."

"Thank God I'm not on a pay-per-call plan with my carrier," I shot back. "I hate billing the city for that sort of thing."

He casually claimed the chair across from me. "But you would have billed us, anyway?"

"You bet."

"You should have come in earlier, like I asked."

"My car doesn't have a windshield, or did you forget?"

"Yet here you are. Imagine that."

He tilted back in his chair like a man settling in for a cozy chat, cocked his head to one side, and studied me.

"Bruises aren't as bad as I'd expected, but you need to redo the coverage on those scrapes."

I could feel the heat rising in my cheeks. Maybe I should have let Amelia patch me up this morning, after all.

"Thanks. That makes me feel way better, Trueblood."

He'd left his sport coat behind and his sleeves were rolled up to his elbows, revealing strongly muscled forearms. The shirt was well made, but it still showed signs of strain across the chest and shoulders.

Worse, he'd shed his tie and unbuttoned his collar. The man hadn't lied yesterday when he'd said chest hair wasn't a problem. It was just a glimpse, but enough to tell: dark, not too thick or curly. Just enough to run your fingers through if you wanted.

Not that I wanted to or anything, but even the best of us can get distracted, right?

"Are you arresting me?" I said, dragging my attention back to the matters at hand.

"Should I?"

"No, and you shouldn't pester me like this, either."

"Is that what you call it?"

"I wasn't the one doing all the shouting. You can ask Geoffrey Dawson if you don't believe me."

"Actually, it wasn't Mr. Dawson's office that called us. The officers were responding to a panicked call from JM Industries, upstairs."

I stifled the urge to swear. "Let me guess. A Miss Sanders, accusing me of murder?"

He beamed approvingly. "Very good! However, we were already on alert after a call from a Jancie Jarrow. She's accusing you of assault."

That made me sit up. "What? She's crazy! What did she say?"

"So you admit you ran into Ms Jarrow this morning?"

"Ran into her? No, I did not run into her," I said, putting air quotes around the 'run into' part. "I did, however, meet her on the steps outside Mr. Leslie Postin's office."

"And...?"

"And she tried to interview me and I said 'no comment'."

"That was it? She didn't push for more?"

"She's a reporter, Trueblood! Of *course* she pushed for more. But I didn't push her, let alone assault her. What do you think?"

"I think there's stuff you're not telling me."

Give the man a star.

"Okay. The sky was blue, high clouds, a light breeze. No rain after all, so a nice day. An old man on the other side of the street was letting his dog take a dump on the sidewalk, which I thought was pretty tacky, and—"

"Peterson?" Trueblood leaned toward me, close enough to stare right down my throat.

"Yes, Trueblood?" I said, letting my eyes go wide and innocent.

"Get to the point."

There were flecks of silver in those deadly Arctic-blue eyes of his. "You want to back off an inch or two first?"

"Why? I make you nervous?"

"No, but I can smell the onions you had for lunch."

He backed off. I swear, he was blushing under that tan.

"I'll bet it was the burger deluxe at Fat Freddy's. Am I right? I'm right, aren't I? Freddy makes great burgers, but he tends to overdo the onions and—"

"It wasn't Fat Freddy's," said Trueblood from between gritted teeth. "Focus, Peterson. Jancie Jarrow?"

"Jancie. Right." I pretended to focus. In reality, I was trying to *stop* focusing on *him*. Even with onions on his breath, being this close to him was turning my brain to mush and stirring up a lot of those annoying hormones that he seemed to disrupt just by walking into the room.

"She tried to get an interview. You said no comment."

"Right. I did. And afterward I headed to the subway and she, I presume, eventually interviewed Mr. Postin, though I can't actually testify to that since I wasn't there."

He sighed. "Because you were on the subway."

I flashed him my biggest, brightest, I'm-so-glad-we-can-all-agree smile. "That's right. At least, I assume I was still on the subway when she was interviewing Mr. Postin. I might have gotten off by then, though, so…" I shrugged and smiled and gave myself two points for being really *really* annoying. "So there you are."

He crossed his arms over his chest and studied me through eyes narrowed to slits.

"You're getting a little squinty-eyed, there, Trueblood. Better watch it or you'll have wrinkles at the corners."

He ignored that, but it cost him an effort. "So you didn't assault Ms Jarrow?"

"Me? Of course not!"

Which is absolutely true. Amelia did, though I'm pretty sure you can't call a freezing spell 'assault' since there's no physical contact involved and no harm. Not counting things like Stewie's potential face plant, of course.

"Not only did I not assault Ms Jarrow, I didn't murder Jameson, and I was *not* the one yelling in Dawson's office. No matter what Gracie says."

"Officer O'Mallon didn't say anything about your behavior at Dawson, Dawson, and Dawson. She was merely being helpful by giving you a ride here."

"In handcuffs?"

"A ride in a cop car wouldn't be the same without them."

"You wanted to talk to me long before Jarrow or Sanders or anyone else called you to complain, Trueblood," I said. "All this yadda yadda is just you being annoying, right?"

He eyed me for a minute like a man trying to collect his thoughts.

I wanted to believe it was because I disrupted his thought

processes as badly as he disrupted mine, but I knew better. Male mental disruption has never been one of my strong suits, not even back in high school when it was a lot easier and really mattered.

"How tall are you, Peterson?" he said at last.

"Me? Five nine. And a half." If he asked me my weight I was going to sock him. "Why?"

"Some of your old buddies here said you're really good with a knife."

"They said *what?*"

"They said you hated your service weapon and never managed much more than minimum on the proficiency tests."

"I don't like guns. Why do you think I quit the force?"

He ignored that, much to my relief.

"One guy remembers a night shift, nothing going on, everybody bored, and then someone challenges everyone to a knife throwing contest."

I remembered. And I started sweating. It was my letter opener in Jameson Montgomery's chest, after all. My extra sharp letter opener that just happened to look like a dagger. Possibly because that's exactly what it was, though I wasn't about to admit it.

"He says they set up a target. A target that you never missed, even when they kept backing up the throw line."

"I—"

"You don't have to answer that," said Amelia, freezing Trueblood as solid as she'd frozen Jancie and Stewie.

Shit. "You know they've got cameras in the room, right?" I said, keeping my eyes on Trueblood and trying to keep my lips from moving.

Trueblood wasn't recording the conversation—legally, anyway—but that wouldn't stop him from finding someone who could read lips if he wanted to. The cameras they use these days make that pretty easy. Of course, that's *if* you've got the right angle *and* the lips are actually moving.

"Took a nap, then thought I'd check up on you, just in case," Amelia said, settling into the chair beside Trueblood. "Good thing I did. You should have hollered. Although…"

She eyed Trueblood appreciatively. "That's a good look on him. No jacket, open collar. You should take a picture while you can. Or did they take your phone away when they arrested you?"

"They didn't arrest me." (Try saying that without moving your lips on the 'm.' I dare you.)

"Same as."

"Unfreeze him. Now." It came out more like *wheeze hih nau*, but it was the best I could do.

"What? Stop mumbling!"

I settled for glaring, which is hard to do if you can't look straight at the person who's annoying you.

Amelia heaved a huge sigh and unfroze him.

Trueblood blinked and his head bobbled a tiny bit.

"I learned the trick when I was a kid," I said, as if Amelia hadn't interrupted us. "So what? You think I killed Jameson by throwing my letter opener at him?"

"Your very *sharp* letter opener."

"Trueblood, you know as well as I do that the world's best knife thrower couldn't guarantee hitting the heart unless he could put a lot more force into it than I can. There's all those ribs in the way. Off by a fraction of an inch and the knife's deflected. Throat? Gut? Sure. Those would be easy. Lots of soft tissue and no bones to get in the way. But not the heart."

"It might explain the angle, though."

"What? Straight in?"

"So you noticed that?"

I snorted. "Of course I noticed. But at five feet nine, if I'd stabbed him with the knife—"

"Letter opener."

"The letter opener," I amended. "It would have gone in at a downward angle. I'd have had a better chance of hitting the heart, but I couldn't have managed that angle. Way too awkward.

But you've already figured that out, so why *did* you call me in here?"

He eyed me. I eyed him.

"He should let his hair grow,' said Amelia. "Not too long, just—"

I kicked her under the table.

Trueblood smiled. "What's the matter, Peterson? Getting jumpy?"

"Bored. My foot's falling asleep."

"Just a little befuddlement. And a persuasion spell," said Amelia. "I tell him to leave you alone and—"

"Don't even think about it," I snapped before I could stop myself.

"You haven't the slightest idea what I'm thinking," said Trueblood. He sounded offended.

"Try and help and whaddya get?" Amelia griped. "Ingratitude, that's what. If I'd been there with that Geoffy guy—"

"You're a cop," I said, ignoring Amelia. "I know how cops think."

"Yeah? So what am I thinking?"

"Yeah, what *is* he thinking?" said Amelia.

I shot Amelia a warning glance. "What? You can't read minds?" Oops. "I didn't mean *you*." That was for Trueblood. I was losing track of this conversation fast.

"I meant," I said, staring straight at him, "I know how cops in general think, so I think you're thinking that I...er...that is..." The words died away.

I blinked, then cleared my throat.

Hell, what *was* I thinking?

He was going to clap me in jail for sure. Indecent stupidity. Crazy with intent. Public display of insanity. There had to be something that fit.

It didn't help that Trueblood was leaning across the table, onions or no onions, with a frown on his face that looked a lot more worried than annoyed. And that worried me. If he thought I was crazy, too, then there might be serious cause for concern.

"Look me in the eye, Peterson," Trueblood ordered. A few inches closer and I could kiss him. Or he could kiss me.

Hell of it was, he was staring into my eyes and ignoring my lips altogether.

He held up a finger in front of my nose. "Watch my finger."

"You're awfully bossy."

"Yeah. Just watch the finger." He moved his finger to one side, then back to the other. It was a nice finger. "Your pupils are normal, and you're tracking just fine…"

He stretched out his hand and gently probed my scraped cheek.

"Ow!"

"Sorry." He was half out of his chair now and so close I could feel the heat of him and catch the faint scent of aftershave and soap. He stretched out his other hand and gently lifted my hair away from the bruise that Mrs Minski's rolling pin had left. We both winced.

"You really should have seen a doctor."

"I'm fine."

"No, you're not. You were starting to babble, and you do not strike me as the babbling type."

"Depends on the circumstances," I muttered, shooting a warning look at Amelia out of the corner of my eye.

She beamed at me approvingly, then winked and vanished.

CHAPTER 24

Some guys just can't resist playing knight in shining armor. Trueblood is one of them. Not that the armor is all that shining—he had me dragged in for questioning, after all—but I suppose, given the implications of that late night competition in the squad room, you couldn't really blame him. And the handcuffs were Gracie's idea, not his. So when he said he was releasing my office and offered me a ride, I accepted.

I shouldn't have.

"You don't have an unmarked car you can use?" I demanded, glaring at the black-and-white whose door he was holding for me.

"It's this or get there on your own, Peterson, take your pick."

Since the second option would involve either a taxi I couldn't afford or another subway ride plus a three-block hike, I picked the black-and-white. Didn't mean I had to like it.

At least he didn't make me sit in the back as regulations required.

Not that it made that much difference. Since he could claim one of the fifteen minute loading zone spaces in front of my building, half the people there must have seen me get out.

You'd think they'd have something better to do than stare out those dirty windows, but I guess not. I didn't get five feet inside the front door before three people had popped out of their offices to check things out. And that wasn't counting Janice Zemelkis, who had taken up a strategic position that blocked access to both the elevator and the stairs.

"Good afternoon, Maxine," she said, as primly composed as an old-fashioned schoolmarm. "And you must be the investigating detective? Trueblood, I believe someone said?"

"Yes, ma'am," said Trueblood politely.

"Is Ms Peterson under arrest?"

That made him blink. "Ma'am?"

"Don't worry, Trueblood," I said. "I've got this." I raised my voice and turned to the three loitering in the lobby with intent. "So you all know, I haven't been arrested yet. Sorry about that."

"Damn," growled one. "Thought I had it there for a minute."

"How nice!" said the grandmotherly one. "That means I've still got a chance." She beamed at Trueblood. "Tomorrow morning at ten, if you can manage it. I'd really like to take my daughter and the grandkids for pizza and a movie. Maybe even the games arcade!"

"Gretchen!" said Ms Zemelkis sternly. "Interference is not permitted. You know that!"

"Sorry," said Gretchen, abashed. "I just thought... Oh, well. While there's life, there's hope!"

The last guy just swore under his breath and retreated into his office, slamming the door behind him. There's always one sore loser in every bunch. The first guy disappeared, as well, but Gretchen lingered long enough to catch Trueblood's eye. *Ten* she mouthed silently. *Tomorrow.* Then she winked.

Trueblood grinned and winked back.

Janice ignored them. She was leaning in to get a better look at my face. "I do trust that is not the result of police brutality."

"Well..." I said, dragging the word out provocatively.

"Absolutely not," said Trueblood.

"Very good. I can't say we've ever encountered the issue before, but I would not condone continuing the pool under such circumstances."

"Is that the office pool Maxie mentioned? Can I buy in?" said Trueblood.

"Absolutely not," said Janice. "Most inappropriate. Though that forces me to ask: Just what, exactly, did Maxine say about the pool?"

He didn't miss a beat. "I'm not at liberty to discuss police business, ma'am."

I tried to look innocent and hoped my obvious physical sufferings would buy me a little leeway.

"Indeed," said Janice. She eyed me, then Trueblood, then me again. "Well, I'll let it go for now, but should you, detective, personally arrest Maxine at the time she selected, I may have to pursue this further. My warning to Gretchen, you understand, would apply doubly to Maxine."

"Of course," said Trueblood.

"Not a problem," I said.

Actually, I was beginning to hope I wouldn't be arrested at all. Trueblood didn't seem to be any closer to a solution than I was, but at least he didn't seem interested in appeasing public opinion by making a quick arrest, warranted or not.

"Come on, Trueblood," I said. "I want my office back."

We took the stairs. Everything seemed back to normal except for the yellow crime scene tape across my door, and Trueblood took that down fast enough.

It wasn't until the lock clicked open that I hesitated.

This was my office, and a man had died there yesterday. A man I didn't even know. A man who'd pretty much taken over my life ever since I'd found him with my letter opener in his chest.

But whenever I'd thought about him, I realized now, I'd thought about him in relation to *me*—the work he was bringing *me*, the money he'd pay *me*, the way his death had disrupted *my* life.

What, I wondered, had *he* been thinking when he'd come

here yesterday morning, earlier than planned? What had he been feeling?

"Peterson?" Trueblood was looking down at me, face shadowed by concern. "You sure you want to do this?"

"Yes. Yes, of course," I said, and pushed the door open.

I'd been prepared to find blood on the carpet, not to mention the coffee stain and broken glass from the pot Amelia had slaughtered. I'd expected to see gray powder everywhere they'd dusted for prints, maybe a few things missing that had been taken away as evidence.

I had *not* expected to find the place had been ransacked by demented elves who'd left every drawer of every filing cabinet gaping, the few framed certificates and diplomas on the wall drunkenly askew, and papers and folders scattered haphazardly across the top of what even I would admit had been an untidy desk. Betsy and her crew had clearly looked at everything, but if they'd put anything back, I couldn't spot it. Even Amelia couldn't have made this big a mess without some serious assistance.

"What the hell?" Trueblood shoved past me.

I started to snap at him, but bit the words back when I realized he was looking as stunned as I felt.

"So this isn't the way you guys leave a crime scene?"

"No! Of course not." He glared at me. "You should know that. You were a cop, too."

"Yeah, but I was always the one standing outside handing out booties and making everyone sign in. I wasn't part of the crime scene team, and I sure as hell was never a detective. But I do know you guys don't clean up afterwards."

"No, we don't. But we don't make a mess like this, either. Don't touch anything, okay?" he said. "I'm calling this in."

Great. Now my crime scene was a crime scene.

My life just kept getting better and better.

THE TWO OFFICERS Trueblood requested showed up about ten minutes later and were immediately assigned to canvas the building to see if anybody had seen or heard anything suspicious. None of us had any hope they'd learn anything useful, but there wasn't much else they could do.

While we waited for the crime scene team, Trueblood had me pick my way through the mess, trying to spot any pattern to the disaster or anything that had gone missing. He gave me a pair of gloves he fished out of his jacket pocket so I didn't leave any more prints than were already there, then retreated to the battered old sofa that sat against the wall by the office door. The cushion made a rude noise as he settled on it, but he managed not to say anything cutting. I guess he could tell from my expression that I wasn't in the mood for jolly banter.

I didn't last very long. I know a hopeless battle when I see one. By the time Betsy appeared, I'd settled for plopping my butt in my desk chair and glaring at everything, Trueblood included. Not that I blamed him for any of it, but there wasn't anybody else to glare at.

Betsy stopped short two inches inside the door. "What the hell?"

"That's what we'd like to know," said Trueblood, struggling up off the sofa in relief—not at Betsy's arrival, but at having a good excuse to abandon the sofa. That thing can be hell on your spine if you're stuck there for very long.

"Your team didn't do this, did they, Betsy?" I said.

"Us? No! No way!" said Betsy indignant.

"What the...?"

"Shit!"

That was from the two team members who, finding it impossible to get past Betsy, had settled for peering over her shoulders. I'd believed Betsy when she denied leaving my office in its current state, but even if I hadn't, one look at the expressions on those guys' faces would have convinced me. They looked pissed as well as surprised, as if they regarded the devastation as a personal attack on them.

"You think you can get anything useful out of all this, Sharanski?" Trueblood asked.

Betsy surveyed the mess sourly. "You got a magic wand?"

He sighed. "That's what I figured."

I refrained from mentioning that I knew someone who did. Amelia couldn't possibly make things worse than they already were.

At least, I was pretty sure she couldn't. If there was any justice in the world, I wouldn't have to find out.

You'd think I'd know better, right?

BETSY AND HER TEAM found absolutely nothing helpful and were wrapping things up when the officers canvassing the building reported back. It was a quick report. Nobody saw anything, nobody heard anything, and no matter what time the incident might have occurred, everyone swore they were somewhere else entirely.

I was beginning to feel like the whole world was conspiring against me. Worse, I'd been kicked out of my chair and relegated to the far end of the sofa. I wasn't sure I'd ever walk upright again.

It hadn't helped that Trueblood had reclaimed the opposite end of the sofa, close enough for me to be intensely aware of him, but too far away to do anything about it. I don't know if he was experiencing the same annoying awareness as I was, but I was darned sure he was right there with me on the physical suffering, not to mention the just plain pissed. He didn't move and didn't speak, but the way he watched Betsy's team try to make sense of the mess said he was thinking as hard as I was and getting just as far—absolutely nowhere.

I suppose I should have been grateful he hadn't booted me out like he did yesterday, but somehow gratitude just wasn't doing it for me right then.

That's when Amelia popped in.

"Holy gerschmolies," she said.

We were back to the tight sweater (fluorescent lime green and yellow stripes this time, bright enough to make my eyes water), black leather mini, and thigh-high boot approach to fashion. After that hooker outfit this morning, it had to be rated an improvement.

I slumped deeper into the sofa and gave in to the incipient headache I'd been trying to ignore for the past half hour. My only hope was that Betsy had spotted the bottle of ibuprofen I kept in my desk and would be able to find it for me once she was done.

Amelia propped her hands on her hips and glared at me. "I leave you with a good looking guy getting up close and personal—first time in I don't know how long!—and *this* is how you take advantage of the moment?"

I glared back. She knew I couldn't say a word. Talk about going into a fight with a handicap.

"So, who did this? Do you know?"

I glared harder. If you only have one option in a battle, you might as well run with it. Especially when your sole alternative is to shut your eyes, roll into a ball, and whimper.

"All right, all right," Amelia grumbled. "You want me to clean this up?"

My glare turned to wide-eyed panic. I leapt off the sofa—all right, squirmed and heaved my way out of the sofa—and, after a painful moment trying to get my spine to straighten, limped from the office without saying a word.

Amelia didn't bother following me—she popped into the hallway before me so I almost ran right into her.

"Well?" she demanded.

"Ssshh," I hissed.

"They can't hear me."

"But I can, so just stop. I don't need any more grief in my life."

"*You* don't need it! How do you think *I* feel? You're ten times more work than all my other fairy goddaughters put together, and less than half the fun."

"So quit. Give me up. Walk away. Leave. Me. Alone!"

"I—"

"Peterson? You all right?" It was Trueblood. He'd followed me out into the hall and found me arguing with a lot of empty air.

"What do you think?" I snapped, then drew in a steadying breath. "Sorry."

"Tell him to go away," said Amelia.

When Amelia tells you to get rid of a good looking male of an appropriate age—which, by her standards, covers an awful lot of territory—you know you've got a problem. In this case, I figured she was spoiling for a fight, and since I was, too, it took a real effort of will to ignore her.

"Talking to myself," I said to Trueblood.

"Sounded more like arguing."

"Yeah. Wouldn't be so bad, except I was losing."

His gaze softened. "I'm going to figure this out, you know. Find who killed Montgomery and why, who trashed your office. We'll get him."

"Or her."

"Or her."

"Not if I figure it out first," I said.

Arguing is good; it gets the heart pumping, the blood flowing. If I couldn't argue with Amelia, I could always argue with Trueblood. Even if he was on my side. Sort of.

"You're just not going to leave this alone, are you?"

"Would you?"

"I'm a cop."

"And I'm an investigations agent. Which means I investigate things. And this thing is getting very personal, very fast."

"That's telling him!" crowed Amelia.

I ignored her.

Trueblood went very still. "That's exactly the point at which you walk away, Peterson."

"Don't you tell her what to do!" warned Amelia, pulling out her wand and pointing it at Trueblood.

"Just like a man!" I exclaimed, throwing my arms wide as if in exasperation. I caught Amelia's wand on my upswing, pushing it up and to the side just in time.

The ceiling light fixture ten feet away exploded.

Trueblood spun into a crouch, his service weapon in his hand before he'd finished turning. It took him about half a heart beat to realize what had happened and relax out of the response.

The man was good. His weapons instructors must have loved him.

"Oh, boy," I said. "Mr. Yaguchi is not going to like that."

I took advantage of Trueblood's back being turned to shoot a warning look at Amelia.

"I was just going to make him apologize," she said, looking aggrieved.

I rolled my eyes, but couldn't do more because people were beginning to poke their heads out their doors, demanding to know what was going on.

"Sorry, folks," Trueblood called, discreetly slipping his gun back into the holster on his belt. "Light fixture exploded. Probably a power surge or something."

"Probably a piece of junk," someone shot back.

"I'm for sure not cleanin' it up," said someone else. "Hall's Yaguchi's responsibility, not ours!"

"I'm going to complain," said a third. "Maintenance here is a disgrace. Especially when you consider what we have to pay for rent and utilities."

"Got that right!"

Poor Mr. Yaguchi. He was going to get a lot of grief for something that wasn't even his fault. Considering all the grief he deserved for all the things that *were* his fault—or his and Mrs. Huffelwitz', anyway—I wasn't going to lose sleep over it.

"We'll take care of it," Trueblood assured them.

"I've heard *that* one before!" one of the gawkers said. I couldn't see who.

"Well *I'm* not cleaning it up," Amelia huffed. "Wouldn't have happened if you hadn't interfered."

At least there was something to be grateful for in all of this.

"Put the wand away," I said, low enough so Trueblood couldn't hear.

"I'm going to—"

"Put it *away*."

"Ungrateful, disrespectful..."

I didn't catch the rest of it, but at least she did what I told her and tucked it back in that magic pocket. For a minute I thought she might go away, too, but no such luck.

"There's a janitor's closet on the third floor," I called to Trueblood, who was trying to collect the biggest pieces in a pile at the side. "I'll go get something to clean that up, then let Mr. Yaguchi know."

By the time I returned, Trueblood had gotten a trash bag from Betsy and filled it with the pieces he'd collected. Amelia was strolling up and down the hallway, poking her head into office doors at random, checking out what was going on behind all those closed doors.

"You call that a broom?" Trueblood demanded, eyeing the decrepit thing I held. It was shedding bristles just carrying it, and it didn't have all that many bristles to lose.

"Around here, this is as good as it gets. You hold the dustpan, I'll sweep."

"No vacuum?"

"Mr. Yaguchi has one, but he doesn't like to wear it out by using it. I bring mine from home whenever I have to clean my office."

And people wonder why that carpet doesn't get cleaned as often as it should. Go figure.

"How are we going to sweep up the bristles that thing will

leave behind?"

"We aren't. I'll leave those for Mr. Yaguchi. I just want to get the glass bits."

"Fair enough." He squatted, steadying the dust pan while I tried to sweep the broken glass his way.

We did the best we could, but I'll admit the carpet looked like it had sprouted a lot of dirty black hairs by the time we finished. Trueblood tipped the contents of the dustpan into the trash bag, then started to rise.

I pushed him back down. "Wait a second."

"You spot some more glass?"

"No, I just had a thought."

"Is that unusual?"

"Seriously?"

"Sorry. You had a thought and...?"

"The killer must have been crouching down, like you are now, when he—"

"Or she."

"Or she," I amended, "grabbed the letter opener. If she'd been coming up out of a crouch, that would explain the angle. I've been thinking it had to be a short person, but it doesn't, does it?"

"No."

"No, so— Wait." I frowned at him. He arched his eyebrows at me. "You've already thought of that, haven't you?"

"No only thought of it, but a half dozen other ways it could have been done." He stood, wincing a little—he wasn't in bad shape, but that sofa really is murder—and dusted off his hands. "We also got the shortest person in the office and the tallest and several people in between to test some of the theories."

"And...?"

"And we still don't know for sure. Could have gone down any one of a number of ways, depending."

My shoulders slumped. "It was a thought."

He patted my shoulder sympathetically. "It was a good

thought. We just beat you to it."

"We're done." Betsy was standing in my office door, ready to go.

"Find anything?"

"Nope. A lot of that mess looks like it was just plain malicious. My guess? We already have what they were looking for, so whoever it was got pissed and took it out on Maxie."

She didn't have to explain. They had my file on Jameson. There wasn't much there, but there wasn't anything else in the office that anyone would have wanted. I wasn't wasting time wondering if all this was connected to some other client. None of them had ended up dead on my office floor.

Amelia sauntered up. I'd lost track of her. I hadn't heard any crashes or screams, so the best thing was to pretend I didn't know she'd been snooping.

"All that time and that's the best they can do?" she said. "Hey! Watch it, sister!" That was aimed at Betsy, who'd almost walked right through her.

"Thanks, Sharanski," said Trueblood. "I appreciate it, anyway."

"No problem." Betsy got a good grip on her heavy case and marched away, but I caught the slight, quick tilt of her head and the way her eyes met mine, then shifted toward the elevator.

"I'll return the broom and empty that trash," I said, snatching up the now-full wastebasket with the dustpan sticking out of it. "Don't leave," I said to Trueblood. "I'm coming right back."

I clattered down the stairs. Everyone above the third floor has long since given up on the trash chutes—there's some sort of blockage that Mr. Yaguchi says he hasn't been able to shift. Personally, I don't think he's ever tried. I had plenty of time to return the broom and dustpan and dump out the glass, then get down to the lobby before Betsy got there. And that's if the elevator was working. It has a tendency to stall between the second and third floors if it's feeling overworked.

"You should leave that stuff," said Amelia, following me.

"You're right."

"It's your fault the thing got broken."

"You bet."

"You're being deliberately annoying, aren't you?"

"You noticed!"

She just fumed while I put everything back, then followed me down to the lobby. We only had to wait a minute or so before the elevator wheezed to a stop and the doors reluctantly opened.

Betsy eyed the doors distrustfully, then hopped out a lot faster than she usually moves when carrying her work case. After two jerky tries, the doors slid wearily shut, followed by a labored clank, then a grinding sound as the elevator headed back up.

"That thing's a menace," she said. "You need to find another office."

"See?" said Amelia. "Exactly what I've been telling you all along."

"I won't need one if Trueblood doesn't get the killer," I said glumly. "Nobody in his right mind is going to hire an investigator who's suspect number one in a major murder case."

"He'll get him," said Betsy. "Trueblood's good."

"Does that mean you've got evidence that gets me off the hook?"

Betsy glanced around the lobby, then dragged me into a little nook at the side where the pay phones used to be, years ago.

"That's why I tried to call," she said, keeping her voice low. "We didn't find anything in your office—and by the way, you really need to vacuum that carpet a little more often—"

"You're worried about my *housekeeping?*"

"Shh! Don't raise your voice like that. I'm just saying."

"Well, don't, okay? Not unless it helps me find the killer."

"Friends like her...!" said Amelia, who was crowding my shoulder, trying to hear what was going on without getting jammed in the space with us.

"Okay, okay. Anyway, we found a message on his cell phone from an attorney named Peter Arnott."

"Borrring," said Amelia.

"Never heard of him," I said.

"Small time, one-man practice in Munroesville," Betsy said, naming a little town that had been swallowed up by River City's sprawl years before. "But that's not the interesting part. The interesting part was he said his client appreciated Mr. Jameson's concerns regarding paternity support, but his client wasn't interested."

"Okay, that *is* interesting," I said. I couldn't see how it helped, but you never knew. Right now, I'd happily grab at straws. "Did he say anything else?"

Betsy shook her head. "Trueblood's met with Arnott, but I don't know what he found out, and I can't ask." She leaned around me to check the lobby. "I've got to get going. The guys are going to be down in a minute. They can't find me talking to you."

"I appreciate it, Bets. You know that."

She gave me a quick hug, then picked up her case. "Good luck. It sucks you got caught in this mess, but it'll work out."

"Sure," I said. I appreciated the info and the hug, but I wasn't quite so optimistic about the working out part. "Now, go. I've gotta get back upstairs before Trueblood wonders what I'm up to."

"That's it?" Amelia said as Betsy left. "A phone call from a lawyer? Whoopie doopie."

"You never know." I could hear the elevator starting to grind its way back down to the lobby. Betsy's team, on their way. Me? I'd have taken the stairs, no matter how heavy those cases were, but then, I've gotten stuck in that thing before. They haven't. Yet.

CHAPTER 25

I found Trueblood leaning out my now open office window. I paused in the doorway for a moment, enjoying the view and grateful Amelia wasn't there to make rude comments.

She'd abandoned me when she found out my first order of business, once Trueblood left, would be to call this Peter Arnott. That rated another "borrring," which was fine by me. If Arnott proved unhelpful, the second thing was to talk to Lucille. There hadn't been any mention of a new kid on the Montgomery family payroll in the stuff she'd given me so far, but, then, we hadn't known she needed to look for it. I hadn't the slightest notion what came after that.

"See anything interesting?" I asked Trueblood from the doorway.

He pulled in his head, then shut the window. It only took him three tries, which is pretty good for those old casements.

"You're right about the dumpster. An escape chute will land you right in the middle of it. Now all you have to do is hope the lid's open and the thing's not empty."

"I also have to hope they haven't moved it. But that's not what you were looking for."

"Nope. I was checking to see if the team had looked."

My stomach dropped. I didn't want to hear what came next. "And...?"

"They hadn't. I stuck my head out just in time to see the last sheet of paper blow away from several file folders spread across the top of the dumpster. I doubt you'll find anything now, but at least the folders will tell you what you've lost."

I stifled a curse. "The way my luck's been going, it's probably all my billables. Not that it matters. I've got as good a chance of those deadbeats paying me as I do of winning the lottery. Less, actually."

"Rough." He eyed me, then added, "Betsy tell you anything useful?"

The man is good—distracts you, then hits you when you're not looking. "What makes you think she'd tell me anything?"

"You really think I wouldn't have found out you two have been friends for years?" He didn't give me a chance to answer. "What'd she tell you?"

I gave in. What else was I going to do? "She told me there was a message from a lawyer named Peter Arnott. Something about a kid and paternity payments."

"And...?" he prompted.

"She said you talked to Arnott, but she didn't know what you'd learned. If anything. Did you learn anything?"

"What do you think?"

I wasn't going to win this one. "I think you won't tell me, either way."

He smiled. "Very good."

"So why are you still here?"

The smile vanished. "You need to be careful, Peterson. This galloping around sticking your nose where it doesn't belong could be dangerous."

"I don't think Julia Carmody is going try shooting me a second time."

"I'm not talking about Julia. I'm talking about whoever murdered her father."

"They haven't shot at me—"

"So far."

"—and you have my letter opener."

"That's not funny."

"Do I look like I'm laughing?"

For sure, neither one of us was smiling. He was still standing in front of the window. I was still standing in the open doorway. That left maybe sixteen feet between us, much of it filled by my desk and chairs and the mess my uninvited visitor had left.

Sixteen feet usually felt a little farther, somehow. Farther, and a whole lot safer.

He seemed to feel it, too, because he dropped his gaze to study the mess across my desk.

"For what it's worth, I'm sorry about the break-in," he said, not looking at me.

"Thanks." I glared at the mess and wished he'd leave. I couldn't think when the man was around, and right now, thinking was what I needed to do most.

That little exchange we'd had about the possible height of a crouching killer had been embarrassing. I didn't like it when people not only got to an idea faster than I did, but actually worked it through, as well. Not that Trueblood was any closer to a solution than I was, but there wasn't any comfort in that thought.

"Can I get my laptop back?"

His head came up. "What? Oh. Yeah, I guess. Other than the history of your background search on Montgomery, we didn't find anything so, yeah, sure. '

He sounded distracted. Whatever he'd been thinking, it was still teasing at him.

Nice to have a thought that's worth more than two seconds of your time. My head was stuffed with thoughts, and not one was worth a bean.

Trueblood shook off whatever was bothering him. "I gotta get back. I'll release your laptop first thing. You can pick it up in a bit, maybe."

I'd have to be content with that. For now.

Once he'd left, I settled behind my desk and surveyed the

mess. It was going to take hours to get the papers sorted into their respective folders. Impossible to tell if anything was missing. Other than what was on top of the dumpster, I was pretty sure nothing was. Missing, that is. There wasn't anything worth taking. I had no intention of retrieving those empty folders. No sense in worrying about what had been in them if I couldn't get it back, anyway.

At least my intruder had left my ibuprofen where it belonged. And the bottled water I kept in one of the file cabinet drawers.

While the stuff worked through my system, I picked up the phonebook that had been included on the pile on top of the desk (the thing still comes in handy every now and then) and looked up Peter Arnott. He might be a one-man office, but I still had to work my way through his secretary first.

I'd scarcely introduced myself before he had his defenses up.

"I don't care what Montgomery hired you to do, my client's answer is still no."

"Could we talk about this, Mr. Arnott?" I said. First tip, keep them talking. Especially when you don't know what they're talking about. You never know what they might let slip.

"What part of 'no' don't you understand, Ms Peterson?"

Oooh. Getting snippy, are we? At least Betsy had given me one bit of information I could leverage. "Mr. Montgomery was willing to accept his paternal responsibilities—"

"He had no proof the child is his son."

His *son*? Now *that* was interesting! "A DNA test—"

Arnott cut the connection. I punched my phone off, thinking hard.

With one simple word, a lot of questions suddenly had answers.

That legacy Jameson wanted to secure? It was for his son. The uncharacteristic willingness to admit liability on the part of the JM Industries subsidiaries? Clearing the board so Jameson number four inherited a business untainted by accusations of

213

wrong-doing.

With all that Lucille and I had dug up on Jameson's wild youth, I'd gotten the sense that part of it—perhaps all of it—was as much a rebellion against his father's expectations as it was the heedless arrogance of a rich, privileged young man who'd never been called to account for his own actions.

The birth of his son, even if out of wedlock, must have made Jameson rethink his feelings. It might have been one thing to reject the idea of being hemmed in by his father's 'legacy,' quite another when it applied to a son of his own.

No matter how much money and power Jameson Montgomery the Third possessed, a Jameson Montgomery the Fourth was his only real chance at a sort of immortality. Even the rich have to die eventually. At least for now.

The trouble with answers, though, is that they inevitably lead to more questions. And not just the most obvious ones like, who was the boy's mother and how was I going to track her down?

To start with, how old was the boy? It would be easy enough to find out exactly when Jameson first announced his intention not to fight those lawsuits, but that wouldn't tell me when the boy was born. If the mother hadn't approached him to demand money, how had he found out he had a son? How long had it taken for Jameson to decide he couldn't ignore his son as easily as he had his daughters?

The mother's refusal to recognize Jameson as the father of her child suggested she was a very different person from the women he had usually acquired. Both Katie Carmody and Angelina Mestes had demanded financial support long before their daughters were born. Add the blatant greed of the two wives I'd met, Annalise and Christine, and it was clear that the unknown mama number three was cut from a different cloth than Jameson's usual fling.

Maybe Lucille could dig out some answers. With a name, I could track down the information on the child and most of the rest of it. Without it, I was going nowhere.

Of course, Lucille might already have found her. She could be one of the dozens and dozens who'd popped up once or twice, only to disappear after Jameson had moved on. How could Lucille possibly sort her from among all the others if we didn't even have a name or a face to look for?

And that was assuming the woman was the flashy, fancy-dressed kind who would have drawn attention in the first place. The paparazzi would follow Jameson, of course—photos of handsome, super-rich bachelors out on the town are always an easy sell—but what if she'd been a shy, retiring sort who'd insisted Jameson take her to places where they wouldn't draw any attention?

Plus, there was the fact she'd retained a nobody lawyer from Munroesville. That suggested she didn't have much money or the kinds of friends who could have hooked her up with a powerhouse lawyer who'd take her on just for the publicity. The kind of friends who might have landed her in the photos because she happened to be standing with them.

What if she'd been a one-night stand he'd forgotten even existed until he'd somehow found out about the boy? There was no way in hell Lucille or I would find her then.

But Amelia could find her, easy. All she'd have to do was poke her head into Arnott's files and—

I sat up with a jerk. Where had an insane thought like *that* come from? I must be getting more desperate than I'd realized, even to consider it.

On the other hand...

I gnawed at my lower lip.

On the other hand, if Amelia could identify the mother for me, and I could retrieve my laptop, I should be able to dig out the rest of it. Lucille might know her way around the gossip pages, but I made my living digging through the kinds of sites that would enable me to track down Jameson's son and his mother.

I squashed the thought. Amelia? Smugly poking around in my business because I'd *asked* her to? What was I *thinking?*

CHAPTER 26

"I'm sorry, pet," said Lucille unhappily. "I'll keep on working on it, I promise, but..." She shook her head sadly. "If only you had a name, or part of a name, or a picture, or something. *Anything* that could help us pick her out of the crowd."

I'd never seen Lucille look so distressed. We'd just spent a couple hours going back over everything she'd dug up for me earlier, and we'd come up with exactly zip. Dozens and dozens of gorgeous potential mommies, but not a hint as to which one of them might have been the real one, if any.

"Not to worry," I said, forcing a cheerfulness I was far from feeling. "I'll figure it out. That's the sort of thing I do, you know."

"I know, dear. Gareth tells me you're ever so good at it, too. But this is really my thing, and I..." She shrugged helplessly. "I just can't find anything that helps. I really am sorry."

"Nothing for me, either," Douglas chimed in. When he heard my news, he'd called someone to take the front desk and settled behind another of Lucille's computers to see if he could find any hints on the legal and financial end of things. "Not even so much as a parking ticket to indicate he'd been somewhere you wouldn't have expected."

"You hacked the city's traffic database?"

"Don't tell Gareth! You know what a stickler he is about that sort of thing."

"I thought Gareth knew everything already."

"Oh, no, dear," said Lucille. "Only what Douglas and I think he should know. He gets so stressed about the silliest things that we decided it was better not to bother him with details."

"Does he know about your infra-red scope?" I asked, curious.

"I'm not sure," Lucille said vaguely. "He usually doesn't pay attention to much of anything except his business, you know."

"The man would forget to eat if I didn't nag him," Douglas added. "But Gareth's not the one we're worried about right now." His handsome brow creased in a frown. "You know there's a lot of calls for the police to make an arrest on this, right, Maxie?"

"I read the stuff you sent me."

"Oh, good. I wasn't sure you would. For a professional, you're really very bad about answering your phone, you know."

"If I answered all the calls I'm getting over this, I'd never get anything done."

"Your mother," said Lucille, nodding wisely. "You really should call her, you know."

My mother doesn't knit, crochet, bake cookies, follow celebrities, or worry about much of anyone except me, so I'd been a little apprehensive when I introduced her to Lucille the year before. I shouldn't have worried. The two had bonded over Lucille's spotting scopes, including the infra-red, and had been best friends ever since. She'd also discovered a common bond with Douglas: They both thought I should dress better than I did, though even she admitted he'd gone too far when he'd dragged out a pile of fashion magazines with pages dog-eared with his suggestions.

That thought made me realize Lucille and Douglas were eyeing me a little nervously.

"She called you, didn't she?" I said.

Lucille beamed, clearly relieved. "Of course, dear. She's naturally quite concerned, so when you didn't return any of her calls and you weren't paying attention to your brother, she called Douglas and me, instead."

"What did you tell her?" I said.

"I said you were very busy solving the murder and would get back to her as soon as you could. You will, won't you?"

"First chance I get." Which should be about Thanksgiving next year, so that wasn't a lie. Not that it mattered. They knew me too well. "I should get going. I've got to retrieve my laptop before all the clerks at police headquarters go home."

"And then what?" they chorused.

"Then I try my approach," I said. "As soon as I figure out what it is."

They didn't look any more reassured than I felt.

I GOT TO THE STATION JUST IN TIME to work my way past the front desk, but too late to reclaim my laptop from the guy in charge of holding evidence and personal property.

"Gone home," the guy behind the counter said. "You'll have to come back tomorrow. He's here by seven."

"You can't—?"

"Nope."

And that was that.

Which left me with two options—catch a bus back to the office and get started on straightening the mess, or catch a bus, then a transfer to get home. The repair company my insurance agent sent had left a message saying they'd replaced my windshield, so that was something. If I left early enough tomorrow morning, I'd miss the worst of rush hour and could be back here in time to reclaim my laptop at seven.

Not to mention I still had six bottles of Twisted Torment in the fridge. I could pick up a sandwich from the sub shop down the street, catch the bus, then eat, watch a movie, and drink myself into insensibility.

It was the best plan I'd had all day.

I got a mixed Italian on whole wheat with all the fixings, endured the two interminable bus rides, hiked the block and a half to my apartment, then settled on the couch with the sub, a beer, and a thriller on the TV. The sub was soggy from the long bus ride, but edible. The thriller suffered from bad writing and worse acting, but since there were lots of guns and explosions I didn't mind. At least the beer was cold.

I made it through half the sub, three-quarters of the movie, and two and a half bottles of beer before I gave up and went to bed. There was something, some comment someone had made today, that was nagging at the edge of my awareness. I just couldn't figure out what, or who, or why it was important. Maybe if I slept on it my unconscious would come up with a solution.

Just goes to show that optimism is an overrated, irrational response.

I DIDN'T QUITE MAKE IT BACK to the station by seven, but, to my amazement, it took less than an hour to work my way through the waiting line and the paperwork, then retrieve my laptop. It seemed like a good omen for the day ahead.

(What did I say about optimism and irrational responses?)

I found a parking space on the street only three blocks from my office, which was another good sign. Things were bustling in the neighborhood, and nobody paid any attention to a woman dressed in neat, if nondescript tan slacks and black blouse...until I walked in the door of my building. Everybody in the lobby, waiting for the elevator, or on the stairs, deliberately avoiding the elevator, frowned at my appearance. A lot of people around here had officially lost their five bucks and a chance at the pot.

Only Jimmy, who had his door open, seemed glad to see me.

"I got confidence in you, babe!" he said, beaming. "Saturday still lookin' good?"

"Friday at two, Jimmy," I called back. "But I appreciate the vote of confidence!"

"Remember! I'll find out if you rig it."

"Never happen."

"I know. Bad habit. You got to get over that honesty shtick. Get you in trouble, every time. Especially in our line of work."

I just waved and unlocked my door. As soon as I had a few extra bucks, I was getting a locksmith in to install a new lock.

And then I took two steps into the room and stopped dead. "Amelia!"

My fairy godmother was seated in my chair, feet propped on the desktop (she was wearing glittery, fire-engine red platform heels that must have added eight inches to her height), and the desktop was cleaner and tidier than it had been at any time since I'd moved in.

In fact, there wasn't a folder or loose piece of paper anywhere in sight. The rug had been vacuumed, the file cabinets dusted, and a new coffee maker, pot happily filling with coffee, was burbling on the credenza. Only the windows retained their usual amount of grime.

"Like it?" Amelia said, looking smug.

It really is possible to hold two diametrically opposed opinions at the same time. On the one hand, I was enormously relieved not to confront the disaster I'd left last night.

On the other hand, this was Amelia. For all I knew, she might have just made all my files and records vanish, never to be seen again, and how was I going to explain *that* to my tax accountant next April?

Fortunately, my mouth might be hanging open, but it wasn't saying anything until my brain kicked in with the safest response.

I kicked the office door closed behind me—I didn't need Jimmy wondering if someone had snuck past his office door without him noticing—and said, "Wow! Just... Wow!"

"I wouldn't do this for just anybody, you know, but you had a rough day yesterday so..." She shrugged as if she were almost embarrassed to accept my praise. I knew better.

"It's amazing. Incredible! Absolutely fan*tas*tic!" With Amelia, you can't go overboard on the gratitude.

"Well, that's my name, you know. Fantastica!"

"Perfect name for you, too." I had a smarmy smile plastered on my face, and I was fighting against a question I knew I shouldn't ask. I asked it, anyway. "Uh... Where'd you get the coffee pot?"

"Nice, huh? Brand new, too."

"Looks it. Looks really expensive, too. Where'd you get it?"

"Second floor. Just sitting on the shelf, still in its box. They had a couple new containers of that half-and-half stuff you like, too. Better than that powdered gunk you normally use. I put one of them in your fridge." She frowned at the fridge. "You need a new one of those, too."

I liked that little fridge. It's one of those pint-sized dorm room things that I'd bought for ten dollars from Hector, who'd found it on one of his scavergings. Since Hector's deluxe packing crate doesn't include amenities like running water and electricity, he didn't have any use for it so he let me have it cheap.

"Which office?" I said casualy, wondering how I was going to replace the pot and half-and-half without having to deal in awkward explanations.

"No name on the door, but it was the big office in the front on the third floor. You know it?"

The bottom fell out of my stomach. That office is occupied by Oleksi Romanenko and his crew. Oleksi runs a perfectly respectable import business specializing in cheap Eastern European and Middle Eastern handcrafts. Being an enterprising businessman, however, he also runs several other import operations that aren't nearly so respectable. The fact that he's best buds with Mikael Konstantin over at Murphy's Pub, and his receptionist is a bruiser who looks like he bench presses three-fifty one-handed and is in serious need of a jacket that does a better job of disguising the dual shoulder holsters, should tell you all you need to know about Oleksi.

"I know it," I said weakly.

"Wasn't anybody in at the time," Amelia continued, "so I just helped myself. I doubt they'll notice," she added breezily. "I don't think they like coffee much, anyway. They only had one thing of coffee, but they had lots of packets of tea and several bags of brown and white sugars just sitting around, taking up space."

"Tea and sugar?" I said weakly. "Really?"

I've tried to talk to Amelia about the ethical issues associated with magical theft before and gotten exactly nowhere. I had no intention of launching a lecture on illegal drugs and the wisdom of stealing from the Russian mafia right now.

"Well, now I've got my laptop back and you've done all the hard work of cleaning up, I can get to work," I chirped instead, plunking my computer down on the desk. "After all you've done, I can't possibly take any more of your time!"

Amelia swung her feet off the desk. "I don't mind. And you don't need to worry about the laptop, anyway. I've already got the information you need."

"Oh, yes?" I said faintly.

"Absolutely." She pushed an index card covered with her almost indecipherable scrawl across the desk to me. "Name, address, and phone number of the boy's mother."

"What? How—?" Once again, my brain was two steps behind my mouth. "You read Peter Arnott's files."

She beamed. "I knew you'd never think of it—"

Oh, I'd thought of it. And then I'd thought better.

"...so I just went ahead and checked last night."

"There's no way he's going to find out, is there?"

"Of course not. I mean, I might have gotten things a teensy mixed up with the files, but he'll never notice. Trust me."

"How mixed up?"

"*Pffft!*" she said with that dismissive wave of her hand. "He has the silliest filing system. Not alphabetized or anything. I'm not absolutely sure I got it all back in the right order, but that could happen anytime, right?"

"Could it?"

"Sure. And I don't *think* I broke the lock on his filing cabinet. Anyway, even if he or his secretary noticed, they'd never suspect *you*."

I hoped not. But Trueblood might. Assuming Arnott reported it, of course. I wasn't the only one who'd be interested in discovering the woman's identity, but I was the only one outside of his investigative team that Trueblood knew for sure was aware of her existence.

Given that he'd somehow managed to find out about every other interview I'd conducted so far, there was a good chance he'd find out if I talked to her. But what choice did I have? If I was going to find Jameson's murderer and clear my name, I needed to hear what the mother of his son had to say.

I picked up the card and tried to decipher what Amelia had written. "Stephanie... um... Gropnet?"

"Grover. Stephanie Grover. The boy's name is Sam. He's two."

"Not as old as Angelina's kid, even."

Amelia nodded and looked sternly disapproving.

"And they're living in an apartment in Munroesville," I continued thoughtfully. "That probably means she doesn't have a lot of money. Yet she turned down Jameson's offer of financial support. Why?"

"Only way for us to find out is to ask, right?" said Amelia.

"Oh, gosh, Amelia. I really don't want to take any more of your time than I already have," I gushed. "It wouldn't be right. After all you've done for me I couldn't possibly—"

"I'll meet you there!" said Amelia happily, and vanished.

When you can't fight 'em, give in. I poured myself a cup of coffee using the purloined half-and-half, then, because I couldn't stand the suspense, pulled out a folder at random from the file drawer in my desk.

The label on the tab read "Bluethorn, Randall." Bluethorn had been one of my earliest jobs and should have been stashed in the old filing cabinet where I kept whatever I wasn't currently working on, but that wasn't something I could expect Amelia to have known.

I opened the folder and flipped through the contents. A flyer for half-off pizza at Giordino's that had expired a year and a half earlier. Receipts from three different hardware stores that I was pretty sure belonged with some past tax records. Five paper clips, one badly bent. (I'd probably used it to pick a lock at some point.) A fraying piece of cotton string, including lint, that might have come from under the sofa. A printout of a scholarly article on Bayesian analysis that I'd never seen before and wouldn't have understood if I had. I couldn't begin to guess where that had come from. A yellowing newspaper clipping about a car wreck in Chicago I didn't remember ever seeing, either, and, last but not least, an aging but, thankfully, unused Lipton tea bag leaking tea leaves. Of Bluethorn, Randall there was not a trace. Surprise!

I drew in a deep, deep breath, then slowly let it out. My recordkeeping was even worse than I thought if I'd never used that pizza coupon. I don't usually let that sort of thing go to waste.

At least the coffee was good. There's nothing quite like a new, high-end coffee maker for brewing a good cup of morning joe, even with the cheap stuff that's all I can afford. The fresh cream didn't hurt, either.

I made a mental note to check the sugar reserves for any white substances that shouldn't be there and returned Bluethorn, Randall to the drawer. Maybe I'd just pitch everything once this was over, then start again from scratch. Possibly under an assumed name in another state on the opposite side of the country.

Oleksi was *not* going to be happy about losing that coffee maker.

CHAPTER 27

Stephanie Grover lived on the second floor of an apartment building that looked as old and worn out as mine. The neighborhood was a little better class, though, and there was a public park across the street that had a newish jungle gym, merry-go-round, and swings for the kiddies.

Amelia was nowhere in sight, which wasn't reassuring.

I parked in a space marked 'Visitor,' then searched for the apartment number on the card Amelia had given me. The woman who cautiously opened the door was as tall, slender, and as gorgeous as all the rest of Jameson's women, but, unlike the others, Stephanie Grover was not dressed in expensive designer clothes. She wore a stained and faded turquoise T-shirt with a fraying hole at one shoulder and even older jeans that hadn't cost more than twenty-nine ninety-nine new. Her long blonde hair was scraped back in a pony tail, she wore no makeup, and she had a smudge of dirt on her chin.

I liked her immediately, which was odd since she was eyeing me doubtfully while keeping her body squarely in the half-open door she still held.

If she wanted to keep strangers out, she needed to install a peep hole and a chain, for starters, but that suggestion would have to wait.

"Ms Grover?" I said, showing her my professional license and deliberately *not* smiling since I wanted to come across as non-threatening, not superficial and fake. "I'm Maxie Peterson. Can we talk?"

Her eyes grew round. She threw a nervous glance over her shoulder, then leaned out to check the hall on either side to see if anyone else was lurking, waiting to pounce.

"I'm alone. I'd like to talk to you about Jameson, Ms Grover. Please." Those huge, blue eyes turned back to me. You could see the fear in them. "I didn't kill him, but I really, really want to find out who did. I think you can help me."

Without releasing her grip on the door, she took my license, frowning at the photo, then at me. "You don't look anything like your pictures in the papers."

"Thank God."

That made her smile. I could see the fear receding. She flipped the license over to read the fine print, then handed it back to me.

"All right," she said, swinging the door wide. "I don't have long to talk, but, please, come in."

"Thank you," I said, and made a point of wiping my feet on the welcome mat before I stepped inside.

I was glad I had. It only took one look to see that, despite the toys strewn everywhere, the little apartment was bright, beautifully decorated, and spotlessly clean.

"I apologize for the mess," she said, snatching a yellow and red plastic truck from the floor in front of me. "Sammy has to put his toys away before he goes to bed, but otherwise I let him just enjoy himself."

"The place looks great," I said, and meant it. It looked like a place where people were happy and little boys were loved.

I retrieved another, smaller toy car from the back of the cushion on the chair she indicated, then cautiously sat. When nothing protested or poked me, I relaxed into the chair.

"Mommy?" A tow-headed munchkin stood in the doorway to one of the two tiny bedrooms, a sock monkey clutched against his chest. He eyed me doubtfully, then edged across the room to his mother.

"Can you say hello to Ms Peterson, Sammy?"

He studied me solemnly for a moment. "Hello."

"Hello, Sammy," I said. "That's a nice monkey you've got." He was cute, but I'm not much good with little kids and never know what to say to them. Which was okay, because he wasn't much interested in me, either.

He held the monkey up for his mother's inspection. "Tootie's got anuver owie."

His mother checked it out. 'Oh, that's too bad. I'll kiss it and make it better for now, then mend Tootie tonight. Will that work, love?"

Sammy beamed. "Sure. *Big* kiss."

"Okay," said his mother.

When she lifted the monkey to give it a kiss, I could see that Tootie had, in fact, endured more than a few owies and been neatly mended every time. I took a closer look at some of the other toys on the floor and chair seats. I'm no expert, but a lot of those toys looked a little more worn and beat up than could be accounted for by one small boy.

To help make ends meet, Stephanie Grover was filling her son's toy box with carefully selected and, if necessary, lovingly restored second-hand toys.

In fact, now I looked more closely, all the furniture was second-hand, too. I had a lot of second-hand stuff in my apartment, and it looked it. Stephanie, however, had taken the time to refinish, repaint, and reupholster. You could see the signs of an inexpert but careful and determined hand at work, but you had to look for them. It made me wonder if the bright, eclectic mix of fabrics and colors was as much the result of what was available from the discount bins as it was a deliberate style choice. Probably a combination of both.

Whatever, it worked, and I couldn't help but admire a woman who could achieve so much so lovingly while trying to support herself and her young son on her own.

Which only made the question of why she would refuse Jameson's offer of support all the more intriguing.

Katie Carmody and Angelina Mestes each had a house and the management of a couple million dollars a year that, while intended for the benefit of their daughters, had also significantly eased their own lives. From the sounds of it, Jameson had been willing to pay as much if not more to support the boy he considered his son, yet his offer had been refused. Not only refused, but, evidently, formally rejected.

As lawyers went, Peter Arnott couldn't be billing a lot for his services, but his fees could still run into the thousands. Especially if Jameson had intended on pressing his demands for paternal rights. And that was money that Stephanie Grover didn't have.

"Ms Grover?" I said, as Sammy, his sock monkey 'healed', happily retreated to the bedroom. "I know Jameson Montgomery was trying to establish paternity in relation to your son. May I ask... Why did you refuse him?"

She looked at me apprehensively, clearly debating what she should say. And possibly wondering if she'd just admitted a murderer to her home.

"I didn't kill him," I added gently. "I don't even know why he wanted to hire me, though I suspect it had something to do with you and Sammy."

She glanced over her shoulder toward the bedroom as if to reassure herself her son was safe, then reluctantly turned back to me.

"Jameson was a mistake," she said after a moment's thought. "Oh, don't get me wrong. He was a nice man, good-looking, charming. And rich, of course," she added, as if she'd just remembered that bit. "But, well... We were from different worlds, you know?"

I nodded. I knew.

"I have a girl friend from college," she continued, getting into the story now. "She's rich, pretty. I had to work my way through, but we clicked, somehow, even though we were from entirely different backgrounds. So when she invited to me a big deal party in our senior year, I went. She even loaned me a dress for it. I'd never worn anything like it before," she added wistfully. "It was like Cinderella, you know?"

That made me wince, but I didn't say anything. So far, I hadn't seen any sign of Amelia. I really hoped she wasn't listening in. You do *not* want to get her started on Cinderella.

"Anyway, there I was, at a fairy tale party in a fairy tale dress, and along comes the fairy tale prince. King, really, I guess," she added thoughtfully. "He was a lot older, of course, but..."

For a minute, she just stared at the wall over my shoulder, remembering. Then she shook it off and dragged herself back to reality.

"I only dated him a couple of times. We had nothing in common. I wasn't comfortable in his world—it didn't seem all that appealing, really, though I don't imagine anybody will ever believe me about that—and he wasn't interested in anything long term, anyway."

"And then Sammy was born," I said.

"I'm not sure he's Jameson's, you know. I wasn't someone who slept around, but..." She blushed. On her, it was rather charming, which isn't something I ever thought I'd say. "But I wasn't a virgin, either."

"How did Jameson find out about the boy?"

Her brow darkened. "My friend told him. She ran into him at another one of those parties. They started talking, and it just sort of came out. He got my number from her. I don't know how he got my address. She swears she never gave him that. I don't think she has any idea that Jameson might have been Sammy's father."

That explained a lot. Once he knew of the boy's existence, Jameson could easily discover her whereabouts.

By now, I was convinced he'd hired me to dig into Stephanie's background. If he was going to sue for parental rights, he'd want to have all the info he could get. He'd especially want all the dirt, assuming there was any, which I doubted.

But there was still the question of *why* he'd wanted a nobody like me to do the digging rather than the people he would normally have used. I had my suspicions. If I could get an answer, maybe I'd know who killed him.

A happy giggle came from the bedroom. Whatever he was up to, Sammy seemed to be enjoying himself.

"Did Jameson demand any proof that Sammy was his son?" I asked.

Stephanie shook her head. "No. I don't think it ever occurred to him that I'd have been with anyone else."

That I could well believe. I looked around the bright, cramped living room. The whole apartment couldn't be more than six hundred square feet, maybe less. A couple million bucks a year would go a long way to upgrading the living arrangements.

"Why didn't you accept Jameson's offer of support? Your apartment is lovely, but it's clear you don't have a lot of money. Jameson was very generous in the support he provided for his daughters."

"But did he love them?" said Stephanie.

From the bedroom came more giggles, followed by what sounded like lots of toys falling down and a childish "again!"

Stephanie glanced toward the bedroom and smiled, and suddenly I could see the pride and inner strength that had enabled her to resist the temptations Jameson Montgomery had represented.

She turned her attention back to me. "Sammy is *my* son, and more than anything else in the world, I want him to be happy and know that he is loved. Money is nice, but it's not nearly as important as being loved. I don't think Jameson ever understood that."

From the bedroom came another crash, only this one was followed by a wail rather than a giggle.

Stephanie was on her feet in an instant. "Oh, dear. It was bound to happen. He's due for his nap and I need to get ready for work. Anyway, did you have any other questions?"

I shook my head, thanked her for her time, and wished her luck. She'd need it. I didn't know if Trueblood had talked to her yet, but once the media got wind of her and her son, this safe, quiet life she'd built for the two of them would come crashing down around them, and there was nothing anybody could do to stop it.

She saw me to the door. I turned around to thank her, and froze.

Amelia stood in the bedroom doorway, scowling, as the wailing from the bedroom increased in pitch and volume.

"I swear," she said, "he *liked* me making all those toys fly! It's not *my* fault that stupid dump truck broke!"

I forced a smile for Stephanie, then dug one of my cards out of my purse and handed it to her. "Call me if you need me, okay?"

She didn't bother to look at it. "Of course. I hope that helped?"

"It did. And...thank you."

I was already talking to the door.

"Unreasonable little snot!" Amelia growled behind me. "I hate kids."

"Must make it tough to be a fairy godmother, then," I said, heading toward the stairs. She wasn't getting any sympathy on this one.

She snorted. "You have no idea."

"You check her nightstand drawers?"

The sarcasm went right over her head. "Pitiful. Kids' toys. A couple mystery and romance novels. Something on natural cleaning products for your home. I mean, really! Who reads stuff like that? Her kid's got more than she does, I swear."

I glanced over at her as I shoved the outer building door open. "And what's wrong with tha— Shit!"

Running into a solid wall of all-male detective is not as much fun as you'd think. Especially if the detective in question is looking mad enough to chew nails.

"Talking to yourself again, Peterson?"

"What do you think?" I said, backing off, but not far enough.

"You do that a lot."

"You have no idea."

Somehow, the fact he kept his voice calm and controlled was a lot more intimidating than if he'd been yelling. At least if he were yelling, I could yell back. This way, it had more the feel of a repressed volcano, waiting to blow. I did *not* want to be in the vicinity when it did.

He stared at me, thin lipped and narrow-eyed and disapproving. I wouldn't have minded so much except, on him, it looked good. And that made me mad.

"Mind getting out of my way?" I said, holding my ground. And the door.

"From where I stand, *you're* in *my* way."

"And I'm in the doorway. You want in. I want out. Someone's gotta give, and since you're the gentleman, I think it oughta be you."

"Gentlemen only give way to ladies, and you're no lady."

"Thank you! I've been telling people that for years. Good to know someone finally paid attention."

I put a hand on his chest, intending to shove him out of my way.

Big mistake.

Instead of backing off like I expected, he wrapped his ginormous paw around my wrist and leaned down until his face was about six inches from mine.

"You and I have to talk."

"Er..." I said. He was starting to get a bit of early five o'clock shadow, and I suddenly found myself wondering how it would feel to run my fingers along that rock-hard jaw.

"Come on," he said, turning away without letting go of my wrist.

My brain abruptly kicked back into gear. I looked back at Amelia and mouthed a desperate, "Do something!"

Instead, she beamed at me approvingly and said, "Atta girl!"

With friends like that, right?

CHAPTER 28

"Let me go, Trueblood! Where are you taking me? I am not going to headquarters with you! Not unless you're arresting me! Are you arresting me? What are you doing?"

For the record, digging in your heels probably works better on something other than asphalt. Trueblood wasn't looking at me, he wasn't letting go of my wrist, and he wasn't stopping. Short of falling on my ass and being dragged, there didn't seem to be much I could do about it, so I gave in and started trotting after him.

I mean, I'm fairly tall, but the man is well over six feet and his legs are a lot longer than mine. When he was mad like this, his walking stride was pretty much a trotting pace for me.

Amelia, of course, was nowhere in sight. Not that she wouldn't make things worse if she did try to help, but I would have appreciated a little moral support, at least.

"Trueblood? You're car's over there, right? I can spot an unmarked cop car a mile off and that's definitely a cop car so— Trueblood!"

That last was to him dragging me out into traffic. Forget looking both ways, he just stepped into the street and kept going, which left me no choice but to keep going, too. Good thing it was a quiet side street and there wasn't a moving vehicle in sight. We might have been run over, otherwise.

He headed toward an opening in the fence surrounding the

play area.

"We're going to the park?" I said in disbelief. "You're kidding me, right? What? You want to play on the swings or something? You try and you'll bust 'em, I guarantee. You're way too big for that sort of thing."

Instead, he dragged me over to a pair of park benches set in the corner of the fenced-in play area.

"Sit," he said.

I opened my mouth to protest, got a good look at the expression on his face, and sat.

This was not going well.

For a minute he just stood there, looming over me and glowering, then he let out an exasperated hiss and thumped his butt down on the second bench and glowered some more.

The benches were set at a ninety degree angle to each other, so we couldn't quite have a head-to-head, but that didn't help much. Both of us were spitting mad, and I had the additional handicap of feeling just a little bit bad about it.

He had a point. I didn't like to admit, but he did.

On the one hand, it was my name that was at the top of the suspect list, my office where Jameson had been found with my letter opener sticking out of his chest, and my career going down in flames around my ears, so which of the two of us was more motivated to solve this thing?

On the other hand, he was paid to investigate crimes, and he had the training and the professional backup to do it right. I was a suspect in the crime and could possibly muck up his investigation if I made a mistake or somehow set the killer off. I might have been a cop, once upon a time, but it wasn't for long. I certainly never had the kind of investigative training or the on-the-job experience he had, so I could understand why he thought I should just keep out of the way and let him get on with it.

Not that it mattered. I was going to keep trying to find out who killed Jameson, regardless, only now I was going to feel a bit guilty about it.

"Do you have any idea how much trouble you're causing me, Peterson?" he said at last.

"Some," I admitted reluctantly.

"Don't you trust me?"

"I don't know you." Actually, I *did* trust him, though I wasn't sure why. He just had that kind of intense, focused approach that seemed to promise success. Eventually. I just didn't have the patience to wait for eventually and never had.

Mama's always said that my impatience is a major character flaw and I should be careful not to let it lead me into trouble, but I haven't paid any more attention to that warning than I have to anything else she's ever said. I wasn't going to start now. Not even with Trueblood sitting four feet away and looking daggers.

Looking a little tired, too, to be honest. Maybe he'd been putting in longer, harder hours on this than I'd given him credit for.

He took a deep breath that made his chest expand impressively, then slowly let it out. "How did you find her?"

I decided to skip the 'whoever could you be talking about' banter. Sometimes it's not wise to tease the tiger, especially when he's liable to snap off your head if you try.

"I can't tell you that."

"Can't? Or won't?"

"Does it matter?"

He considered that, but decided not to press the issue. "So, what did she say?"

"She said Jameson was a nice man, but they weren't together for more than a few days. And nights, I suppose. She's not even sure he's the father, though she swears she never really played around much."

"And you believe her?"

I nodded. "I do. I like her. She's a nice woman who's working hard to make a decent life for her son."

He looked skeptical. I couldn't really blame him, but then, he hadn't met her or little Sammy yet.

"And she's not interested in a cool million or two a year to ease the hardship? Really?"

"You're such a cynic."

"I'd call it realist, but I'm willing to be convinced."

So I told him what I'd seen and what we'd talked about, putting in as much detail as I could remember.

In the end, he looked convinced, though I don't think he'd willingly admit it.

"She said she had to get ready for work," I added, "so if you want to talk to her—"

"And leave you free to cause more problems?"

That stung. "I don't cause problems! Point out one single prob—"

"Geoffrey Dawson's office keeps calling, wondering if you've been arrested. Mrs. Christine Montgomery seems to think you bewitched her, then invaded her house—"

"That's ridiculous!" And news to me. Guess Amelia forgot to lace that spell with a little forgetfulness for afterwards.

"Ms Jarrow and Mr. Nicholson—"

"Who?"

"Mr. Stewart Nicholson? The photographer accompanying Ms Jarrow yesterday?"

"Oh, him."

"Him. They're still want to press charges for assault and—"

"I told you! I never assaulted them!" Now *that* was annoying. Still, it explained why I hadn't had any voice messages from her today. That I knew of, anyway. I hadn't checked my messages lately.

"Which I've pointed out to them more than once. That doesn't stop them from wasting police time threatening to do it, anyway."

"You guys get the crazies all the time. Not my fault that some of them just happen to be in this case."

"I—" His voice trailed off. His eyes widened. He blinked, swallowed hard, then tried again "Do you, uh... Do you see that?"

I turned to see what he was staring at, then sighed.

Amelia was perched on the merry-go-round, feet in those ridiculous platform pumps held high and wide off the ground as her wand kicked up little puffs of dust, pushing the thing around and around and around. She looked up to see us watching her, grinned from ear to ear, then gave the wand an extra flourish that set the thing spinning faster and started the swings on the swing set rocking. I'd never seen her look so happy.

"See what?" I said.

Bad enough he was seeing an apparently empty merry-go-round spinning around and empty swings swinging. I wasn't going to tell him about the invisible woman in platform pumps, too-short shorts, and a totally inappropriate tight tank top that spelled out 'Rock Star!' in glittering spangles across the chest.

"Uh... Nothing," he said, forcing himself to look back at me.

I tried to remember that he'd been yelling at me and, worse, making me feel guilty, but I couldn't help feeling a little sorry for the guy. He didn't deserve Amelia any more than I did.

At least he didn't have to look at those shorts and tank top. Nobody should have to do that, including me.

"Trueblood?" I said, dragging him back to attention.

He blinked, looked at the still-spinning merry-go-round out of the corner of his eye, though he tried to pretend he didn't, then scraped a hand across his face, and blinked again.

"You've been working too hard," I said sympathetically.

"Huh? Oh, yeah. Definitely."

"So... You through yelling at me?"

"What?" The man needed to get a grip. There are a lot worse things in this world than thinking you're going crazy and seeing things. "Oh. Yeah. I'm through yelling at you. For now."

I got to my feet. "Great, 'cause I got a lot to do and—"

My phone rang. If I hadn't been so distracted, I would never have answered it without checking the caller ID first, but right then a little diversion seemed like a good idea. *Big* mistake!

"Maxie Peterson," I said crisply.

"Maxine. It's about bloody time you answered the damned phone!"

"Mom," I said, and felt the ground spin out from under me as if it were Amelia's merry-go-round.

"I'VE LOST TRACK of the number of times I've called you these last couple of days, and you couldn't return even one of those calls?"

"I've been busy, Mom."

"In trouble, you mean."

"That, too." I sank back on the park bench. This was going to take a while. "I'm sure Nic kept you posted."

"He told me about the shooter. The murdered man's daughter, right?"

"That's right. Can you hang on for a minute, mom?" I didn't wait for an answer, just hit mute. "We done here, Trueblood?"

He dragged his puzzled gaze off the gradually slowing merry-go-round—Amelia had vanished, which wasn't necessarily reassuring—and scowled at me.

"For now, Peterson. But if I find you've stuck your nose where you shouldn't one more time..." He didn't need to finish.

I had no doubt we'd reach a point where his tolerance ran out before my determination to keep poking at this, but we weren't there yet. 'Yet' being the operative word.

"I'll keep you posted, I promise," I said.

I caught a low growl that came from somewhere deep in his throat, but he didn't say anything, just shot me a sharp-eyed look of warning and stomped off. His departure might have been a bit more impressive if I hadn't caught him glancing back over his shoulder at that merry-go-round. Twice.

I punched off mute and stuck my phone back to my ear. "Sorry, Mom. I was in the middle of an interview when you called."

"An interview with whom?" Trust my mom to keep her pronouns straight. She's a real stickler that way.

"I was talking to the police."

A car pulled out of the apartment house parking lot, headed back toward River City. Dark blue, solid, nondescript. Trueblood's unmarked police car. I hadn't lied when I said I'd spotted it. For one thing, it had been washed in the last week. In my world, that's just not normal.

Whatever it was that had been nagging at me last night gave me another poke. Not hard enough for my brain to figure out what was bothering me, but enough to remind me there'd been something...

"Maxine?" said my mom, snapping me back to attention.

"Sorry. I was thinking."

"Nice to know you can."

"Hah hah."

"So what did the police want?"

"It was the lead detective on the investigation. He was telling me to butt out."

She sniffed disdainfully. "I hope you told him where to go with that one."

"It was a friendly exchange."

I didn't want to go into details. Give my mom an inch with that sort of thing and she'll think she owns you. Besides, I've sat through more than my fair share of her lectures on handling interrogations. From both sides. I'm not keen on setting myself up for more.

"So, is there a reason you called, mom?" *Besides wanting to tell me how to run my life?* I didn't actually say that last part.

"I've talked to Cheng Lee. He's in Istanbul and really busy right now, but he says if you need help he might be able to send one or two of his operatives—"

"I don't need any help."

"This Montgomery was a big deal in international business, Maxine. The kind of international business that can attract some very, let us say, unsavory connections?"

"I know, but I'm pretty sure this has nothing to do with anything like that. And I'm handling it, okay? He ended up dead in my office with my letter opener stuck in his chest, so that makes it sort of personal."

There was a long silence on the other end, then, "I appreciate that, Maxine, but, really, I think—"

"And I appreciate your appreciation, mom, but I gotta go. Bye!"

I cut the call, but not before I caught an enraged, "Maxine!"

Still, I ended the call first. In my book, that counts as a win.

As long as I had the phone out, I decided I might as well see if there were any messages. Thirteen, an unlucky number. I deleted them all without checking to see who called, then pocketed the phone.

On to the next thing.

I sincerely hoped I'd have some idea what that next thing might be by the time I got on the highway.

CHAPTER 29

"So! What's our next little thing?" said Amelia cheerily as I slid behind the steering wheel.

I jumped. I couldn't help it. She hadn't been there when I unlocked the door. Two seconds later, there she is, feet propped on the cowl and still in those short shorts that wouldn't have worked on anyone except a hundred-and-ten pound super model, which Amelia most definitely is not.

"*Our* next thing?" I said.

"I was thinking maybe we storm his company's headquarters. What's it called?"

I opened my mouth to tell her, but she breezed on. In Amelia's world, answers are generally irrelevant.

"I'm thinkin', raid their files, maybe listen to a few of the top brass plotting, sit in on top secret calls. You know. A little espionage stuff."

"And how, exactly, do you suggest I do that?"

Did I mention that sarcasm is wasted on my fairy godmother?

She sat up, beaming. "I'm glad you asked."

I groaned. You'd think, after all this time, that I'd have learned to keep my big mouth shut.

"It's going to take two of us," she said. "I do the espionage stuff. You park and go sit in the lobby or something and keep watch."

"They can't see you," I pointed out. "Why would I need to keep watch?"

"Uhmm..." She squinted, unseeing, at the car's headliner, thinking hard. "I know! You'll eavesdrop on their conversations while they're going in and out of the building."

"You expect whoever it is to be talking about how he murdered Jameson while he's walking across the front lobby? Are you nuts?"

That made her rear back. "Don't you talk to me like that! Have you no respect for your elders and betters?"

"No. Just ask my mother." Anyway, as far as I'm concerned, Amelia only falls into one of those two categories. "I have a better idea. I'm going to talk to Julia Carmody."

"That little twit? Why?"

"Or her mother. I want to know how Julia found out where I live and what car I drive."

"You're in the phone book."

"Actually, I'm not. Not personally. That only lists people who have a land line. All I have is a cell phone. And even if I had a regular phone, I could have been unlisted. My only listing is in the Yellow Pages, and that's my cell with my office address. Anyway, it definitely doesn't explain how she knew it was my car she was shooting at."

That thing that had been nagging at me? Seeing Trueblood's car pull onto the street had finally made it click into place. If Douglas could hack River City's traffic database, so could someone else. And if Julia had managed to ferret out my car and license plate number—she'd known exactly who and what she was shooting at, after all—what else might she have dug up from other sources? And what might she have done about it once she had?

I WAS IN LUCK. SORT OF. Katie Carmody was at home, but she wasn't at all happy about me showing up on her doorstep unannounced.

"What do you want?" she demanded. "I told the police I'd pay for your windshield. You didn't have to drive out here to harass me and my daughter."

She was standing in her front doorway, one outstretched hand pressed against the door frame, the other still clutching the doorknob, blocking the way. Two days ago, she'd been teary-eyed and perfect, a grieving lover bravely facing her loss. Today, she was tense and hostile, her features strained, eyes narrowed into ugly slits that dug dark lines at the corners.

All that anger was aimed squarely at me, but I wasn't the one who'd set her off. She'd been vibrating with fury when she'd wrenched open the door. Seeing me had simply given her a physical target to aim at.

"Actually, I wanted to talk to Julia," I said, keeping it calm and low key.

Katie wasn't armed and I doubted she'd had any training in fighting, but she was taller than me and those long fingernails could do a lot of damage. I'd been caught in the middle of a human cat fight once when I was a cop. It had taken weeks for the scratches to heal.

"She said she was sorry," Katie spat, not budging an inch.

"Did she?" I said sweetly. "I'm sorry. I must have missed that part when I got knocked out protecting your daughter from a totally pissed off old lady whose vintage Mustang Julia riddled with bullets."

All right, I admit the 'riddled' is a bit of an exaggeration. And while Mrs. Minski would undoubtedly have creamed Julia with that rolling pin if I hadn't gotten in the way, she probably wouldn't have killed her. Still, she *had* been awfully pissed, so who knew. I deserved a little appreciation, regardless.

"Anyway, that's not what I want to talk to Julia about."

"Lemme help," said Amelia, shoving past me, wand out, ready to go.

Amelia, helping, was the last thing I needed. I hurriedly

reached past her and smacked the front door out of Katie's grip.

"Come on, Katie. Where is she?"

Katie backed up. "You leave us alone! You don't have a warrant to search my house. And you're not a reporter! You *lied* to me!"

I'd wondered if she'd get around to that.

"I didn't lie," I said, stepping past Amelia into the house. Katie backed farther away. "I mentioned the magazine. You assumed everything else." I wasn't going to waste time debating the ethics of that particular tactic, especially since I wasn't sure I'd win even if I were the only one debating. "I also didn't murder Jameson, in case you're wondering."

By this point, Katie had backed halfway across that big marbled foyer. I hadn't hesitated to follow. From here, I could see the patio and pool where Julia was seated at one of the umbrella-shaded tables, a laptop open in front of her. Her back was to us, and if she'd heard what was going on between her mother and me, she gave no sign of it.

"Never mind," I said, brushing past Katie. "This shouldn't take long."

"Yeah, never mind," said Amelia, cheerfully following me. At least she'd put that damned wand away.

"Oh!" I added, turning back to Katie. "If you're thinking about calling the cops or whatever, you might just consider how it would play if the media learned about up-and-coming fashion designer Katie Carmody's daughter being arrested after trying to kill her daddy's private investigator and shooting up a whole parking lot full of cars."

The 'whole parking lot' bit was an exaggeration, but she got my point.

"Bitch," she hissed. There was nothing pretty about that face when she said it, either.

"Hey!" Amelia objected.

I waved her down. "Like I said, this shouldn't take long. Up to you if you want to make a bigger deal of it than it is."

Protect her daughter or risk me informing the media of that same daughter's little shoot-'em-up? For Katie, there was no contest.

"Fine," she spat. "Talk to her. Then get the hell out of my house."

I wondered what had gotten her so worked up before we showed up on her front step. There was more to her temper than resentment at my deception.

"Go away," said Amelia, pointing her finger at Katie and giving it a little wiggle.

In fairy godmother land, finger pointing magic is minor stuff, but useful. Katie went away. Too bad I couldn't do the same for Amelia whenever I wanted.

The sound of my footsteps on the stone dragged Julia out of her computer trance. She took one look at me and leapt to her feet. "You! What are *you* doing here?"

"We need to talk." I pulled out a chair for myself, then pointed at hers. "Sit."

"No way! I'm not—"

Amelia did her finger-wiggle thing.

Julia sat.

I gave Amelia a quick smile of thanks. The smile vanished an instant later when she pulled out a third chair for herself.

"I like lots of room," I said to Julia, deliberately slouching into my chair as if I'd shoved Amelia's under the table.

My thirteen-year-old sniper just sneered at me and tried to pretend she wasn't nervous. I didn't waste energy trying to put her at ease.

"Your mom will be getting the bill for my windshield," I said. "There'll be more bills to come, of course. I haven't had time to deal with the bullet holes yet."

"Piece of junk like that? Why bother?"

"Because, unlike you, I don't steal my mother's car when I want to get somewhere."

"If hers is as crappy as yours, I can see why."

247

The kid had sneering down to an art form, but the snotty attitude was getting old fast.

I sat up abruptly and leaned toward her. Her eyes got wide as she shrank back in her chair.

"What do you want to bet it's all coming out of your allowance?" I said, and grabbed her laptop.

Amelia laughed and gave me a thumbs up.

"Hey! That's mine!" Julia protested.

"That's a relief. Your mom's probably wouldn't be nearly as interesting." I batted away her attempt to grab it back. "Oh, my, my, my. Do you really think you can order a rifle like that on-line? At your age? What would your probation officer think if she knew?"

She had her mother's delicate, natural-born blonde complexion, so the angry flush that washed across her cheeks glowed like neon. "I don't have a probation officer."

"You will," I said, my attention focused on the open tabs at the top of her browser. Nothing interesting there. Well, not unless you're interested in gun dealers. Julia clearly was.

"No, I won't. My mom's lawyer—"

"Won't be able to get you out of this. Not with the damage you did and with your fingerprints all over that rifle your daddy bought you." I gave her a nasty smile. "You have heard of ballistics and finger prints, right?"

"Bitch."

Like mother, like daughter.

I opened the browser history and scrolled down. Thank heavens Julia was one of the millions who never remember to clear that potentially incriminating record of where they've been.

There, as I'd expected, was the url for the city's traffic database.

"Tsk, tsk, tsk," I said. "Does your lawyer know you've been hacking the city's databases?"

"Don't you dare—!"

This time Amelia, bless her heart, had her wand at the ready.

Julia froze in her chair, mouth half open, eyes still shooting fire.

Okay, so maybe that wand isn't such a bad thing, every now and then.

"Thanks," I said.

"You're welcome."

"I need a couple minutes to copy some files. You think you can hold her and keep everyone else away while I do?"

"Piece of cake," she said, giving a wave with the wand.

I couldn't help flinching at all the golden sparkles that flicked off the star's points, but rather than create any mayhem in our vicinity, the things obediently floated off, slipping through the open glass doors to the living room and ducking around the ends of the house as if in search of a victim or three.

Working with Amelia might not be so bad, after all. In judicious doses.

"Well?" Amelia snapped. "Don't waste time staring. Those spells aren't going to last forever."

Then again, maybe not, judicious dose or no.

I dug into a zippered inner pocket on my purse and fished out one of the large-capacity flash drives I carry with me for just this sort of thing. You never know when you're going to need to copy something or other. The drives are especially handy if the information's owner isn't sharing it willingly.

"I'm gonna check out some stuff," said Amelia.

"Go for it," I muttered, focusing on the computer screen in front of me. Amelia stalked off, annoyed. Just as well. I didn't need her hanging over my shoulder being "helpful," especially since those spells weren't going to last forever.

Most computer users have a preferred browser, but that doesn't mean they don't occasionally use another, so I made sure to get the histories from all of them. The nice thing about modern browsers is they can mirror everything across multiple computers, so even if Julia owned more than one computer, chances were good I'd captured it all. I couldn't guarantee she hadn't used a school computer or another friend's, of course, but a girl can't have everything.

Her email wasn't opened, and when I clicked on it, it demanded a password, so I reluctantly skipped that. No time to try and hack it, and I wasn't about to call Amelia back to make Julia tell me. I checked the files on the hard drive, too, and sighed. Unlike those of us who learned our computer skills when you needed to create folders and subfolders if you wanted a snowball's chance of finding whatever you'd been working on a month ago, Julia used tags, long file names, and search to track her stuff. Worse, she had an awful lot of stuff to track. I didn't have time to dig around in there, let alone copy it all. The browser histories were going to have to suffice.

I'd just clicked on the command to disconnect the flash drive when a distant, panicked cry of "Dang it!" brought me out of my chair.

Amelia, wide-eyed, bolted out of the house as fast as if a pack of ravening orcs were on her tail.

"Lawyer! Here! They're headed this way!" she exclaimed, brandishing her wand. I think she was aiming at Julia. She killed a potted day lily at the opposite side of the pool, instead.

"Breathe!" I said. "Aim!"

I yanked out my flash drive, made sure the laptop screen was the one Julia had been on when I intervened, spun the computer around so it was facing her, then sat back in my chair, trying to look casual and relaxed even though my heart was pounding.

Amelia breathed, did her own spin, hit another pot—more day lilies—then, finally, zeroed in on Julia.

"...touch my computer!" Julia screeched.

"What are you talking about?" I said, feigning innocence. "Do I look like I'm touching your computer?"

"Julia? Darling! Are you all right?"

Katie burst from the house, a tall, good-looking guy in a suit hot on her heels. Amelia had gotten the lawyer part right—the man fairly oozed high-class slime. This must be Don Larson. He didn't really look like a Don, but what do I know.

Katie had the concerned, protective mother act nailed. Now that she had an appreciative male audience to play to, the anger that had distorted her features when we arrived was gone completely. Instead, she was a beautiful mother hen worried about her adorable little chick.

Forget high fashion. The woman should have been an actress.

"What's going on?" Larson demanded. He glanced at Julia and as quickly dismissed her, then turned his attention to me. "Aren't you Maxine Peterson? What do you want? What are you doing here?"

I gave him a friendly smile, leaned back, and casually crossed my legs. "Which of those questions do you want me to answer first?"

"What happened? Is Julia okay? Where is she?"

Larson's head snapped up as Ricky, clad in a scrubby T-shirt and shorts two sizes too big for him, came barreling around the end of the house, a hoe brandished in one fist. I was guessing Julia's screeching had drawn him. Double dang it.

"Who are *you?*" Larson demanded. "What are you doing here?"

Definitely the lawyer. I swear, one of the first rules they teach them in law school is, when you're losing control of the situation, ask more questions.

"I'm Ricky," said Ricky, unimpressed. "I work here. You've seen me plenty of times, but you don't pay much attention to the hired help, do you?" His attention was focused on Julia. "Are you all right?"

"Ricky!" Julia leapt out of her chair and raced across the patio to throw herself into the boy's arms. I'm pretty sure she didn't even notice her mother, who had to take a step back to avoid being bowled over.

Ricky tossed the hoe aside, narrowly missing another pot of day lilies, then protectively wrapped his arm around her shoulders, drawing her close as he glared at the rest of us.

"What were you guys doing that upset her?" he demanded. "What are you bastards *thinking?*"

"Ricky!" Katie gasped. Once again, that angry flush swept up her throat and over her face, obliterating all trace of the worried, loving mom look she'd been wearing. "You should be ashamed of yourself, insulting Don, talking like that in front of my daughter! You let her go this instant! And from now on, you're banned from my house, do you understand? I'm telling your father!"

"Ooohhh!" said Amelia, who was thoroughly enjoying the spectacle. "She's going to tell his caddy! *That's* got him scared!"

Actually, it had him pissed off.

"You go right ahead and tell my dad," he snapped back. "He knows you ignore Julia, too. He knows you lock her in her room when you have all those wild parties and all those men who sleep over. Some of 'em men you never even met before!"

Larson glanced at Katie, clearly shocked. She didn't notice. She was glaring daggers at Ricky. ' Shut up! Just shut up!"

Ricky laughed. "Make me! I know all about you. In fact, I'll tell that *cop* about you, shall I? I'll bet he'd like to hear about all the empty booze bottles I have to pick up around here after one of your parties, and all your talk about how much money you were going to get out of Julia's daddy. And the pot and that white powder stuff I find on the tables sometimes? How about I tell him about *that?*"

Larson blenched.

"*What?*" shrieked Katie, perfectly manicured hands curling into pink-tipped claws. "Lies! That's all lies! How *dare* you say things like that? How dare you threaten *me!*" She whirled to challenge Larson. 'Don! Tell him. Tell him he can't threaten me like that!"

The lawyer coughed, clearly unhappy at being drawn into this fight.

"*Tell* him!"

"Now, see here, young man. You apologize to Ms

Carmody."

"And you're gonna make me...how?"

Julia sniffed dolefully and clung tighter to her hero. I'm pretty sure I'm the only one who caught the flash of satisfaction in her face. Instead of being frightened, she was enjoying this.

Amelia should adopt her. They'd make a perfect pair because Amelia was enjoying the hell out of all this, too.

I needed to get out of here.

"Family chats are wonderful things," I said, getting to my feet, "so I'll just leave you to it."

"Good riddance," Katie spat at me. "And I'm not paying for that windshield. *Or* the bullet holes!" she added triumphantly.

"Now, Katie," said Larson, looking even more alarmed. "We don't want to discuss any of that right now, remember?"

I wasn't worried about the windshield bill. He'd be eager to talk out of court settlement in order to keep Julia out of juvie and Katie off the nightly news. Especially given Ricky's threat to tell Trueblood what he knew.

To make things easier, I handed Larson one of my business cards.

"In case you want to get in touch to discuss those repair bills," I said helpfully. "Also, you might want to take a look at the webpage Julia's got open on her laptop right now."

"What?" screeched Julia, abandoning Ricky. "No! That's *my* laptop! Don't you dare touch it!"

Katie got there first. She clicked a key to clear the screen saver, then gaped at the image in front of her, horrified.

"Julia! What are you thinking? That's a *rifle!*"

"It's none of your business what I look at!"

She made the mistake of shoving her mother away from the laptop, which gave Larson the chance to snatch it up, out of her reach. What he saw made his jaw drop.

"Shit! That's a semi-automatic!"

He snapped the laptop closed, then swung on Julia. "I'm taking charge of this. As of now, you will not be allowed on the

Internet. For any reason!"

"You're not my daddy! Just because you're screwing my mom every chance you get doesn't mean you can tell me what to do!"

Poor Ricky, Julia's knight in baggy armor, could only stand there and stare, caught between the urge to rescue his fairy tale princess and what looked like a dawning realization that maybe there was a darker side to his princess than he'd realized. Which was too bad. He was a good kid, and he deserved better than Julia, no matter how rich and good looking she was.

Amelia didn't even notice I was leaving. She was focused on offering encouraging advice to Julia, who was alternately pummeling the lawyer and trying to crawl up his suit to grab the laptop he still held out of her reach.

"Kick him where it hurts!" Amelia crowed as Larson tried to keep hold of the laptop and fend off Julia at the same time. "Shins! Kneecaps! Aim higher, girl!"

Good thing no one could hear her. The last thing Julia needed was encouragement. She was doing just fine on her own.

CHAPTER 30

I picked up a late lunch of an extra-large coffee and a cheese panini at the Last Caff, then trudged up to my office. Thanks to Amelia, the place was as clean as it was ever going to get, even if my files were a mess.

I didn't spot anyone on the stairs and didn't pass any open office doors, which meant I should have a little peace and quiet to go over Julia's browser history. Anyone who could hack the city's databases could hack other places that might prove more useful. Places like her daddy's private email.

I'm not a hacker, but Douglas had given me a flash drive with a program that could test for passwords. The software isn't state of the art—and I wouldn't know what to do with it if it were—but it's better and faster than guess work or trying to dig up the name of someone's first dog or where they went to grade school, which is the sort of information most of us use as our passwords. Of course, I always make sure to check the obvious stuff first. Things like 'password' used as a password, or birthdates, home phone numbers, or kids' names, all of which are pretty easy to find if you know where to look.

I set the coffee and panini on the desk, then dumped my purse and the bag with my laptop and the info Lucille had given me on the floor beside it. First things first—I was hungry.

I kicked off my shoes and got down to business.

The Last Caff's sandwiches are generously sized, but I

flattened it as best I could, then fished around in my desk, hunting for the not-quite-a-switchblade knife I used for this sort of thing. Assuming Betsy and her crew hadn't taken it as evidence, of course.

A little searching revealed that Amelia's cleanup efforts had landed it in the file for "Repairs, Office" along with a sales brochure for surveillance devices and miscellaneous documents and bits of evidence from five separate case files, none of them related to the others. (I don't have space for separate boxes to hold the miscellaneous bits I pick up on a case, so I just keep 'em with the paperwork.)

I didn't spot anything connected to repairs, office or otherwise.

I used the Last Caff's napkins to wipe the blade, then divided the sandwich into more manageable portions. Before I could take a bite, my phone rang. I checked and felt my eyebrows sliding upward. The caller ID said Leslie Postin.

I set down the sandwich and picked up the phone.

"Ms Peterson? Leslie Postin." There was an edge to his voice that didn't bode well for the conversation ahead.

"Mr. Postin," I said warily. "What can I do for you?"

"I understand you've tracked down a woman who claims she's the mother to Jameson's son."

"No," I said, dragging out the single syllable. "I can't say that I have."

Absolutely true. Amelia tracked down Stephanie Grover, not me. And Stephanie hadn't claimed that Jameson had fathered her son. Since she'd engaged legal counsel to prevent Jameson from forcing that claim, I was on solid ground with this one.

"Did Jameson father a son?" Postin demanded.

"I believe he thought he had."

A pause. A long one. Then, 'You should have studied law, Ms Peterson. That's a lovely equivocation."

"Why, thank you. Coming from a lawyer with your reputation, Mr. Postin, that's very flattering."

"Let me rephrase my question. Did Jameson hire you to prove the boy was his son?"

"What boy?"

"You know what boy. Samuel Elliot Grover. Mother, Stephanie Marie Grover of Munroesville."

"Why are you asking me?"

"Did you know of the boy's existence when you came to see me?"

"I did not."

"So you admit—"

"That I know of the boy's existence now. I didn't then. Nothing more than that, Mr. Postin. Everything else is speculation because Jameson is dead."

That earned me a long silence. Postin was one of those careful lawyers who never says anything without thinking through every word and its implications first.

"Have you seen the boy?"

"Yes." I could just hang up on him, but I wanted to know where he was headed with this, and why. Besides, I sort of owed him for that disaster in his office yesterday, even if it was Amelia's fault, not mine.

"And...? Do you think he's Jameson's son? Does he *look* like him?"

"He's two years old, Mr. Postin. He looks like a kid. And for the record, his mother hired a lawyer to defend *against* Jameson's claims of paternity."

"What! Who?"

I told him.

"Humph! I don't know this Arnott, but I can't imagine there's any lawyer in Munroesville who would stand a chance against Jameson and his lawyers."

"Probably not, but Arnott was going to try. I doubt Ms Grover can really afford him, let alone anyone more influential." And because I owed him, I added, "But here's a thought. Jameson could afford anyone, yet he hired me. Geoffrey Dawson doesn't seem to have heard of Stephanie Grover and her son, so who did Jameson hire to represent him in the case?"

More silence while Postin weighed his options. I was pretty sure he knew.

"Jameson hired a Mark Ruson to represent him on this," Postin said at last.

"Don't know him."

"Young. Bright. Tough. He and a college friend, John Graves, are partners in their own firm here in River City. They're pretty much starting from scratch. Neither one comes from a family with money or influence, so far as I can tell. I'm not sure how Jameson found him. Like you, Ruson has no previous connection to Jameson or JM Industries that I know of."

"Which means that Jameson intended to make sure he had what he wanted before he let the world know what he was up to."

"I assume so, yes."

"How do you know about Ruson?"

"He surfaced today with a new will that Jameson wrote. The will leaves just about everything to the boy he claimed was his son."

I almost fell out of my chair. "*What?* Holy sh—" I drew a deep breath. "Sorry. I suppose Dawson and Mrs. Montgomery are contesting?"

"I'm sure they will. I don't know if they're aware of it yet. I only learned about it through a friend in the judiciary."

"That's going to make for an entertaining court case."

"And make a few lawyers a great deal richer than they are right now," said Postin dryly. "On both sides."

That made me think of something else. "Do the police know?"

"I'm sure they do. A new will leaving millions and a major international business to a two-year-old boy no one's heard of before? That could well change everything."

I eyed my congealed sandwich, thinking hard. "At least now

you know why Jameson said he was thinking about his legacy when he wanted to settle all those court cases."

He chuckled. "Once again, you've hit the heart of it, Ms Peterson. Will you keep me informed if you learn anything else?"

"A quid pro quo, Mr. Postin?"

"Exactly," he said, and hung up.

It was going to take a very, very big quid to measure up to his bombshell quo.

A new will that left everything to a boy whose mother refused even to recognize Jameson as the father? That was going to be lot of fun. It also provided a hell of a motive to anyone and everyone who'd lose out on that transaction, starting with Mrs. Christine Montgomery and her favorite attorney, Geoffrey Dawson. Then there were the investors of JM Industries, who presumably wouldn't like to see the company being run by executors. And how about Katie Carmody and Angelina Mestes, the mothers of Jameson's daughters? Jameson might have made provision to continue his support, but that was paltry compared to what the boy would receive.

Katie, at least, was bound to be furious. Angelina might not mind so much, providing her Saudi sheikh came through with a better arrangement. Annalise was probably going to have a heart attack when she heard, though I suspected she'd find at least some comfort in the knowledge that Christine had been cut out of the will, too. Presumably Shannon Montgomery, Mrs. number two, was still in Florida. No way to judge how she'd react without having met her, but given the nature of Jameson's other women, my educated guess was, not well.

And what about the daughters themselves? Angelina's daughter wasn't old enough to appreciate what had happened, but Julia was. I didn't know whether she honestly believed her father had loved her, or if it was just something she told herself and everyone else in the hopes it might come true. Either way, that second will was bound to hurt. It was the emotional equivalent of driving a knife into someone's heart, then viciously twisting it to do even more damage.

I frowned at my now-cold coffee and panini, then reluctantly shoved them to the side and retrieved my laptop. When I'd commandeered Julia's laptop, all I'd wanted was to confirm what I already suspected—that she'd hacked the city's traffic database to find out where I lived and what kind of car I drove. I'd hoped to find evidence of her having gone further, but that was all it was, a hope.

Now, I had a whole lot more reason to see what else I might find.

A part of me—the driven, answers-at-all-costs part—wished I'd had Amelia 'persuade' Julia to give me the laptop so I could do a lot more digging.

As it turned out, I didn't need to do that much.

THE FIRST HINT was the rusonandgraves.com in the browser history. The most recent hit was two weeks ago, but some digging revealed Julia had first visited that site about a month earlier.

When I checked the site, there was a clearly visible "contact us" tab that led to two separate email addresses, one for each of the two partners.

I slumped back in my chair, staring at the lines in that copied browser history. When they were online, thirteen-year-old girls lived on whatever social media sites were currently favored by their generation and not yet discovered by their parents. They visited websites for fashion, cosmetics, gaming, the latest popular rappers and teen rock groups, and whatever else they were passionate about. They did *not* go to the websites of young, relatively unknown lawyers, no matter how handsome (Graves was almost movie star good looking, Ruson not so much, though he did look like an athlete who'd strip nicely).

The second hint was all the hits to JM Industry's website. It wasn't clear to me that Julia had actually managed to hack her father's private email, but some of those addresses, with all their numbered codes at the end, suggested she'd been to places on the site the general public normally didn't see. When I tried to open them, most demanded passwords I didn't have.

I wasn't willing to use Douglas's password-cracking software yet, but at least I knew Julia had been trying to get into places she wouldn't have gone unless she was prying into her father's secrets. I'd be willing to bet a search of her hard drive would turn up a cache of her father's private emails regarding the boy Jameson had been determined to claim as his son and had already named his heir.

It wasn't hard to figure out what that would do to a girl who wanted, desperately, to believe her father loved her despite all proof to the contrary. But...murder? In my office? Julia was *thirteen.*

Thirteen, maybe, but she hadn't hesitated to use a rifle to shoot at me, a woman she'd never met and knew nothing about other than that her father had died in my office.

Nothing except for what she might have found in her unauthorized searches.

There were still gaps. Big ones. Finding links to a lawyer's website and a publicly held company in Julia's illegally obtained browser history was a far cry from proving she'd had access to her father's communications, let alone that she'd committed murder.

There were still too many unanswered questions. Why had Jameson arrived an hour earlier than he'd planned? Assuming it was Julia he'd met here, how had she arranged it? And why would Jameson agree to meet her if she had? One or the other had to have picked the lock, but which one? Why meet here and not at her house, or his office, or a restaurant? Hell, even the Last Caff would be a better place than this crummy little fourth-floor hole in the wall.

Plus, even if she'd hacked his personal computer and found a mention of the letter he'd written to me, setting the meeting, she wouldn't have gotten anything beyond my name and address and the time of the requested meeting, because Jameson hadn't given *me* any information. Unless he kept something like a computer journal, which I doubted, or he'd mentioned me in emails to someone else. Someone like Ruson, for instance.

Another thing: Jameson's murder had been spur of the moment, not premeditation—why use my letter opener, otherwise?—and Julia was about the right height for that oddly angled thrust. But her shooting at me had been planned. She'd not only have had to hack the city's database to get my address and license plate, she'd also have had to pick the lock on her school's gun locker—I sincerely doubted her fancy girl's school allowed students to keep lethal weapons lying around, not even single-shot twenty-twos. And then she'd have had to smuggle that rifle out of the school and into her house, all of which argued for more planning.

Of course, she could have taken the rifle before she knew about me. For an angry kid wanting revenge for what she'd see as her father's betrayal, the rifle might have simply been accessible and familiar. The letter opener had been accessible, but there was no hint that Julia played with knives as much as she did with guns. Which didn't mean she couldn't have adapted.

All speculation, of course, since the only "proof" I had of anything was those urls in her browser history, which weren't admissable. At least, not from me. Not to mention, the urls didn't actually prove anything. Even if Julia had hacked every last email her father had ever written, it didn't mean she'd met him here, let alone killed him.

So far, illegally snatching Julia's data hadn't got me much of anywhere. Worse, I couldn't even tell Trueblood about my suspicions.

As if conjured by my thoughts, my phone rang. I looked at the ID. Speak of the devil. I picked it up.

"Trueblood," I said.

"Peterson." He didn't sound friendly. "How many hours has

it been since I gave you one last warning about keeping your nose out of my investigation?"

"Are we counting?"

"*You* aren't paying attention."

"Who's complaining about me now?" As if I didn't know.

"I can hold you for interfering with an investigation, you know."

"Can you? Seems like an awful lot of paperwork. Why don't you just solve the murder, instead?"

"It would be easier if I didn't have to waste time with you."

"Then don't. Besides, I've got some information you might find helpful."

"Yes?" He sounded more wary than skeptical.

"Jameson left most, if not all, of his estate to Sammy Grover, the boy he was trying to claim as his son."

"Day late and a dollar short, Peterson. Ruson contacted me yesterday."

Well, phooey.

"Julia Carmody knew about her father's contact with Ruson," I said. I was getting annoyed. It'd be nice to get one up on him on *something*.

He hesitated, clearly surprised. "Did she? How do you know?"

Yes!

"She and I were having a friendly little chat before Katie Carmody and her lawyer interrupted."

"That's not quite the way they reported it. And what were you doing talking to Julia, anyway?"

"I wanted to know how she'd found out where I lived and what car I drove."

"I already know. She hacked our traffic databases."

That made me sit up. "And you didn't tell me?"

"She's a juvenile, so she's not my problem. We have specialists trained to work on cases involving kids that young. She told them. She said she was mad at you for killing her father, that she'd just wanted to scare you, not kill you."

"And you guys believed her?"

"No, but we didn't not believe her, either."

"If she's clever enough to hack your databases, she might be clever enough to hack her father's emails, so she might have found out about Ruson. And me," I added, though I still wasn't convinced of that last point. Or even that Julia was the killer.

"It's possible."

"She tries to pretend that her daddy loved and adored her, but I'm pretty sure, deep down, he didn't much care about her, one way or the other. Have you considered how she'd feel if she discovered that the father she seems to have worshiped had left just about everything he owned to a two-year-old boy who wasn't even legally recognized as his son?"

"You think I'm stupid? Of course we've thought of it. We've thought of a lot of other possibilities, as well, including the possibility that there was something between you and Montgomery that we don't yet know about, something that would have led you to murder him in your office, then try to cover it up."

I snorted. "You believe that?"

"I said we've *thought* of the possibility. I didn't say we believed it."

"Okay, but—"

"This is my last warning, Peterson. Keep out of this investigation and keep away from everyone associated with it, or I really will arrest you for obstruction. Got that?"

I didn't answer because I was no longer listening.

The faint metallic clicks of someone trying to pick the lock on my office door had just drowned out Trueblood's lecture.

CHAPTER 31

"Someone's trying to break into my office, Trueblood," I whispered into the phone. "I'm going to go look, but I'm leaving this line open, okay? Put your phone on mute, just in case, and be ready to call in backup if I need it."

"Shit!" He must have done as I asked, though, because I couldn't hear anything else.

I slid the phone under the edge of the paper wrap for my abandoned panini, then tip-toed across to press my ear against the door.

From the sounds of it, whoever was trying to break in wasn't very adept at picking locks, but then, that deadbolt was supposed to have been hard to pick. And didn't *that* work out well?

I glanced down and stifled a curse. I'd forgotten to lock the thing.

So that made me careless, and whoever was trying to break in not too bright, since they were trying to pick a lock that wasn't even locked.

I couldn't hear anything else from the hall. By now, Jimmy was probably down at the jail house with his afternoon crop of customers. Some of the others farther down the hall might be in, but they wouldn't necessarily leave their office doors open, or be interested in anything that didn't threaten themselves if they did.

I considered my options. Wait to see who came through the door, giving them a slight advantage even if I hid behind the door and caught them as they walked in? Use my fire escape ladder, with all the risk and attendant unpleasantness that entailed? Or open the door now, while the intruder was unprepared?

No contest.

I got a good grip on the door knob and yanked the door wide open.

My would-be invader squawked and staggered forward, off balance. I gave them an assist with a hard shove from my foot. That sent them sprawling, face first, onto the floor. They yelped. I flung the door wide open, then planted my foot in the small of their back.

Her back.

"Hello, Julia. Fancy meeting you like this. You steal your mother's car again?"

"Let me up, bitch!"

"I don't think so. As long as you're down, you might as well relax and put your hands out where I can see them."

She squirmed, fighting to get away, which threw me off balance. I wobbled, she squirmed some more, so I settled matters by sitting on her. Hard. I seemed to be doing a lot of that lately.

"Oof! Fat pig!"

"Bitch? Pig? I'm not sure I appreciate your references. And I happen to like dogs and pigs. I'm pretty sure I don't like you, though. What were you doing, trying to break into my office?"

"Who says I was trying to break in?"

"You sure as hell didn't knock."

I gave a little bounce, settling myself more securely. She whuffed like a seat cushion, suddenly compressed. She probably felt like a seat cushion, too. I must weigh at least ten pounds more than she does. All right, maybe more like twenty, but this was no time for quibbling.

"I was listening. I heard voices."

Her voice sounded a tad bit strained. With her nose buried in that old carpet, she was probably trying not to breathe. I couldn't work up any sympathy.

"Eavesdropping as well as breaking and entering. I guess I should be grateful you didn't shoot the lock off and have done with it. But, then, the police still have your rifle, don't they?"

"Thanks to you."

She didn't sound grateful, but my mama raised me to be polite. "You're welcome. If you're lucky, they might give it back by the time you turn twenty-one."

She squirmed some more. I bounced some more. She whuffed. Twice.

"Your hands still aren't where I can see them," I said.

She considered that for a minute, then reluctantly pulled them from under her. That meant she had even less leverage if she wanted to throw me off, which suited me just fine.

"Good girl. So why'd you trash my office yesterday?"

"I didn't—"

I bounced. Gently, this time. "Don't lie. Why'd you trash my office?"

"What are you talking about? I didn't trash your office, but I wish I would've! I ended in *jail* because of you!"

"You ended in jail because you committed a crime. Several crimes, in fact. So why break into my office?"

Another bounce. This time, she groaned.

All right, maybe I was thirty pounds heavier. I'm older, taller, and bigger boned. I'm entitled. But she was young. She'd survive. I wasn't about to let her up until I had the answers I wanted.

I just hoped Trueblood was still listening in. I'd hate to get a confession and end up being the only one who heard it.

"Julia?" I said. "You like having your face in my carpet?"

"I'm looking for something, all right?"

"What?" When she kept silent, I shifted my weight a fraction. It wasn't really a bounce, but she still noticed.

"Nrrrh! I wanted to see what my daddy sent you!"

"What makes you think he sent me anything?"

"He hired you, didn't he? He must have told you something. Email, letter. Whatever. I want to know what he said."

I considered that. Jameson had sent me a handwritten note, not an email or typed letter. If Jula hadn't come across my name before his death, then he probably hadn't mentioned me in any of his private emails. Not even in his emails to Ruson. Assuming he'd emailed Ruson, of course. Which was a pretty safe assumption because she wouldn't have gone to the lawyer's website, otherwise. But that didn't guarantee she'd found any mention of me or of Sammy Grover and her father's plans for the boy.

Didn't guarantee she hadn't, either.

The question I really wanted answered right now was, when had she known her father had hired *me?* Before he was murdered, or after?

"You hacked your father's email, didn't you?"

"What?"

I shifted again.

"I didn't hack his email, all right? He left me in his office one day when he got called out. It was pathetic." Even nose-deep on that godawful carpet, she did a great sneer. "His email was already open, and, anyway, he had all his passwords written down in his desk calendar. Not my fault he was so stupid! Most of it was stupid stuff, anyway."

"Like what? Business?"

"As if! He has other accounts for that. This was his personal stuff. Messages to his girl friends, and making golf dates, and...and stuff," she added with a snicker.

"What...stuff?" I said.

Her upper lip curled in a nasty little grin. "My dad blocked my mom's emails. I looked, 'cause I knew she was mad at him and there she was, blocked. He wouldn't even talk to her!" And then she laughed.

I considered that. She wasn't lying, but she wasn't telling me everything, either. "The whole truth, Julia. What else did you see?"

She went still. The laughter hadn't been pretty, a protective mechanism against the hurt of her parents' indifference, but this was something darker. Something that hurt even more.

"You saw messages to a lawyer whose name you didn't recognize, right? Messages about a child."

Not so much as a peep out of her. I poked her in the ribs. "Julia?"

"He wanted to adopt a stupid boy!" she snarled. It sounded as if the words had been ripped out of her. "He wanted to *adopt* him! Give him his name and everything! He never adopted *me!*"

Now it was my turn to go still. Adopt. Not merely claim paternity. Jameson had actually wanted to adopt his illegitimate son and give him his name.

Trueblood must have known. He hadn't said anything, but if Julia read about her father's plans in his private email, so had Trueblood. Which explained why he was so annoyed with my visit with Stephanie Grover. He'd known about the will *and* the planned adoption, though that didn't seem to have gotten him any closer to the identity of the killer than I was.

Stephanie Grover's resistance definitely made more sense. It wasn't just that Jameson wanted a part of their son's life; he wanted *all* of it.

And Julia Carmody, who'd adored her father and tried hard to pretend he loved her, had found out. I was pretty sure Trueblood hadn't known about that.

"Did he say anything about marrying the boy's mother?" I said.

"Not that I saw. Anyway, he's already married, right?"

"He was getting a divorce."

"So?"

Good point. Jameson had never let a wife get in the way of what he wanted, and Julia knew it.

"So I'm thinking—"

"Get off her!"

The angry shout made me jump, which didn't make Julia happy. What happened next must have delighted her, though. A long, boney body slammed into me, knocking me backwards off Julia. My head hit the floor. Sharp elbows and knees dug into me, making me grunt.

Ricky the pool boy had come to his fair maid's rescue.

He grabbed my shoulders and pinned me against the carpet. "You leave her alone! She—!"

He didn't finish. He couldn't. I'd slammed the heels of my hands against his chest and shoved. The instant his knee came out of my midriff, I rolled him over and planted *my* knee in *his* midriff. He had a solid set of abs for somebody so skinny, but that didn't stop me worrying I'd squish him right down to his spine. That weight differential thing again.

In his case, though, young, fast, and fit easily trumped those extra twenty pounds. He shoved me aside, then rolled back on top of me. My turn to whuff as his knee flattened my ribs.

"You shouldn't have hurt her" he snarled.

"Hit her, Ricky! Hit her!" Julia crowed. She was on her feet, safely out of the way and doing some sort of celebratory jig while miming swinging a fist, presumably into my face. "*Hit* her!"

That got his attention. He glanced over his shoulder just in time to see her take a good swing for the kick she was aiming at my ribs.

"Julia! Stop!"

He launched himself off me, trying to tackle her just as her foot reached the most powerful point of its arc. Her toe caught him on the point of his chin, snapping his head back and throwing her off balance. He grunted and tumbled off me. Flailing wildly, she toppled backwards into the chair in front of my desk. Something gave a loud, wooden *crack* as the thing slammed into the edge of my desk. Chair and Julia collapsed into a tangled heap.

From my vantage point, flat on the floor, I could just see the top of my still full, extra-large cup of cold coffee wobble, then pitch forward, spilling its contents across the desk top and everything on it. Creamy brown liquid cascaded over the edge into Julia's face.

Julia screeched, then swore, swiping wildly at the mess while she tried to dodge the drips and untangle herself from the remains of my chair. "Bitch!"

"Mind your mouth," I shot back, getting awkwardly to my feet. "*I* didn't try to kick *you*, and I sure as hell didn't make you spill coffee all over my desk or break up my furniture."

It was good furniture, too. Not more than third or maybe fourth-hand from the used furniture dealer over on Garmin Street. It hadn't been easy to find stuff I could afford that didn't look as if it had belonged to a team of drunken, belligerent rugby players who hadn't been housebroken.

Ricky, still shaking his head dazedly, had made it to all fours.

"Julia?" he croaked. "You okay?"

"Ricky? Ricky! I'm so sorry! I didn't mean to kick you!" Julia dragged herself out of the remnants of my shattered chair and crawled over to her friend. "You okay?"

I edged back, out of her reach.

"That's smart. She's a tricky one. I've decided not to recruit a fairy godmother for her after all."

My head snapped up. Amelia was standing in my open doorway, wand carelessly dangling from her hand. This time she'd gone for wild blonde hair and black leather with a million silver studs on collar, cuffs, and down each side of the way-too-tight pants, right to where they disappeared in yet another pair of thigh-high, high-heeled black leather boots. It was a new look for her. I didn't rate it an improvement.

"Put that thing away," I said. I should have kept my mouth shut.

Julia's attention riveted on me.

"What thing?" she demanded, eyes narrowing in suspicion. "What are you talking about?"

"Rotten thing to do, kicking him like that," I said.

"What'd you expect?" Amelia demanded, abandoning the doorway. "She's a rotten kid." She leaned down to get a better look at Ricky. "Poor guy. That's going to leave a nasty bruise."

Julia jumped to her feet so fast Amelia almost tripped getting out of her way. "Hey, kid! Watch it!"

Ricky was staring up at the girl he'd come to rescue. "Julia? Why'd you kick me?"

"I didn't mean to, Ricky! It wasn't my fault." She spun on me, finger pointing accusingly. "It was *her* fault! *She* made me kick you!"

"Huh?" said Ricky. Poor kid probably had a minor concussion. He was usually a lot sharper than this.

"You have a serious problem with taking responsibility for your own actions, Julia, you know that?" I said. Any sympathy I'd once had for her was gone, replaced by a strong urge to shake her till her teeth rattled. "But I still don't get it. You already trashed my office once and didn't find what you wanted. Why come back and try again?"

"Julia?" said Ricky again. He looked like he was having a hard time focusing.

Julia ignored him. All her attention was fixed on me. "You're crazy."

"Well, if you didn't, who—?" I cut the question off short. "Where's your mom?"

"My mom?" Julia's lips twisted in a ugly sneer. "Stupid bitch is probably home screwing her new boy toy."

"Young lady!" Amelia exclaimed. "Watch your mouth!"

"Who?" I said. As if I couldn't guess.

Julia laughed. It wasn't a pleasant laugh. "You don't think she's actually *paying* that lawyer she hired, do you?"

"Good thing she had one around if you're going to shoot up innocent people's cars."

I should learn to keep my mouth shut. With a screech of rage, Julia launched herself at me, outstretched hands curved like claws. Ricky rolled, reaching to grab Julia. Out of the corner of my eye, I spotted Amelia raising her wand.

"No!" I shouted.

Julia was half in the air. Ricky grabbed her ankle just as she launched off her back foot, throwing her off balance. Amelia's sparkly stuff missed Julia, sailed over my desk, and blew out my window.

Instead of digging into my throat, Julia's nails raked down my chest, gouging my breast and popping my shirt buttons. I screeched. Julia swore. Ricky gasped.

Amelia just said, "Dang!" and stood there, eyeing my shattered window as the three of us collapsed in a tangled heap on the floor.

"Do something!" I roared at Amelia an instant before Julia let go of my shredded blouse to drag her nails down my cheek. It was the side with all the scrapes, too.

I swore, scrambling to get free. Ricky shouted, "Julia!" again just as Julia hauled back her fist, ready to punch me.

Dimly I caught a very masculine "What the hell?" from the open doorway, but I was too busy trying to grab Julia's wrists to look. Julia was still swearing. Ricky was still yelling, "Julia! *Julia!*" And Amelia was shouting, "Get out of the way, kid! I'm gonna nail her! Get out of the way!"

There was a rush of footsteps across the floor, followed by Julia being pulled off me, still screaming and swearing.

"Stop it, you little spitfire!" said Trueblood, dragging her to her feet. That was immediately followed by a "Shit! What the hell!" as his arm suddenly froze at his side.

"Oops!" said Amelia.

I glanced at her. She had the grace to look guilty, just for an instant, then she gave another wave of her wand and unfroze his arm.

"What?" she said, aggrieved. "It was his fault. I was aiming at her when he got in the way."

I looked back at the combatants towering above me just in time to see Julia's foot headed straight at my head. I ducked, but not fast enough.

"Oof!" My head snapped backwards into the floor. Again. Pain shot though my temples.

"Stop it!" Trueblood wrapped his arms around Julia and lifted her bodily off the floor, then swung her away from Ricky. It wasn't his fault she accidentally clobbered the boy as she kicked and flailed, fighting to get free.

"Unh!" Ricky tumbled back, clutching his battered head.

Julia was going to have to do a lot of apologizing if she ever hoped to patch up that relationship.

I slid backwards on my butt until I was safely out of range, then staggered to my feet. I blinked and shook my head, trying to shake off the effects of Julia's kick. Big mistake. It just made my newly acquired headache pound harder.

Wincing, I probed my cheek with my finger tips, then tucked in my chin and tried to peer down at my chest.

Not a good idea. Blood welled in the four parallel gouges slashed across my breast. I could see all the way to my navel, but I couldn't see a single button still attached to the front of my blouse. In a couple of places there were gaping holes where the fabric had given way before the thread on the button.

Thank God I put on good underwear this morning. I'd needed the extra boost that wearing black silk and lace can give a girl, but I hadn't planned on showing it to the world.

"You okay, Ricky?" I reached down to give him a hand.

He looked up, got a good eyeful of boobs, bra, and cleavage, blushed scarlet, and hastily looked away. "I... I'm fine, thanks."

Amelia snickered. "Bet that's the high point of his day."

I glared at her, then pointedly drew my blouse together and turned my attention back to Trueblood and his prisoner.

"Thanks," I said. "I wasn't expecting you to show up."

"I was already headed here. Uniforms should show up in a minute. I called them when I started hearing screams and thumps."

It might have been my imagination, but I had the feeling he

was trying hard not to look at my chest, too.

Julia, squirming mightly in his grip, drove her heel into his kneecap.

"Oww!" He set her on her feet but without letting go. "Assaulting an officer in the performance of his duty is a felony, young lady."

"Bastard!" she spat.

Trueblood's, "Hey! None of that!" didn't faze Julia in the least. She stuck her tongue out, then tried to kick his other knee.

"Julia!" Ricky exclaimed, appalled.

"Right," said Trueblood grimly. "That's it."

With practiced efficiency, he pulled his handcuffs off his belt and cuffed her. Then he grabbed my sole surviving guest chair and dragged it over.

"Sit," he said.

Julia opened her mouth to protest, took one look at the expression on his face, and sat.

Amelia looked disappointed. To my relief, she reluctantly tucked her wand in her pocket where it belonged.

I turned my attention back to the boy. "Did you drive Julia here?"

He glanced at Julia, who scowled at him, then looked back at me and nodded miserably. I couldn't help but feel sorry for him. Shattered illusions suck, especially when you're that young.

"I got my license two months ago. But I didn't know she meant to break in. Honest! I thought she was just going to wait while I found a place to park, then we were going to talk to you. That's all, I swear!"

"Did you hit Ms Peterson?" Trueblood asked, but without taking his eyes off Julia, who was looking mutinous.

Ricky shook his head. "No, sir. Not this last time. I mean, yeah, I tackled her first off because she was sitting on Julia. I didn't know— I mean, this time I was just trying to stop Julia. Honest!"

As explanations went, it was a little jumbled, but Trueblood seemed to get the point.

Amelia wasn't impressed. "Fat lot of good it did," she grumped, her gaze on the shattered window. "If it hadn't been for him—"

From the hall came the grating sound of the elevator at its crankiest, followed by a couple of loud clangs, an even louder *whump!* then silence. We all turned to look, even though there was absolutely nothing to see except the scuffed beige wall on the opposite side of the hallway.

Since I was expecting it, I was the only one who didn't jump when the elevator alarm started shrilling thirty seconds later.

And people ask me why I walk up all four flights of stairs.

"I hope that wasn't the officers you called," I said.

Trueblood looked grim. "Should I go—?"

I shook my head. "Don't bother. Mr. Yaguchi will handle it. He's had lots of practice." I turned my attention back to his unrepentant prisoner. "So, Julia—"

This time it was the heavy thump of footsteps on the stairs that interrupted me. A minute later, Gracie O'Mallon, red-faced and huffing from the climb, stomped into the office.

"That's Fred in the elevator," she informed Trueblood sourly. Her gaze narrowed, then slid from Ricky, to Julia, then me. She almost smiled when she saw my scrapes and bruises.

"I knew it. The minute we got the call, I knew it had to be you, Peterson."

I held up my hands in surrender. "Not me. Not this time, I swear."

"Yeah?" She eyed me with disfavor, then turned back to the detective. "I sure as hell hope you didn't want us to arrest anyone, Trueblood, because it's going to be hours before they get Fred out of that damned elevator!"

CHAPTER 32

Gracie was wrong. It only took an hour and fifty-six minutes to liberate Fred, who passed the time by settling onto the floor in one corner and taking a nap. The elevator shaft acted like an echo chamber so we could hear his snoring all the way from the fourth floor, even over the sounds of Mr. Yaguchi and Gracie down on second yelling at each other while the repair guys worked on the problem.

Trueblood used the time to call in another unit to take custody of Julia, who, to everyone's relief, refused to say another word. Ricky was allowed to slink away with no more than a warning. From the expression on his face, I figured his guilt and growing disillusionment would be punishment enough. I suspect Trueblood agreed, though he didn't say so.

As the sound of Ricky's footsteps on the stairs faded away, I shut my eyes and took a really, really deep breath and stretched my shoulders, trying to ease the tension that had been building ever since Trueblood stormed in.

Big mistake. First one, then another and another of the paperclips I'd rigged to hold my tattered blouse together gave way. The slight breeze coming through my shattered window brushed against my bare skin. My eyes flew open.

Trueblood was standing three feet in front of me, his attention glued to my chest.

"You checking out my injuries or my boobs?" I said, trying

to tug my ruined blouse together.

"Both," said Trueblood. "I have to admit, I hadn't taken you for the lacy black bra type."

"Hah!" said I, abandoning the fight to fasten a blouse that now had neither buttons nor paperclips. I settled for crossing it over my front then, with what dignity I could muster, firmly tucking the tails under my waistband.

I might have managed the dignity bit if one of the damn paperclips hadn't poked me somewhere to the right of my belly button.

With a hiss of frustration, I fished out the errant bit of wire, then redid the tug and tuck. To hell with dignity.

"Still shows your cleavage," Trueblood said helpfully.

"Enjoy it while you can," I sniffed, and pointedly turned away.

I think he said something like, "Believe me, I will," but it was under his breath so I can't absolutely swear to it.

Fortunately, Gracie interrupted us by bellowing up the stairs, "Hey, Trueblood! You wanna come help me? Fred turned off his radio, and we need him to wake up to punch a button or something."

Trueblood sighed and did as he was ordered.

The tension in my shoulders started to ease...until a beaming Amelia sauntered back in.

"What a circus! There's some guy down on third floor who's got somebody wanting to deliver some new furniture but they're refusing to carry it up the stairs and they don't want to wait so he's shouting at that Yaguchi, telling him he has to pay for the reschedule and the double delivery charges, and Yaguchi's yelling at him saying he isn't going to pay a dime and that cop lady's yelling at everyone in sight and—"

"And you're enjoying yourself," I said. It wasn't a question.

"Beats watching you sitting around here, getting nowhere," she sniffed.

Her gaze dropped to my blouse. I looked down and swore.

It was gaping. Again.

Amelia's lips curled in a sly smile. "If you've been walking around like that for the last ten minutes, I'll bet I'm not the only one who's been enjoying himself."

"The paperclips fell off "

"Oh, yeah?"

"Yeah," I said. "I'm quite sure Trueblood wasn't enjoying this any more than I am."

Besides, *enjoyed* might be going a little too far. *Appreciated*, maybe. I thought of that mumbled, "Believe me, I will" and had to repress a smile. *Appreciated* was good.

"Hah!" said Amelia with a knowing grin.

I ignored her. I was trying to decide if I should start cleaning up this latest disaster or just go home and finish off that six pack of Twisted Torment.

The six-pack was winning until I caught Amelia frowning at the pile of kindling wood and fabric that had been my guest chair, then the sodden desktop with its congealing coffee. There was a glitter to her eyes that set off my inner alarms.

"Glad I went to so much trouble to clean this place," she grumbled. Her attention swung to the window she'd broken. "Although I suppose..."

"That's all right! Really! I—"

Too late. She had her wand out, aimed, and fired before I could grab it.

I turned to see what additional havoc she'd wrought. And then I blinked.

Crystal clear new glass now filled the window frame where jagged shards had clung a moment earlier. She'd even remembered to clean up the bits on the sill and carpet.

"Oh!" I said, gaping. "Wow!"

She hadn't gotten it absolutely perfect—that sparkling clean pane didn't match the smudged and dusty panes that had survived the original assault—but I wasn't about to complain.

"Should I—?"

"No! No, that's fine. Really. Absolutely wonderful, in fact."

"You're sure? I—"

"I'm sure! Besides, Trueblood will notice if you go too far."

"Hah!" said Amelia, inspecting her handiwork with satisfaction. "You really think he's going to believe what he sees? If anything, he'll tell himself he was confused or something and that'll be it."

She had a point. Instead of arguing, I wandered down the hall to cadge a few safety pins off Wendy Rosenstein, instead.

The screaming and shouting hadn't gotten Wendy out of her lair, but Trueblood had. The minute she realized he was there, she'd started a regular pilgrimage to the ladies' room at my end of the hall, with frequent stops at my open office door to sweetly offer her assistance. Safety pins when Trueblood wasn't in tow evidently didn't rate because she grumbled the whole time she dug through her desk for them. I suspect she still blamed me for not getting arrested on schedule, though she didn't say so.

I returned to find Trueblood picking up the pieces of my shattered chair. I hesitated in the doorway. The man looked as good from the back as he did from the front. It took an effort of will not to stand there and enjoy the view.

Amelia had no such qualms. She was perched on my credenza, head appreciatively cocked to one side, grinning like a fool.

"You should have break-ins more often," she said. "I haven't enjoyed myself this much in ages."

"Glad we could entertain you," I said dryly.

Trueblood straightened, brows drawn together in annoyance. "You think this is entertaining?"

"No. Sorry. I wasn't talking to you."

Fortunately, there were footsteps in the hall just then, followed by the sound of an office door shutting. Those dark brows smoothed.

"Oh," he said.

I smiled. If Trueblood chose to think I'd been talking to

whoever it was, I wasn't going to set him straight.

"You don't have to worry about the chair," I said, crossing to take the splintered hunk of chair leg he held. "I'll clean it up. I'm getting used to it."

Then I took a closer look, and frowned. I'd swear there were a whole lot more pieces than there'd been before. I shot a look at Amelia. She shrugged.

"I tried to fix it, but it didn't...um...quite work. Sorry."

She didn't really look all that sorry, but there wasn't anything I could do, anyway. Fortunately, Trueblood hadn't noticed that there not only were more pieces than before, but that one of the chair's feet was now firmly cemented to the broken back. He had other things on his mind.

"You must have been here till all hours last night cleaning up," he said. "Julia really trashed the place."

"She says she didn't."

"And you believe her?"

I looked up into those pale, pale blue eyes fixed so intently on me, and immediately wished I hadn't. He was waaay too close. *I* was way too close. We seemed to be doing that a lot lately. It was going to have to stop.

I hastily bent to retrieve a piece of the chair arm. "I do. She came looking for something. She wouldn't have done that if she'd had any idea the place had been completely turned over yesterday."

"Mmm," he said noncommittally. He wasn't making any effort to put any distance between us. "You want help carrying that out?"

"Nah," I said, backing away. "Thanks. If the bin lid's open, I'll just pitch it all out the window."

I shouldn't have mentioned the window.

He laughed. "Makes it even easier if the window's already bro—" He stopped short, mouth agape, gaze fixed on a clean, unbroken pane of glass.

Amelia giggled.

"Yes?" I said helpfully when he didn't finish.

"Er... Nothing. Sorry. You...uh...you want me to open it? The window, I mean."

I beamed. "Please."

It was mean of me to enjoy his discomfiture, but being around him tended to rattle me. It was only fair that he got rattled occasionally, too.

He walked around the desk, gaze glued on that pane of glass as if he expected it to fall in pieces right in front of him. I tried not to snicker when he cautiously poked it. Amelia wasn't nearly so polite, but then, she wouldn't be.

"Want me to break it again?" she asked.

I shot her a warning look, then crossed to join Trueblood. Much more of that wide-eyed stare and I was going to have to slap him to snap him out of it.

"Is it sticking again?" I asked. "Let me show you—"

"No, no. No problem," he said hastily.

He flipped the old-fashioned latch and slid open the window, then, under the pretense of checking the bin four floors below, stuck his head out to take a closer look from the other side.

"Huh," I heard him mutter. "I could have sworn..." He pulled his head back in. "Want me to pitch that out for you?"

"No thanks. I've had plenty of practice. See?" I added, after both pieces landed where they were supposed to.

It was a little harder getting the seat and back through, especially with that odd bit of leg where it wasn't supposed to be, but with a little careful maneuvering and some totally useless suggestions from Amelia, I managed. I shut and re-latched the window, then turned to find Trueblood frowning at the blank wall opposite.

"Trueblood?"

"Mmm?" That dragged him back. "She could have done it, you know. Julia. She could have killed her father."

"You said you didn't believe it."

"I also said I didn't *not* believe it. It's called keeping an open mind." He transferred his frown to me. He was doing a lot of that lately. "I got the impression she knows about the boy."

"You mean, that Jameson wanted to adopt him?"

"So you found out about that, did you?" He didn't seem surprised.

"Julia told me."

"Did she say how she knew?"

"Her father left her alone in his office one day when he had his personal email account open. Seems he's got all his passwords written on his desk calendar, and she found them. Since he didn't email me, I'm guessing he mentioned me in one of the emails to Ruson, so she knew about me even before her daddy was killed."

"That works."

"Yeah, but it doesn't prove anything."

"No."

"Talk, talk, talk," griped Amelia, hopping off my credenza. "You two are positively boring. Why don't you make him take you out to lunch?"

I ignored her. "So, Julia knew about me. Ruson knew about me. I can't think of anyone else who would have known about me. So how did whoever it was end up here? Were they following Jameson? And why did he come early? He—"

I stopped, trying to remember.

"He...what?" said Trueblood.

"He got confused," I said. "That's all."

"This thing about the boy was pretty important to him. Why would he make a mistake like that?"

"Because that's the sort of thing he did," I said, relieved the explanation could be that simple. "Sharon Demetrios told me. She said Jameson couldn't keep his own schedule straight without the help of his secretary. And he doesn't seem to have told his secretary about any of this."

"Sheesh!" said Amelia, distracting me. I shot her a warning

look. She stuck out her tongue.

"Maybe," said Trueblood. He stuck out his lower lip, mulling possibilities. Yet another distraction. It was a nice lower lip. "So if he…"

His words trailed off, whatever he'd meant to say forgotten. His mouth curved into a smile and his eyes brightened.

"I know! Why don't I take you to lunch?"

"Wha…?" I jerked around to find Amelia, arms crossed over her chest, a smug smile on her face. Her smile widened as she wiggled her index finger at me.

"Sure! Lunch, maybe a glass of wine to go with it?" said Trueblood, suddenly enthusiastic. "I know this great little Italian place—"

"*No!*" I almost shouted. "No lunch. Thanks," I added, a bit more calmly.

If I could kill Amelia, I would. Trueblood couldn't charge me with murder if he couldn't even see the victim, right? Talk about the perfect crime.

"No?" He looked like a puppy that had just been kicked, hurt and betrayed, all at the same time. "How about Mexican and a beer? We could—"

"No. Thanks. Really," I said.

"What?" Amelia squawked.

"Pizza?" Trueblood said plaintively.

"No. No pizza." I took his arm and turned him so he was pointing at the door. "I'm busy. You're busy. You need to get back to the office."

"I do?" said Trueblood.

"No, he doesn't!" said Amelia.

"Yes, you do," I said firmly, giving him a shove.

"What am I going to do in the office?"

"Investigate stuff," I said.

Even dazed and bewitched, the man was hard to move. I planted both hands on his back and shoved harder, then wished I hadn't. Under that suit jacket was a really *solid* back. He definitely worked out. Plus I could feel the edge of the harness for his shoulder holster. Guns make me nervous.

"Bye," I said firmly, and shoved him out the door.

He turned, mouth open to protest.

I shut the door in his face, then turned to find my fairy godmother glaring bullets at me.

"Well! Of all the ungrateful, unappreciative— I *never!*" said Amelia, and vanished with a pop.

CHAPTER 33

My office seemed bigger without the two of them in it. I leaned back against the closed door for a moment, eyes closed, drinking in the silence, then reluctantly went to deal with the mess on my desk.

The spilled coffee had missed my laptop but soaked both the panini and my phone, which was deader than a doornail. I ought to clean up the mess, but the damage was done. It wouldn't get any worse. Right now I was hungry, frustrated, and the worries that had been dogging me ever since I'd found Jameson dead on my office floor were seeping back.

Figuring out why Jameson had been early was good, but it still didn't explain who had murdered him, or why they'd met him here.

I decided to ignore the temptation of that unfinished six pack in my fridge in favor of a beer and nachos at Wild Bill's. Maybe a few carbs with the alcohol would get the little gray cells working again. If I went home now, I'd never get moving again.

The safety pins down the front of my blouse got a raised eyebrow and a smirk from Bill when I placed my order, but the waitress who'd served Trueblood and me the other day had a different take. She took one look at my bruised and battered face and my ripped blouse, and set my order down with a thunk.

"You should call the cops on the bastard," she said, hands fisted on her hips, a pugnacious set to her jaw.

I glanced down at the pins. From that angle, I could see the scratches Julia had left, but I didn't think anyone else could.

"Believe it or not," I said, "the face is thanks to a concrete sidewalk and a ninety-year-old lady with a rolling pin. The blouse was a thirteen-year-old girl with a temper and a really foul mouth who thinks I murdered her father."

"You shitting me?"

"Nope."

She shook her head in awed disbelief. "And I thought I'd heard everything."

"Cheers!" I said, lifting the beer. "My name's Maxie, by the way."

"Linda." She gestured at the beer. "You finish that, I'll bring over another one. On the house. Looks to me like you could use it."

Forget the lousy wine. The beer was cold, the nachos some of the best this side of the Mississippi. Wild Bill's might be a dive, but they had the essentials down pat.

I slowly worked my way through both, trying to force some sense into the tangle my life had become.

For starters, who trashed my office yesterday? The "why" of it was the same as for Julia today—whoever it was wanted to know what Jameson had been up to and thought there'd be something in my files that would tell them.

Whoever it was, they hadn't needed to know I existed before they killed him. They could have been following Jameson and simply taken advantage of finding him alone in a place they had no connection to. Only later, when the media reported he'd hired me, would they have realized that I might have something they needed. Or needed to destroy.

As with all high-profile news stories, the coverage of Jameson's murder had ranged from the dryly factual (and still occasionally inaccurate) to the luridly speculative (with only limited connection to reality). All of them had reported that I didn't know why Jameson had hired me. Even if the murderer believed those reports, they might still suspect I had something important even if I didn't realize it.

And if that convoluted line of reasoning wasn't enough to give me a headache, there was the additional possibility that whoever had ransacked my office had been searching for information that had nothing whatsoever to do with Jameson's murder. Not that I was going to waste time worrying about that particular possibility. That way lay madness. With two angry ex-wives and one bitter, greedy almost-ex wife, two former lovers, one hot-tempered, gun-toting kid, a dozen hostile board members, numerous outraged investors, and uncountable angry individuals who considered themselves victims of JM Industries' operations, I had way more suspects than I could manage as it was.

And that was just for starters. What had Julia said about emails to his girlfriends? I hadn't heard about any recent additions to Jameson's long list of conquests, but that didn't mean they didn't exist, or that they wouldn't have a grudge against him if they did.

Added up, that was a lot of speculation with not much of anything concrete to bring it all together.

I stared glumly into the now-warm dregs of my second beer, considering.

What, after all, did I know for sure?

I knew Jameson had hired a new lawyer to handle the adoption of the boy he believed was his son, even though the boy's mother wasn't willing to swear Jameson was the father. A mother who, despite her limited resources, had hired a lawyer to defend against it. I definitely needed to talk to Ruson, so add that to my list of Things To Do.

I knew that Julia was aware of her father's plans for adopting the boy and had bitterly resented them. I knew she insisted Jameson had loved her, though I wasn't convinced she honestly, deep down, believed it. I also knew she didn't hesitate to resort to violence when it suited her.

I knew Julia's mother, Katie Carmody, had used her daughter as leverage with Jameson, and had somehow convinced herself, without any foundation so far as I could tell, that Julia would be Jameson's heir. Katie's temper and sense of entitlement seemed as oversized as her daughter's, but at least she hadn't resorted to guns and physical violence. That I knew of, anyway.

Mama number two, Angelina Mestes, was busy cavorting with Russian millionaires in London, so she was clear of the murder and the raid on my office. Probably. Since Angelina's daughter was barely four years old, I was pretty sure she could be counted out, too.

I knew that Leslie Postin represented a large segment of stockholders who were seriously unhappy with Jameson's new, and far more costly, direction on corporate responsibility and were trying to do something about it, though how they hoped to accomplish anything when Jameson—or, now, his heirs—held more than half the outstanding stock was more than I could figure. I couldn't see Postin resorting to physical violence, but that didn't mean some of his followers wouldn't.

Sorting through all those possibilities was way beyond my capacity, however, so set that aside for later consideration.

Ditto the angry board members, all of whom would be shareholders, as well. Given the reaction of the emotional Miss Sanders, I probably wouldn't be getting past any other front desk in a JM Industries office. At least, not without Amelia wreaking unimaginable havoc on my behalf, which didn't even bear thinking about.

And then there were the wives. Number one, Annalise, would have happily cheered on anyone with a murderous bent, but she wouldn't have dirtied the soles of her Jimmy Choos by setting foot anywhere near a high class neighborhood like mine.

Shannon Montgomery, wife number two, had been in Florida when Jameson was killed and, so far as I knew, still was. That let her off the hook unless I learned something to the contrary.

Which left Christine, wife number three and, until the revelation of Jameson's new will, principle heir to Jameson Montgomery's considerable fortune. A fortune that had been about to slip out of her hands until someone conveniently stuck my letter opener into her soon-to-be-ex husband's heart. Plus, thanks to Amelia, I knew Christine had married Jameson for his money even though she'd long had a hot thing going with Jameson's attorney, Geoffrey Dawson. Christine was mercenary and unprincipled and had the best motive, but she didn't strike me as a murderer.

As for old Geoffrey, I'd gotten the impression he hadn't much liked Jameson, despite what had evidently been a long-standing and, to Dawson, highly lucrative business relationship. But I couldn't see the lawyer murdering anyone, either. He wouldn't have found that nearly as satisfying as publicly ripping them to shreds in the courts.

All of which left me with more suspects than I could count and not one scrap of hard evidence against any of them.

The headache Julia had given me earlier was back with a vengeance, and I still had to clean up the spilled coffee that had been solidifying on my desk and in my phone.

Thinking of the phone cheered me up a little. At least I no longer had to worry about harassing calls from Jancie or mom or anyone else I didn't want to talk to. It wasn't much, but sometimes a girl's gotta settle for whatever she can get.

THE SENSIBLE THING was to go home, take a shower, and go to bed. Instead, I walked over to the Bargain Basement clothing store on Barclay to see what they had in the way of blouses. If I was going to track down Ruson, I needed a new one.

You've heard of those snazzy discount stores where they sell last month's designer styles at reduced prices? Bargain Basement isn't that kind of place.

BB's, as it's fondly known in the neighborhood, is located—surprise!—in the basement of a decrepit brick building that should have been demolished sometime early in the last century. It's owned by a little old Polish lady who goes by the name of Rosie because her real name has more consonants than the alphabet has letters and no one except another Pole can pronounce it.

Rosie's got connections to every illegal sweatshop and down-market clothing manufacturer in the state and, for five cents on the dollar, stocks her store with whatever they can't sell. It only requires one look at the merchandise to know why it didn't sell, but she still manages to turn a profit because there are a lot of people around here for whom a really good month means merely struggling to make ends meet instead of watching those same ends slide completely out of reach. For those folks, cheap wins, every time.

And sometimes, like now, you just need a shirt, style be damned.

As usual, Rosie was perched on a tall stool at the front of the store as I strolled in. She took one look at my blouse, said, "Aisle seven," then went back to keeping an eye on an elderly woman with a walker who was checking out a rack of glittery things that were probably meant to be party dresses.

I wasn't sure if it was the bulging bag hung on the front of the walker, the old lady's odd choice of merchandise, or the fact there didn't seem to be any other customers to watch that had drawn Rosie's attention, and didn't really care. If Rosie could handle a six-foot-two, coked up druggie with the hots for a knock-off Walking Dead T-shirt, she could handle a geriatric shoplifter with really bad taste.

In case you haven't guessed, the problem at BB's isn't finding something, it's finding something you'd be marginally willing to be caught dead in.

I found three black blouses in aisle seven that were roughly my size, but I'd seen hookers trolling for business in clothes that weren't that see-through. A white blouse gave me a moment of hope until I pulled it out and discovered someone had sewn red sequin nipples with gold tassels where front pockets usually go.

In the end, I settled for something in an odd purply-brown color that was not skin-tight, not see-through, not nipple-embroidered, and had buttons and button holes that not only mostly matched up, but buttoned high enough to cover Julia's scratch marks. The price was right—two bucks fifty plus tax—and since it only needed to get me through a few more hours until I could honestly justify giving up and going home, I pulled it off the hanger and headed to the front.

The old lady had finished her shopping and was there before me. She let go her death grip on the walker, shook out the multi-colored tangle of satin and sequins and beads draped over the front of it, then carefully spread the outfit—what little there was of it—out on the counter.

Even Rosie, who'd sell sequined G-strings to an undertaker, seemed a little taken aback. "You gonna *wear* that thing?"

The old lady tittered. "Me? Oh, goodness, no. It's for my granddaughter."

Out of curiosity, I craned forward to get a better look. Anyone who wore that thing would have all the essential bits covered, but only just.

It took me a minute to realize I'd seen that sort of design before. It was a Katie Carmody, or, rather, since this was BB's, the sort of thing Katie did. She must be more successful than I'd realized if they were already making knock-offs of her designs.

"Not much of it, is there?" said the old lady with another titter. "But my little girl, Anita—her name's Anita and she's pretty as they come!—she showed me a fancy magazine with pictures of stuff just like this. I thought I'd have a heart attack when I saw the prices! My gracious, nothing but little scraps and bits and they cost way more than my Walter and I get in a month, what with his pension doing so poor and Social Security not giving us anything like a raise, you know?"

"That's—," said Rosie.

The old lady wasn't stopping, not even for Rosie. She probably didn't get out much and was determined to make the most of her audience while she had one.

"So I told Anita, I said, dear, your granddaddy and I just can't afford that, you know? And she's such a good girl, she just said she understood but she wanted to show me anyway, and wasn't that sweet of her?"

"That's—" Rosie tried again.

"But then I saw this. I just wanted a new shirt for my Walter, really, that's what I came in for, but I saw this and I thought I'd fall through the floor when I saw the price. So I decided Walter could just wait till next month, you know? Anita's going to be so happy. I can't wait to show her!"

"That girl's gonna be even happier when you tell her that's the real deal, then," Rosie said when the old lady paused to catch her breath. "O-rij-in-al. Guaranteed."

The old lady's eyes got big as saucers. "No!"

"S'truth. Told me they couldn't even give them things away," said Rosie. "I got a couple dozen, you want more. Figured around here, there might be more of a market."

I managed to turn my laugh into a cough, but only barely. There were plenty of working women around here who'd find that kind of thing useful in their business, but for the old lady's sake, I hoped her granddaughter wasn't one of them.

Ten minutes later—most of which were spent waiting for the proud grandma to fish the money for her purchase out of her bag, then bustle out of the store at a clip slightly slower than a crippled snail's—I had a new blouse.

Rosie reluctantly let me change into it once I'd paid, but she refused to let me dump the torn one in her trash. I didn't argue, just walked around to the alley behind the building and shoved it in the first bin I came to, then set off for my next stop.

CHAPTER 34

My two fifty plus tax had not only bought me a really ugly blouse that gapped embarrassingly, even when buttoned (I'd salvaged Wendy's safety pins before dumping the old blouse, which helped a little), it had given me an unexpected lead.

I headed around to Garr Analytics and, to my relief, found Douglas still there.

Douglas took one look at my new wardrobe and closed his eyes in pain. "Puce? You had to buy *puce?*"

I frowned at the odd purply-brown color that was so unlike my normal black. "I thought puce was green."

He opened one eye and groaned. "And *safety pins? Really?*"

"*Pin.* As in, one. Not pins. And you can't even really see it. Not much, anyway. You should have seen me an hour ago."

"Thank God for small favors. ' He reluctantly reopened both eyes. "Why are you here?"

"I need your help."

"Maxie, even *Dior* couldn't help you with that... that *obscenity.* Why you *ever—*"

"Forget the blouse. I'm talking about research. You and Lucille. I need some information."

That got his attention. "What kind of information?"

I told him.

He smiled, called for backup, and led the way to Lucille's office.

LUCILLE HIT THE STYLE AND FASHION PAGES, Douglas hit the business sites. While they were furiously clicking away, I paced, unable to sit still. I already knew what they would find, but I needed to be absolutely sure. Not that it would prove anything except I had yet one more possible motive for Jameson's murder, but it still *felt* like I was making progress. Sometimes, you just gotta go with your feelings.

And speaking of feelings: my new shirt was beginning to itch. I should have gotten the one with tassels. At least I'd have had something to entertain myself with while I waited.

"Looks like Rosie was on to something," Douglas said at last with satisfaction, pushing away from Lucille's work table.

Lucille didn't look nearly as cheerful. "I'm so sorry, dear. I really should have dug deeper that first time you asked. I had no idea! Really!"

"What'd you find?"

"You were right," said Douglas. "Katie Carmody's clothing launch was a bust."

"Totally," Lucille said, unconsciously echoing some of Gareth's staff, a few of whom weren't old enough to vote.

"She got a lot of advance coverage because of her name," Douglas continued, "and I guess some of the early, more adventurous shoppers and reviewers gave her a bit of a boost. But it didn't last."

Lucille shook her head mournfully. "I should have caught it, Maxie. I'm so sorry. It was there, just...not at the top of the searches."

"It's okay, Lucille. Really." I couldn't keep from grinning. "I hit you with a lot and didn't give you much time for anything. Without you, I wouldn't have known where to start, let alone gotten this far. So what's the bottom line?" I added. "For Katie, I mean."

"Huh!" said Douglas. "That line's so low it's almost out of

sight. She didn't get picked up by any but a few custom boutiques. I'd guess she didn't even cover her expenses. Forget funding for a second round. What you saw is all you got. Looks like her lawyer, that Larson fellow you mentioned, was in it for a bundle, too."

My ears perked. "Really? Now *that's* interesting."

"Yeah. In fact, Larson may have been her main backer. Well, and Jameson, I guess, since I imagine she siphoned off a few bucks from her daughter's support money to do it. She might even have talked him into investing, though I didn't find anything to confirm that."

"And now you can get her dresses at BB's," said Lucille sadly. "After only one season, too That's so sad!"

Lucille relishes scandal and disaster, but only when it's not attached to someone she might know. Even if she only knows them second- or third-hand.

I gave them each a hug, then took myself off. I still had Ruson to track down tonight, if I could, but there was something I wanted to do first.

The failure of Katie's high fashion venture wasn't proof of anything, certainly not anything involving Jameson's murder, but it was *something*, and it was a whole lot more than I'd had earlier when her daughter had cussed and scratched and ripped my blouse to shreds.

It was a *motive*, and I purely love a good motive.

Even more convenient, it was the same motive as the current Mrs. Montgomery's: money.

Whenever the two of them had looked at Jameson, they'd both seen dollar signs and lots of them. That first visit, when Katie and I had bonded over coffee and her teary-eyed grief, it hadn't been hard to figure out her priorities.

Plus Katie had had a career until Jameson came along and knocked her up. She might have enjoyed the past thirteen years of living high without having to work for it—especially since she'd bundled Julia off to nannies and boarding school, right from the start—but that didn't mean she hadn't missed the glamorous life of a high fashion model, complete with apartment in Paris. Or at least told herself she had.

Her failure to become the glitter world's substitute for Dior had to rankle, and Katie didn't strike me as the type to blame herself if there was someone else she could pin it on.

What if, when that first venture into fashion design went south, she'd asked Jameson for more money and he'd refused? I could easily imagine her trying to convince him she just needed a little more time and a lot more cash. Just one more season. Really.

But Jameson, for all his failings, hadn't been a fool. He couldn't do much about Katie using his support payments for Julia to fund her own luxurious lifestyle, but he didn't owe her a dime of support for anything else. Even if he had invested money in her new line, when the line fizzled he wouldn't have thrown good money after bad by funding a second season.

Besides, I was pretty sure he'd no longer cared about Katie or Julia, if he ever had. Things had changed. He had a son who was going to get everything. He'd already paid for the daughters, who wouldn't carry the family name and so could be conveniently forgotten. Why would he care if Katie's big dream was a bust?

But Katie cared. What had her daughter said? That Jameson had blocked her mother's emails on his private account? He wouldn't have had any reason to do that if she only contacted him when it involved their daughter or the support payments or something like that. But he might have done it if Katie had become insistent, hounding him, demanding money.

Depending on what email system he used, there'd be no way for the police or anyone else to see all those blocked emails. All they'd know—all Julia had known—was that Jameson had set his system to not accept an email from her mother, his ex-lover.

Katie could easily have been following him, looking for an opportunity to argue with him, convince him to change his mind.

They'd talked, he'd refused again, she'd gotten angry, lashed out. Heck, maybe she'd even been fiddling with my letter opener like she had that coffee spoon in her kitchen, and then it just sort of ended up in his chest when she lost her temper.

Forget the angle the thing went in. Hadn't Trueblood said they'd identified a number of ways it could have gone down? So Katie could have done it.

Julia was a lot easier to blame for the knife—right height, same temper—but she'd come after me with a rifle. Had she really thought I'd killed her father? Or had she just figured it was a good way to cover her own guilt?

But why draw attention to herself like that if she really had killed him? Until she'd starting shooting up my apartment parking lot, nobody except Ricky had paid her any attention, not even her own mother.

Plus, Julia had to either steal her mother's car to get around or talk Ricky into driving her, and I couldn't see the boy as get away driver on a murder. Not even for Julia. Katie, however, was all grown up with her own transportation, right at hand. She didn't need any help in following Jameson around.

Speculation, every bit of it. But an interesting line of questions to work with…provided you were in a position to ask the questions.

My chances of getting through Katie Carmody's front door again rated in the slim-to-none range. Trueblood, however, didn't have the same handicap.

Unless things had moved a whole lot faster than they usually did, Julia would still be in police custody and her mother would still be trying to bail her out. It would make a nice cap to the day if Trueblood could use this information while the two of them were still on his turf. Questioning suspects is so much easier if you don't have to track them down first.

At the thought of seeing Trueblood, I tugged at my shirt tails, then froze.

He'd liked the lacy black bra, as well he should, but I didn't think this purple thing—puce? I mean, Douglas would know, if anybody did, but...*puce?*—was going to enhance my reputation.

Not that it mattered or I cared. Nuh huh. Nope. Not a bit. Did not care one least little bit.

Still, I tugged at the front of the shirt, trying to get it to lie right, then stopped in the middle of the sidewalk to shift the safety pin to the inside, out of sight.

"Ditch the pin, honey," suggested a passerby sporting sideburns and a suit that probably fit him ten years and twenty pounds ago. "And the buttons," he added helpfully, slowing down for a better look.

I ignored him, clipped the pin closed, then tucked in my shirt tail.

I mean, seriously? Who's going to take fashion advice from a guy with sideburns?

EVEN THOUGH the subway would be faster, I decided to take my car so I could look for Ruson afterward. I didn't think I'd be looking very hard—I was tired and the shirt was really beginning to bug me. Go too long and I'd have a rash to rival Larry the Lobster. Besides, if Katie really was the killer, and Trueblood nabbed her, I wouldn't have to bother with Ruson at all.

Since my car was parked on the street near my office, I figured I'd reclaim my coffee and cream-soaked phone, as well. If I couldn't resuscitate it with the old trick of rinsing it under the tap then burying it in uncooked rice until the rice had absorbed all the water, I'd have to drop by the phone store tomorrow and investigate options. I didn't object to my mother being unable to reach me, but the prospect of not being able to call for pizza was terrifying.

It was long past beer thirty, as Jimmy liked to say, so the lobby was quiet, the doors to the offices on either side firmly shut. Opposite the stairs, a hand-scrawled "Out of Order" sign was plastered over elevator doors criss-crossed with caution tape.

Ditto the doors on the second and third floors. The situation had to be pretty dire if Mr. Yaguchi was publicly admitting the thing wasn't working. I hoped he wasn't blaming Fred.

Since they'd fished Fred out at the third floor, Mr. Yaguchi hadn't made it to the fourth floor with his signs and tape. He and the elevator guys hate stairs so they generally never go any higher than they have to. You ought to hear them cussing when the thing gets stuck on six.

The red emergency exit light for the fire stairs door was on again. The two overhead lights between the stairs and my door had burned out, however, so you couldn't count it as a win. The place was silent and, thanks to the burned out lights, shadowy and grim. Wes Craven might have done something with it, but around here, everyone was too used to the vagaries of the old building to worry about it.

That and the fact I was digging for an itchy spot on my left shoulder blade I couldn't quite reach probably explains why I was two feet from my office door before I noticed the line of light seeping out at the bottom edge.

I froze for an instant—just long enough to make sure there were no obvious sounds coming from the room—then strolled on past, heart racing, making no effort to muffle my steps. Whoever was in my office couldn't have missed hearing *someone* coming up the stairs, but they had no way of knowing it was me unless I walked in on them, they opened the door to check, or I drew their attention by turning around and running like hell down the stairs. That last would definitely tip them off.

I'm not stupid enough to walk in, alone and unarmed, on someone who might have already killed a man, but I didn't like the idea of running away before I'd learned who they were. Not to mention, I didn't really want a possible murderer hotfooting down those stairs after me.

Besides, I'd look a right fool if I finally found a phone and called the cops, only to discover I'd forgotten to turn off the lights before I left. It wasn't likely—electric isn't part of our already extortionate rent so I'm generally pretty careful—but it wasn't impossible.

There was, however, another way—lull whoever it was into thinking I was another tenant by wandering on down the hall, then sneak back and listen at the door so I could figure out who it was and what they wanted.

Then I could quietly tip-toe down the stairs, find a phone, and call the cops.

I couldn't see lights under any other doors, but that didn't mean no one else was around. Wendy would be gone by now, but Bill sometimes worked late. If he was in his office, the light wouldn't necessarily reach to the front door. Ditto anyone else whose offices consisted of more than one room.

Even if someone else was around, there was no guarantee they'd be any help. Unlike my apartment building, most of the folks here weren't likely to call the cops unless they were the ones being shot at. If then. A few were more likely to just shoot back.

I stopped by the emergency exit. I'd already had my keys out, ready to open my door, so I made scrabbling sounds against the stairwell door, as if I were fumbling with a lock, then shoved the door open—thank heavens Trueblood had loosened it up the other day—waited a second, then let it shut. It didn't sound quite the same as a regular office door, but it was the best I could manage.

The silence in the hall after it closed was deafeningly loud. If there was anyone else in any office on this floor, they were keeping awfully quiet.

Next step: creep back to my door and start investigating for all I was worth.

I remained right where I was.

"*Move!*" I told my feet.

"*Like hell!*" my feet said, adamantly refusing to budge.

Great. My heart was pounding so hard I couldn't hear myself think. My stomach was threatening to bring up whatever I'd had for lunch—assuming I'd had lunch, which I couldn't for the life of me remember right then—and now the rest of me was in revolt, too.

I'd just flunked the nerves-of-steel qualification for private investigators. If anybody found out about this, my professional reputation was toast.

What little was left of it, anyway.

For the first time in my life, I wished I'd listened to my mother and at least carried a little snub-nosed revolver or something. If Maxie Peterson Investigations survived all this, I was definitely getting a gun that would fit in my purse.

That appalling thought—the listening to my mother part, not the snub nose in a purse part—was finally enough to get me moving.

And thinking of my purse...

I unzipped it and reached in, searching for my knife. It wasn't in the pocket where I always kept it.

I frowned, then rummaged around. Still nothing. Shit. When I'd retrieved it from the crime scene team, I hadn't bothered to check that everything had been put back where it was supposed to be, including the knife. Now was not the time to start looking, either. Especially since the emergency sign didn't provide nearly enough light for the job.

Okay, so no knife. That didn't mean I didn't have any weapons.

I rezipped the bag, cautiously slipped it off my shoulder, then folded the strap into my left hand like a handle. It wasn't a big purse, as such things go, but it was solidly packed. You'd be surprised what three or four pounds of purse can accomplish when it's held firmly, then swung into someone's face with as much force as you can muster. Helps even more if it's got large decorative buckles like mine.

Satisfied with the heft of it, and that I could release it if I had to without getting the strap tangled around my wrist, I turned my attention to an even more potent weapon.

Without letting go of the purse, I used the thumb and forefinger of my left hand to adjust the keyring in my right hand so the three longest, sharpest keys stuck out from between my fingers. I settled the ring and remaining keys flat into my palm, then curled my fingers and thumb into a fist around them. Brass knuckles it wasn't, but I could do a lot of damage to someone's face and eyes if I had to. Other parts, too, if that was all I could reach.

I waited, straining to catch any sounds from the direction of my office. Nothing. No one switched off the light and no shadow moved across that slim yellow bar at the bottom of the door.

Maybe I really had forgotten to flip the damn switch off when I left.

Keeping close to the wall to avoid the creaky boards in the center, but not so close I couldn't swing my right hand if I had to, I crept toward my office, testing each step before taking the next. As my eyes adjusted to the gloom, that bar of light seemed to get brighter and brighter the closer I got.

Still no sound or movement.

I was two feet from the door when I heard the soft creak of a floorboard and a shadow broke that yellow bar of light.

I had my makeshift weapons up, ready to defend myself if I had to, when the door opened and Katie Carmody cautiously poked her head out and looked right at me.

She had a gun in her hand, and she held it like she knew how to use it.

I decked her with my purse.

CHAPTER 35

Katie's head snapped back. She grunted, dropped the gun, slammed into the half-open door, then toppled backward as the door swung away.

"Ooof!"

I hopped over her feet and into the room, keys up, purse back enough I could get a solid swing if I had to. No one else was there. With my foot, I nudged the gun out of Katie's reach, then turned my attention back to her.

She writhed on the floor, her hands cupped over her mouth and nose. Blood was beginning to trickle over her fingers.

I'd mashed her nose, maybe flat out broken it. Whichever, she wasn't going to be doing any cover model shoots for a while.

"My doze!" she moaned. "You bwoke my doze!"

I lowered my hands, but kept out of range of her feet, just in case.

"Get up."

"Can'd! My doze!" The moan had turned to a wail. Tears were joining the blood. If she wasn't careful, that nice, expensive blouse she was wearing was never going to be the same.

"Fine." I turned, preparing to yell for help at the top of my lungs.

Don Larson was standing in the doorway, mouth open, eyes wide as saucers.

"What the hell's going on?"

I drew a steadying breath. He didn't look like a man who'd come prepared to commit a crime, but that didn't mean he was on my side.

"I'm not sure. You might want to ask your client. She's the one who broke into my office," I said, indicating Katie, still writhing on the floor.

"She bwoke my doze!" Katie wailed.

Judging by the blood now gushing from between her fingers, I really might have. Another few minutes and that blouse was going to be past any hope of salvation.

I couldn't dredge up any sympathy.

"Katie?" said Larson, bewildered. "What are you doing here?"

"She was searching my office," I said. "What are *you* doing here?"

"Me?" He looked at me blankly.

I hoped his clients didn't rely on him to be a quick-witted Perry Mason type, because they were doomed to disappointment.

"You," I said. Katie was too busy wailing to get much sense out of her just yet.

"I— We were supposed to meet at the station, bail Julia out," he said at last. "But I spotted Katie going the other way so I followed, thinking maybe she had Julia..."

"She didn't call you?"

He shook his head. His gaze was once more fixed on his client. "Didn't return my calls, either. And then she came in this building. I knew your office was here, but I had a hard time finding a place to park, and..." The words trailed off. He shook his head again, slowly, as if that might jar the little gray cells into action. Didn't look like it was working.

"My *doze!*"

I glanced down, then hopped out of the way just as Katie squirmed around to kick at my ankles.

"Feeling better, are we?" I tossed my purse and keys on the desk, then bent to drag her to her feet. "Come on. Up you get.

Cut that out!"

"Bidjz!"

"Did you just call me a bitch?"

I thought she might swing on me, but she kept her hands clamped over her nose, and that threw her off balance. Just as well. Those four-inch heels she was wearing could do real damage to my instep if she got her weight behind them.

I dragged her over to the sofa and shoved her down. Hard.

She squealed.

I didn't apologize. I really wasn't in the mood.

I didn't have any handcuffs, but the sag in that sofa would keep her pinned. No way she could climb out fast enough to get to me before I clobbered her. Although I was sort of hoping she'd try.

"Right," I said, stepping back to admire my handiwork.

"Is this a *gun?"*

I froze, then slowly pivoted to find Larson holding Katie's gun. And he was pointing it at me.

I don't know a lot about guns, but I did know that thing was more than adequate to put a nice hole in my chest, especially at this distance.

"That's right," I said. My mouth had suddenly gone dry. "It's your girl friend's gun, to be precise."

"Katie's? Katie has a gun?"

Man, if he was this sharp in a court room, it was a wonder he had any clients at all. Even the ones that were innocent wouldn't have stood a chance. They'd have been convicted of hiring an idiot, if nothing else.

He swung the muzzle toward Katie.

I don't think he realized what he was doing—the way he was holding that thing, it was clear he wasn't familiar with handguns—but that only made him more dangerous, not less. You can be killed just as dead by a fool as by a villain.

"You want to put that thing down?" I said. He wasn't listening to me.

"Katie? Why did you have a gun?"

Katie whimpered, playing the fragile-female-needing-protection shtick for all she was worth. Over her blood-stained hands, her eyes were wide and tear-filled and beautiful.

"Oh, baby," said Larson soulfully. He crossed to sit beside her, arms outstretched as if to comfort her. Then he got a better look at her hands, glanced down at his suit, and settled for patting her on the shoulder, instead. "There, there."

I couldn't help rolling my eyes. The two deserved each other.

He rested the gun on his lap, though he didn't let go of it. I couldn't tell if Katie had noticed it or not.

"How about if I take that thing?" I said casually, edging closer.

They both ignored me.

"I thought you were going to meet me at the station?" Larson said. "Why did you come here, instead?"

Katie just looked tearful and abused. Larson fell for it.

"It's okay if you don't want to talk about it right now," he said.

"Want some tissues for your nose?" I asked. If I had an excuse to get close enough, maybe I could get Larson's attention long enough to get him to give me the gun.

He shot me a distracted look. She just kept on looking pitiful.

"The blood's going to ruin that beautiful blouse if you don't do something." Helpful, that's me. "Be a shame, gorgeous blouse like that."

"My gall gors," said Katie.

It took me a minute to figure out she'd said Michael Kors. Her nose was busted, she was going down for breaking and entering, at the very least, her boyfriend had her gun, and she was boasting about the designer?

Then she made the mistake of looking down at the front of her blouse. She jumped to her feet—she had to be in pretty good shape to manage an exit from that sofa that fast—and started shrieking and desperately brushing at the front of her blouse, flicking blood everywhere.

"My bwouz! Oh, dod, my bwouz!"

"Oh, for—!" Larson was on his feet, swiping at the red drops that had landed on him.

I wouldn't have worried if he hadn't been doing it with the hand holding the gun.

While they were pleasantly occupied, I scuttled over to the desk. I didn't give a damn about the tissues, but I did want my other knife, the not-quite-a-switch blade knife I'd used to slice up my panini before Julia interrupted me. I figured they would notice if I dug for the one that might not be in my purse after all.

It was right where I'd left it. While I fished in the file drawer where I'd spotted the packet of tissues (they normally had a home in the junk drawer, bottom left), I kept my right hand out of sight and flicked the knife open and closed a couple of times, working out any sticky residue left by the coffee and cream.

Satisfied, I flicked it close, then cupped it, hidden, in the palm of my right hand, and returned to my unwelcome guests.

"Here you go," I said cheerfully, extending Katie the packet with my left hand. "Just screw them up and shove one or two up each nostril. That should do it."

"Nrrgh!" Katie bleated, but she stopped pawing at her blouse long enough to take the things. At least she wasn't wailing.

"Be even better if you lie back on the sofa and tilt your head back, maybe pinch your no—"

"Arrrrhhhhhh!"

"Can I have a couple of those?"

Larson had his hand out. From the expression on his face, he was about to snatch the tissues right out of Katie's hands. He must really like that suit.

He was no longer holding the gun. It took a moment to spot the bulge in his side jacket pocket where he'd stuck it. I couldn't tell if Katie had noticed. Probably not. She seemed totally preoccupied by the destruction of her Michael Kors blouse. I relaxed slightly.

"Sorry," I said. "That was my only packet. Don't worry, though. Except for that spot on your collar, it doesn't even show."

He tucked in his chin and tried to look down his nose at his collar.

I sighed.

He grabbed the almost empty packet out of Katie's hands, dragged one out, then stuffed the remainder in the pocket with the gun. I don't think he even remembered the thing was there.

I thought about just reaching over and snatching it out of his pocket, but he was dancing around too much, trying to get at the tiny drips of blood on his clothes

Rather than do as I'd suggested, Katie had settled for holding a wad of rapidly reddening tissues under her nose, which gave me my first good view of the damage I'd done. Yup, definitely broken. By tomorrow, no amount of makeup would cover the bruising. I thought I could see scrapes left by the decorative buckles, too. I always liked that purse.

For the first time since I'd clobbered her, I was the center of her attention.

"Wheh is id?"

I blinked. "Where is what?"

"My bway zlud," said Katie.

I had to think about that one for a minute.

"What bracelet?"

"Mie!"

Hers. Wow. That was helpful.

"I don't know about any bracelet."

"*Mie* bway zlud. Jamezur gave id do me."

I had a sudden vision of her nervously rubbing her bare wrist that first time I'd visited her.

"When did you lose it?" I said as the bottom of my stomach seemed to drop away. I was pretty sure I knew the answer, and I didn't like it.

309

She eyed me balefully over the wreckage of her nose. I glared back.

The destruction of my office finally made sense. If you can't find what you're looking for, tear the place up out of spite. You'll feel better and the office's occupant will be just as unhappy as you are. Fair's fair.

"You searched my files, didn't you?" I said.

"Nurgh."

"You snooped on your daughter's laptop. No reason, really, but you got curious, wanted to know what she was up to."

"Zhe dot I was doo zdupid do figuw id oud, bud I did," Katie said, an ugly, triumphant glint in her eye. "Id was wicky. Hah! She waszn zo smahd afdew aw."

Ricky, the pool boy. My heart twisted. Julia had made her password the name of the only person in the world who cared about what happened to her.

Larson just stood there, tissue poised over his lapel, stupidly staring at first Katie, then me, then Katie again, totally lost.

"So you guessed her password. Good for you. Whatever you were looking for, I'm pretty sure you weren't expecting to find the stash of her father's private emails that she'd copied when she'd hacked his computer."

Her eyes were getting wider, warier.

"You certainly weren't prepared to read the ones to a lawyer you didn't recognize, talking about a boy Jameson was convinced was his son. I'm pretty sure one of those emails mentioned me and the appointment he'd made with me. So you came here to see what you could find."

I was guessing, but I was sure I was right. The pieces of the mental puzzle were clicking into place, one right after the other. And unlike Lucille, I didn't have to cheat to make them fit.

"What are you talking about?" Larson demanded. "Katie, what's she talking about it?"

We both ignored him.

"You came here earlier—I'm guessing the night before—

because you had to find out what was going on. You're plenty smart enough to have realized that Jameson adopting a son was going to seriously undercut your expectations. That's when you lost your bracelet, isn't it? When you were snooping in my files. And you were afraid Jameson might see it, recognize it, so you came back early to look for it."

Even with that wad of reddened tissue in front of her face, she looked guilty as hell.

I was on a roll now. I could almost hear the pieces falling, fitting, making a whole. A very ugly, murderous whole.

"Only trouble was, you forgot that Jameson had a tendency to get confused about appointments and schedules if his secretary wasn't there to remind him. And this was something I'm pretty sure he hadn't shared with his secretary. Or anybody else except that lawyer he'd hired. The young, competent, ambitious lawyer whom no one associated with Jameson Montgomery had ever heard of."

Larson was finally catching on. He was staring at me as if I'd suddenly grown two heads, but I could see the wheels turning in his, and I don't think he was very happy about it.

I wasn't very happy about it, but there was a grim satisfaction in seeing everything clearly, at last.

"I'm pretty sure you didn't intend to kill Jameson. Did you, Katie?"

Katie flinched.

Larson squawked. The wheels hadn't yet turned quite far enough. "What?"

"I'm guessing the two of you argued. You cried, tried tears, but they didn't work, did they, Katie? Not any more. Jameson was determined. He had a son at last. A boy to carry his name. Beside that, nothing else mattered, did it?"

She shook her head. Slowly, as if dazed, battered. She'd been living all of it for days, but hearing it put into words must have made it hurt all over again. She'd forgotten the blood-soaked tissues she still held, forgotten her still leaking nose. I was forcing her to relive it, step by ugly, painful step.

I forged on. "As far as Julia was concerned, he'd meet his obligations. Probably exceed them, actually. But that wasn't good enough for you, was it? You wanted more. You wanted...everything."

"I *wuvved* im!"

"No, you didn't. You loved the idea of his loving you, of being Mrs. Montgomery and living in the Montgomery mansion and having all the money and status that the name and the money conferred. But you didn't love Jameson, and you couldn't bear that he not only didn't love you, but that he wasn't even interested in you or your daughter and never had been."

"E cawd me a zdoopih bidz!" she cried, unable to keep silent any longer. "I'm gnaw a bidz, an I'm *gnaw* zdoopih!"

I didn't need to translate that. The emotion behind it came through loud and clear.

"So you grabbed the letter opener and..." I shrugged. I couldn't quite bring myself to say it out loud.

Even Larson didn't need it spelled out. He was staring at Katie, face twisted in shock and horror.

"Doan ook aa me da way!" Katie snarled.

"I—" He knew, but he didn't want—couldn't bear—to believe. "Your poor nose..." he said, reaching for the almost empty packet of tissues he'd stuffed in his pocket on top of Katie's gun.

She was there before him. He froze, clearly thinking she was groping for the tissues.

She had the gun out and was backing away before he realized what she'd really been after.

Okay, so she'd been paying more attention than I'd given her credit for. So sue me.

"What? No! Give me that!"

Too late. She had the gun in her bloodied hand, pointed at him. She held it like someone who knew what they were doing.

Looked like Julia wasn't the only one who enjoyed a little

target practice, now and then. I wondered if Jameson was the one who'd introduced her to guns, then squelched the thought. It didn't matter how she'd gotten the gun or learned to use it. It only mattered that she had.

"Katie!" Larson pleaded, taking a step toward her.

She raised the gun.

Larson took another step.

"Larson, no!"

He ignored me, took another step.

The idiot really didn't seem to grasp that the woman in front of him was not the pretty, helpless thing he'd thought he was protecting. This was a woman who'd already killed one man and was perfectly prepared to kill another rather than give up the fantasy world she'd been living in for so long.

If only he'd stayed where he was.

He didn't. He lunged, grabbing for the gun.

Katie stepped back out of reach and shot him.

The shot took him in the chest. The sound of it echoed in the enclosed space.

His eyes rolled up as he stumbled backward into my remaining guest chair. It skittered sideways, then tipped over as he fell on it in a tangle of limbs and snapping wood.

All I could do was watch in horror.

I'd wanted to distract them, find a way to get out so I could run like hell for help. I hadn't intended for anyone to get killed. Certainly not Larson, whose only crime had been stupidity and allowing himself to be influenced by what was in his pants rather than what was between his ears.

For a moment, Katie and I just stared, appalled, as a small red rose blossomed on Larson's breast. His eyes stared sightlessly at the ceiling. There was a twitch, then another, weaker. I caught a faint sigh, then his entire body went slack.

I'd never seen anyone die before, but there was no doubt in my mind: Don Larson, attorney-at-law, was very, very dead.

Katie and I looked at each other. If my eyes were half as big and round as hers, they were taking up half my face. I was pretty sure my mouth was gaping just as wide.

I could see in her eyes when the full enormity of what had just happened began to sink in.

"Shid!"

Her mouth closed. Her eyes narrowed. Her chest rose and fell as she steeled herself to deliberately do to me what she'd just done to Larson accidentally.

She raised the gun. Not fast enough.

My not-quite-a-switchblade knife sang across the space between us and buried itself in her right bicep.

"Wha—?"

The gun slid out of her fingers as she clutched at her arm.

"Jimmy! Jimmy Jones! That you?"

The angry voice from somewhere on the stairs brought Katie around with a snap.

"Damn it, Jones! If you're shooting up the place again—"

I'd never been so glad to hear Mr. Yaguchi's voice.

"Help! Murder!" I bellowed, surging toward the door. "Call 911!"

"Shid! Shid shid shid *shid!*" Katie was spinning, still clutching her arm, uncertain what to do.

I raced past her and through the open door.

"Call 911, Mr. Yaguchi! Call the cops!" I screeched, charging for the stairs.

I'd tried to slam the door shut behind me but I could hear it bounce back open, hear Katie's footsteps pounding after me. Four inch heels or no, the woman could move.

The head of a troll peeked up through the stair railings.

"Mr. Yaguchi!"

"Peterson!"

"Bidjz!"

I whirled to see Katie, my knife in her left hand, poised to throw.

She missed by a mile. I knew she would. The grip was

wrong, and she was right handed.

And now she'd conveniently handed my knife back to me. I snatched it up from the floor where it had fallen after bouncing uselessly off the wall.

"911, Mr. Yaguchi!" I shouted. *"Now!"*

To my relief, I heard the clatter of his footsteps headed back down the stairs.

Katie stood in a half-crouch, unwilling to challenge me now I was armed with a weapon I'd already proved I could use, uncertain what to do next.

"It's over, Katie," I called.

I was armed, she wasn't, but that didn't mean I wanted to run down those stairs with her hard on my heels if I didn't have to.

"Why don't you just lie down there on the floor, put your hands behind your head, and wait like a good little girl till the police get here? Make it easy for everyone, that way."

"You wisz," she sneered.

Yeah, I did wish. Oh, well.

"This isn't going to make things any easier for you, you know."

She took a step toward me. I held my ground. If necessary, I'd start running, get her to chase me. Anything to not give her a chance to remember her gun was still on the floor of my office just a few feet from her.

Mom's warning about knives at gun fights had been spot on. Not that it did me much good right now.

At that moment, the red emergency exit light flicked back to life. I hadn't realized until just then that it had gone out again, or that the only light up here was coming up the stairs from below or spilling out of my open office door.

Not to mention, that red exit light was pointing straight at Mr. Yaguchi's main storage area slash death trap, commonly known as a fire escape.

"Here's a suggestion," I said. "There's a fire stairwell behind

315

you. Opens straight out on the alley. You slip out that way, no one will see you. You waste time tackling me, that's that much less time you have to get away." I hefted the knife to remind her I still held it. "You already know I'm pretty good with this thing. You really want to take the risk?"

She wavered, glanced over her shoulder at the exit light, then back at me.

I raised the knife higher so she could get an even better view.

She turned and ran for the stairwell.

I didn't think anyone could run that fast in heels like those. Just goes to show how wrong I can be.

She hit the door. It stuck. Katie glanced back at me, then slammed her shoulder against it. It lurched open. She plunged through without stopping to look.

As fast as she was moving, she probably got halfway down the first flight of steps before it dawned on her there weren't any emergency lights in the stairwell, but there *was* a lot of stuff in her way. By then, it was too late.

I heard her scream, then an indecipherable jumble of thumps, bumps, and more screams before it suddenly all went silent.

The click of the door finally closing behind her sounded awfully loud in the silence.

I took a deep, unsteady breath—I hadn't realized I wasn't breathing—and carefully, fingers trembling only a little, snapped the knife closed and tucked it in my pocket.

Then, because my legs were shaking way too much to stand, I slumped against the wall and slowly slid down it until I was sitting on the floor. And then I just sat there, shivering and trying to breathe and desperately listening for the sound of sirens.

Until I finally caught their distant wail, coming closer, I hadn't known just how sweet that sound could be.

CHAPTER 36

"Broken right leg," said Trueblood. "Twisted or fractured left ankle. Dislocated left shoulder. Broken nose. Various contusions and abrasions. Oh, and she may have to wear a neck brace for a while. Katie Carmody will live, but she's not going to be very happy about it."

"Good," I said. "I think."

"She admitted she shot Larson. More or less. Kept saying she didn't mean to do it, it was all his fault, blah blah. So you're off the hook. Sort of."

"Sort of?"

"She's accusing you of assault and battery. For starters."

"The knife was self defense. She was threatening to shoot me. And since she'd just shot Larson…" I shrugged.

"And the stairwell?"

"I just pointed out it was there," I said virtuously. "She didn't ask for details."

The corner of Trueblood's mouth quirked upward in that disconcerting way he had. The five o'clock shadow on his chin only made it more distracting.

We were sitting on a decrepit sofa in an unused office Mr. Yaguchi had reluctantly opened for Trueblood's use, sipping coffees from the Last Caff because I hadn't been able to convince Trueblood to get them with a little something extra from Wild Bill's. From the looks of him, he would have gone for

Wild Bill's version if he hadn't still been on duty.

My office was currently occupied by the crime scene team, who probably knew every inch of the space by heart by now. They'd taken Katie away first then, about an hour later, Larson's body.

It didn't help that the elevator was still out. I was going to have to haul a ton of donuts to the station one day soon if I expected to have any friends left on the force.

The worst part of the whole mess was that Gracie and Fred had once again been the first ones on the scene. As if that weren't bad enough, they'd already been on overtime and were on the point of finally calling it quits for the day when Mr. Yaguchi's call came in. Even Fred wasn't feeling very friendly. As for Gracie...let's just say that if I was about to be run over by a bus, she'd make a special effort to push me farther under the wheels.

At least they hadn't made me go back in there to identify Larson or walk them through what had happened. I liked to tell myself I was plenty tough enough for my job, but I wasn't quite ready to face all that. Not yet.

Not that I was going to admit it to anybody, least of all Trueblood. I'd simply said I didn't want to risk destroying any evidence. To my relief, he'd been willing to leave it at that.

"It's just so..." I searched for the word I wanted. I couldn't find it. I changed tack. "It's not right. Two people dead, all because a few silly things went wrong. Katie lost her bracelet. Jameson got confused about the time. I decided to retrieve my cell phone instead of go home." I shook my head, trying to come to grips with it all. "If just one little thing had changed, none of this would have happened. It doesn't... It's not right."

"No," said Trueblood. "But most of the time, that's the way it is. It's not the big things that trip us up, it's the little ones we aren't watching for."

"I suppose." It was a rotten answer, but Trueblood was right. That was the way it was. Even if he'd had a better answer, it wouldn't have made Jameson or Larson any less dead than they already were.

I could feel Trueblood studying me, but kept my gaze fixed on the cooling cup of coffee I held. The dark, dingy little office suddenly seemed a long way away from everything else that was going on in the building, and he was sitting awfully close. Not that he could help it, given the size of the sofa, but still.

"You like all the pieces to fit, don't you, Peterson?" he said. "Everything explained, all the dots connected."

I looked up, surprised. "Yeah. Yeah, I do. So?"

"So why'd you leave the force? You had a good record—well, other than your marksmanship." Again that disconcerting little quirk at the corner of his mouth. I blinked, but found I couldn't look away. "You could have tried for detective—you would have been good at it. So why didn't you?"

It took me a minute to find the right words. The safe words. "Long story. Maybe I'll tell you someday."

He let that hang between us for a minute, as if he were weighing whatever I *wasn't* saying.

"I'll be here," he said at last, which I didn't find quite as reassuring as I might have.

He set aside his half-empty cup and got to his feet. He seemed a lot taller and broader, looming over me like this, though maybe it was just the deep sag in the sofa cushions that made it seem that way—if I leaned forward a few inches, I could rest my chin on my knees.

"I gotta get back to the station," he said. "Julia's still in custody, poor kid—Katie never showed up to bail her out—and I gotta brief the chief. I asked the team to process your purse first thing so you can have it back."

"And my keys? They were on the desk with my purse."

"You bet."

The room seemed a whole lot bigger and darker once he was gone.

The keys would be easy. I wasn't counting on getting the

purse since they'd want it to match the marks the buckles had left on Katie's face, but I needed my wallet and credit cards—a six pack of Twisted Torment was definitely on my schedule for the evening. Eventually.

It would probably take them hours to find Katie's bracelet since Amelia could have stashed it anywhere. And since I tended to store odd bits and bobs on some of my cases, they wouldn't have noticed it the first time around because it wouldn't have seemed that out of place. Assuming Katie had really lost it in my office to begin with. It hadn't helped that I couldn't tell them what it looked like.

In any case, it wasn't likely there'd be two expensive bracelets stashed in any of those files. I would have remembered something like that.

The whole thing was just so...sad. Two people dead, a troubled teenager left with no father and a murderer for a mother, another little girl and boy without a father, and for what? Pride and greed.

Not that Katie deserved any sympathy, but Julia did. No matter what arrangements Jameson had made for her in his will, the money would never make up for the love and support she'd deserved from her parents but never gotten.

Maybe I'd ask Amelia to find her a fairy godmother after all. If she had the right one, someone with good sense who didn't go off half-cocked—

"I cannot *believe* you didn't call me!"

Speak of the devil...

"Sorry, Amelia." Okay, so I do lie sometimes. But only little ones, and only to Amelia. Well, and maybe my mother, though that one's a lot trickier. She has an uncanny nose for sniffing out a fib. "I was a little distracted."

"Musta been. I dropped into your office while they were hauling out the stiff." I winced, but Amelia sailed on, oblivious. "It was a lot more fun watching them try to dig that skinny broad out of that mountain of paper that came down on top of her."

She giggled, but it came out more of a snort.

"Where'd she finally land?" I'd forgotten to ask, and Trueblood hadn't said.

"Halfway between third floor and second. Old Yaguchi's not going to be happy about the mess."

"He's going to be even unhappier when the fire inspectors descend on him and Hufflewitz. They can't ignore this building now."

"Yeah, well…" She'd already lost interest in favor of poking around the unfamiliar office. "And I thought your place was a dump. Sheesh!"

"Better than sitting on the floor in the hall."

She plomped down on the sofa beside me, and popped right back up. "Yeouch! There's something sticking out of that thing."

"Broken spring. Trueblood found it, too."

Her eyes lit up. "You two were cuddling on that sofa?"

"We were *sitting* here. Talking. About what happened."

"Should have been cuddling. You wouldn't look like such a grumpy-guts if you had."

She had a point, but I wasn't going to give her the satisfaction of admitting it. I dragged myself to my feet—not that easy, given the sag in that sofa—and wearily stretched, then scratched ferociously at my left side. In all the commotion, I hadn't noticed the growing itch from that awful blouse.

"I'm tired," I said. "I'm going to retrieve my keys and junk, and then I'm going to go home, shove this shirt in the trash, and go to bed and try to forget about all of this."

"You're no fun."

"I know. Just ask Larson."

That shut her up.

There was still a busy parade of cops and crime scene experts going up and down the stairs.

"You look like hell, Peterson."

"Thanks, Mac. Kind words always appreciated."

"Nice blouse, Peterson."

"Like it? I'll sell it to you, cheap."

"Nah. Already got more clearing rags than I can use."

"You got any more clients you're planning on bumping off, Peterson? My knees are killin' me. Much more of these stairs and I'm gonna put in for a transfer."

Make that two tons of donuts

As if all that weren't bad enough, Gracie was hovering right outside my office door, and she wasn't looking happy. My steps slowed.

Keys. Credit cards. Beer. Bed. I wanted them—*needed* them—and Gracie was standing between me and the first two, both of which I needed to get to the last two. If I backed down now, I'd never get home. I forced myself forward.

Gracie hunched her shoulders, fisted her hands on her hips, and stepped into my path.

"Where do you think you're going?"

It took an effort, but I kept my voice polite and nonthreatening. "Trueblood said I could collect my keys and purse and go home."

"Yeah?"

"Yeah." That wasn't quite so polite or nonthreatening.

"You have any idea how much grief you've been causing us, Peterson?" she demanded. She was starting to rock back and forth on her feet, which was never a good sign.

"*I* didn't cause any of this! I'm the innocent victim here."

"Tell that to the dead guy."

We stood there, squared off like beady-eyed banty roosters, both of us tired and cross and pretty much at the end of our patience with crime and each other and life in general.

"Want me to freeze her?"

I could feel my shoulders get tenser than they already were. "No."

"Too bad," said Amelia.

"You getting snippy with me, Peterson?" Gracie demanded.

Before I could say something I'd regret, Mr. Yaguchi

emerged from the emergency stair well, followed by another couple of cops. My guess, the cops had made him clear a path on the stairs so they could get Katie out, then kept him working at it in case there was any evidence buried in the mess. He didn't look happy.

He took one look at me and came storming down the hall toward us, clearly spoiling for a fight.

"You! Peterson! You're out, you hear? I'm telling Mrs. Hufflewitz to cancel your lease. You're nothing but trouble."

"Oh, yeah?" I said. I was *not* in the mood to take anything off Mr. Yaguchi right now.

Gracie grinned nastily and stepped to the side so she wouldn't be in the way if Mr. Yaguchi took a swing at me, then started rocking again, clearly looking forward to the show.

Mr. Yaguchi kept on coming. "Yeah. I'm gonna make sure you pay—"

"I got this," said Amelia, stepping forward, hand coming up to zap him with the wand she now held.

I squawked and grabbed for Amelia's wand, trying to make it look like I was waving my arms in exasperation. And then Betsy stepped out of my office and into my way.

"You mind clearing a path here?" she growled. "We're done and—"

My forearm caught her on the chin, knocking her back into the room. That threw me off balance. I lurched toward Gracie, arm still swinging to grab the wand, but Amelia had already hopped back, out of the way.

The spell intended for Mr. Yaguchi hit me dead center. Since I was already turning and off balance, I toppled forward, right into Gracie, unable to move a muscle to stop myself.

"Oops!" said Amelia, and hit me with an un-freezing spell a split second later.

Too late. It didn't help that Gracie had been rocked all the way back on her heels when I hit her.

We landed in a sprawling heap, her flat on her back, me on

top of her.

I rolled, trying to get off her and onto my feet.

I swear, I did *not* mean to plant my hand on her D-cup chest.

I also hadn't realized just how much give there is in a boob that size.

I splatted back flat on my face on the floor beside her.

She yelped, but she'd clearly paid a lot more attention in the mandatory self-defense and hand-to-hand fighting classes in police academy than I had. Before I could gather my wits, she'd punched me in the side, then rolled over on top of me, smashing my nose and chin into the carpet and driving the air out of my lungs.

And then she grabbed my hand and yanked it up high behind my back.

I screeched. That move hurts, especially when done with that much enthusiasm.

"You're under arrest for assaulting an officer, Peterson," she said gleefully. "Two officers, actually. I can't believe you clobbered your own best friend."

To add insult to injury, she wasn't even breathing hard.

I, on the other hand, was trying not to breathe at all. I'd thought my carpet was in bad shape, but out here in the hall… Yuck!

I was dimly aware of two more pairs of feet in regulation shiny black cop shoes milling around a few inches from my nose, and Amelia's glittery gold pair nervously dancing around another couple of feet behind them.

"You want me to freeze 'em, Maxine?" Amelia demanded. For the first time in all the years I've known her, she sounded nervous. "There's an awful lot of 'em, but—"

"No! Don't even *think* about it!"

"Don't tell *me* what to do!" said Gracie, dragging my other hand behind my back and cuffing me. "Help me get her up, will yuh?"

"Ah, come on, Gracie," said one of the cops. "She tripped

and fell. If she'd been meaning to hit you, she could've done a lot better than that."

I didn't recognize the voice, but whoever it was, he was my new official Best Friend.

"You really want to do this, Gracie?" That was Fred. "I'm sure Maxie will apologize."

Good old Fred. When his kid finally popped, I was buying it a boatload of toys even if I had to hock my car to do it.

"Honest, Gracie," I squeaked. (It's hard to talk when you can't breathe.) "I'm sorry. I didn't mean to land on you. I tripped."

"Let her go, Gracie," Betsy chimed in. "She didn't intend to clobber me, either. She was just waving her hands around, and I walked right into it. Let her up."

"Come on, Gracie," I pleaded. "I'm tired. You're tired. We're *all* tired. You really want to spend an extra hour down at the station booking me?"

I could feel Gracie's weight shift, as if she was reconsidering. I drew in air. Too bad the oxygen didn't hit my brain before my mouth started moving.

"I mean, nobody's going to say anything about you landing on your ass—"

If only I'd kept my big mouth shut.

Gracie managed to put her knee on my back as she got to her feet, making me grunt.

"It was assault," she insisted grimly, grabbing my arm and dragging me to my feet beside her. "You're all witnesses."

Fred sighed. The other cop threw up his hands. I couldn't see Betsy, but I thought I heard her mutter something about stupid broads under her breath. I wasn't sure if she meant me, or Gracie, or both of us. Probably both.

"So, you're arresting her?"

That made us all jump. I wasn't the only one who'd forgotten Mr. Yaguchi was there, too.

Gracie glared at him. "That's right. You want to argue about it, too?"

"You're really *arresting* her?" he insisted.

"Watch me," she said, shooting a warning look at Fred. He didn't say a word. She turned back to me. "Maxine Peterson, you have the right to remain silent. Anything you say can and will be used against you in a court of law."

"I won! I won the pool!" Mr. Yaguchi crowed. "Wait till I tell everyone! I *won*!"

I gaped at him. I'd never seen him so much as crack a smile. Now he was dancing a jig and laughing like a loon.

"I won! I won! I won!"

Gracie snorted and jerked on the cuffs to get me moving toward the stairs. I gave in and started walking. What else was I going to do?

"You have the right to an attorney. If you cannot afford an attorney—"

"I'll meet you down at the jail house," Amelia called encouragingly an instant before she vanished. "Don't worry! I *know* I can get you out of *there!*"

CHAPTER 37

I spent a sleepless night in jail, mostly thanks to Amelia, who insisted on sharing, in excruciating detail, her various schemes for a spectacular breakout.

My personal favorite was the sleeping spell cast on everyone in the building. Sadly, my suggestion that she amend the plan by adding an impenetrable wall of thorns around the building sailed right over her head.

Amelia, on the other hand, lobbied hard for blowing up every locked door between me and the front steps while I dodged the inevitable hail of bullets as I escaped. I tried to be enthusiastic—I mean, what's not to like about fireworks, explosions, and a hail of bullets? Especially if you're the star attraction?—but I still couldn't help thinking she'd watched the ending of *Butch Cassidy* a little more often than was good for her. Or me.

Regardless, I promised to consider her suggestions for possible future applications. It was the only way to get rid of her so I could get a little sleep.

Thank heavens there was no one in the adjoining cells to complain about the crazy lady muttering to herself.

Double thank heavens that, shortly after I was shoved in the cell, Betsy had snuck me a T-shirt to replace the puce monstrosity. She said the skin rashes were beginning to show. I didn't even take it personally when she held the thing out at arm's length as she hauled it off. I'd have done the same.

I suppose I should have just called Nic to come bail me out, but I couldn't bring myself to ruin his love life twice in the same week. Lucille and Douglas would have come, but I didn't feel right about rousting them out, either. I didn't even consider trying my mother. She'd have bailed me out, but she'd never have let me forget it. A few hours in jail beats years of snarky reminders about one's transgressions, every time.

I was just settling down for a nice nap after a breakfast of watery scrambled eggs and a slice of over ripe tomato when I was dragged out of my cell and told I was being released. They wouldn't tell me why. I'm guessing no one was willing to support Gracie's contention I'd deliberately assaulted her. I wasn't about to argue, so I signed where they told me, and that was that. All charges dropped, I was free to go, don't let the door hit me on the butt on my way out.

As expected, I didn't get my purse back, but I did get the contents, my car keys, and a nice, new plastic bag to carry it all in. Good enough to get me back to my car—assuming it hadn't been towed or stolen in the interim—and home for a shower and change of clothes. What I was going to do after that was anybody's guess. Personally, I hadn't a clue.

The plastic bag cum purse didn't draw any attention from my fellow subway passengers, but my battered face and obvious need of a shower did buy me a little more space than usual.

My car was right where I'd left it, but it now sported a parking ticket tucked under the driver's side wiper. I looked up to see all five foot ten, two hundred and fifty pounds of Derick Johansen, the neighborhood meter maid, happily strolling away. Nothing makes Derick's day more than giving one of the regulars a ticket.

I tucked the ticket in the bag with the rest of my stuff, then remembered I'd never retrieved my phone.

That made me hesitate. If I hadn't gone back for my phone last night, I'd never have run into Katie. If I hadn't run into Katie, Larson would still be alive.

On the other hand, if I hadn't run into her, I would still be under suspicion for Jameson's murder and desperately trying to convince Trueblood that her creations being on sale at the Bargain Basement was sufficient reason to suspect her of Jameson's murder. I'm not sure that would have worked out too well. When I'd told him about it the night before, Trueblood had looked dubious, but he hadn't been able to argue with everything that had happened after, so he hadn't pushed it.

I wasn't sure how I felt about the situation, and wasn't sure I really wanted to know.

Regardless, I still needed to retrieve that phone, and now was as good a time as any. I squared my shoulders, got a good grip on my plastic bag, and forced my feet to get moving.

Yet one more mistake to add to my rapidly growing list of mistakes.

Three-quarters of the buildings' occupants had taken over the lobby in a churning scrum that was rapidly turning hostile. No one noticed my entrance—they were too busy shouting and waving their fists, their attention glued to the two individuals standing on the stairs in front of them: Mr. Yaguchi and Miss Zemekis.

The two were both over seventy and under five feet two, but that didn't faze either one of them. Yaguchi stood, shoulders hunched and hands balled into fists like a prize fighter itching to take on all comers. Miss Zemekis, on the other hand, was as stiff and straight and disapproving as a Sunday school teacher faced with an unruly herd of five year olds.

She spotted me first. "Ah, Miss Peterson. So kind of you to join us."

I swear, she didn't raise her voice above what would be proper for tea in the rectory, but the crowd went totally quiet, then turned as one to see what she was looking at.

"If you'll all make way for Miss Peterson? Yes, that's it. That's it. Thank you." She looked up from the crowd that was beginning to divide like the Red Sea parting before Moses and looked straight at me. "If you'll join Mr. Yaguchi and me here...?"

It wasn't a request.

I flashed what I hoped was a friendly, confident smile and did as I was told.

"Yes. Right there. That will be fine," she added, indicating I was to stand two steps below them. The woman knows how to maintain her authority, and keeping me no higher than eye level was part of it.

Mr. Yaguchi eyed me suspiciously without relaxing his fighting stance. I offered him a not-quite-so-friendly but still plenty confident smile, then turned to face the crowd in front of us. They didn't look the least bit friendly. I felt my own smile falter.

That's when I caught sight of a grinning Trueblood, arms casually crossed over his chest and shoulders propped against the wall on the far side of the lobby, watching the proceedings.

My smile widened. He winked and gave me a two-fingered salute.

Suddenly, I felt better than I had in days.

"Now then, Miss Peterson," said Miss Zemekis, drawing my attention back to the matter at hand. "Your arrival is most fortuitous since you will be able to confirm the precise nature of your encounter with the police last night."

"Ah... I was arrested for assaulting a police officer," I said. "Two of them, actually."

"Indeed," said Miss Zemekis. "And what time was this?"

I told them.

The crowd stirred uncertainly.

"Were you arrested for murder?" Miss Zemekis continued, as coolly as if she were inquiring about the freshness of the rectory's cucumber sandwiches.

"No."

No sense in elaborating. Trueblood and I were the only ones here who cared about the details.

"Excellent. Now, if you would be so kind, please read what's written at the top of this page. Out loud, so everyone can hear." She handed me the now slightly rumpled, legal-sized sheet of paper with the betting pool grid and the names of the participants in their respective boxes.

I took the paper, cleared my throat a little nervously, then read what was written across the top. "Arrest of Maxine Peterson." I looked up to find everyone's gaze fixed on me. I don't think anyone was breathing. "That's it. Just, arrest of Maxine Peterson. Nothing else. No mention of what I'd be arrested for."

A long, sad, collective sigh swept through the crowd, almost, but not quite drowned out by Mr. Yaguchi's jubilant, "Yes!"

I smiled at everyone indiscriminantly, handed the paper back to Miss Zemekis, and stepped down. This time, I had to shove my way back through the dejected crowd, which was slowly dispersing. No one so much as glanced at me.

I crossed to Trueblood, who lowered his arms and shoved away from the wall.

"If you're planning to arrest me for anything else," I said, "you might want to wait until everyone's gone.

"Actually, I'm off duty. I finished up all the paperwork I could last night. When I called in this morning, they said they were about to release you. So I came here."

I cocked my head, studying him. He'd shaved, bathed, and put on an after shave with a tantalizingly earthy scent. He was dressed, as always, in slacks, sport jacket, and button-down shirt, but had dispensed with the tie and left the top couple of shirt buttons unbuttoned.

He looked damned good and smelled better, but I wasn't about to tell him that.

Besides, mentioning his after shave was bound to invite unflattering comparisons with my own eau-de-jailhouse aroma, so less said, the better.

"Why?" I said at last.

"Why what?" he said, blinking. I was pretty sure I didn't

want to know what he'd been thinking.

"Why'd you come here?"

"I heard about your run-in with Officer O'Mallon last night, after I left, and wanted to see how you were doing."

"Fine," I said. "Just fine. Really. Nothing a shower and clean clothes can't fix, anyway."

It was his turn to cock his head and study me. "Yeah?"

"Yea..." I couldn't quite finish the lie. I shrugged uncomfortably. "I... I'm coping," I admitted at last. "I think."

I'd swear his gaze warmed, though I thought that was just something that happened in fairy tales and romance novels and stuff like that.

"Coping's good," he said gently "Coping's very good."

"Yeah." I couldn't look at him when I said it.

"A beer's better."

My head snapped up. "What?"

"I'm off duty and Wild Bill's is open. I checked."

"But it's only, what? Ten? Eleven? In the morning."

"Ten thirty three. But the pubs opened hours ago in London."

I thought about that. "They've got a head start on us, then."

He nodded and took my arm. "That's what I was thinking."

I hesitated. "You're paying, right?"

"Well..."

"You're paying," I said, giving in to his touch. "And I want nachos."

Out of the corner of my eye, I caught a flash of hot pink glitter, but I didn't turn to check it out. I already knew what I'd see.

"Nachos?" A dark eyebrow arched He held the door for me. "At this hour?"

"Beats pickles and stale crisps," I said, sailing past him.

He grinned. "When you put it like that..." he said, and followed me out the door.

Made in the USA
Lexington, KY
04 March 2019